I0706270

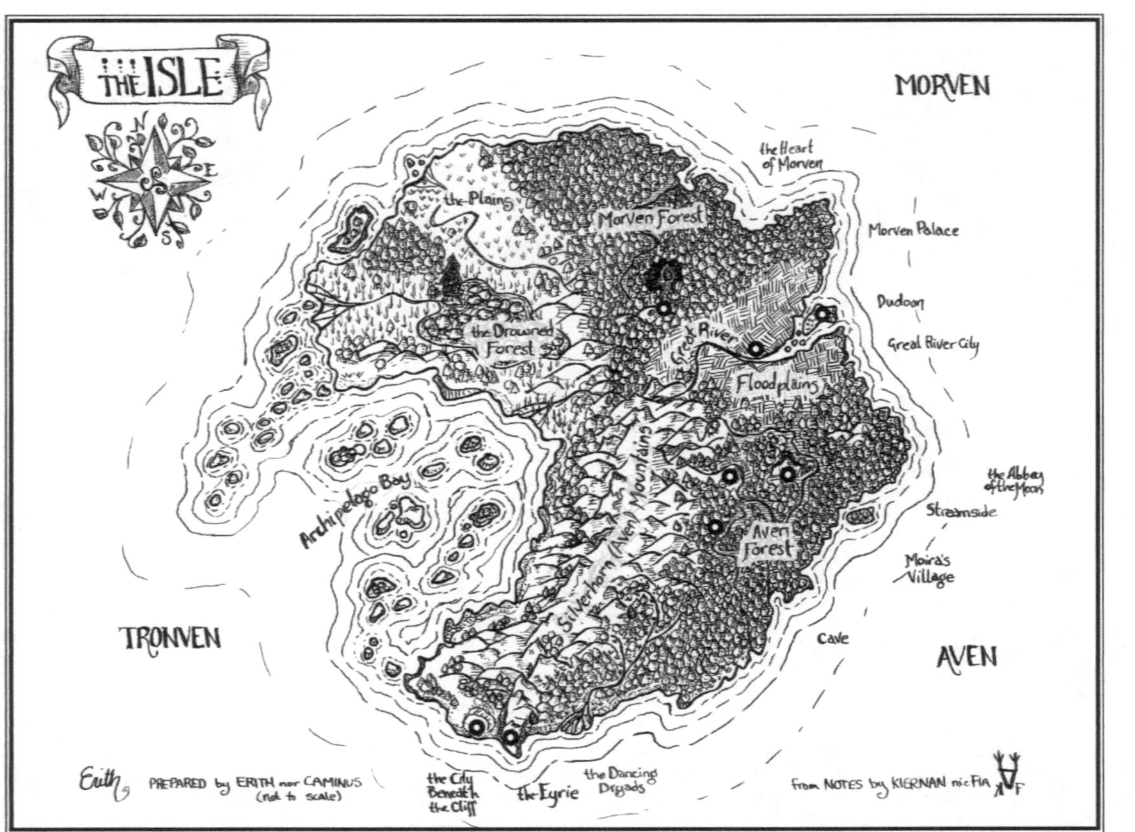

THE ISLE
N E S W
MORVEN
the Heart of Morven
Morven Palace
Dudoon
Great River City
the Plains
Morven Forest
the Drowned Forest
Great River
Floodplains
the Abbey of the Moon
Streamside
Silverhorn (Aven) Mountains
Aven Forest
Moira's Village
Archipelago Bay
Cave
TRONVEN
AVEN
the City Beneath the Cliff
the Eyrie
the Dancing Dryads
Erith
PREPARED by ERITH nor CAMINUS
(not to scale)
from NOTES by KIERNAN nic FIA

A TASTE OF EARTH

Three Realms, Nine Monarchs

A TASTE OF EARTH

written by

NICO SILVER

illustrated by

NIK SYLVAN

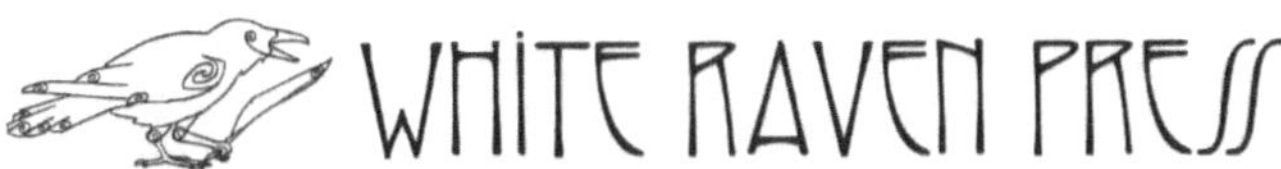

WHITE RAVEN PRESS

ISBN 978-1-998212-11-8

White Raven Press
North Cowichan, British Columbia, Canada

Cover illustration: "Kier and Fionn: Reunited" © 2024 by Nik Sylvan.

Cover design and border by Nik Sylvan.
Title typefaces: Rivanna NF Pro by Nick Curtis and Eva Antiqua by Spiece Graphics, used under license via MyFonts, www.myfonts.com.

Author's Note

ONCE AGAIN, there is a lot of enthusiastic, consensual sex in this book between two men in love. It gets pretty graphic, so if that's not your thing, maybe this book isn't for you.

There are also scenes of sexual harassment, dubious consent, and sexual assault (this does not happen between our main characters, who are sweet and gentle with each other). These scenes are not meant to be titillating; they're terrible and that's how they should be viewed.

There are brief mentions of pedophilia, though no actual scenes including it.

There are scenes of violence, which include broken bones, blood, and death-by-stabbing. There is also an attempted suicide scene, and there are general references to not wanting to be alive.

There is a lot of swearing, including (especially) the f-word. Kiernan swears a lot, sorry.

And, finally, there is no happily ever after—yet. This is book two, and it ends with our heroes in an okay place, but there is more to come. I promise there will be a happily ever after for Kier and Fionn before the series finishes.

1: CUT ADRIFT

1
Kiernan

Morven forest was a part of me, had always been a part of me. From my very earliest memories, even before I came into my magic, it was there, a connection deeper than awareness that let me feel its moods, its health, the green pulse of its magic.

The forest was home, and the Heart of Morven, a huge old oak deep in the woods, was also *my* heart.

Or it had been.

Yet the closer I got to the Forest, the more I was coming to hate it. Because being in Morven Forest now meant being captive. It meant my mother, my Queen, owned me as surely as she owned her lowliest dryad servant.

And the closer I got to Morven, the farther I got from where my heart now lived. My heart, my beloved, my silver-eyed seer of the Eyrie. Sometimes I couldn't breathe with thinking how far away he was, how untouchable.

I knew there would be a price for defying my Queen and not returning to Morven as soon as I escaped the Abbey of the

Moon. It wouldn't matter to her that I hadn't *planned* not to return. It wouldn't matter to her that I did what I thought was right, that I followed the laws of the Isle, and took Fionn to his own people in the Eyrie.

It would especially not matter to her that I tried to stay away from home out of love. Because it was not love for her.

No, she would feel the need to demonstrate how fully I was back in her power, and she would probably do it very publicly. Just in case anyone else's loyalty might be wavering.

My best hope was that she would strip me of my title and my inheritance. Maybe even banish me. But if she chose that route, she would also lose direct control over me, and I doubted she would ever do that.

I had once suspected she planned, eventually, to marry me off to whomever would bring her the most advantage. Now, perhaps, she would choose the most repulsive possible match, to put me in my place. But again, she would be surrendering direct control if she did.

Really, I had no idea what she might do. Take my antlers, perhaps, to make my disgrace visible to anyone who looked at me. It was not a pleasant thought, but I had been through it before. Once when she sent me to live with my human father, when I had only been a child. And once, at thirteen, when I made that choice myself, wedged my prongs in the branches of a tree, and tore them free with my own strength.

It would hurt. It would damage my connection to my magic, but not destroy it. And they would regrow, eventually.

I tried very hard not to think about my fate as the ship turned into the delta of the Great River with the tide. I just tried to be happy that Fionn was safe – or as safe as he could be – and that he loved me, even if we couldn't be together. We were connected by magic, and I could feel him like a warmth in my belly, growing fainter as we sailed father from the Eyrie, but there all the same.

I was surprised that my Queen had chosen to sail up the Great River towards the Heart of Morven instead of continuing along the coast and mooring to the north. This route would have us passing my father's stronghold of Dudoon, and my mother usually avoided anything to do with him. She didn't like to be reminded that she was married to a human man.

Bad enough that she had *me* to remind her. It was lucky, I suppose, that the only part of me that resembled my father was my curly brown hair.

I didn't turn when I heard her step on the wood planks of the deck. Presumably, she wanted me to know she approached, because if she had wanted to be unheard, even I wouldn't have noticed the sound of her feet.

«My son,» she said, putting her hands on the railing next to where I leaned. For a moment, it felt strange to hear the Sidhe language again. «Are you glad to be returning home?»

«Of course, my Queen.» Half human as I was, I *could* lie, but my words were true. Mostly. I had missed Morven Forest like an ache in the core of who I was. Coming home soothed me, made me feel whole again. But it was also true that I would have given up ever returning if it meant I could be with Fionn. His absence was far worse an ache.

«And yet you seem distant.»

I had no answer for that would not either anger her or expose too much of myself. I had learned early on that letting her know me too well opened me up to pain; she would use any advantage she had, even against her own son.

«It's been a long Moon, my Queen,» I finally said. «I don't feel entirely well yet.» My body still hurt, even after the careful ministrations of one of the best Sidhe healers.

«You do look unwell,» she said, and someone who didn't know her might have mistaken her look for concern. «Do your injuries still pain you?» She put a hand on my arm – my right arm, only recently healed from a bad break – as if she actually cared about my wellbeing. And I suppose she did, in the way a craftsperson cares for their tools.

Once, I would have believed that she did care for me, that she loved me, even. Over and over, I had believed it, and over and over it had broken me to find out she only cared how useful I was. If she had any maternal feelings at all, they were expended on my older sisters.

I looked at her hand and didn't move. «I'll be fine, my Queen,» I said, and glanced back at the passing landscape.

Dudoon – the Black Hill – occupied an island in the mouth of the Great River, and it seemed to take an eternity to sail past. I watched the men on the walls, and knew they watched us back, knew my father would know whose ship glided by.

«May I ask, my Queen…?» I had good eyesight, but it wasn't keen enough to recognize individuals on the fortified walls. Fionn would have been able to see what each of them looked like, though he didn't know my father to pick him out from the other men.

«You may.» She didn't remove her hand from my arm, and I wondered if I was about to feel the sting of her claws in my flesh.

«Why did we sail this way?» I had been about to ask if she thought Father would be watching, but changed my words before they came out of my mouth.

«It seems like a good idea to remind them who rules over them, once in a while.» Her voice was matter of fact, and she looked at me as if I should have known the answer. As if a near-crippling annual tithe from the human's vassal Monarchy to the Sidhe wasn't enough to remind their ruler – and my father, his best general – who held their leash.

The Queen looked at me a moment longer, then turned and

walked back the way she'd come, leaving me to brood again.

I watched as the trees along the near bank of the river increased in size and depth of greenery, from the thin, reddish salt-leaf near the ocean, to the grand spreading oaks and firs farther upriver.

Gradually, the air became less salty, less tangy, more *earthy*, and the breeze changed from cutting to fickle. I closed my eyes as we sailed back into the shelter of Morven Forest, my home and my prison. It already felt empty for the absence of one sweet, gentle man who had somehow become everything to me.

S HE GAVE ME MORE than a ninenight to recover before she sent for me.

I was sitting on the bank of a stream, deep in the forest, dangling my feet in the ankle-numbing cold water, and watching dragonflies hunt smaller insects over a still pool where the flow of water bent and slowed under a fallen tree. Not so long ago, though it was starting to feel like a lifetime, I had sat on the bank of a different stream, nursing a dislocated nose, watching dragonflies hunt insects, and feathered tree serpents hunt dragonflies. Fionn had been sitting next to me, and the worst thing on our minds had been an overly pushy werewolf. We had been avoiding confessing our feelings to each other for days. Or, *I* had been avoiding it, and Fionn had been adhering to my request not to talk about it.

Finally, sitting there on that mossy creek bank with Fionn wiping blood from my nose, I knew I had to say something. I'd said, "I'm yours." It wasn't, "I love you," though that was what I had meant.

I saw a bright flash of red fur low to the ground in the

bushes across the stream, so I sat up and pulled my feet from the water. And then, a glimpse of equally red hair and the spark of her magic touched mine.

It was not my mother, the Queen, but her Seer. The mother of my heart, Fionn would call her. Her fox friend, Ember, emerged from the undergrowth first, leapt across the stream, and burrowed her head under my hand until I scratched behind her ears.

«Hello, Ember,» I said, and I heard her return greeting more in my mind than in my ears.

Treats? she said. I dug a piece of deer jerky from my pocket. I'd been saving it for later, so I could avoid returning to the palace for as long as possible, but I couldn't resist Ember's cute fox smile.

«Hello, Seer Siona,» I called, and the tiny woman stepped out into the open. She was blind – had been blind for many years – but her *sight* allowed her to move through the world almost as easily as if she had vision in her eyes. It was Ember's job to warn Siona of any obstacles her magic might not show her.

«You look better rested,» Siona said, and I smiled. I knew she was referring to my magic, and not whether or not I had dark circles under my eyes.

She picked her way down the mossy stream bank and stepped across the water by way of the cobbles that broke the surface. Like me, she preferred to be barefoot in the forest.

«Will you sit with me a while?» I said. «We haven't had a chance to talk.» I suddenly felt shy, as if this woman hadn't seen me in every emotional state I was capable of, and in every state of dress or undress. She had changed my diapers, wiped tears and snot from my face, and soothed my anger at my mother more times than I could count.

And our Queen had kept her so busy since our return that

we had barely had time to pass basic greetings.

«I want to tell you about Fionn,» I said.

She smiled, but her voice was grave when she spoke. «She sent me to bring you to her.» She didn't need to specify who "she" referred to; one never had to, here.

«She's decided on my punishment, then.»

«I believe so.» She put her hand on my head. «You cut your hair.»

I laughed, though I didn't suppose it came out very merry. «Our Queen wanted me presentable, when we were guests of the Vogel King.» I felt my smile twist into something darker. «Once he was done letting his minions break various parts of my skeleton.»

I leaned into her hand, knowing her fingers that stroked the curls off my face would never turn mean, as my mother's so often had.

«You were becoming a little unkempt,» she said. «Even before you left for Aven.» Her hand moved to one of my antlers and hesitated over the moonsilver adorning each tine, turning the blunt points into sharpened weapons. «There is magic here.»

I had felt the tingle of magic, but hadn't known what its purpose was, and it didn't surprise me that my mother would use any excuse to attach her spellwork to me.

«Can you sense what it's for?»

She withdrew her hand. «Whatever it is, it doesn't appear to be active.» She cupped my face in both hands. «Son of my heart,» she said. «I am afraid for you. I don't know how she plans to punish you, but I do know you angered her.»

I sighed and closed my eyes. «I only wanted a little bit of freedom.» That was only partly true. At first, I had wanted a taste of life away from my Queen, as something other than her tool. I had wanted a small and temporary escape, a tiny defiance to keep me company when I returned to captivity in her court.

But then there had been Fionn, and falling in love, and I had wanted very much to escape for good, to claim a life – and a partner – of my own choosing. And even though I knew Fionn and I couldn't be together – even if he'd been allowed the freedom to take a lover, it was illegal in the Eyrie for a Vogel to fuck anyone other than bird folk – I had still hoped to be near him. To protect him as best I could. To make sure he was happy.

And I had hoped that maybe one day we could find a way to change the world, or find a new place to live, so we could be ourselves, and be in love.

A very small part of me found it difficult to forgive him for forcing me to live, for refusing to allow me to give up and die, because the only way to save my life had been to return me to my Queen.

I got to my feet slowly, not wanting to give up the peace of the evening or even the melancholy of my thoughts, and brushed leaves off my trousers. Summer was coming to an end, and some of the trees were dropping their foliage already.

«Should I change?» I was dressed in travel clothes, sturdy linen trousers and shirt in shades of green and brown, instead of the stiff, uncomfortable court dress my mother preferred.

«Don't keep her waiting,» Siona said, slipping her arm in mine, as if she needed me to guide her. I think she knew I found the contact comforting. I think she found it comforting, too.

As we walked, I tried to let the calm of the forest seep into me, to make me imperturbable. It should have worked; the sun on the needles of the firs made the air sweet and tangy, and somewhere, blackberries were ripening.

What calm I managed evaporated as soon as we came in

sight of the Heart of Morven. The huge old oak was encircled by a spiraling walkway that led into the canopy where the Queen's Hall occupied a wooden platform, walled around by living greenery for most of the year.

Noblefolk in full court finery were making their way up the walkway, more of them than I was used to seeing here at the same time. Whatever punishment the Queen was planning to give me, she'd have an audience for it.

«Are you sure I shouldn't change?» The low Palace, built into a natural hill, if hills had doors and windows and chimneys, was not far away; I could be there and back before the last of the nobles had ascended into the treetop.

Siona drew me forward, ignoring my question. I kept my chin up and met each set of eyes that turned to look at me. I was the Prince, after all, and they should fucking remember it. I outranked them all; only my sisters and my Queen were above me. And Seer Siona, though that was only a courtesy, because as a Seer, she belonged to her Monarch.

The noblefolk paused, every one of them, to watch as I passed. Their servants and attendants dropped to one knee as I drew near, and the lesser nobles bowed their heads to me. Some of the higher-ranked dared to meet my eyes, but it didn't last; I had grown up around them, and not one of them could stand up to me in the end.

At the top of the walkway, I let go of Siona's arm and she bowed to the Queen and took her place behind the throne, Ember crouched at her feet. I sank to my right knee and bowed my head. «My Queen,» I said.

«My son,» she replied. «Come forward.» I stood and crossed the floor. Her throne was an elaborate chair that grew from the living wood of the Heart itself, shaped by some long-ago magic worker. My mother would have looked tiny perched on it, except it was impossible to look at her and not be aware of the immense power she held – both political and magical.

She looked around at the assembled nobility, frowning at those who scurried in late and jostled for a good place to stand. «Do you not bow to your Prince?» she said, her voice light, but anyone who knew her even the slightest amount would hear the deadly edge in it.

All around the room, servants sank to the ground, lesser nobles dropped to one knee, and higher-ranking folk stood from their chairs and bowed their heads.

«That's better,» the Queen said. «You may relax.» Everyone in the room obeyed. I heard a snicker and turned to see one of my sisters covering her mouth. The two of them sat on padded stools at our mother's feet, both looking like exact copies of her, only with smaller antlers. One even had her deep red hair, while the other had black like their father.

They were twins, my sisters, and even they didn't know which had been born first. Only our mother knew – and Siona, presumably, as the only one who had attended their birth.

The Queen looked back at me, and her frown deepened, her displeasure at my clothing and my bare feet apparent in her expression. She was not one to hide her feelings. She didn't need to because she controlled everyone around her.

«I thought you would rather I arrive quickly than perfectly groomed, my Queen,» I said.

«I would have preferred both, but no matter. At least you have some consideration.» She stood, and everyone not already standing stood, too. The servants knelt, and the nobles bowed.

The Queen ignored them.

«My son,» she said. «I made you my third heir, Prince of Morven Forest, nearly fours years ago, did I not?»

The room became quiet, everyone in it recognizing that

whatever was going to happen had begun.

«Yes, my Queen.»

«And in return, you promised me your loyalty, your freedom, your obedience?»

«I did, my Queen.»

«And yet, you failed to report back to me after attempting the mission I sent you on. Instead, you fled.»

«I –» I knew there was no point in arguing with her. She had already decided on my punishment and would carry it out, no matter what I said. But I couldn't let the gathered noblefolk think I had failed to succeed at the task she had set me.

«I prevented the Alfar from completing their blood sacrifice,» I finally said. «They were unable to raise the magic that would have allowed them to conquer the entire Isle.» I dared to meet her eyes, the same green as mine, only hers held no warmth. «Was that not the aim of my mission, my Queen?» It was probably a bad idea to question her in front of the court – or at all, really – but I *had* done what she sent me to the Abbey of the Moon for, and I wanted all those assembled to know that.

I hadn't failed, I had only declined to return right away.

She raised an eyebrow and put a hand on my face. I could feel the tips of her claws resting uncomfortably close to my right eye. «You did prevent war, yes,» she said, and I breathed a little easier, though I should have known better.

«You were born for preventing war.» She smiled, but I knew she was probably not pleased. I had been born from her arranged marriage to my father – a human war hero – to solidify a truce that ended the uprising of the human Monarchy in Morven.

«You should have brought their sacrifice to me,» she said, her voice gentle, like she was correcting a wayward but well-meaning child. «Perhaps we could have claimed that power for the Sidhe and used their own plan against them.»

I was hardly surprised that my mother was as power-hungry as the Alfar King, and just as unbothered about starting an Isle-wide war. I was a little taken aback that she would admit to it in front of her whole court, though.

«My Queen,» I said. It was useless to argue that a blood sacrifice would have left her and those who assisted her tainted with death magic, or that the Sidhe instigating bloodshed was no better that the Alfar doing it. But there was one tack left to me.

«Their sacrifice was no longer perfect,» I said. «His blood would not have brought you a fraction of what it would have given the Alfar King.»

She snorted and one claw dug into my face, then quickly withdrew. She removed her hand and sat on her throne again and the noblefolk around the room relaxed.

«Explain,» she said.

«The ritual was intended to draw on the magic of the Lady of the Moon,» I began. «It would not have been as effective away from her center of worship, or on a night when the moon was not full.»

«You said the sacrifice itself was not perfect.»

I didn't like her referring to Fionn as "it," but I didn't dare say anything. I didn't want her to guess my feelings for him.

«He was born on the solstice, under the full moon, and reached his majority this solstice past. Once that date was gone, he was too old to be perfect. And –» This was harder to say, because she would easily guess the part I had to play. I might not have said it, except I suspected she had known what might happen when she chose to send me in the first place.

«And?» She leaned her elbow on the arm of the throne and her chin on her hand.

«To be perfect, he needed to be a virgin.»

One of my sisters snorted and only a flick of my mother's eyes to one side showed she heard. «And you, naturally, made sure he was no longer a virgin,» my Queen said.

Someone in the audience snickered.

«It seemed the easiest way to reduce the efficacy of the ritual,» I said.

One of my sisters sat up straighter and said, «Of course, Mother, my Queen, you knew he was the right person to send, if you needed someone fucked.»

«Give our little brother any chance to get laid and he'll take it,» said my other sister.

The Queen swatted the ear of the nearest, but lightly. «Language, my daughters,» she said.

She looked back at me. «So, you prevented a war, and declined to bring me a ruined sacrificial offering.»

I knew she was ready to declare me guilty of fleeing, that she would let me talk my way right into it, but there was nothing in her words I could deny.

«Yes, my Queen.»

«And yet, accomplishing this, you failed to return home.»

«I was… sidetracked, my Queen. It was not my intention to stay away.» To be fair, I hadn't even really been gone that long. I think it was that she had had to fetch me home herself that was my real crime.

«Sidetracked?»

I had nothing else to say in my defense, so I just waited.

«You made me travel across the Isle to fetch you, where I found you close to death, and you call it *sidetracked*?»

«I am sorry, my Queen. I didn't mean to inconvenience you.»

She sighed, as if she were only a mother with a wayward young son.

«I did leave the Vogel indebted to us,» I said. «To you.»

«So you did. Perhaps I will be lenient with your punishment. Make it temporary instead of permanent.»

I felt dread settle like cold in my guts and only the faint warmth of my connection to Fionn gave me hope.

He believed we had a future together, so I must also, no matter what happened next.

2
Fionn

I WASN'T PERMITTED to visit the docks the day the *Spirit of Morven* sailed away on the tide.

The King still didn't trust me – and I suppose I had given him reason for his distrust – and so I had to watch the elegant, fleet little ship sail past from my balcony. I suppose I should have been thankful they hadn't decided to sail around past Tronven, or I wouldn't have seen her at all.

I hadn't seen her arrive; it had been night, and my eyes weren't good in the dark. And besides, I hadn't known to watch for her. I was determined to watch her leave.

And while my eyes were poor in low light, they were excellent in daylight and at distance. The Queen of Morven Forest's personal vessel sailed as close to the shore as was wise, both to keep the journey shorter and because the Sidhe, though fine sailors, were a forest people, not a sea people. I could see the faces of every crew member as they set sails and tied knots and did whatever else sailors did.

There were men and women both, and some who might be

both or neither, and I realized that while the Sidhe Monarchy might be as corrupt and strict as any other, at least they were more egalitarian in who could do what sorts of jobs than my own people were. Here, only men could be sailors, or soldiers, or any of a number of other supposedly masculine jobs.

And, too, in the Eyrie, every citizen was assigned their sex at birth, and the choices were only male or female. Kiernan had told me that among the fey, people could choose how they were identified, and there were more choices. People could also choose how they married; in the Eyrie, though same-sex couples were accepted, they could not wed.

<Do you see him?> My attendant, my friend, Neeka, leaned over the balcony railing and shaded her eyes.

<Don't fall over the side,> I said, though of course unlike me she had functional wings. "And no, I haven't spotted him yet." I slipped back into Islish. I knew I mustn't let the King hear me speaking the common tongue – Vogel must only speak Vogelspek, unless to strangers – but it was my first language. It was the language I spoke with Kiernan, because I knew only a little Sidhe, and he had no Vogel.

But then I did see him. He emerged from belowdecks and slipped past the busy sailors to lean on the rail and look up at the Eyrie.

"There he is," I said, softly, and there must have been some emotion in my voice, because Neeka took my hand and leaned her head on mine.

"I see him. He looks very handsome." She squeezed my fingers. "Do you think he sees us?" She waved.

"His distance vision isn't as good as ours," I said, but I waved, too, just in case. He looked sad, I thought, but even I couldn't tell for sure at this distance.

Between us and where the ship sailed by, a pair of feathered tree serpents twisted and spiraled through the clear air.

They chittered at me to let me know how they felt about Kier leaving.

Dark goes, said Flame. Her voice in my mind was reproachful, as if she thought I should have gone with him.

Bright stays, said Smoke. I was fairly sure she thought I should have found a way for Kiernan to remain here.

<Did you know the Sidhe have woman warriors?> Neeka said. I knew she switched back to Vogel to remind me to be more cautious. Our King wasn't a cruel man, but he had a quick temper and he was jealous. Possessive.

He knew Kiernan and I had been lovers, and though I tried to convince him otherwise, he probably guessed my heart still ached for my Sidhe Prince.

As I watched, Kiernan straightened and turned, as if someone had called for him. He glanced once more towards the Eyrie, put his hand over his heart, then kissed his fingertips and turned them outwards, as if to send the kiss my way. Then he left the rail and disappeared back into the ship.

<He knew you would be watching, my Seer,> Neeka said quietly. <Even if he couldn't see you.>

Love and sadness both burned deep in my belly, where I could feel the strange magical connection to Kier.

<Yes,> I said.

We stood without speaking for a while, watching the ship sail away and finally disappear into the distance, around the curve of the Isle's coast.

<Did you want to be a warrior?> I said, when we went back inside to wash for the evening meal. I hoped the King would let me eat alone tonight. I hoped he hadn't yet forgiven me for saving Kiernan's life and that he would keep trying to punish me by staying away.

<Since I was this big,> Neeka said, holding a hand out to indicate a child about hip-high. On her. It was closer to belly-

high on me.

<I wonder how hard it would be to change the law preventing women from becoming whatever they choose?> I went to my bathing room to wash my face and hands and took the towel Neeka handed me when I was done.

<Add that to the list of other laws you want to change,> she said, smiling, and taking her turn at the sink. As my attendant, she was supposed to wait for me to give her permission, but I had made it clear on her first day that, as far as I was concerned, she was my equal. As long as we were alone, at least.

I laughed. <There are a few,> I said. <For a culture descended from a grand and glorious civilization lauded for its egalitarian policies, our current laws certainly are…> I groped for an appropriate word.

<Backward?> Neeka said. <Restrictive?>

<Primitive,> I said. <Uneducated.>

<Stupid,> said Neeka, and dissolved into laughter.

<All of those things.>

A tap at the outer door made us both fall silent. My stomach lurched. Please let it be anyone but the King.

The relief I felt when it was only the evening meal being delivered reminded me that, if I was going to survive here, to do *well* here, I needed to find a way to accept my position. I needed to re-discover my resolve to be my King's lover, to be pliant and obedient. I needed to hide the hot streak of rebellion that burned in my belly next to my connection with Kiernan.

THE KING LEFT ME ALONE for more than a nineday, letting me know by his absence how displeased with me he was. But one evening, while again awaiting my late meal, there was another knock at my door.

Neeka went to answer it, while I checked the mirror to make sure I was presentable. I still wore the long flowing tunic I had been dressed in for the day, and though my makeup had long since been washed off, I didn't look too awful.

My eyes always looked too big, makeup or no, and now they looked a little wild, too, from watching my beloved sail away from me and from remembering it every day since.

I reminded myself that even if he had stayed, had been allowed to stay, we would never have been permitted to be together. At least he was alive.

<Leave us,> I heard a voice say, deep and imperious.

I muttered "fuck" under my breath – Kier's favorite swear – and forced myself to be calm. I let all emotion drain away and watched my face go still and serene in the mirror. Then I walked calmly across my bedroom and emerged into my sitting room, where a cluster of servants was setting out dishes on the low table and scurrying away as quickly as possible.

Neeka stood in the small anteroom by the main door with the King's attendant next to her, and when the last of the servants left, she shut the inner door, closing herself out.

<My King,> I said, bowing my head.

He said nothing, and I dared a look at him. He was watching me, and his usually readable face was blank. Then his mood seemed to shift, and he smiled.

<I hope you don't mind,> he said. <Me inviting myself to dine with you.>

As if I had a choice. But he did like to keep up pretenses. And I was the one who had told him I missed him.

It had been a lie; I only wanted him to think I had no more feelings for Kiernan, that I was loyal and obedient. And though the King could read lies from truth, he had to do so deliberately, and he wanted for me to miss him, so he hadn't looked.

<You may join me whenever you like,> I said. That was *not* a lie, but only because it was literally true. He was the King and as a seer, I was his property. He *could* do whatever he liked.

<Will you sit?> I gestured to one of the couches near the table and when he sat, I chose the other.

<You did well,> he said, <at the farewell ceremony.> He began lifting lids from dishes without waiting for an invitation. <I would never have been able to guess you ever had feelings for that self-important little shit.>

I put a slice of roasted goose in my mouth to keep myself from saying something the King wouldn't like. He was testing me, so I was careful not to react, even though if anyone in that room full of nobles had been self-important, it wasn't Kiernan.

<I belong only to you, my King,> I said, when I had chewed and swallowed. I managed a smile. It felt wrong on my face, but he seemed to accept it.

<I am sorry I have been so distant these past days. Will you let me stay with you tonight?> he said, reaching across the table to take my hand. <Or will you come to my rooms? I know you like to keep your space private.> He gestured towards the bedroom door I had closed when I came through to the sitting room.

I wanted to ask him if those two choices were my only options. My room or his? But I knew the answer, and that reminding him I knew would be a bad idea. He seemed to be in a good mood, now; he would be gentle with me if I didn't anger him. Careless words might get him to leave, or they might make him decide I needed to be reminded of the power he had over me.

I had resolved to play my part, to be the meek and willing servant, the meek and willing bedmate, because doing so would not only keep me safe, it would gradually bring his trust. When he trusted me, he would give me the freedom to explore the Eyrie, and the City Beneath the Cliff. Perhaps even the countryside. And that illusion of freedom would make my captivity bearable until I could find a better way to live.

But that was before I had watched Kiernan sail away, taking my heart with him.

I opened my mouth to answer but was spared by a commotion at the door. One of the King's guards burst in, closely followed by his attendant.

<Forgive me, my King,> said the guard.

<What is it?> The King kept my hand in his, tracing my fingers with his own.

<Your daughter, my King.>

King Sarkot rose to his feet, my hand forgotten.

<What has happened?> Suddenly, between one breath and the next, the King looked more regal than I had ever seen him.

<The messenger only said Healer Kah sends for you.>

The King nodded sharply, then looked at me, put a hand on my face, and stroked my cheekbone with his thumb. It was moments like this that made me wish I could like him better, could want him, even.

<Perhaps I will see you later,> he said.

<May I accompany you, my King?> I didn't know the King's daughter except to recognize her face, though of course I hoped she was well, as I would wish for any child, but I liked watching Healer Kah work. Sometimes she would tell me what she did and why, and when she used magic she would describe it for me, so I might someday try for myself.

He nodded and strode from the room. I had to scramble to keep up. Vogel were tall, except for me, and the King was tall even among other Vogel. His step was long, and by the time we reached the hall I was almost running.

Neeka scurried behind me and after her came a pair of my guards and a pair of the King's.

I realized, after we had gone down several long hallways and made numerous turns, that the King's children lived in a completely different part of the palace that the King did. *My* rooms were only a couple of turns away from his, practically next door. I wondered if it was for reasons of security, or if it was that he didn't like the noises of children playing.

I refused to think about why he wanted me so close.

After nearly a moon in the Eyrie, this would only be my second time meeting the Princess, and I spent time with the King nearly every day.

Healer Kah met us at the door to the Princess's rooms and gestured for us to be quiet.

<Your attendants may wait in the anteroom,> she said. <And your guards outside the door.> She glanced at me, nodded in greeting, then looked closely at the King. She was one of the only palace employees of any rank who could get away with not bowing to him – she usually did, but when haste was necessary, she was allowed, as healer, to skip the formalities.

<It hit very suddenly,> she said.

<What did?> said the King, speaking through clenched teeth.

<The fever, my King.>

He went very still and looked over her shoulder into the room.

<No,> he said, softly.

<I don't understand,> I said, keeping my voice low and directing my words at Healer Kah.

She touched my arm as if to ask my patience, then said, <There are masks on the table. Past this point, you must wear one.> She gestured. <Wash your hands in alcohol before you

leave and change your clothes for a smock. I will not have this spread.>

<Should I wait outside?> I asked, anxiety gathering in my belly. I tried to push it away; Kiernan would feel it, and I didn't want him to worry.

<No,> the Healer said. <You should see this.> She pointed at a pile of fabric on the anteroom chair. <Change your clothes. You may change back when you leave.>

We did as Healer Kah instructed and, dressed like infirmary attendants in white knee-length garments – almost to the ankles on me – and mouth-covering masks, we stepped into the room.

The first thing I noticed was the smell. It was strange, sweet like the natural odor of a Vogel, only too strong and much too sickly to be pleasant.

When the King approached the Princess's bedside, I stayed back. I noticed the child's hollow cheeks and sunken eyes, her too-pink skin and too-bright glance.

<How long has she been like this?> I said.

<She began to feel unwell this morning,> Healer Kah said. <Her nurse found her collapsed on the floor just before the evening meal was brought.>

I looked at her, feeling stupid. <So quick?>

She nodded. <This same fever killed our Queen, her attendants, her guards, and some of the cleaning staff, most of them in the first two days.>

I bit my lip. I knew the Queen had died of an illness, but the King had made it seem like it took time.

<Papa?> The girl's voice was hoarse. She seemed not to see the King standing at her bedside, though she was looking right at him. He sat on the edge of the bed and took her hand.

<I'm here, lovely girl.> His voice was gentle, caring. I had never heard him sound like that.

<We call it Royal Plague,> said the Healer quietly, drawing me over to a table nearby where jars of herbs and preparations scattered the surface. <Because, while it kills all Vogel, it hits the royal family and the noblefolk quickest and hardest.>

She looked at me and I could see the strain in her eyes. <For royals, it is almost always fatal. Healing magic doesn't touch it, so all we can do is make tisanes to keep the fever down and hope the body's own healing is strong enough.>

<Should the King *be* here?> I said.

<Would you try to keep him from his child?> Kah asked. <With these precautions,> she gestured at my clothes, <He should be safe enough.>

<Cool water?> I said. <For the fever?>

<Of course.> She frowned and pointed at a basin near the bed, where a cloth floated, ready to wipe perspiration from the Princess's face.

<A cool bath?> I said, knowing I was probably not being helpful, that nothing I could suggest would be new to Healer Kah. But there had been a sister at the Abbey of the Moon, who ran the main infirmary, who swore by cool baths for fever. Well, for any sickness, really, but it actually seemed to work for fever.

The healer cocked her head at me. <Such a simple, reasonable suggestion,> she said. <One might wonder why we hadn't tried it before.> She glanced at the King. <When he goes, we'll try it.>

<Do you think he'll leave?> I said. <If this sickness kills royalty so easily?>

She sighed. <No. I suppose he'll stay.> She tapped her fingers on the table.

<Put him to work,> I said. <Have him draw her a bath and lift her into it.> She looked at me curiously. <He's her father. Let him feel like he's doing something to help her.>

<You should go,> she finally said. <I don't know if the fever is as bad for seers as it is for kings, or how easily you might catch it.> She glanced at the King again, then back at me. <My precautions *should* be enough, but…> She trailed off.

<Should I ask his permission to leave?> The King was murmuring softly to the Princess, holding her hand in both of his, and she was smiling.

<I'll tell him I sent you back to your rooms.> She picked up a jar, studied it a moment, then handed it to me. <Make a strong tea and drink it if you feel even the slightest bit of fever.>

Then she led me to the door. <There's a hamper for the smock and mask.> She pointed. <And clean your hands and arms.> She gestured at the alcohol. <Bathe when you get to your rooms and send your clothing for laundering, but make sure they know to treat it with caution.>

<Yes, Healer,> I said, not knowing what else to say. I followed her instructions and let Neeka lead me on the long, complicated path back to my rooms where I bathed and disposed of my clothing and sat down to my now long-cold evening meal.

I FELL ASLEEP THAT NIGHT skimming a thick and rather boring old history of the Eyrie and the Vogel Monarchy, looking for references to Royal Plague. There was probably nothing I could do, especially if it didn't respond to magic, but I couldn't sit by and wait while a child sickened.

I dreamed I was walking along a beach, holding hands with Kiernan, only when I turned to speak to him, he was gone, and I held only a handful of twigs. They were reddish-brown, with thick grey-green leaves, and bark that crumbled and peeled in my hands.

Hadn't I read a passage in one of the boring history books, something about salt-leaf?

It was hot on the beach, in the dream, and when I woke, I thought I was still dreaming, because I was still hot. I pushed the blankets off and it helped a little, but I couldn't fall back to sleep. I rolled onto my side and a trickle of sweat down my ribs had me stripping off my sleeping tunic.

Vogel didn't perspire much, and I couldn't remember the last time I had been hot enough to cause it.

I rolled onto my back again and rested a hand on my hip and had to move it almost immediately because where skin met skin, the heat was unbearable.

Maybe if I opened the balcony door? I stood up and nearly fell, dizzy and disoriented. There was something I was sup- posed to remember about being too hot. And something about leaves? My brain didn't seem to want to work.

Clinging to the furniture, I made my way across the room to the balcony door and pulled it open. It was late summer, but the air felt cooler outside. At least it was moving. I followed the breeze out onto the balcony and leaned on the railing.

The ship was, of course, long gone, a nineday and more. Kiernan's ship, stealing him away from me. And why hadn't I jumped from the balcony to follow? I had wings. I spread them out and remembered that only part of them was my nat- ural wing, and it was too small to carry me. The rest was only decorative.

I was suddenly very tired and wished it wasn't so far back to bed. I slumped against the rail and the stone felt wonder- fully cold against my burning skin.

Kark. It was a familiar sound, something I had heard in the forest with Kiernan. And… before that? Was it Kier? No, that was silly.

Kark. I heard the soft rustle of wings and saw a speck pale against the dark sky, soaring closer. *Tok*, it said.

"Hello, bird." Wasn't I supposed to be able to understand the speech of birds? Wasn't that something they said of the Vogel people?

Tok. It got closer, bigger. And bigger. It was huge, and white, and looked at me from eyes too intelligent for a bird.

I reached for my magic, still not very practiced, but I had done this once to be able to understand my own people's speech. Surely, I could do it for a bird.

I was vaguely aware of two long, sinuous shapes streaking out of my bedroom to scold me.

Bright bird, said one.

Get up, said the other.

The huge bird landed on the railing and stared at me. *Tok*, it said. I reached for my magic again.

Child, the bird said. *It seems you have learned a thing or two since we last met.*

It was a raven. Kiernan said they were sacred to the Sidhe, and my name – Branfionn – was partly raven, because Bran meant raven, he had said, only ravens were supposed to be black. This one was silver-white. Like me.

"Hello," I said. "But I don't think we have ever met." The serpents swirled around me again, chittering their distress, but they didn't get too close to the bird.

The raven cocked its head at me. *Follow*, it said, and launched from the railing to soar into the open sky. When I didn't follow, it circled, watching me.

Seer, child, it said. *Follow me. You are needed elsewhere.*

"Am I?" I pushed myself up straight against the railing, then climbed up. "But I can't fly." I opened my wings and craned my neck to look at them. Without the added decorative rows of feathers, they were small. Too small. I knew I could probably manage to glide well enough to not die when I hit the water. I might even make it around the cliff to the beach. But I could not fly.

I could have sworn the bird snorted. *As I have said several times before, you do not need physical wings for this flight.*

"Oh." I spread my wings wider and saw they were glowing, my long hair was glowing. *I* was glowing. "That's never happened before."

It has, child of my name. Now come.

"Child of your name?"

Branfionn. White bird. The Abbess did not give you that name by accident, though she probably never suspected its significance.

It circled again. *Now come. You are needed and we have far to go.*

I realized I no longer felt dizzy, and I was no longer too hot. I stepped off the rail and felt the wind catch under my wings. I flew.

I looked back at the balcony as I turned to follow the raven and saw my body sprawled on the pale stone.

And I remembered that to the Sidhe, ravens were not just a sacred bird; they were also omens of death.

3

Kiernan

THE QUEEN LOOKED AROUND the hall, as if considering the crowd. As far as I could tell, no one dared meet her eyes.

Finally, she leaned back on the throne and said, «Leave. All of you.»

There was a confused stirring and a few nobles closer to the exit bowed and shuffled slowly toward the walkway. The rest just looked at each other.

«Was I unclear?» The Queen stood and a wave of kneeling and bowing moved around the room. «Leave.» She gestured with one hand and people finally began to move, at first slowly and then more quickly, like no one wanted to be the last to get through the grand doors.

«Siona,» said the Queen. «You may stay. And you.» She pointed to one of the dryad servants standing near the wall. They spoke an almost inaudible, «My Queen,» and stayed in place while the others moved quietly away and out.

I was only half-aware of my mother ordering my cousins Sean and Padraig to leave, and then my sisters, who pouted like children but finally swept out, arm-in-arm.

My attention was instead on the tall, slender dryad who waited next to the wall to find out why the Queen had singled them out. My suspicion was that they were simply the first one she focused on – like most Sidhe, most fey, she saw dryads more as things she could use than as people.

But I knew this dryad. Or I *had* known them. Most dryads were fully male and female both, but he had used male pronouns then, and we had been boys together, companions, before my mother decided it wasn't appropriate for me to have non-fey friends. After that, I had no real friends at all, only a handful of age-mates who wanted to get close to the royal family, and I was the easiest way to do it.

Daphnis had been my first lover. We had explored our sexuality together, and he had gently taken my virginity and eagerly surrendered his to me. The last time I had seen him was around the time my Queen began to experiment with dryads as living topiary, and then changed her mind and sent all her dryad servants to the pleasure gardens. Now, it seemed, she was using them as household servants again.

His eyes flicked up to meet mine briefly and I almost drowned in a memory of a deep brown gaze looking down at me as tendrils of vegetation grew out of him to caress me in my most sensitive places.

I looked away first.

«Close the doors and wait outside.» My Queen's personal guards obeyed silently and efficiently, leaving only the four of us inside the huge leaf-walled hall: The Queen, her Seer, her wayward son, and a dryad servant who would be ignored as if he was a part of the furniture until he was needed for something.

The Queen looked at me and said, «Kneel,» and I knew exactly why she wanted me on my knees. Standing, I was taller than her, and I looked enough like my grandfather that she might not feel entirely dominant. Kneeling, she could look down at me.

I knelt.

«You are too powerful for your own good, my son, unless you can remember to obey me.» I had always thought she wanted me obedient because she wanted everyone around her obedient; it had never occurred to me that she might find my magic a threat to her own. But that seemed to be what she was implying.

«It would do you some good to be powerless, I think. To learn to survive without it.»

«Without what, my Queen?» I knew what she was saying, of course I did. But I didn't want to face it yet. My voice was rough, like I was desperate for a drink, and the feeling of dread in my gut was like a weight, dragging me under to drown in fear. I tried to set it aside, to concentrate on breathing. I knew Fionn was too far away to feel what I was feeling, but what if he *could*? I didn't want him to worry about me.

«Power, my son,» she said, her voice going pointedly patient for having to repeat herself. Then she said the thing I had expected and feared. «Magic.»

I opened my mouth to protest, though I knew very well there was nothing I could say to move her once she had made up her mind. She raised a hand, and I felt her magic close around me, holding me silent and still. My magic might be a threat to hers someday, but for now she was still the most powerful of the Sidhe.

Siona's eyes widened in horror when she realized what our Queen was about to do, and I wondered how she could not have known what she planned. Even Daphnis shifted his weight, when dryads could stand without moving for days.

«My Queen,» said Siona, managing to keep her voice even

and emotionless. «Are you sure –?»

The Queen stopped her with a gesture. «It's for his own good.» She glanced at Siona, then back at me and made a dismissive wave of her hand. «Oh, I won't make it permanent, as long as he behaves.»

She stepped closer, looked into my eyes, and reached for my antlers. I closed my eyes, shutting out the green that was so like my own, *too much* like my own, and I braced for the wrenching tear as she used her inhuman strength to pull my antlers off. She had done it before, and I had survived. It would cripple my connection to my magic, to the Three Realms, but not kill it entirely. I would not be able to use magic, but at least I would still be able to feel it.

Fionn had told me I must live, so for him, I would endure this.

But it never came. She didn't grab my antlers and wrench them off, she merely touched the sharp tips of moonsilver for a moment, one touch for each tine, and then stepped back.

Blood dripped from the tips of her fingers. Six fingers for six tines, and as I stared, they healed, and the blood vanished.

«My Queen?» I said, and she smiled, just the barest twitch at the corners of her mouth. And then the burning started.

Sidhe antlers are not dead bone, like deer antlers. They are alive and full of feeling and magic. Fionn could caress my antlers and make me hard, never touching me anywhere else.

And now they felt as if they had been set on fire. My mother's blood ran into the engravings on their moonsilver tips, and I could feel as each spiral in the decoration was filled and the spell she had written there took effect. And I realized she had been planning this punishment since she had arrived at the Eyrie to fetch me home.

It was only pain, I told myself. I could endure pain. If only it had been mere pain.

It was not my actual antlers that burned, it was the connection to my magic. And it was not only my connection to Land, Sea, and Sky, but the magic that lived within my bones, in my soul and my very being, that burned.

She released me from the force that held me still and I collapsed forward onto my hands and knees.

«My Queen, please,» I said. Her blood flowed into silver and set it burning and the burning crept into my head and consumed my magic, my *self*. The fire of her spellwork sucked away my magic as a blaze sucks air.

«My Queen,» said Siona. «I don't think this is wise.»

«I didn't ask you to think.»

I forced myself to look up at her, my Queen. She looked bored.

«Mother,» I said. I hadn't called her "mother" since I was a small child, still believing she loved me. «Mother, please.»

Her face blurred and vanished, and I couldn't see anything. All there was was fire and growing emptiness.

I opened my mouth to beg again, and no sound came out. Instead, I vomited up everything in my stomach, sending a vile pool spreading out towards her royal feet.

«Find someone to clean that up,» said the Queen. «And you.» She gestured to the dryad. «You belong to him now. Take him to his rooms and see that he does no harm to himself. It would hardly be a punishment if he escaped to the afterlife.»

I DON'T KNOW HOW I got to my rooms; I assume Daphnis carried me. Dryads are as strong as the trees they share kinship with, and I was not exactly large, though Fionn assured me once that I'm heavier than I look.

I didn't remember much at all, save glimpses of shocked faces as we passed, whispers, a look of wicked glee from one of my sisters and a smirk from my cousin Sean. I wondered how much of my begging they had heard, how much of the screaming that followed. I tried to escape into darkness and darkness – always my friend before – let me hide in its shadows.

I remembered, too, begging Daphnis to kill me, to end my suffering. I think I may have shouted at him, sworn at him, called him terrible things when he refused, as if he had a choice. Part of the magic that kept dryads enslaved also prevented them from harming their captors. Soon, it all faded into a grey blur, and then the shadows came again, and everything went away.

I remember throwing up whatever he tried to feed me, every cup of water he convinced me to swallow, over and over until my throat burned with my own stomach acid. And I remember how, eventually, he laid a hand on my forehead, and I felt healer's magic – magic no dryad should have been able to use – and I slept.

I woke scrambling for something to puke into and Daphnis was there, holding a delicate ceramic vessel that looked too nice to hold vomit. When I stopped heaving, I examined the design.

«Isn't this from the Queen's favorite set of dishes?» My voice sounded hoarse and abused.

Daphnis took the bowl into my bathing room to empty it in the commode. I thought I saw a fleeting smile on his face as he turned away and wondered why he didn't hide it. Dryads, as a rule, did not show emotion. It was safer that way.

«It seemed appropriate, my Prince,» he said, and I snorted.

He returned and helped me lie back down. When he started to move away, I took his hand, and he went very still.

«Daphnis,» I said.

«I did not think you would remember me, my Prince. I'm told all dryads are alike to your people.»

«We were friends,» I said. «When we were boys. Do you still call yourself 'he'?» I realized I was squeezing his hand too hard, so I let go.

«Were we friends, my Prince?»

«I —» Had he seen our friendship differently? «Did you think I used you?» I said. «That I wanted someone… that I wanted a pleasure boy?»

«If you knew a Sidhe lord and a dryad slave were lovers, what would you assume their relationship was?» He turned to the nightstand and took a cloth from a bowl of water, wrung it out, and wiped sweat from my forehead.

I stared at him with my mouth open, wanting to protest, but knowing he was right. Finally, I said, «I always saw you as a friend, Daph. Never as a servant.»

His hand on my cheek made me stop whatever else I might have tried to say. I knew I sounded desperate, that I was reliving the same boyhood hurt I had felt when my Queen told me I wasn't to see him again, that he would be sent to the gardens with the other dryads, and I wasn't to visit.

"You promised to free me," he said, switching from Sidhe to Islish, and I winced at the simple matter-of-fact tone in his voice.

"Because you were my friend," I said. "Not to get you to fuck me." I pushed his hand away and tried to sit up. I only managed to throw up all over the bed.

"Fuck," I said, trying to pull the soiled bedding away. Trying not to cry. He took the blanket from me.

"Dryads are not permitted to be friends with royalty," he said, still no emotion in his voice. "We are and always will be your servants. Your slaves."

"I tried to convince her to gift you to me. Back then. So I could free you. Instead, she sent you away. Then I found out I couldn't have freed you anyway, because Isle law dictates that dryads are an enslaved people and always will be."

"There," he said. "You see."

I watched him bundle the soiled blanket into a basket of laundry and fetch clean bedding from a cupboard across the room.

"I don't want servants," I said. "I don't want slaves."

"Would you return me to your Queen, then?" he said. Not "our" Queen. No dryad would refer to her that way if they could avoid it.

He lifted me from the bed like I was a child and carried me to the bathing room, where the stream running through its floor had been blocked off to allow the pool to fill. An empty cauldron, steaming slightly, sat next to it and I realized I had lost time somewhere, that I hadn't seen him move the hot water from the fire to the bath.

He lowered me into the pool and straightened up.

"What do you want me to do?" I asked, as he headed back into the bedroom to change my sweat- and vomit-soaked sheets. I leaned back on the stone lip of the bathing pool and tried to find the energy to reach for the soap.

He glanced at me as he went, a faint frown of surprise between his deep brown eyes. I didn't suppose he was asked what he wanted very often.

"I think I would have a better life as your servant, my Prince, even if I am an unwanted one."

"You're not unwanted," I said.

"Of course, my Prince." I didn't think he believed me.

I was able to wash, finally, and climb out of the bath, dry off, and make my wobbly way back to the bed without help.

"Why do I feel like I was beaten with mallets and force-fed

spoiled oysters?" I said.

Another fleeting smile. "I suppose your body doesn't know how to react to your magic being torn away."

And as soon as he said it, it came flooding back, in every excruciating detail. Everything I had blocked out, every small ache of missing magic, and every tiny pain of it being torn away. I felt the burning start in my antlers all over again and spread, and I felt the trickle of my Queen's spellwork seeping under my skin and into my bones, stripping away my magic like scraping the insides out of a root vegetable to make a haunt lantern.

"I'm a fucking lantern," I said and laughed at Daphnis's confused look. And the laughing turned to screaming as I felt every scrape, peel, pick as I relived every trace of magic being burned and torn out of me until I couldn't feel half of my own self anymore.

I had been without magic before. Twice, I had lost my antlers and had my connection damaged, but it had not touched the magic in the core of my being.

Once, at the Abbey of the Moon, I had been trapped behind magic wards that walled me off from my access to the three sacred realms of Land, Sea, and Sky. It had been unpleasant, and I had not even been able to do a child's magic like calling a flame or a wisplight. But I had still had my connection to the forest, my connection to my heritage, and my strange new connection to Fionn.

And once I had nearly burned myself hollow trying to stop a magical fire from consuming the Forest of Aven. I had used too much magic too quickly and nearly consumed everything I had. But even then, I could still feel the forest, myself, and Fionn. And I had healed, and the magic had returned stronger than before.

But this was different. It was as if a sort of anti-magic had crept into my being and burned away anything that wasn't entirely mortal, leaving me a hollow husk of who I had been, of who I should be.

And I had begged her not to do it. "Please, Mother," I had begged, as if using that word might stir some maternal instinct in my Queen, instead of just making me seem pathetic. It hadn't worked even when I was a child, cute and obedient and eager to please her.

"Please, Mother," had never brought me anything but scorn – from my sisters, my cousins, my aunt. I hated myself for resorting to those words. And I hated her for making me think they might work.

I felt a cool cloth on my forehead and opened my eyes. Warm brown met my green, and there was concern on his face.

"Daphnis," I said. "Bring me my knives."

He wiped my face again and pulled the sheet back to wipe my neck and chest. I had soaked the bed with sweat again.

"I can't do that, my Prince," he said. "And even if I could, I would not."

"Fine, I'll do it myself." I tried to sit up but found his hands on my arms holding me down.

"Daphnis," I said. I would not beg. Not again.

He shook his head. "My Prince, you must live."

"Don't call me that," I said. "My name is Kiernan."

"I know your name. And you are the Prince of Morven Forest."

"Please, Daphnis." Okay, maybe I *would* beg. Again.

"When you were raving," he said. "Feverish from your Queen's magic stealing yours and burning you hollow…"

I winced and looked away. His hands gentled on my arms, but he didn't let go.

"You kept calling out a name."

Tears formed in the corners of my eyes, and I tried to hold them back. I blinked rapidly, willing them to go away.

"'Fionn,' you said. You called him 'beloved'."

The tears spilled over.

"I understand you may not wish to live for yourself, that your life feels empty and wrong without your magic."

I gasped, like I was drowning and couldn't get enough air. I almost laughed at the thought of drowning in my own tears and snot. At least I wasn't puking anymore.

"But I believe, my Prince – Kiernan – that you would want to live for him."

He let go, and gently wiped the tears and mucous from my face.

"Why are you being so kind to me?" I said. "My Queen only told you to keep me from harming myself."

He tucked a curl of hair off my face, like Fionn used to do. "Because you were my friend once," he said. "Because it didn't matter to you that I was a slave, and you were the son of a Queen and a famous general."

I looked up at him and saw the barest hint of moisture in his eyes.

"And anyway, seers are sacred to my people, and if a seer calls you 'beloved' you must be worth helping."

"How did you know Fionn is a seer?"

"You talk a lot when you're feverish, my Prince."

He smiled and put his hand on my forehead, and I slept again.

I HAD THOUGHT, THEN, that I was through the worst of it, but if I was, it didn't feel that way. I continued to throw up food and could only sometimes keep down water.

The Queen's spellwork continued to burn through me as a fever, and I lost track of how many times Daphnis carried me to a cool bath while he changed my sweat-soaked sheets.

I remembered, like through a fog, Siona coming to check on me. The first time, I felt the faint spark of her magic, but after that, I only knew her by her voice.

«Son of my heart,» she said. «You are stronger than this. You will survive.» And later, «Please, my child, my Kiernan, my own boy, I need you to hold on. To return to us. To me.»

And then, finally, emptiness. Compared to the fire, the lack of it felt like a relief. And the next time I woke, I no longer burned quite so hot under my skin, and I no longer sweated all over the sheets.

Daphnis sat on the side of the bed, watching me, and for just the barest moment, I felt peace. No agony, no fire, no scraped-out root vegetable feeling.

And then I realized I could feel nothing. No little sparks and glows of magic from all the other people around me in the palace; no background buzz and swell of Land, Sea, and Sky, ready to come to my asking.

And worst of all, no sense of the forest.

Except, no, that *wasn't* the worst.

The worst was the loss of that small warm feeling deep in my belly that told me Fionn was alive, that we were still connected, that he was mine and I was his.

I must have made some sound, because Daphnis looked at me closely.

"I can't feel him anymore," I said.

"My Prince?"

"Fionn. We're connected. We *were* connected. By magic. I can't feel it. I can't FEEL HIM." I realized I had shoved Daphnis aside, had climbed out of bed and was shouting.

I stared at him, and he stared at me.

"I'm sorry, my Prince."

I sat back on the bed, all the anger gone. The terror gone. Only emptiness left.

My stomach rumbled and I stared at it, like it wasn't part of me. I felt as if I had been taken apart violently and shoved back together with pieces missing.

"Are you hungry, my Prince?" Daphnis said.

"Kiernan."

"Are you hungry, Prince Kiernan?" That slight smile again, there and gone.

"I should eat," I said, knowing it was true, but not caring even a little.

"I'll fetch you something from the kitchen. The evening meal is past and it's some time yet until midnight."

I waited quietly, calmly, for him to leave, and then I got up and locked the bedroom door. I went to my dresser and slid one of my knives out of its sheath, and briefly ran a hand over the other one. I would only need the one.

I touched the hilt of my sword, too. "Winterborn," I said. I had named it after my first love, Declan Winterborn, after he was murdered by my cousin for the crime of being a commoner, a werewolf, and daring to fuck a fey noble.

"I'm sorry," I said. Declan had told me I had to live when I would have followed him into the afterlife. He would have told me I was being selfish, and stupid. But he hadn't had to learn what it was like to have an essential piece of yourself carved away. When Sean had separated Dec's head from his body he had died instantly; I didn't think I had the strength to die slowly.

I turned away from my sword, walked towards the bathing room, thinking I should get in the bath so as not to leave a mess for Daphnis to clean up. Avoiding thinking about how he might be blamed for it, anyway. As I passed my desk, something white fluttered on its top and I paused.

A large, silver-white flight feather fluttered in the breeze of my passing, twisting in place where it stood in the cup holding my quill pens. I touched it lightly with my fingertips. Fionn had lost it when we were making our way out of the caves under Aven Forest, on our way to the Eyrie.

"Fionn," I said, my voice barely audible even to myself. "Beloved. I'm so sorry."

"You're sorry for a lot of things," he had said to me, once.

There was a sharp tap at my window, like a stray branch had hit it, then a *Tok* that sounded like a raven. The candles guttered and almost went out, and I had no magic to call a wisplight or to re-light them.

I shifted my knife to my left hand and waited.

Nothing more happened, so I continued to the bathing room. I was still naked from my bout with magical fever, so I climbed into the pool and leaned back, let the cool water flow over me. I traced the inside of my wrist with the tip of the blade. I had never believed I was one for self-harm, had always thought I was too fucking stubborn to give up on life, but I realized this was not the first time I had wanted to die, nor even the second.

Tok, said the raven.

Fionn would be angry with me. I pushed the knife against my skin a little harder. He would cry, but he would be free to love someone else, someone he would be allowed to make a life with. A small voice in my head reminded me that the Vogel King would only allow Fionn to love *him*.

"I think I'm stuck on the windowsill." Fionn's voice. I smiled. But he wasn't here. He was in the Eyrie with his King, and I couldn't even feel our connection anymore.

"I'm sorry, Dec," I said. "I never did kill Sean for you." I looked at the blood welling up around the blade of my knife. Not deep enough.

"How can I be stuck when I don't even have a physical body?" Fionn's impossible voice again. I ignored it. He wasn't here, and I was no use to anybody, least of all my beautiful silver-eyed seer.

I closed my eyes and pressed the blade against my skin, harder this time.

"Beloved?" He sounded like he was right next to me.

"You're not real," I said. "I love you, but you're not real."

"I am. I'm not *here*, exactly, but I *am* real. And I love you."

I opened my eyes and saw him, transparent and wavering. A ghost. "Oh, Goddess, no," I said. "Fionn. If you're a ghost, then you're…" I pressed the knife down again. If Fionn was gone, then there was nothing at all to keep me here.

"I'm not dead, Kier." I felt my skin slide under the blade, beginning to part, like everything was in slow motion. "I'm just… having a very strange vision."

He moved closer, his bare feet silent on the stone, even the click of his claws muffled. He knelt and took the knife from my fingers. He didn't seem to be able to hold it, and it clattered to the stone floor.

"Fionn?" I said, watching his shape waver and fade. I heard the desperation in my voice, the need, and I was ashamed at how weak I was. How could he ever want someone so weak?

"I'm here, Kiernan," he said. "I'm here, and I'm still your Fionn."

But he faded and vanished completely before I could say anything else.

4
Fionn

WHAT KIND OF EXCUSE for a seer was I, anyway, that I got stuck climbing through a window when I wasn't even in my physical body?

But the whole time I struggled to get both legs over the sill and both wings between the panes, I was thinking about how Kiernan would laugh when I told him. How it would light up his eyes and he would tease me about how ridiculously long my legs were. And then he would tell me how pretty my legs were, and how he loved that they were long because I could wrap them around him when he fucked me.

So I was smiling when I finally dropped to the floor in what I assumed was Kier's bedroom, followed the sound of running water, and found him in the bath.

My smile vanished. "Beloved?" I said, afraid to move closer, to startle him, but I could see blood already welling up under his knife.

"You're not real," he said without opening his eyes. His voice sounded empty, devoid of hope, missing the good humor

I was used to hearing in it, even when he was in pain. "I love you, but you're not real."

"I am," I said, taking a careful step closer. "I'm not *here* exactly, but I am real." I kept my voice soft, tried to fill it with everything I felt for him, every bit of love and caring. Of desire. Of need. "And I love you."

He opened his eyes and I saw the hopelessness there, too, devastating emptiness. I forced myself to hold my tears in, because if I started to cry, I would dissolve into weakness, and I needed to be strong.

"Oh Goddess, no," he said, and I realized I was not quite solid to his vision. "Fionn, if you're a ghost, then…" A tear slid down the side of his nose and I had to work hard to keep my own from falling.

"I'm not dead, Kier," I said, and in my head I was repeating *IloveyouIloveyouIloveyou* over and over as if he might hear what I was thinking. "I'm just… having a very strange vision."

He was frozen, in that moment, staring at me, wavering between belief and despair. I could see that he wanted to believe I was there, but he had been hurt, his faith in everything shaken badly.

There had been a moment when, following the raven here, I had nearly fallen out of the sky, incorporeal magical wings or not. I had felt Kier's apprehension, and then, suddenly, a tearing force ripped at him, and our connection was gone. If the raven hadn't been there, squawking at me to fly, I don't know what would have happened. If I crashed from a vast height in my spirit body would I be unharmed or would it be as if I were my physical self?

I knelt next to the bathing pool and reached for the knife. Was it because of the loss of our connection that his eyes were so empty, or was there more? I knew I felt the lack; I could see him, but I had no idea of what his emotional state was. I couldn't *feel* him, and it hurt.

"Fionn?" he said, as I lifted the knife from his fingers and almost immediately dropped it, unable to keep a solid hold on it.

The sound of the blade hitting the stone floor was loud in the small room.

"I'm here, Kiernan," I said, touching his face. He didn't feel quite solid, and he didn't react to my touch at all, so I wasn't sure he even felt it. "I'm here, and I'm still your Fionn."

He lurched forward in the pool as if he could grab me, but his hands passed right through me, as if I truly was a ghost. He couldn't see me, and couldn't feel me, and I wasn't sure he'd heard me, either, after those first few words. How was I supposed to help him?

I pushed the knife farther away, scowling at it as if that could make it more solid under my hand. Kiernan groped for it, but I had moved it out of his reach. He stood up to climb out of the pool.

Halfway out of the water he paused, listening. His ears were better than mine, and at first I didn't know what he had heard. But then I caught the sound: quiet footsteps somewhere beyond the door, a door opening, footsteps again. The bedroom door rattled, but it was locked.

Kiernan reached for the knife again and said, without looking up, "I'm sorry Fionn. Beloved. I'm so sorry."

"I'm *here*, Kiernan," I said, my voice turning desperate.

A knock on the bedroom door startled us both, though we had both heard the footsteps.

"My Prince?" came a voice. "Kiernan?"

"Go *away*, Daphnis," Kier said. He swayed on hands and knees on the stone, his head hanging between his arms, close enough to the knife to reach it. He looked defeated. Even injured and close to death, I had never seen him give up before.

Not like this.

What had happened? What had that horrible feeling been right before our connection was cut off?

The door rattled again, gently, as if someone was playing with the knob, and then it swung open.

A tall, thin dryad stepped briskly in, carrying a tray. When they saw the bedroom empty, they set the tray on a dresser and turned towards the bathing room. They spotted me through the open door and stopped. Their eyes went to Kiernan and widened when they saw the blood dripping down his arm.

"What?" they said.

"He can't hear me," I said. "I stopped him, but now he can't see me."

The dryad said, "My Prince, your beloved is here."

How did they know who I was? Had Kiernan told them about me?

"He's not real," Kiernan said, misery in his voice and every quiver of his muscles. "I thought he was here but it's just the fever."

"He is here, my Prince. And your fever is gone. Your Seer is here next to you. You can't see him because…" The dryad hesitated, like he didn't want to have to say the rest of the sentence. "Because your magic is gone."

I heard a thin keening sort of sound and for a moment I thought it was me. Kier was half-made of magic, how could it just be gone? But then I realized the sound was him. He collapsed to the floor and the dryad crossed the room to pick him up.

"Come sit with him, my Seer," said the dryad. Not, "Seer Fionn" or "Seer Tokka," but "*my* Seer." That seemed significant.

"He can't see me," I said, feeling stupid. "He can't hear me or feel me."

"But I can." The dryad carried Kiernan to the bed and tucked him under the blankets, leaving his injured arm uncovered. They smoothed the covers over his chest, as I would have done, and I felt a sudden stab of anger. *I* should have been the one caring for Kier, not this stranger.

But of course, the dryad was not a stranger to Kier. I swallowed back my jealousy.

I watched, helpless, as the dryad cleaned and bandaged Kiernan's arm, draped a damp cloth over his forehead, and tucked a curl of hair back from his face.

"Tell him…" I said, and then didn't know how to continue. This felt wrong. I was the seer; I should be the one relaying messages from unseen occupants in the room.

"My Prince," said the dryad softly.

"Why can't you just let me die?" said Kiernan and something painful stabbed at my heart.

"Aside from the fact that I am not *allowed* to let you die, my Prince, I am fairly sure your beloved would find some way to have revenge on me if I did, seer or no."

Kiernan turned miserable eyes on the dryad, and I took a half step forward, wanting to touch him, to comfort him.

"It hurts," he said. "At first, the connection was just… gone. Like my magic is gone. But where it used to be…" Beneath the blankets, he pressed a hand to his belly. "It hurts."

"I know, my Prince," said the dryad.

"I can't do this, Daph."

"You can."

"I'm not that strong."

"You are. And your Seer, your own Fionn, he has come to help you."

Kiernan's eyes darted around the room, looking for me, but not seeing me. "Is he really here?"

"He is, my Prince. Right here next to me."

He turned his face to the pillow and closed his eyes. "I don't want him to see me like this."

That hurt. I knew why he didn't want me to see him so weak, but it still felt like someone had stolen all my air.

The dryad met my eyes. His were dark brown and depthless.

"Tell him I don't care. Tell him I love him. Tell him…" The tears I had been holding back spilled over and I pressed my hands over my mouth to keep from wailing like a frightened child.

"My Prince, he loves you, no matter what state you are in. And he already knows how strong you are, and he says you are allowed to be weak sometimes." They smiled softly and Kiernan turned his eyes back to meet theirs. "He does not think any less of you."

"Tell him… Tell him this makes me love him even more. That he keeps *me* strong. Tell him I need him. *I* need him to live." I grasped the dryad's arm as I spoke and found him solid to me as Kier was not, as the knife had not been.

The dryad relayed my message, changing my words just enough that somehow they sounded better, stronger, more loving. Then they said, "I may know a way you can see each other."

I didn't know if they were speaking to Kier, or me, or both of us, but the two of us stared at them.

"My Seer, if you would allow yourself to be absorbed into me, you could borrow my body."

"I couldn't ask that," I said, just as Kiernan said, "We could never ask you to give up your body."

A small smile touched the dryad's mouth. "It would be very temporary, but it would allow you to talk. To… touch."

The dryad met my eyes. "My Seer, I don't mind. Speak to him. Hold him. Kiss him, even."

There was something more in his expression I could almost read, that if he had been human or fey or even Vogel, I could have read with my seer abilities. But he was a dryad, and opaque. It felt like maybe he wanted me to use him because he could never do those things for Kier himself, and I wondered what their relationship was. I felt a little like I was the intruder in something I didn't understand.

"But you're solid to me," I said, putting my hand on his arm again.

"Yes, but that's why I believe this will work." He shook his head. "I can't explain, but because you can touch me, you should be able to use my body."

I looked at Kiernan. He seemed small and young and broken and I wanted to comfort him. The raven had brought me here for this, hadn't it?

I nodded. "If you're sure you're willing," I said. "I don't want to… to use you against your… without your…"

"I am willing, my Seer."

I nodded again. "What do I do?"

"Close your eyes. Connect to the Realms, to your magic as a seer."

"Can I do that without a physical form?"

"I should think it would be easier." There was humor in their voice and it made me wonder what sort of secrets dryads kept from those who controlled them, what sort of magic they had that no one knew about. And why this one was so willing to help Kiernan.

"You're trusting me with an awful lot," I said, and I think they knew I meant more than just the use of their body.

"I am aware, my Seer."

"Why?"

They shrugged. "My people revere seers. And your people and mine once lived in harmony, honoring the same spirits, and speaking the same sacred language."

I bit my lip. I had only read a very little about dryads in my investigations into Vogel history, but now was not the time to ask questions about how we were related.

Kiernan had closed his eyes again and almost seemed asleep, but his body was tense.

"Okay," I said. I closed my eyes and began one of the calming breathing exercises I had learned at the Abbey of the Moon. I connected to the three Realms the way Kiernan had taught me to, and to my own magic the way the human Seer Moira had showed me.

"Now," said the dryad, aware without having to be told when I was ready. "Take a step towards me."

I stepped.

"And another."

I took another step.

"Now imagine you are embodied inside me," they said. "That my physical self is a suit of clothes you wear." *I am still here, but only in the background.*

I realized his last words had not been spoken aloud, that I heard them only inside my mind.

Now open your eyes.

I opened my eyes and almost fell over. Everything looked strange, like dryads saw the world differently, a different range of colors, or… something.

I looked down at myself and saw the dryad's body and mine, superimposed. Then something shifted, and it was only me.

For a moment, I thought it hadn't worked and I was back to my half-corporeal spirit body. Then I heard Kiernan gasp. He sat up.

"Fionn?" he said, his voice full of hope. And fear.

I sat on the edge of the bed. "I'm here," I said, and I realized I sounded almost as broken, and as relieved, as he did.

And then his arms were around me, his face buried against my shoulder, and I held him, stroked his hair, kissed his head between his antlers.

He sobbed as if he'd thought I was lost forever. Which wasn't really an unreasonable assumption, after all.

"My beloved," I said into his hair. I was crying, too, and trying not to drip mucous onto him. "I'm here. I love you. I'm here."

Eventually his sobs eased, and he sat back, groped for a washcloth on the nightstand, and wiped his face. Then he wiped mine, his hands as gentle as they always were with me.

"How?" he said.

I put my hand on his face and traced the curve of his cheekbone. He closed his eyes, then opened them again, like he didn't want to let me out of his sight.

"I don't know," I said. "I think I'm having a vision, only somehow my spirit traveled here, to you." I touched his full lower lip; how I loved his lips. "A raven brought me." I shrugged.

"You're finding your magic," he said, and smiled. But then his smile faded. "She took my magic, Fionn," he said, and his voice broke. "That's how she decided to punish me."

"I'm so sorry," I said. It seemed such a pathetic few words. "I felt it happen. I didn't know what it was, only that it was terrible."

"She said I was too powerful. That I need to learn to live without magic." He searched my eyes. "Fionn, I can't do this."

Once, I had said those same words to him, when I had known we had to part, that I had to go to the Eyrie and leave him behind. This was so much worse than what I had had to face – what I still faced every day – and I felt cruel for asking him to suffer.

But I needed him to live.

"You *can* do this, beloved. I know you can. You are the strongest person I've ever met, and I wouldn't ask this of you if I didn't know you could do it."

He held my hand in his and traced my fingers. My hands were thin and smooth and soft, except in a few places where I had small callouses from spinning and weaving. His were strong and muscular, with callouses on every finger from practicing with his knives and his sword. We were so different, but we fit together so well. And though he touched me then the same way my King had touched me, it didn't feel the same at all.

He met my eyes, and I could see that something in his mind had shifted.

"Will you forgive me, beloved?" he said, and I had to catch my breath at the way he pronounced that final word: like it meant everything.

"For what?" I felt a trickle of dread down my spine, afraid that he might be about to tell me that he was going to leave me anyway.

But he said, "For doubting you. For doubting *us*."

I rested my forehead against his. "There's nothing to forgive."

"Forgive me anyway."

"Of course I forgive you."

He sighed, and tension eased out of his muscles. "Goddess Below, I love you so fucking much."

"Now that sounds like *my* Kier."

He found a smile for me, and even a small laugh. "Will you kiss me, pretty bird?"

"I'm borrowing a body," I said. "I'm not sure."

Yes, said Daphnis. *Kiss him. He needs you.*

"Daphnis says I should kiss you," I said.

"But do *you* want to kiss me?" There was a teasing note in Kier's voice that eased something in my heart that I hadn't realized was pained.

"Always," I said and leaned closer to brush my lips against Kiernan's. His response was just as gentle, almost uncertain, and I remembered the first time we had kissed. I had been so afraid I would do something wrong, that I would be bad at it, but when he'd flicked his tongue against mine, I had moaned, and he'd laughed gently and did it again. And it had been perfect.

He parted his lips, and I was suddenly so hungry for him that my worries melted away and I just wanted to be as close to him as I could get.

I slid my tongue into his mouth, and he was the one to moan softly this time, to open his mouth wider to let me in.

His hands found my face, my neck, my shoulders, and before I even thought about what I was doing, I had pushed him back on the bed, my hands stroking over his chest, his belly, and back up his ribs.

I pulled away, suddenly remembering Daphnis. Kiernan laughed quietly. "I missed you, Fionn," he said, tucking my head against his chest.

"I missed you, too."

"Is he good to you, your King?"

I almost pulled away then, and I knew he felt the change in my demeanor.

"He's… he's fine. Most of the time."

Kier nuzzled my hair. "I'm so sorry, pretty bird. I didn't want to leave you with him. Fuck." His hand tightened on the back of my neck.

I shifted to tuck myself more closely against his side. "Neither of us had a choice," I said.

"Has he hurt you?"

"No."

He sighed and stroked a hand down my back. "It's so strange not to feel your wings," he said, and I'd have sat up in startlement, twisted to look over my shoulder to make sure my wings were still there, but he held me close to his chest. "I can feel the feathers on your back." One hand stroked my back again and his fingers slipped between the feathers to touch my skin. "But I can't feel your wings."

I could grow wings, of a sort, said Daphnis in my head. *If it would make you more comfortable.*

"I can feel them," I said. "It feels strange when your hand passes through them."

We lay together a while longer, not speaking, just taking comfort in the presence of each other.

I thought I heard a rustling of feathers outside the window, and I ignored it.

"What do we do now?" Kier said.

"I don't know." I ran a hand over his chest, pausing to touch one of his nipples and smiling when it stiffened under my fingers. He laughed, just a soft breath of sound.

"I think you're obsessed with my nipples," he said, teasing.

"Of course I am," I replied, pinching the one under my fingers so he drew his breath in sharply. "I don't have any."

Tok, I heard, and ignored it.

"Do you want me to come to the Eyrie and steal you away?" he said.

"Yes," I replied. "But first you must get your magic back."

Tok, said the raven again. *Kark.*

Kier shifted beside me and lifted my head up so I had to look at him. "Do you mean that, pretty bird?"

"That you have to get your magic back?"

The corner of his mouth twitched. "That you want me to steal you away." He looked so serious. So deadly, calmly serious.

"Yes," I said, realizing it was true. There were things I wanted to learn about my ancestors, ways I wanted to help my people, but more than that, I wanted to do all of it with Kiernan standing beside me. "I think… I think I can do a lot for my people if I can figure out how to get the King to actually let me be his fucking seer." I stopped.

"You must be serious," Kier said. "You said a swear."

I stuck my tongue out at him.

Tok, said the raven. *Come, child. We must go.*

Only if you let me come back, I thought at it fiercely.

I felt its amusement. *You figure out how, little one, and you may return as often as you like.*

"So, you *don't* want me to steal you away?"

"What if there was a way… a way to help all peoples, and not just mine?" I said.

"How?" His fingers were soft on my hair, like he still couldn't quite believe I was there.

"I don't know yet." I chewed the inside of my cheek. "But you figure out how to get your magic back, and I'll figure out how to be a real seer. The rest we'll figure out together."

He gazed at me, eyes shining. "And then?"

"And then come steal me away from my King and we'll change the fucking world."

I could feel something like approval from Daphnis as the raven's magic pulled me away and I saw Kier notice the moment I left the dryad's body.

He gently pushed Daphnis away and though he couldn't see me anymore I knew his smile was just for me.

"I will come get you, beloved," he said.

"I know." And then I climbed out the window – and didn't get stuck – and let the raven lead me back over the forest to where my body waited, sprawled on the stone on my balcony.

5

Kiernan

Daphnis stood up from the bed and tucked the blanket back over me.

"Are you feeling better, my Prince?"

I looked away, wanting to touch him again, to see if there was any remnant of Fionn left in him. But of course there wouldn't be.

"He said a raven brought him here."

"He did, my Prince. Will you eat? I brought bread and cheese. Blackberry preserves. They say the blackberries are sweet this year."

"How did you do that?" I said.

He didn't wait for my answer about eating; he just brought the tray to the bed and began to layer bread and cheese and fruit for me.

"How did I do what, my Prince?"

"Let Fionn borrow your body. He looked like himself, felt like him. Fuck, Daphnis, he even *smelled* like Fionn."

He stopped arranging the food and looked at me, sighed,

and pulled a chair over from my desk. "May I sit?"

"You don't need to ask permission to sit."

"I am your servant. I *do* need to ask."

"Fine. As your master, I order you not to ask my permission to do every basic fucking everyday thing."

He snorted – amused, I think – and sat on the chair.

"I am trusting, my Prince, that you truly are the friend you claim to be."

My stomach rumbled and I picked up a slice of bread and looked at it. Daphnis had put a thick layer of preserves on it and topped it with a cheese that smelled sharp and salty.

"I *am* your friend," I said, and took a bite. It was good. Better than good. I shoved the rest of the slice into my mouth.

Daphnis looked amused again and said, "Slowly, my Prince. You've been ill and haven't eaten for days. Go too quickly and I'll be washing your vomit-soaked sheets again."

I picked up another slice, took a small bite, and raised an eyebrow at him as I chewed it slowly.

"Your Queen, any of your noble relations, would kill me if they knew. Or perhaps torture me." He looked at his hands. "They might even use it as an excuse to slaughter my people." He looked back at me, his brown eyes so dark I almost couldn't tell his pupils from his irises.

I swallowed my bite of bread and cheese. "Perhaps it's best you *don't* tell me, then," I said. I set the bread down and put a hand on his knee, staring at the white bandage on my arm, bright against my skin. I was curious, of course, but I knew the value of secrets kept, and the danger of letting the wrong people know things.

He shook his head, squeezed my hand, and moved his knee out of my reach. "Then I shall only say this: My people still have magic, beyond those tricks that make us such good pleasure slaves, though we are very careful how we use it. And for whom."

I pushed aside thoughts of those magics that made dryads a preferred choice of bedmate – I knew about their ability to grow tendrils to the exact size and shape their partner preferred – and focused on the unknown.

"You have healing magic," I said.

He shook his head sadly. "Once, we were the greatest healers on the Isle. Now, we have only a few fragments."

"Could you regain your magic?"

He stood and put the chair back next to my desk. "Perhaps. The spellwork that keeps us enslaved could be reversed. Some of the magic we once had is no doubt lost forever, but some could be regained." He met my eyes again. "One of our Mother Trees is gone, and one is… turned to a new purpose. The third flourishes, but few dryads live in Tronven now."

I looked at him, chewing my food thoughtfully, and swallowed. "Your Mother Trees?"

"The Heart of Aven was a great salt-leaf that once stood in Aven Forest not far from the Eyrie. It was destroyed centuries ago, the last time the Royal Plague swept through the Vogel royal family."

"The Heart of Morven…" I said, forgetting my meal.

"Is now a hall and a throne room for our Sidhe overlords, yes. Once a dryad priest would have sat in that chair and acted as Seer."

"But… dryads don't have seers," I said. "If dryads had seers, they'd be a monarchy. They'd never have been enslaved." Because when the Nine Monarchies were formed, it was peoples who had seers that became states, and peoples who didn't who became subjects.

His smile was wry, just a small hint of a twisted curve to his lips. "We have no seers," he said. "But there is a little bit of seer magic in all dryads, and when a priest sat in the crown of a Mother Tree, my people could join those bits together and the priest would channel them and be our Seer for a short time."

"But… isn't this something the Monarchs should know? That you should be free and have your own rulers?"

He shook his head. "Perhaps, but with the Monarchs we have now, I think it would be an excuse to end my people entirely, so we could never be a threat."

"I should have guessed," I said. "About the Heart of Morven, at least."

"At least she is alive and healthy," he replied. "Even if we are not permitted to put a priest on her throne or hold our rites at her feet."

"I'm so sorry. It's all so wrong."

"It happened long before either of us was born."

"How can the spellwork be broken?" I said. I put the tray aside and pushed back the blankets. I need to move, to walk in the forest even if I couldn't feel its magic.

"I don't know. I'm not even certain it *can* be."

As I went to stand, I realized I was naked. Because of course there would have been no point in dressing me when I kept sweating and puking all over everything.

It didn't embarrass me to be naked; in fact, I rather enjoyed not having clothes on. But I couldn't help thinking it might bother Fionn, that he might not like me to be unclothed in front of others – in front of Daphnis, especially, as we had history together. I pushed the thought aside and stood up, crossing the room to my dresser and wardrobe.

As I rummaged in a drawer, Daphnis stepped beside me.

"If I may, my Prince," he said.

"I'm not such an invalid that I need help dressing." I wouldn't admit out loud that just standing upright made me feel weak.

"Of course, my Prince. But your Queen expects you to be waited on, now. And she expects you to dress as befits your station."

"Why now? She never cared before."

"I expect she cared more than you knew. And I suppose she believes you have had enough freedom."

I started to say something about never having had *any* freedom, but saying something like that to a member of an enslaved people would be insensitive, at the least.

"Fine," I said. "I suppose she has supplied me with a wardrobe."

"I believe the tailor is to attend you once you're well again. This evening, perhaps."

I wandered back over to the nightstand and took another slice of bread and cheese from the tray. It was early in the season for blackberries, but they *were* sweet.

"In the meantime," Daphnis said. "I found a few suitable items when I was cleaning."

"You cleaned my bedroom?" I looked around. It did look much tidier than usual.

"All of your rooms, yes. I needed something to do besides sponge your brow while you were unconscious."

"There are people who are paid to clean," I said. "You don't have to do that." I didn't point out that I rarely even let any of the paid staff clean my rooms. I didn't like other people touching my things.

He ignored my comment and turned from the dresser with an armful of clothes that he began to hand to me, one item at a time. As I put each garment on, I realized I was dressing in the same clothing I had worn at the farewell ceremony in the Eyrie. They were the clothes I had been wearing the last time I saw Fionn, when I had whispered my promise to be his as I bent over his hand.

I sat down on the edge of the bed, only half dressed.

"My Prince?" said Daphnis, laying a tailored jacket in dark moss green with subtle embroidery on the bed next to me and tugging at the shoulders of my shirt to get it to sit better.

"I'm fine," I said, but my heart ached. My chest ached from lack of magic, and my belly ached from the broken connection to Fionn.

I looked at my hands. "Where is my ring?"

"There," said Daphnis, satisfied with the drape of my shirt and turning to point to the wooden box on my dresser.

I stood and crossed to it, opened it, and scowled at the assortment of trinkets I never wore. "It's not here."

Daphnis appeared behind my shoulder and reached out to touch a wide band of moonsilver with the nicFia stag engraved on it. "Here," he said.

"Not that one."

"Oh," he said. "The cloud silk band." He held the jacket out for me and waited, silent, until I put my arms in the sleeves, and he settled it on my shoulders. He turned me around and began to fasten the buttons.

"Yes, the cloud silk one, Daphnis. Where is it?" I tried not to snap, to keep the edge from my voice, but that ring was the only thing I had of Fionn aside from the white feather in my ink stand.

"With your antler pendant, my Prince." His mouth twitched slightly, as if he was trying not to smile. "It seemed a better place for it."

"And how did you know where I keep my antler pendant?" I turned back to the dresser, felt around behind its back edge until I located the hidden catch and a small compartment between the two top drawers popped open.

"I found it when I was cleaning," he said.

"Of course you did."

"You were unconscious for a long time, my Prince. I had time to be thorough."

I snorted and looked into the compartment. It held only three objects: a ring of gold with my father's coat of arms on it, a delicate set of miniature antlers carved of wood and strung on a plain string, and a silver-white ring braided of Fionn's hair.

"You plan to wear it, my Prince?" Daphnis's voice held caution, like he believed I should keep that ring secret. He was right, of course. He waited for me to turn around again and held out a pair of soft knit socks in one hand and my nicest boots in the other.

I lifted the thin circle of white out of the compartment and snapped it shut. I slid the ring onto the middle finger of my right hand – because I was left-handed, my right was what the Sidhe call the "hand of promise," where we wear wedding bands, promise rings, and symbols of our patrons or masters on the middle finger. I looked at the line of gleaming white across my dark skin for a moment, before sliding the wide nic-Fia ring over it to hide it.

"I made a promise to him," I said. "So yes, I will wear it." Hidden, because my life wasn't really my own to promise to anyone. My promise to *myself* was to find a way to change that.

Daphnis held out the socks and I scowled at them. "Perhaps once we're actually *in* the forest, my Prince, you can go barefoot."

"We?" I said. "Are you to follow me everywhere, then?" I sat on the desk chair and pulled on the socks, and then my boots. If I had to wear footwear, I'd have preferred my well-worn travel boots, but I supposed they wouldn't exactly go with the outfit.

"I am your attendant, your servant, your valet," he said. "Unless you send me on a task, I am to go where you go."

"Does my Queen require you to stand over me while I take a shit?" I said, and immediately regretted it. It wasn't his fault.

"Your Queen can no longer command me to do anything, my Prince, because I belong to you now. But I have duties I must fulfill, no matter who owns me."

I opened my mouth to apologize, but he held up a hand.

"And no, I am not required to accompany you to the latrine." He smiled a little more than his tiny, amused smirk. "Unless you wish me to."

"Well, at least I like your company," I said, standing and stamping my feet to settle the boots. "I am very glad, Daphnis, that you happened to be standing in the right place when she decided I needed someone to carry me to bed and catch my puke in a bowl."

"Thank you," he said. "I think." Then he smiled again. "But you assume I was there by chance."

"Weren't you?"

He only turned away to hold the door.

I TRIED TO LET THE CALM of the forest settle over me, to breathe in its green smells, its dampness, its stillness that was somehow never still at all.

It was better than the confines of the palace, but I couldn't *feel* it. For as long as I could remember, the forest had been a part of me. I could read its moods, its health; I could let it read me in turn. With a little magic, I could almost see it spread out like a map around me, could sense where rivers ran and how deep, where caves lay hidden, where animals bedded down.

Now I felt nothing. I tripped over fallen tree limbs, got branches and leaves tangled in my hair, and had to rely on sight alone to tell me where I was. And before long, I realized I was lost. It was not that the place I found myself was unfamiliar – I knew every smallest part of this forest as well as I knew my own body – but I couldn't remember where I was in relation to any other part of the forest, and I didn't know how to get back.

I had never had to *think* about these things before. And for the first time in my life, I felt afraid in the woods. Afraid that I might wander forever and never find my way back to the palace. And that small part of me that had made me press a knife to my arm in despair whispered that maybe it was better this way, that losing myself in the dark between trees until there was nothing left of me was an even better way out.

"Fuck," I said under my breath. I had promised Fionn to be his, and he had asked me to live. For him, I would do my best to carry on.

Daphnis said nothing. He stood patiently, nearly invisible in the shadows in his plain brown tunic and trousers. If I hadn't already known his people were kin to trees, I would have realized it then.

"I suppose we shall have to ask the tailor to make you some suitable livery," I said, just to say something, to distract myself from the awful fact of being lost in my own forest. "I don't think the Queen would deem a drudge's clothing suitable for a Prince's attendant."

"Probably not, my Prince."

"Can't you just call me Kiernan? At least when we're alone?"

"And if someone were to overhear?"

I frowned, chose a direction, and began to walk. I followed a deer path and, like most animal trails, it eventually dwindled to nothing and left me standing between trees with nowhere to go. But I glimpsed sky ahead, and stars, so I pushed through the undergrowth until I came out at the edge of a meadow.

The grass was long dead, still tall but dried to stiff stalks. Whatever flowers grew here in warmer days were gone, save for a few stubborn daisies that still turned their faces skywards.

I turned to look down the slope of grass, knowing what I would see and almost afraid to look. There, its back to us, crouched a small cabin. It looked cozy in the dark, but I knew it was three years abandoned, cold and empty. In front of it ran a swift stream full of fat trout. I had fished here often, before my Queen decided to acknowledge me as her heir and make me her lackey.

Why had my feet brought me here, of all places? Had my unconscious mind, hurting at the loss of Fionn, decided to remind me of another loss, to pile sorrow on sorrow until I might drown in it?

"My Prince?" said Daphnis, softly. I hadn't heard him approach. "Kiernan?" He put a hand on my shoulder, and I resisted the urge to lean against him. "Do you know this place?"

For a moment I didn't answer. I couldn't answer. In the dark, I could almost imagine the werewolf who had lived there coming around the corner of the cabin to fetch more logs from the woodpile, grinning when he caught sight of me.

For a moment, I couldn't breathe.

Finally, I forced myself to draw in a lungful of air, slow and deliberate. "I had… I knew the man who built the cabin," I finally said.

"He was a friend?" Daphnis moved his hand to my other shoulder, so his arm draped across me. Again, I had to resist the urge to lean on him, to take comfort in his touch.

"More than a friend," I said, and stepped away from him, out onto the grass. I crossed the meadow to the cabin and looked up at the single dark window on its back wall. Beyond that window, I knew, was the bedroom. I had looked out on the meadow from the other side of the glass many times.

Daphnis's feet shushed through the grass as he followed me.

"His name was Dec," I said. "Declan Winterborn."

"You named your sword for him."

I looked at him in surprise. I hadn't realized he knew the name I'd given my sword after I took it from my cousin Sean. It seemed there was a lot about Daphnis that I hadn't realized. "You were… still in the gardens when I met him," I said. "And when… when he was murdered."

He looked up at the sky. "I was sent to the pleasure gardens for three handsful of years," he said. "I was nineteen when I entered the gardens and I only came out this summer, when you were on your way to the Abbey of the Moon. I thought, once, that it was punishment for… for being with you."

He looked at me and met my eyes. "But I realized, when your Queen released me and the others I had gone in with, that she probably couldn't even tell us apart. She didn't even know who I was, let alone who I spent my days with before the gardens." He sighed. "When she returned us to the palace to work as attendants and drudges, I doubt she even knew what we had done before. I still don't know if our release was because we were being rewarded for doing well as pleasure slaves or if we weren't good enough to remain there. Or, more likely, it was simply whim."

"I'm sorry, Daph," I said, knowing as I said it that the words were useless.

"Did *you* miss me, at least?" he said, and for the first time I heard something in his voice besides carefully measured tones or mild amusement. He sounded… wistful? Sad?

"Of course," I said. I touched his hand, and he moved

closer, looking down at my face, studying me, perhaps to determine if I lied. He knew, he had always known, that unlike my full-fey relatives, I could lie. I stared up at him, overcome by a memory of him looking at me in just that way, fifteen years ago, before he had kissed me and confessed I made him want to do much more than kiss.

"Daphnis?" My voice came out as a whisper. For a long moment I thought he would kiss me, just as he had in that long-ago memory, but then he stepped away.

"Your Dec was a werewolf?" he said. "Your Queen must be disappointed that her son and heir kept choosing partners who were not of his own people."

"I'm only third heir, and *she* never said anything. Besides which, I've fucked plenty of pretty fey courtiers." I made myself go around the side of the cabin and trailed my hand over the chimney stones as I walked. "It was my cousin who was fond of pointing out that I liked to fuck vermin."

"I assume 'vermin' was his choice of word?"

"Of course it was." I glanced back at him, stung that he could think *I* might say such a thing. "I've never thought werewolves were in any way lesser than fey."

"What about dryads?" he said. "Or Vogel?"

"Do I need to answer that?" I rounded the corner towards the cabin's front door, but decided I didn't want to go inside. Dec was gone and seeing his home dusty and cold would only bring back the hurt of his loss even more.

"I suppose not."

I turned to the stream and paused on its bank, staring down into the water. "How am I supposed to do this?" I said.

"Do what, my Prince?"

"Carry on, as if everything is fine. As if my magic wasn't stripped away, my connection to the forest wasn't severed, my beloved…"

He moved close again, standing near enough I could feel his warmth, but not quite touching me.

"You could do as I do," he said.

I glanced at him. His eyes were focused far away, looking into the forest on the other side of the stream.

I touched his hand and he blinked.

"What do you do?"

"I look for the good, the beautiful, the interesting," he said. "And I get through each day, one day at a time."

"Tell me what good you see." I let my fingers wrap around his and squeeze.

"There is the glint of starlight on the stream," he said. "The way the breeze smells as if it has touched every leaf in Morven." He turned his hand so our fingers twined together. "There is the music of swaying trees and howling wolves."

I closed my eyes and inhaled deep through my nose. I couldn't feel the forest, but I *could* smell it, and like Daphnis said, it seemed like the breeze had touched every leaf in Morven and brought the scents of all them to my nose. I opened my eyes again and saw how the stars, bright white against the black sky, picked out every ripple of the stream and edged them in faint silver. And I listened and heard the wind playing the leaves and the tree trunks like a huge living instrument. Far off, wolves sang to each other. I couldn't understand them anymore, but I could still hear the music in their voices.

My chest still ached, but the forest made it feel a little less terrible.

"What else?" I whispered.

He turned to face me and tightened his fingers on mine.

"People," he said. "My people still have each other, and we have a hope for a better future. We may not be able to hold our rites at the feet of our Mother Tree, but we can still honor the spirits."

"That sounds lovely," I said, and he smiled, just a slight up-lift of the corners of his thin lips.

"We can still have children to carry on after us, to pass our magic to," he said. "And we can still speak to the trees, if only a little."

He took a half step closer, so his chest brushed mine and I had to tilt my head back to look into his eyes.

"What else?"

He touched my face with his free hand. "We have friend-ships," he said. "And we have lovers."

"Daphnis."

He brushed his fingertips across my lips.

"When your Seer was borrowing my body," he said, bend-ing his neck so his forehead was against mine. "He reminded me…"

I knew I should step away, should keep him from saying too much. He was my friend, but he could not be more than that. I would not break my promise to Fionn.

"Your Seer is far away," he said. "But he loves you so."

"I love him," I said.

"He loves you and…" He hesitated. "My Prince. Kiernan, I…"

Finally, I managed to step away. I felt suddenly cold. "Please, Daph, don't."

He kept hold of my fingers for a long heartbeat, then an-other, then finally let go. "He made me remember, my Prince, that I loved you once. That you were my *first* love." He turned away to look at the stream again. "A love I could never have, no matter that you were willing to share my bed."

"Daph…"

"I am your servant, my Prince, not only because I have to be, but because I *want* to be."

6
Fionn

I WAS SO FULL OF JOY when I climbed out Kier's window and let the raven's magic and the night wind lift me into the sky that I felt like I might float up and up until I disappeared among the stars. Instead of just following along as the raven led me over Morven Forest, across the Great River, and into Aven, I swooped around it, tilting and turning my wings and tail.

I had dreamed of flying my whole life, but with stunted wings I had believed it was something I could never have. And maybe I wasn't in my physical body, but I could still *feel* it. I could feel the air moving around me, the thrill as I closed my wings and dipped, and the stomach-clenching delight as I snapped them open and swooped suddenly upwards.

One would think you'd never flown before, said the raven, its tone amused.

"I haven't," I said.

It couldn't curve its beak into a smile, but I heard the humor in its tone. *You have. You just don't remember yet.*

I banked closer and tried to peer into the bird's seer-silver eyes. "What do you mean?"

I mean, child, that I have collected your spirit from your body before, and you have flown with me.

The bird suddenly rolled over to fly upside down for a few wingbeats before righting itself and continuing its slow, steady pace. I tried to copy the maneuver and laughed when it worked.

And shrieked when I suddenly dropped towards the trees. I caught myself and beat my wings hard to catch up.

"Where did you take me, before?" I said. "How many times? Why don't I remember?"

You will remember soon, it said. *It is nearly time.*

"Did you take me to Kiernan? Does he remember?"

He remembers no more than you do.

"Will he remember this time?"

With a dryad to help, he just might.

"Will I remember this time? Please let me remember."

That depends on you, but I would be surprised if you did not remember.

I saw the hills of Aven gathering below us and knew we would soon be back at the Eyrie, and my body. And then there would be no more time for questions.

"You said I could go back," I said.

If you can figure out how.

"Won't you tell me?"

You already have a clue, the raven said.

"What clue?"

Remember what you were dreaming before I came to fetch you. That was as much a vision as this is.

I flew straight and steady for a while, trying to recall any dreams I had before I woke too hot and stumbled out onto my balcony. Nothing came to mind.

"I can't remember," I said.

The bird snorted. *Do you not have magic for the recall of damaged memories?*

"But I can't use that on *myself*. Can I?" I touched my forehead, thinking about how I had helped Kiernan regain a memory in the Abbey of the Moon, and how I hadn't had the first idea of what I was doing when I did it. I had only known it was possible, not how.

I don't advise trying it until you're back on solid ground, back in your body, the raven said.

I moved my hand away from my forehead. "Of course."

I tried a few more dips and swoops, a few more aerobatics, but my mind was too full of thoughts, of questions, of ideas, to really enjoy the play, so I finally settled down to follow the raven along the course of a river to the shore, and along the beach to the outthrust cliff that held the Eyrie.

"Will you come to fetch me again?" I said, when we landed on my balcony. I felt a smile curve my lips when I thought of kissing Kiernan, of his eyes when he realized I was really there, of his teasing when I touched his nipples.

Perhaps if his need is great enough and you haven't figured out spirit flight on your own.

"Only *his* need?"

The bird looked at me from one eye and then from the other. *You will learn that soon enough.*

"But I can go to him on my own, if I find out how?"

The raven nodded. *So I have told you at least twice now.* It sounded stern, but its silver eyes glistened.

"If I separate my spirit body from my physical body…" I mused, feeling like I had begun to solve a puzzle.

The bird made a chuckling sound, then hopped off the balcony railing to disappear into the darkness below.

"But how do I do that without dying?" No answer came.

I turned to re-enter my body and stared. The stone floor of

my balcony was empty.

"Raven?" I said. "Are you still there? My body's gone."
How long had I been out of my physical form? I supposed someone must have found me and brought me inside. I couldn't be dead, could I?

That thought froze me for a moment. The idea that I had flown across most of the width of the Isle to ask Kiernan to live, only to arrive back and find myself dead made me want to scream.

But if I was dead, surely I would feel the spirits calling, the afterlife pulling at me. Wouldn't I?

I peered into my sitting room, but it was dark, only the faint moonlight peeking in to trace the edges of objects with a silver outline. But I could see a glow from under my bedroom door.

I walked the length of my balcony to the smaller door that led to my sleeping chamber, and warm yellow lamplight spilled out there. Not a lot – only a single lamp burned on the far side of the room – but enough that I could see my huge bed and the silhouette of someone sitting in a chair next to it.

Neeka. She was slouched in the chair, wrapped in a blanket. I thought I could also make out a shape under the blankets on the bed that must be me.

I put a hand out to open the door and was reminded of how nothing was quite solid when I was in my spirit body. I had managed, only just, to push Kiernan's knife out of his reach. Now, I could grasp the door handle, but I couldn't manage to move it. It felt almost spongy under my hand.

I gritted my teeth and added my other hand, leaning my

weight down on the handle. It shifted slightly, but only enough to rattle the latch, like a gust of wind had hit the glass. Neeka looked up, and away again.

<Neeka!> She shifted in the chair and glanced over her shoulder, but I don't think she really heard me.

"Fuck," I said, and scowled, as if acting like Kier would help me figure out what he would do in such a situation.

I grasped the door handle in both hands again and leaned on it as hard as I could, jerking it up and down, and willing it to move. It rattled. I threw my weight on it again and it began to give. Until my hands passed through and I lost my balance and fell to my knees.

And why did the stone feel solid enough to leave bruises?

I leaned against the glass and refused to cry. At least my body was safe inside, and not sprawled on the stone where I might die of exposure. I had no idea how long my body could remain alive without me in it. What if I remained trapped outside and had to watch my body waste away? What if I died safe in my bed?

I struck out at the glass, and it was like hitting a soft pillow. I hit it again and it felt the same.

"Stop panicking," I told myself sternly. "Kier wouldn't panic. Just *think*."

I placed both hands on the glass and closed my eyes and tried to focus my mind on the problem. I had been solid enough in Morven to get stuck on Kier's windowsill, but not solid enough to do more than nudge his knife away. I hadn't even been able to touch him without the dryad's help.

But the dryad was solid before he told me to connect to my magic, to close my eyes and step *into* him. Then he had not been solid, or not in the same way.

I took a deep breath, then another, using one of the Abbess's lessons in mindfulness. Then I connected to my magic and to the Realms, imagining their energy flowing through me. I got to my feet, dropped my hands from the glass, and squeezed my eyes tight.

I took a step forward and felt a tingling, like a vertical line through my body.

Oh Goddess, what if I got stuck halfway through?

I made myself breathe slowly again, touch my magic again, and I took another step, and another, until I was sure I must be in the middle of the room.

Hoping fervently that I hadn't stopped in the middle of a piece of furniture, I opened my eyes. I was, as I had hoped, in the clear space in the center of the room, between the desk near the window and the bed.

Neeka sat next to my bed staring at a book but not turning the pages. She had dark circles under her eyes and her clothes – even her feathers – were rumpled.

I turned to look at myself and was surprised at how small I looked, how young and vulnerable. Was this how the King saw me? No wonder he could pretend I was still a boy.

Even closed, my eyes looked too big for my face, and though my cheekbones were prominent there was a softness to them, too. Was this how Kiernan saw me? He called me pretty, and I supposed I was, but did that mean he thought I looked like a girl, or could I be pretty and handsome both? Did it even matter? I knew he loved me. Before our connection was severed by his loss of magic, I had been able to *feel* how he loved me, how he desired me.

I blushed in my spirit body, to think of myself that way, and I thought I saw a slight touch of pink on the cheekbones of my physical self.

It was so strange, seeing myself from the outside. You might think it couldn't be that different from looking at yourself in a mirror, but it *was* different. I had the oddest urge to protect myself, as if the me on the bed was a separate person, lost and in need of a friend.

But I *had* friends. I had Neeka and my guards. I had Moira and Col, who I might never see again, but who I felt sure would welcome me into their home if I ever made it to the werewolf village to visit. And I had Kier, far away but still trying to be strong for me.

I straightened my spine and stepped around the bed, moving to the side opposite Neeka. How did one get back into one's body after leaving it? I touched my own hand where it rested on the quilt and felt my fingers pass through.

But no, they didn't pass through, they went *into*. I felt myself drawn back into my physical self. I closed my eyes and let it pull me in until I felt whole again.

I hadn't realized how *incomplete* I had felt in my spirit body until I was back in my physical self.

I sighed and opened my eyes.

I STARED AT NEEKA for a long time before she noticed, and while I waited, I could feel a thousand different aches and pains. My joints ached. One of my wings felt like it had been twisted. My back muscles twinged from seizing. And behind my eyes the headache I always got after a vision was building, only worse than any I'd had before.

Finally, I croaked out, <Neeka?> I really needed a sip of water.

She lifted her head, met my eyes, and stared. Then she shrieked and I tried to burrow into the covers; the sound jabbed at my head like a thorn.

<Tokka!> she said, almost yelling. <My Seer!> She stood

and took two steps away then turned back, like she didn't want to leave my side.

<Konta!> she bellowed, and I hadn't known she could be so loud. <Trikta!>

The outer door banged open, then my sitting room door, and finally my bedroom door, and my two guards peered through, bird masks in hand, to stare at me.

<Hi,> I said.

They stared until Neeka shoved them back out the door. <Go get Healer Kah, you dolts. And one of you stay by the door where you're supposed to be.>

They obeyed – the way she was ordering them even the King would have been tempted to obey – and she turned back to the bed, grinning.

<You're awake,> she said, and I pulled a pillow over my face.

<I'm glad to see you, too,> I said, my voice a rasp. <But can you be quieter?>

She laughed but sat on the side of the bed without saying anything else. Her hands were gentle as she pulled the pillow away and rested her palm on my forehead.

<Headache?> she said softly.

I nodded.

<Thirsty?>

I nodded again.

She pulled me into a hug, suddenly careful, like she thought I might break. <I'll make you that tea you drink after you've had a vision.>

I sighed and she grinned again before bustling out of the room and into my sitting room, where I always had a kettle hanging over the fire.

I tried to sit up and found myself too weak to do more than shift on the mattress. Had I ever had a vision that left me so weary before? I didn't think so, but then I didn't remember ever having a vision where I left my body before, either, and the raven told me I had.

Maybe more than once.

As I lay and waited for Neeka and the pain relief tea, I went over every moment of the vision, of leaving my body and flying to Morven. Of Kiernan and the dryad, Daphnis. Of my conversation with the raven on the way back.

There was something else I needed to remember. Something about a dream? I tried to think back to before I had awakened in the night, so hot I must surely have had a fever. But thinking made my head hurt more.

Oh Goddess, fever. The Princess. Was she all right? Had she lived through the night? Was this even the same night? I didn't recall seeing any daylight, but visions can be strange in the way time passes.

When Neeka came back, I started to ask, only all my questions seemed to want to come out at once, and I couldn't make a coherent sentence.

<Drink first, my Seer,> she said, and helped me sit up. I found out very quickly how weak I was when I nearly dropped the cup into my lap.

Neeka just smiled and held it for me, her strong hands steady, even when there was a sharp knock at the door and the sound of people entering my sitting room.

<Back to your post,> said Healer Kah's low, soothing voice. Although she never failed to sound kind, she was someone who could face up to the King; neither of my guards would intimidate her.

<I only want to see that he's all right,> said Trikta.

<You already did see,> said Konta. <Come on lad, let the Healer do her work. We'll see him when she says we can.>

<But...>

<You'll see him when your replacements arrive,> said the Healer. <And then you will both go to your rooms to sleep.>

I heard feet shuffle and smiled.

<I know very well neither of you has let the other guards take over for more than a few hours at a time, and never both of you at once, since our Seer fell ill. Now go, wait outside.>

I heard them both mumble and then the outer door closed.

Neeka set the cup of tea aside and stood as Healer Kah entered. <Healer,> she said, and dipped into a half-curtsey.

The Healer nodded and set her bag on the end of the bed. <When did he wake?>

<Just now,> Neeka said. <I sent Konta for you right away, and only had time to make the tea.>

Healer Kah nodded and turned to me. <You gave us a fright, my Seer. Neeka found you on your floor caught in a vision and she and your guards put you to bed.> She moved around the bed to take Neeka's place and laid the back of her hand on my forehead. <I was able to stop your seizures but couldn't wake you.> She removed her hand. <The fever is gone. That's good.>

<I had a fever?> But of course I had, I just hadn't realized it while it was happening.

<What do you remember?> She leaned across the bed to grab her bag and rummaged inside it. <Boil more water, would you, Neeka?>

<Yes, Healer.>

<I was dreaming,> I said. The tea had eased my headache enough that I could think without stabbing pain. <I dreamed about...> I stopped myself from describing how I had dreamed of walking on the beach with Kiernan. <Salt-leaf,> I said. <I read something about salt-leaf and fever before I fell asleep.>

<And then?> She found what she had been looking for in

her bag and placed three bundles of herbs on the table next to my bed.

<I was hot. I pushed off the blankets and decided to open the balcony door, to let in some cooler air.>

I watched the Healer measure out herbs into a small dish, crush them together, and pour them into a sachet of loosely woven linen.

<Then you had a vision?> she said.

<Yes.> I didn't want to tell her I had left my body. I would if it seemed necessary, but not yet.

<Healer?>

<Hmm?> She stood and walked to the sitting room door to pass the herbs to Neeka. <Steep until the water is dark green,> she said, <Then take the herbs out and let it cool.>

She turned back to me.

<Did the Princess…?> I couldn't finish the question.

Healer Kah crossed the room to sit on the side of my bed again. <Your idea of cool baths worked much better than we could have hoped,> she said. <She still lives, but every day she wakes up a little less coherent.>

I pressed both hands over my mouth to keep from letting out the noise that was building in my chest. Both from horror that a child had suffered so, and at the thought that I had been unconscious, unable to help, trapped in my vision, for… how long?

She sighed and shut her eyes. <When you were found, caught in a vision and then feverish, our King was beside him-self, and angry that he couldn't stay with her and with you at the same time.>

<Does he know I'm awake?>

<I've given orders to let him sleep as long as he can,> she said.

<But… How long have I been… gone?>

<More than a nineday, my Seer. I sedated the King because he was frantic that he was going to lose you and the Princess both.>

7

Kiernan

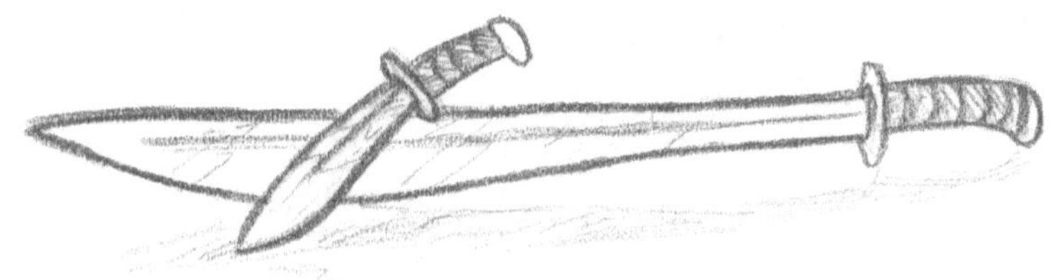

My Queen mother left me alone that night and the next, though as Daphnis had expected, the royal tailor made an appearance and measured us both. I spent much too long looking at fabrics and styles for something I really didn't care about, and finally told Daphnis to just choose what he thought was best. I was fairly sure that he cared more about how I looked than I did.

The next night, however, I had barely finished my breakfast when there was jaunty knock at my door.

"Don't answer it," I said, retreating into my bedroom to find the book I had been reading so I could return it to the palace library. I had been planning to spend the night there, researching things I thought might prove useful in the near future. Top of my list was information on breaking spellwork, especially that engraved into metals. I also wanted to read more on the early history of the Nine Monarchies and the role the dryads had played in the conquest of the Isle. And I hoped to find something about the obligations and responsibilities of monarchs to their seers.

I could also vaguely remember a treatise on artificial flight I had once thought would be interesting as a boy, until I discovered it was full of mathematical calculations and complex diagrams. I wasn't any better at math now than I had been then, but I hoped more of it would make sense.

"It could be a summons from the Queen, my Prince," Daphnis called, and I heard him open the door.

"Fuck." I knew the knock, and it probably *was* a summons from the Queen, but I didn't want to talk to my cousin Sean just then. Or ever, if I could help it. The only things I wanted from him were his blood on my sword and his head separated from his body.

I tucked the book under my arm and entered my sitting room to find my cousins Sean and Padraig lounging on my couches, their booted feet propped on my table. Daphnis had retreated to stand stiffly against the wall, eyes downcast, blending in like furniture. I hated that his people were expected to be that way.

«What do you want?» I said, crossing the room to a sideboard where I poured myself a cup of cider, and didn't offer them any. My mother would no doubt have scolded me for being so rude, but my cousins didn't deserve the courtesy of politeness. Or Sean didn't; Padraig I wasn't sure of yet, though he seemed to enjoy Sean's company too much for my liking.

«Not even a 'how are you?' cousin?» said Sean, cleaning under his claws with the tip of a small dagger and flicking the detritus onto my floor.

I crossed my arms and stared at him until he looked away. He had no more love for me than I had for him, but he hadn't been able to stare me down since I grew taller than him. We had been raised together and should have been as close as brothers, but that became impossible when Sean had let me know at a very early age that he considered half my ancestry to be barely more sentient than the deer we raised as beasts of burden.

«Our Queen sends for you,» said Padraig. Sean was a couple of years older than me, and Padraig a couple years older than that. He had not been raised at court, being a more distant cousin, though he looked enough like the rest of the royal family he could have been much closer. It's possible he might have deserved better than my contempt, but I hadn't spent enough time around him to know, and I didn't much care to.

«Are you here to escort me to her, or merely to sprinkle dirt on my table?»

Padraig moved his feet to the floor and looked sheepish. Sean grinned and thumped his heel on the edge of the table, knocking a clump of something dark and moist off the bottom of his boot and onto the polished wood surface.

I wanted to punch him in the face, to feel his nose crush under my fist and hear the satisfying crunch. It would hurt, but it would hurt him more. I had been forbidden from killing him, but my Queen hadn't specifically said I couldn't give him a few bruises occasionally.

«We'll take you to her,» said Padraig.

«I expect it's difficult to find your way around without magic,» said Sean. «We wouldn't want you wandering about lost like your human kin.»

I declined to point out that plenty of humans had magic, but even if he was wrong, he'd known the comment would sting. I hated that he knew me well enough to know that it would. Fortunately, I was used enough to his barbs and cruel attempts at humor that I didn't react. I just gestured to the door.

Both my cousins stood, and Padraig opened the door.

«After you, cousin,» said Sean.

«I think you forget yourself,» I said.

He hesitated.

«After you *my Prince*,» I said, and swept from the room. I hated to turn my back on him, but I was pretty sure he wouldn't stab me with Padraig there. «I'd ask you to go first,» I added, «But you probably don't have the guts to stick me in the back unless you can think of a way to blame someone else.»

«My Prince,» he said, and muttered something under his breath that was almost certainly unflattering. I knew he was probably glaring at me from narrowed eyes because I knew him as well as he knew me, and I knew he hated having his honor questioned. Most likely because he didn't have any.

Padraig chuckled, whether at my comment or Sean's I didn't know.

«One day, *my Prince*,» said Sean, and he didn't need to finish the sentence. He wanted me dead because I offended his conception of what made a proper Sidhe prince. I was half human. I liked to fuck, and not just other noble fey. I made friends of werewolves and humans and treated everyone like they were just as important as everyone else. I made a terrible prince.

It was a pity my Queen couldn't see that, disinherit me, and save us all a lot of grief.

I only wanted to kill him because he murdered someone I loved, and I really do think my reason was better than his.

My Queen waited, not in the Hall high in the branches of the Heart of Morven, but in her private sitting room. When my cousins delivered me, she waved at them to depart. Daphnis took his place against the wall, next to her trio of blank-faced servants – another dryad, and a pair of fauns who looked like they could be brother and sister.

The Queen gave Daphnis the barest glance, raising an eyebrow at me as she turned away.

«I'm having a suitable livery made for him,» I said, and I could see her interest vanish as if Daphnis had ceased to exist once she had determined he would soon be a respectable servant.

She rose from her couch and crossed the room to grip my shoulders. It would have looked like a motherly gesture to anyone watching, but it had too much of the pinch of her claws in it to be comforting.

«You look well, my son,» she said. She put a finger on my chin and tilted my face down so she could look at me better. I was tall for a Sidhe, and the Queen was not. She moved my head from side to side and I wondered if it was my face she was examining or my antlers and the spellwork she had done on them. «A little thin, still, but much improved.»

«Thank you, my Queen,» I said.

«I trust you are having more clothes made for yourself as well?»

«Of course, my Queen.»

«You don't wear your sword?» She let go of me to walk around me and I knew I was being inspected for the slightest flaw. I was glad, then, that I had let Daphnis go over my clothes with a lint brush and a tiny pair of scissors to trim off stray threads. He had strapped my knives to my belt, but I had refused my longer blade as too bulky for everyday wear.

«It seemed unnecessary, my Queen.»

She frowned. «It is not merely a weapon,» she said, stepping back from me and gesturing to a plush chair. «It is also a symbol.»

«Of course,» I said. «I should have remembered.»

«What was the name you chose for it again?»

I very much doubted she had forgotten; the Queen of Morven Forest didn't forget anything.

«Winterborn.»

«Ah, yes. Because you took it from your cousin at Midwinter.»

That wasn't the reason I chose that name, but I had never told her what the reason was, and I didn't intend to tell her now. I sat in the chair she indicated, not liking how it seemed to want to envelop me. It would not be an easy chair to get out of quickly. That was probably why she offered it. She probably offered it to all her guests.

«See that you wear it in public,» she said. «Remind your people that their Prince is strong and capable with a blade. They will remember how you put your cousin in his place.»

«Yes, my Queen.» I waited for her to tell me why she had summoned me.

«Have you resumed your lessons, now that you're home safe and healed from your ordeals?»

I managed to reduce the frown that drew my forehead in to a slight wrinkle between my eyebrows. «Which lessons, my Queen? I intend to resume combat training tomorrow night, now that I can stand again.»

She snorted delicately. «I have no doubt you will soon return yourself to peak condition.» She perched on her couch and considered me. «You always were fond of exercise.» She tapped her lips with one finger. «No, I refer to your diplomacy lessons.»

«I was not aware there was still a tutor for me,» I said. «I had thought you sent the last one home when I left on my latest errand for you.»

«Did not your last tutor leave you with some topics to research on your own? The Archivist will know.»

«I was intending to visit the library tonight. I will consult with them once you're finished with me here.»

She nodded and watched me some more. I managed to hold her gaze for several heartbeats before I had to look away.

She was the only person at court I couldn't stare down. I kept trying but had never in my thirty-six years succeeded.

«Your attitude is much improved,» she said. «You seem to be making an effort to use courtly manners.»

I wasn't sure how to answer so I just nodded, and her lips curved in a slight smile when I had to look away again.

«I had the notion, my son,» she said, and I looked back at her, focusing on the spot between her eyebrows so I could appear to be paying attention while not actually making eye contact.

«My Queen?»

«We have been far too… isolated, of late,» she said. «Since the human uprising was dealt with, we Sidhe have concerned ourselves with others only inside our own borders.»

The human uprising had been dealt with by marrying their Monarchy's greatest general – who was also their King's brother – to my mother. An uneasy peace, and my birth, had been the result.

«What did you have in mind, my Queen?»

She leaned back and lifted a glass of wine from a side table. She didn't sip, she just gazed into the ruby red liquid before setting it down again.

«Although I was not pleased to have to fetch you from the Eyrie,» she said, turning the glass in place on the table so it fractured the light and splashed a bloody glow on the wood. «It did open up opportunities for contact with the Vogel Monarchy. I would like, I think, to explore more possibilities of diplomatic relations.»

«Indeed?» I said, groping for something to say that would sound intelligent, but not as if I might have an opinion to contradict hers. «Further contact with the Vogel King, or with other Monarchies?»

«Both, I should think.»

«Is it wise to maintain relations with a Monarchy that is vassal to the Alfar?» And I almost winced. Why did I have to question her reasoning?

But she only smiled. «Perhaps not wise, my son, but amusing. Imagine if our Monarchy had better relations with the Vogel than their own overlords?» She tapped her glass. «Perhaps we could even forge an alliance of marriage. Does the Vogel King have any offspring I could offer your hand to?»

I was immediately glad she hadn't given me a glass of the wine she was still toying with, because I'd have choked on it. «I believe he has a daughter and a son,» I said. «But both are still young children.» I paused, then added, forcing a regretful tone into my voice that I didn't entirely have to fake, «And Vogel law forbids marriage outside their own people.»

«A pity. I could only imagine the Alfar King's face when I told him you were to marry the Vogel Princess.»

It wasn't the Princess I wanted, but I would never tell her that.

«I am also considering extending an invitation to the Huldr court to visit us. And to our own vassals, of course.»

«The humans or the Hirsch?»

«Both, eventually.»

«That is… a lot of diplomacy, my Queen.»

«Indeed,» she said. «But I don't intend to handle all of it myself.» She smiled so that her sharp canines showed. «I've asked your sisters to organize an envoy to carry an invitation to the Huldr.»

«Fitting,» I said, and she nodded. My sisters' father was a Huldr lord, after all.

«I might eventually look into extending an invitation to the Hirsch, as well. Perhaps that might be something you could undertake.»

«If you wish it, my Queen.»

«You do get on well with our non-fey neighbors. They like you.» She lifted her glass and finally took a sip. «To that end, I'd like you to compose an invitation to the Vogel King to send a delegation here. For Second Harvest, perhaps, if that isn't too soon. Or Autumn Balance. Let them view the festivities, participate, even, and open a dialogue for trade and other relations.» She sipped her wine again. «I should like them to enjoy our hospitality as we enjoyed theirs.»

What she didn't say, but that I knew, was that she felt indebted to them, and she didn't like feeling indebted to anyone. It didn't matter that I had saved their Seer, making them just as indebted to us. I also didn't point out that the Vogel had nearly killed me before Fionn had revealed that I was the Prince of Morven Forest. And I very carefully hid my excitement at the prospect of opening contact with the Eyrie. I shouldn't hope that Fionn might be part of the delegation the Vogel King sent, assuming he agreed to meet, but I *did* hope.

«And,» the Queen said, looking away from her glass to meet my eyes. What I saw there was not comforting. «Once the Vogel have been suitably impressed with our harvest festival and our generosity, I plan to send you to the human court, to be my ambassador there.» She stood and I rose with her, automatically, my years of training kicking in and keeping me acting appropriately, even though my brain seemed to be shutting down.

«I'm sure your father will be delighted to welcome you home.»

I WAS IN SUCH A DAZE when I left the Queen's rooms that I hardly noticed Padraig following me until he cleared his throat. I was really starting to hate not being able to sense other people's magic nearby.

«What?» I said, heading away from the palace and into the forest, hoping to find my way to the stream where I liked to sit and think. I was badly in need of calm and a clear mind.

«Can I ask what the Queen wanted you for, my Prince?»

«No.»

«Wow, you really are as friendly as everyone says,» he said, sarcasm edging his voice. «Would it be better if I pretended I wanted to fuck you?»

He was grinning when I turned, but an instant later the humor was gone, and I held him pinned against a tree by his throat.

He tried to say something, but it came out as a croak. His nostrils flared as he tried to draw in more air. I leaned closer and bared my teeth and was gratified when his eyes widened.

«You want someone to pal around with, cousin, try Sean. I'm sure he'd especially love it if you polished his boots with your tongue and laughed at all his attempts to be funny.»

I let him go and turned away. Anyone else in the court – even Sean – would have taken the hint and left me alone, but Padraig was obviously not used to being told off by someone of higher rank. Maybe he had been spoiled as a child.

«Sorry, my Prince.» He left a gap between us this time, but still followed me farther into the trees. It wouldn't have been enough space if I'd decided to go after him again, but I didn't feel inclined to tell him so.

«I really was under the impression that you were a lot more friendly.»

I glanced back at him, and he rubbed his throat and closed the distance between us by half. «And that you could take a joke,» he added.

«My apologies,» I said, taking a random turn in the path

that seemed like it was heading in the right direction. I really needed to start learning to navigate the forest with my eyes and ears instead of by magic senses since I had no magic to use anymore. «I forgot it was supposed to be funny that the Prince of Morven Forest enjoys getting laid.»

«Well, when you put it that way, it just sounds normal.»

«I used to be a lot more inclined to joke before I realized most jokes we tell about one another are cruel.» I had been very careful about the jokes I repeated after I had said something mean about the bird folk before I learned Fionn was Vogel. He had very effectively shown me that many of things I assumed were funny really weren't when you looked at them from a different perspective.

I stopped walking suddenly and turned, and Padraig walked right into me. I might not have been that much taller than him, but I was considerably more muscular, and it must have felt a bit like walking into a tree for him.

«Oof,» he said, putting his hands on my chest as he stepped back. «Fuck, my Prince, you're… um…»

I raised an eyebrow and his cheekbones flushed pink.

«Solid?» he said, turning it into a question. He dropped his hands and wiped his palms on the thighs of his trousers.

«What do you want?» I said.

He bit his lip and looked away and I was suddenly – absurdly – reminded of Fionn. «When I was a boy,» he began.

I crossed my arms, and he shifted his feet.

«I begged my father to offer to foster you and Sean in our hall.» He gave me a tentative smile and I just stared back. «My mother was done having children after me, but I thought it would be the best thing ever to have a brother or two.»

«And?» I was starting to feel just a little bad for being rude. I knew how it was to be sent to a new place and to have no one to call a friend. Of course, I had been a child when it happened to me, not a grown man sent to take up a prestigious post as Queen's Guard. He looked enough like Sean to be nearly a clone, but that didn't necessarily mean he was *like* Sean.

He shrugged. «And… Sean's mother wanted him trained at court, to be sure he'd be selected for the Queen's personal guard.» He cocked his head and looked at me. «And you were sent to your father for three years.»

«Did you have a point with this story?» I still wasn't ready to confess all my sorrows to Padraig, but I had to admit his tale was effective in getting me to reconsider my first impressions of him.

«I never got a brother, or even a good friend who was Sidhe. When I was allowed to, I played with the local fauns and humans and other non-fey peoples.»

«Don't tell Sean you consorted with non-fey,» I said, turning to follow the path again. «He'll hate you on principle.»

«I'm not sure I care that much what Sean thinks of me.»

«And yet I always see you together. You work together in the Queen's Guard, carry her messages together, you even drink and carouse together. If I didn't know Sean doesn't fuck men, I'd assume you were sleeping together.»

«What, I can't make a comment about who you fuck, but you can comment on who *I* sleep with?» He raised his eyebrows and when I didn't comment, he added, «My Prince.»

«Fuck off,» I said, but without much conviction.

«The Queen wanted us to spend time together,» he said, trotting to keep up with me. «She said she didn't want me to feel alone at court, so she had Sean show me around. I guess I just got used to him.» He paused. «Now she wants us to make sure you… well, have friends befitting your station I suppose.»

«I think that's her new favorite phrase,» I said. «At least where I'm concerned. She ignores me most of my life, finally finds a use for me when I reach my majority, and now that I've started to figure out what I want for myself, she requires me to be the good little Prince, and wear clothes befitting my station, own slaves as befits my station, acquire odious friends as apparently fits my fucking station.»

«I'm sorry she took your magic,» he said, ignoring my implication that he was odious.

«Has she told everyone how I was punished, then?»

«No, but… enough people could feel it that it got around. I can feel it… that you're hollow.» He sighed and gripped my shoulder as we walked. I didn't pull away. «I don't have the strongest magic, but it must be awful. I can't imagine not being connected to the forest.»

I looked at him more closely. All Sidhe are connected to Morven Forest to some extent, but I doubted many of them would even notice if that connection were cut off. Or care.

«It's not pleasant,» I finally said.

«Is Sean really that bad? He seems incredibly pompous and self-absorbed, and his sense of humor's shit, but he's been all right. To me, anyway.»

«How long have you been here?»

«I've been to court with my father plenty of times. We used to play together as boys.»

«I remember,» I said. «You and Sean liked to tease me for being half-human.»

He looked embarrassed. «Yeah, well. The Queen called me to her Guard just after you left on your last errand for her.»

«So not long, then.»

«No, not long.»

«You must have heard the rumors.»

«I've heard plenty. I've heard our Prince likes to fuck, which by the way, is not considered a negative. Plenty of pretty girls and boys are hoping to catch your eye.»

I snorted. «If I haven't fucked them already, they might as

well give up.»

He gave me a look but didn't comment. «I've heard our Prince has more friends among the non-fey than he does among his own people.»

I shrugged one shoulder. «Not so many since I became the Queen's favorite lackey.»

«And I heard you had a falling out with Sean when he accidentally killed a friend of yours.»

I laughed, but it was a strained and harsh sound. «Sean and I were never close in the first place. I was always too human for his taste. And it wasn't an accident.»

«It wasn't an accident?»

«No.»

«But…»

«Oh, he didn't *lie*. He can't lie. He just said it looked like Dec was restraining me, and from the angle he was watching from, it probably did look like that, though he knew very well it wasn't.»

«Your friend wasn't restraining you?»

I stopped walking to face him directly, keeping my face blank. I wasn't sure I wanted to be so open with him, but it wasn't like everyone at court didn't already know. Someone would tell him eventually.

«He wasn't my friend, and he definitely wasn't restraining me.»

«I don't understand.»

«Dec was my lover,» I said, and waited, watching as realization slowly came over Padraig's face.

«He was…»

«He was fucking me,» I said. «And I was very much enjoying it until Sean cut his fucking head off and oops, there went my boner.»

«Oh, fuck,» Padraig said, very quietly.

«And then he acted like I should thank him.» My nostrils flared and my eyes burned, but I didn't cry. I never had cried for Dec. «He killed the man I loved and wanted me to be grateful.»

«Oh, fuck,» he said again.

«And Sean didn't even get so much as a scolding for it.»

«But…»

«I was allowed to fight him, to take his sword, to humiliate him in front of the court. But I was not allowed to kill him or even maim him. So I did take his sword, and I broke his nose and snapped his wrist. I dislocated his shoulder, and I cut his pretty clothes off him, so he stood naked and bleeding in front of all those fucking nobles who probably thought he was in the right.»

I snarled, but it wasn't at Padraig, not really. «I wasn't allowed to kill him, and I wanted so badly to cut off his fucking head to avenge Dec.»

«But… how could even the Queen allow him to just… murder someone?»

«Because, cousin,» I said, turning to walk away again. «Declan Winterborn was a werewolf.»

8
Fionn

GONE FROM MY BODY for more than a nineday? It couldn't have taken so long to fly to Morven Forest and back, could it?

I tried, again, to remember what had happened before I flew away in my spirit body. I had been dreaming, and the raven said I had dreamed something important. Maybe the dream was part of the vision, too.

<Healer Kah,> I said, and she returned from where she was speaking to Neeka in my sitting room. I heard doors open and close, and two streaks of feathers and scales arrowed past her and flung themselves at me.

Too hot, said Smoke.

Went away, said Flame.

<I'm okay, my little friends.> They burrowed into the quilt on each side of me, chittering at me until I stroked their little feathered heads.

Healer Kah looked at the feathered tree serpents and smiled. <They were very hard to persuade to leave your side,> she said. <But I wasn't certain the sickness couldn't affect

them.> She held a cup and helped me sip from it. I almost spat it out.

<That's terrible,> I said.

<It is, but it will help you regain your strength.>

I scowled, but I drank it all.

<What did you want to ask me?> the Healer asked when I had swallowed the last drop.

<Where was I found?>

<Where, my Seer?>

I nodded.

<Neeka?> she called, and my attendant poked her head around the corner.

<Where did you find me?> I said, and ran my tongue over my teeth, trying to rid myself of the horrid taste of Healer Kah's medicine.

<On the floor,> she said.

<Out on the balcony?>

<No,> she said, looking confused.

<But the balcony door was open?>

She shook her head. <You were there, right next to the bed.> She pointed. <Your serpents were making a terrible racket, so I came in and there you were. You'd pulled off half the blankets when you fell.>

<Was I… Was I feverish?>

<Not then. You were twitching, though, like you do when you have a vision.>

<I gave you a draught to relax your muscles,> said Healer Kah. <I've been working on a way to ease your visions, and it seemed like a good time to test it.> She smiled. <It took four of us to get you to swallow it, but it worked.>

<You were so still I thought you were dead,> said Neeka. She moved closer to the bed and took my hand.

<The fever came on a handful of nights ago,> said the

Healer. Her voice was soft. <The King lifted you into the cooling bath himself, and refused to leave until I drugged his tea.>

I'd have smiled at the thought, except I couldn't find it in me to feel any softness towards my King.

<Has anyone else caught the fever?> I asked.

<We don't know for certain that you had the Royal Plague, my Seer. I've never heard of such a long delay between encountering the sickness and coming down with it.> She sighed. <Though the only experience I have is when the Queen died, and many of her household were affected. I've no notion of how it might affect a seer.>

<But no one else has been ill?>

She shook her head.

<Thank the spirits,> said Neeka. She sat on the side of the bed and squeezed my fingers. <Did you have any useful visions?>

<I don't think I've ever had a useful vision,> I said.

She opened her mouth to protest, then glanced at Healer Kah, and said nothing. I know what she would have said, though. The same thing Kier had told me once: my visions were useful to *me*, even if they weren't useful to anyone else.

<I dreamed about salt-leaf,> I said. <Or maybe that was a vision.>

<So you said.> Healer Kah laid a hand on my forehead again, nodded, and began to pack her bag.

<I read… Where's that book?> I looked around the room and didn't see the history book I had been reading – or attempting yet again to read – before I'd fallen asleep or into a very long and strange vision. I looked up at the Healer as she shouldered her bag. <Does salt-leaf have any healing properties?>

She shook her head. <A tea of the outer bark can make the drinker feel warm. It was once popular as an additive in winter

beverages, but I've never heard of any medicinal uses.>

<My gran had a little rhyme she'd say, whenever we passed a stump,> said Neeka. <Or a sapling, though there's few enough of those around.>

Healer Kah rolled her eyes. <The peasant folk have sayings about the healing properties of shiny rocks and pig dung,> she said. <I wouldn't put too much value on your gran's rhyme.>

<What did your gran say, when she saw a salt-leaf?> I asked. I had a book of Vogel folklore in my sitting room that I hadn't started yet. I was saving it as a reward for making my way through the tedious history, but maybe I should read it sooner.

<Inner for outer, outer for in, leaves are for cooling a feverish skin.>

<Well, I'll leave you to ponder your old gran's sayings. I expect the King will be by tonight before too long. You should sleep, my Seer. Real sleep. And bathe, but not in the hot pool. It's too soon for that.>

<Yes, Healer.>

She left and Neeka stood up from the bed. <I'll run you a bath,> she said, and I nodded absently.

I looked around the room again, checking every surface, but didn't see the book I'd been trying to skim through for references to the Royal Plague. It had been incredibly boring, and I didn't remember most of what I had read, but I was sure there had been a mention of salt-leaf.

I patted the blankets, thinking I might have left it on the bed when I'd fallen into my vision. Smoke raised her head to glare at me for disturbing her, and Flame flicked her tail, smacking me with the end of it. It was like being tapped by a very tiny feather fan. I leaned over the edge of the bed to see if I'd knocked it to the floor, and Smoke wriggled out of her place on the blanket to join Flame on the other side of me.

<There it is!> I said, spying the corner of the worn cover just sticking out from under the bed. I leaned farther to grab it but couldn't quite reach.

I was so tired, too, that it was tempting to just push all thoughts aside and lie back on the pillows until Neeka came to fetch me for my bath, but the problem kept whirling around and around in my head. Salt-leaf. Fever. Spirit traveling. Visions. Fever. Salt-leaf.

I leaned over again and stretched. I could almost reach. My fingers brushed the cover. Just a little farther.

I lost my balance and tumbled over the side of the bed, dragging most of the bedding with me. The tree serpents launched into the air and swirled around my head, chittering and scolding. I must have shrieked or yelped, because Neeka rushed out of the bathing room with a towel dangling from her hand.

<My Seer! Are you…?> She saw me, and her lips pressed together. She clamped a hand over her mouth and wrapped her arm across her body as if to still her shaking.

<You're laughing at me,> I said, from my inelegant huddle on the floor.

<I'm sorry, Seer Tokka,> she said. Even her voice shook with laughter, and I couldn't help smiling, too.

<I suppose I am a bit ridiculous,> I said.

<Oh, never.> She bent over me, pulled my arm across her shoulders, and helped me stand. <Your bath's ready, anyway.>

I was as wobbly as a new-hatched chick, but Neeka was strong and half-carried me into the other room and over to the metal bathtub.

I dipped a hand into the water. It was hardly what anyone would call hot, but at least I could get clean. I leaned on the side of the tub while Neeka dragged my sleeping tunic over my head, then clung to her hands as she helped me in. When I was sitting, she said, <You wash. I'll change your sheets.>

<You don't have to…> She held up her hand and I stopped.

<It would take too long to call a cleaner, and I know where everything is.> She smiled. <I expect you would do the same for me, were we in opposite positions.>

<Of course I would.>

I relaxed into the water for a moment, then reached for a bottle of my favorite soap. It had a light musky scent, complemented by undertones of something that reminded me of the forest. I rubbed in into my hair and over my skin, then slid down into the water to rinse.

I hadn't realized how grimy I had felt until I was clean. I held the bottle of soap under my nose and inhaled. Fir trees, I thought. It smelled like fir trees. I set the bottle aside again and closed my eyes. Kiernan smelled like fir trees, like oak leaves and moss. Like the night wind. I wished I was alone so I could think of him while I touched myself. I had kissed him, at least, in my spirit travel, but I wanted more, I wanted all of him.

<Better?> said Neeka and I opened my eyes.

<Better,> I said.

<I put your book on the table by the bed.>

<Thank you.>

<Let's get you settled, then, so Trikta and Konta can come and gawk at you, alive and well, and maybe they'll go get some rest.>

<You, too,> I said.

<I'll stay.>

<You won't. If I need anything, I'll call my guards.>

She frowned at me and put her hands on her hips. <Fine.>

I grinned and she grinned back.

Once my guards were gone and their replacements were in their places outside my door, and Neeka had gone off to join her sweetheart in her own room, I pulled the book onto my lap and opened it.

Which part had I been reading when I'd fallen asleep? I flipped pages, glancing at headings and random sentences. It had been so dry I remembered almost none of it. The founding of the Monarchies. The last Vogel Seer. The felling of the Heart of Aven.

I paused. *That* seemed familiar. I knew the Heart of Morven was a huge oak tree that the Sidhe revered as the center of their Monarchy. There was a throne in its branches for their Monarch, and it was so tall it towered above all the other trees.

But according to this book, there had been a Heart of Aven once, too. Had it been sacred to the Alfar? And did that mean there was a Heart of Tronven, too, sacred to the Huldr? I scanned the page. Once, it said, not far from the Eyrie, there had been a huge salt-leaf tree, bigger than any other, that the peasants and lesser folk – by which I assumed the writer meant non-Vogel people – believed was sacred.

When the Royal Plague swept the Eyrie – yes, this was the part I vaguely remembered reading – the countryside was quickly stripped of smaller salt-leaf trees, because the common folk believed it was a cure for fever, and the nobles were desperate to try anything.

The book repeated Neeka's Gran's rhyme, only with more words.

Inner is for outer heat
Outer is for in.
Make a poultice of the leaves
for cooling feverish skin.

When all the salt-leaf in the area and for days' travel around had been stripped of bark and leaves, cut down and even the wood ground up in desperation, and the plague still ravaged both the nobles and the peasants, threatening to reduce the Vogel Monarchy to a land of ghosts, the King ordered the Heart of Aven felled.

The thinking was, if ordinary salt-leaf trees brought some relief, the ancient and sacred Heart of Aven would surely bring a cure.

The plague had ended, but the book didn't say if it was the leaves and bark that did it, or if the sickness had simply run its course.

I had to suppose that with almost no salt-leaf left in Aven anymore, no one remembered it as a cure except the long memories of peasants with their passed-down rhymes and lore. It could mean it was no cure at all. Or it could be that no one knew how to prepare it, that no one had known then, either, which was why they had gone through so much.

"Make a poultice of the leaves for cooling feverish skin" seemed clear enough. But what of "Inner is for outer heat, outer is for in"? Inner and outer what? Bark seemed logical; it was common to use the bark of medicinal trees in herbal preparations. One of the key ingredients in my pain relief tea was the inner bark of a type of birch tree. The inner bark was, usually, especially effective.

And when I had dreamed of salt-leaf, it was of branches with bark that crumbled in my hand.

So what, then, was I to make of inner and outer *heat*? Fever from illness was felt on the skin, but it existed deep in the body, too. That's why it was so dangerous.

But perhaps the rhyme meant that part of the bark could be used to treat a fever from inside the body, from an illness, and another part of the bark… The raven had said there was a clue to spirit flight in my dreams. Did it mean salt-leaf? Could salt-leaf *cause* fever, allowing the spirit to slip free from the body? Healer Kah said it could make a person feel warm.

I needed some salt-leaf leaves and bark to test. It was rare, though, at least in Aven, and I didn't want to further endanger something that might save lives.

Truly, even if it were entirely useless, I'd feel bad killing it all.

But I felt excitement building. I might have a way to induce spirit flight. Maybe even a treatment for the Royal Plague if I could figure out how to prepare it. But I finally had to admit defeat for now when my eyes kept drifting closed. I put the book on the bedside table, turned down the lamp, and snuggled under the covers, the tree serpents curled on my pillow, one on each side of my head.

I DREAMED OF KIERNAN, of walking on the beach below the Eyrie, hand in hand. Or maybe I was remembering the vision I had had, before leaving my body to fly to Morven.

This time, instead of vanishing when I turned, he was still there, smiling, holding out a bundle of salt-leaf twigs like it was a bouquet of flowers. I took it and smiled back, and he reached up, put his hand behind my neck, and pulled me into a kiss.

Then the dream, or vision-memory, or whatever it was, shifted and we were sharing a large chair in front of a stone fireplace. We didn't really fit – I was in Kier's lap and my legs dangled over the side and I kept sliding, and he would laugh and pull me back into place.

His hair was threaded with silver and white, and long, the

unruly curls loosened into ringlets, held in check by braids over his ears and between his large antlers. There were fine lines around his eyes and his high cheekbones were more prominent, and the hair that edged his jaw was *almost* enough to call a beard.

His eyes caught the light strangely, and I realized he was blind.

"Will you kiss me, pretty bird?" he said, his voice still strong and smoky.

"Always," I said, and when I leaned over to do just that, something in my back cracked – only briefly painful, but loud – and I laughed.

"My beautiful old man," he teased, and pulled me closer, and maybe we were old, but the fire between us had not dimmed. I felt myself grow hard inside my sheath and shifted position so I was astride his legs so I could more efficiently get my tongue in his mouth.

Just when I was sliding my hands under his shirt the vision shifted again and I was kneeling in a cave, a shadowy figure standing in front of me, long hair flowing over her shoulders and huge antlers rising from her brow.

"I will help you," she said, and then I was standing side by side with Kiernan on a bare hill, looking down at a cluster of tents and campfires and wagons in the valley below.

"It's not me they follow, my Seer," he said, turning and smiling at me. "It's you."

"So I'm 'my Seer' now," I said, teasing. "That's not what you called me last night, General Druison."

It was hard to tell on his bronze skin, but I thought he might have blushed.

"Did you want me to call you 'my Seer' while I fuck you?" he asked, and ducked when I swatted him.

"If I can call you 'General' while you're pleasuring me with your mouth," I replied.

"You can me call anything you like, beloved," he said, and then I was on the beach again, alone, a bundle of salt-leaf twigs in my hand, the bark crumbling off under my fingers.

I WOKE TO ARMS SLIDING around me, to someone climbing into my bed with me, and for a long, joyful moment, I thought it was Kiernan.

Then I caught the thick floral scent of the perfume my King preferred. I held very still, hoping he would think me asleep and fall into slumber next to me.

But he leaned closer, kissed my neck, and said, <I felt you wake, little seer.>

<My King,> I whispered, letting my words slur a little, as if I were still very sleepy. I held thoughts of Kiernan in my head, his hand in mine, his smile that was only for me.

<I thought I would lose my daughter and my Seer in one night, little one.>

<I'm sorry, my King.>

<She still lives,> he said. <And you have recovered.> He nuzzled my neck and placed a kiss behind my ear. I shivered, and he must have taken it for arousal, because he gripped my hips and pulled me close against him.

<I am still very weak, my King.> He could read lies and truth, if he bothered to try. But it was true, I was weak. I wanted to go back to sleep.

<Then you shall lie still and let me take care of the exertion.> He stroked my wings, gathering them together on my back, then moved one hand over my belly, up to my chest, and back again.

I squeezed my eyes shut, forced myself to be still and my body to relax, and I thought fiercely of Kiernan. I remembered the way he would stroke my skin, first gently, barely touching me at all, and then more firmly, massaging my muscles. I thought about how he would run his hand over my belly, his palm smoothing the fine feathers of my sheath, and then trace one finger over my seam, softly, teasing, until my muscles relaxed and my seam parted and my erection slid out.

And then he would trail his hand over my hardness, tell me how lovely I felt, then coat his fingers in my lubricant and slide his hand between my buttocks to massage my anus, teasing me until I pushed against him. Then he would push his fingers inside me, shift his weight so he could fuck me with them, and stroke my hardness, too.

He would move maddeningly slowly until I cried out, until I begged him to go faster, to fuck me properly. And he would do as I asked, sliding his fingers out and pushing his erection inside me instead. And still he would stroke me, tease me, pump his hand over me until I pulsed, once, twice, and I would beg him not to stop.

And he wouldn't stop. He would tell me how good I felt, that he loved the noises I made, that he loved *me*, and I would pulse again. And I would feel him throb inside me, and moan, and tell me how fucking magnificent I was.

And when I could feel my orgasm was over at three pulses, I couldn't pretend he was the one fucking me anymore. It was my King who wiped my semen off his hand onto my sheets, my King whose harsh breaths hissed in my ear, and my King who thrust into me and pulsed three times, one quick release after the other.

<You see, little seer,> he said. <You're regaining your energy quickly.> He rolled away from me. <I'd keep you company all night, but I do have an early morning meeting with

the council, and I haven't slept well of late.>

<Shall I attend the meeting, my King?> I said, somehow managing to keep my voice even, though I wanted to cry.

It seemed all I wanted to do lately was cry.

<No need, little seer. We've managed without you for generations. I'm sure we'll find a way to decide how best to manage the harvest tithe.> I didn't miss the mild condescension in his voice.

<Of course, my King.> But I resolved to wake early and attend the meeting anyway. Somehow, I had to find a way to make him – and all the council members – take me seriously.

9
Kiernan

Wʜᴇɴ I ᴇᴠᴇɴᴛᴜᴀʟʟʏ found my way back to the palace – without Padraig any the wiser about my difficulties navigating my own forest – I headed for the library.

I had my list of topics I wanted to research, and now I'd have to add whatever my tutor had left for me to work on. And I'd have to look into what methods had been traditionally used for official communication with the Vogel Monarchy. If any such information existed.

I supposed I could have just asked the Queen – she had hosted a small delegation of bird folk when I was younger – but I hadn't thought of it until I was long gone from her rooms, and I wasn't inclined to go back and ask.

Padraig followed me to the library door and then stopped.

«What, afraid of books, cousin?» I said, and he made a rude gesture.

«I enjoy a good book now and then,» he said. «But I'm not sure I'm allowed in there.»

I looked around. It had never actually occurred to me that

only certain people were allowed in the palace library. Being the Queen's son, I'd had the run of the place since I was old enough to know that books were objects to be respected. Even though I hadn't been the most accomplished scholar, always being more inclined to physical pursuits, I couldn't imagine growing up without this place.

When I had lived at Dudoon, I'd had only my father's collection of tactical manuals and combat techniques to explore. And while I made good use of the available material, you couldn't exactly call it *enjoyable*.

«I probably spent more time hiding here than reading,» I said. «But since I returned from the Eyrie I've been more interested in reading for enjoyment.»

«Do they have many sex manuals here, then?"

I returned to him the rude gesture he'd given me earlier and said, «Would you like me to ask the Queen to allow you to borrow from the collection?»

He laughed. «What made you want to read more at the Eyrie?»

I shrugged. «Facing my own mortality, perhaps.» The lie slipped easily off my tongue, and I almost regretted it. But I sure as fuck wasn't going to tell him it was because I wanted a pretty young man to think better of me. That I wanted something more than great sex and shared trauma to connect me to the man I was completely lost for.

«Well,» he said. «I'll leave you to it.»

I didn't immediately get to work once he was gone. I put my borrowed book on the archivist's desk – they hated for people to return them to the shelves because too many got returned to the wrong place – and wandered aimlessly among the stacks.

It was a beautiful room, all dark wood and rich upholstery, with wood floors softened by carefully woven rugs. It was dim, to better protect the books and documents stored here, but even without magic I had good night vision. Even if you weren't inclined to read, this was a pleasant place to get lost in.

I breathed in the scent of paper and leather, of parchment and ink, of dust and floor polish, glue and graphite. It wasn't as comforting as the forest, but it wasn't too far off. I found myself imagining a little house for myself deep in the woods, equipped with shelves like these. One or two in the living area, or maybe even a whole room, though nothing so grand as this. And every gift-giving occasion I would find a new place to take Fionn shopping for a volume to add. Or maybe we'd find a nearby town with a book shop that would become a favorite haunt. And in the evenings, or in the sunlight of late morning, we'd read together, and talk about what we read. He would probably read three or four books to my one, but he'd never make me feel lesser because I couldn't keep up.

«You're very far away, my Prince,» said a dry creaky voice, and I looked up from contemplating the forest scene on a long runner to see the Archivist perched on a stool, dusting the top of a row of books.

«Just daydreaming,» I said.

«As you have been since you were a small creature, all wild hair and pointy elbows, sneaking in here to escape your cousin or your sisters, and ending up entranced by the colorful pictures in a book of fairy tales.» They climbed down from the stool and peered up at me.

Presumably the Archivist had a name, but I had never learned it, and I'm pretty sure I had asked more than once before I learned it might be rude. They were of middling height but bent and hunched from a childhood affliction. They had fine strong cheekbones and curious hazel eyes.

Their infirmities had ruled out dreams of becoming one of the Queen's Guard, but a knack for handling delicate paper had eventually led them to the royal library, where it seemed to me as a boy they'd been here since the depths of time and would still be here when the world ended.

They used to frighten me, at first, but they had always let me stay when I crept in here, looking for a peaceful corner. Now, I felt fondness for a person who had tolerated the curious but overactive boy I had been, who had let me loiter in the library even though I hadn't shared their love of words.

I smiled. «I enjoyed the book you suggested, though I'm not sure I understood all of it.»

They smiled back. «Poetry can be slippery. One day you're sure it means something, and the next it means something entirely else.» They brandished their duster at another shelf. «I am glad you made the effort. What can I help you find today?»

I rubbed the side of my nose. «I have a whole list, but I don't suppose I should try to learn everything at once. First, I'm to ask if my last tutor left me any lessons to complete. And then, I need to know about past relations with the Vogel Monarchy.»

«For the first, your tutor said he was going to leave you some research questions but failed to do so.» They smiled tightly, as if such a failure of memory was a sign of bad character. «And as for the second, didn't you just return from the Eyrie?»

«I did.»

They led the way back towards their desk as they spoke. «I should think you know more about relations with the Vogel already, than any book in this library can tell you.»

I snorted. «I guess I don't need an account of what I experienced myself.»

«That's good, because there won't be one until you write it.»

«My writing is only marginally better than a trained magpie's,» I said. «Though perhaps a fraction more legible.»

They laughed. Most people thought the Archivist was as dry and dusty as the library they never seemed to leave, but I had spent enough time here when I was younger that they'd perhaps let me see a more personal side of themself.

«Your composition skills weren't flashy, as I recall, but you were always capable of writing a clear sentence.»

«High praise from you,» I said. «Though a little flash might not be a bad thing when writing an invitation to a King.»

They raised their eyebrows at that. «I believe there was a short account written of the two Vogel ambassadors who visited briefly many years ago. You would have been ten or eleven years old, I think.»

«Eleven,» I said. «I thought they were ridiculously tall and liked showing off their tanned legs. I envied them their wings.»

«And you spent the entire summer after they'd gone trying to design a set of artificial wings for yourself.»

«Sean dared me to jump from the canopy of the Heart, and I broke my leg.»

«As I recall, you beat him at swordplay for the first time the next day, with your leg in a splint.»

«You remember *that*? I didn't think you ever left the library.»

«I do like to watch swordplay, from time to time.» There was something a little wicked in their smile, and I suddenly remembered they had had a partner in the Palace Guard. And I realized I didn't know if he was even still alive.

«I didn't manage to beat him again for most of a year,» I said. «I think he was taking it easy on me because of my leg. He never made that mistake again.»

The Archivist had been rummaging in their desk while we spoke and they finally straightened up with a triumphant flourish to hand me a battered book, thin and bound in deep green leather that had been embossed with leaves around the edges and had the nicFia stag in silver on the front cover.

I took it and opened it carefully. This book hadn't been out of my possession once that whole summer after the Vogel's visit. The first page had written on it *The Top-Secret Flying Experiments of Kiernan Druison nicFia, Future Prince of Morven Forest, With Notes on the Bird People of the Eerie* in painfully careful script. It had taken me far too long to write it and I was furious when I still managed to write the second line crooked. I'd have been even angrier if I'd realized I spelled "Eyrie" wrong.

Under the words I'd drawn a stylized pair of wings that looked like a bizarre composite of bird, bat, and insect appendages.

«Where did you find this?» I said, flipping pages to look at my childish attempts to draw the artificial wings I had dreamed up. There was page after page of diagrams and notes, calculations that made no sense or that didn't come out to the correct answer, and stiffly posed attempts to draw tall, thin people with wings and feathered tails.

«Where you left it,» said the Archivist. «On the shelf between *A Treatise on Bird Wings* and *Artificial Modes of Flight*.»

«I was a cheeky little shit,» I said. «Sneaking my own book onto the library shelves with the work of real scholars.»

«I was going to leave it there, for posterity, but then I thought you might like to see it.» He tapped the page I held it open to. «I remember you attempting to read both those books and getting frustrated at the dry prose.»

«I thought I might tackle them again,» I said.

«You've a notion to invent artificial wings for Sidhe nobles?» they asked, leading the way into the shelves again.

«Just curiosity,» I said, but I was thinking about a silver-eyed seer with wings too small to fly on, jumping from a tower and trusting me to catch him. And later, that same seer, crouched over my lap, small perfect wings beating as he raised and lowered himself on my cock, magnificent in his ecstasy. I loved him exactly as he was, but I knew he longed to fly and if I could, I would give him that.

I snapped back to the present when the Archivist pushed two books into my hands and then led the way to another bookcase where they pulled down a thin report on the Vogel visit to Morven and another equally thin volume on the possibilities of trade with southern Aven and the Eyrie.

«If you have any suggestions on how to send an invitation to the Vogel King, I'd love to hear them,» I said.

«Oof,» said the Archivist. «I don't envy you that task.» But they took two more books from the same shelf and added them the ones I was already holding. I tried to examine the spines without dropping the whole lot. One was a thick history of the Vogel, "with particular reference to the founding of the Nine Monarchies." The other was *Beliefs and Customs of the Vogel People*.

I looked at the Archivist, eyebrows raised in question, and they waved a hand vaguely. «You never know what might prove useful.»

I nodded, wondering if I might find anything about the custom of tying woven cloth and small trinkets to the branches of trees. And that sparked another thought. «Is there anything on the… the Heart Trees?»

«As in the Heart of Morven?»

I nodded. «I understand there was once such a tree in Aven and might still be one in Tronven.»

They looked thoughtful. «All I can think of is a book of folk beliefs surrounding the Heart of Morven.»

«That's something, at least.»

«If you could tell me what it is you want to know, I might be able to find references in other volumes.»

«I don't even know, really,» I said.
«Just curiosity?»
«Yeah.»

DAPHNIS APPEARED as I left the library and insisted on carrying the books back to my rooms and then suggested, with his tiny smile, that I might perhaps make room for a bookcase in my sitting room, if I planned to take up reading as a hobby.

I sat on my favorite couch and picked up my childhood notebook. "I doubt I'll be reading more than one book at a time under normal circumstances." I couldn't have said why I kept choosing to speak Islish with Daphnis, except that it was the language I spoke with Fionn, and it was comforting.

He arranged the other books in a row on the sideboard, behind the fancy crystal glasses my mother had sent over with a bottle of her best wine.

"If you're to be an ambassador, you might find yourself doing research in many books at once more often than you think, my Prince."

"If that's the case, I'll do my research in the library."

"But not this time?" He stood next to the sideboard, still except for his eyes.

I looked at the row of titles. Nearly half of them had nothing to do with any of my upcoming diplomatic tasks. I flipped through the notebook, looking at the increasingly fanciful designs for artificial wings I had come up with, and my awkward attempts to draw the tall, elegant Vogel and their glorious, colorful wings. I had been imaginative, at least.

"Will you try to construct functional wings for him?" Daphnis said softly, and I snapped my gaze to his face. He was as expressionless and utterly still as only a dryad could be.

"Shouldn't you go root for a while, Daph?" I said. Dryads needed to periodically root in the soil they were sprouted in to flourish, and I knew he hadn't left my side for some time. I tried not to think about how the dryads my Queen had gifted to the Vogel King were faring, with only a small pot of earth each.

"Are you trying to be rid of me, my Prince?" His thin mouth curled at the corners.

"I'd like to be alone for a while," I said.

"Of course, my Prince. I'll bring your morning meal when I return."

I nodded and turned back to my notebook. On one page near the beginning, I'd drawn a careful, if unskilled, diagram of a bird's wing, only I'd attached it to the body of what was supposed to be a bird person. I'd outlined each individual feather with as much care as I could manage. I had bribed a sparrow to sit for me, one wing outspread. I only got a few feathers drawn before it got bored, and I'd had to bribe another. It took me six birds and an entire sack of seeds and nuts pilfered from the kitchen, but I'd managed it.

I leaned back and closed my eyes and tried not to think about the aching hollow place in my chest where magic should have been, or the sharp pain behind my belly button where I should feel a connection to Fionn, but instead felt nothing.

How the fuck was I supposed to send a message to the Eyrie without magic? Once, I'd have paid a magpie in dried fruit and shiny trinkets to deliver a letter. But without magic, I couldn't even *talk* to a magpie, let alone hire one as a messenger.

I thought, briefly, about petitioning my mother to restore my magic so I could function as her ambassador more effectively. But I suspected this was a test, that she meant to make me work to get my magic back, and part of that would be proving I could function without it.

So, fine. I was the fucking Prince, I'd command someone else in the court to hire a magpie. It couldn't be Siona, even though she would have helped if I asked. She was the Queen's Seer, and not mine to command.

Daphnis might be able to help, but he wasn't supposed to even *have* magic. And with all the lovers I'd taken in my Queen's court, not one of them was someone I'd trust to help me perform even the simplest task. And of all the friends I'd once had outside court, I couldn't think of any who would be willing to do anything for me once I became the official heir, and the Queen's spy, assassin, and general lackey. It didn't help that most of them considered me responsible for Dec's death, even if I hadn't been the one holding the sword.

After a moment, I got up, locked the door, and went into my bedroom. I locked that door, too. Then I stripped down to my undergarment, drew my sword, and began to practice forms. I felt sluggish and weak, but I pushed myself to continue.

I had a large bedroom without a lot of furniture, but even so I had to be careful where I swung. It wouldn't be princely to accidentally shred a priceless tapestry or reduce a carved chair to kindling.

I swung and stepped, whirled and lunged until my muscles burned and sweat dripped down my back. And then I switched hands and kept going.

Finally, so tired my arms were shaking, I sheathed my sword and stepped out of my undergarment.

There was a cauldron of water heating over the fire, and the fire itself had been well-tended; Daphnis liked to be prepared. I lugged the steaming vessel into the bathing room, kicked over the lever to block the flow of water and fill the bath, and poured the hot water in.

When it was full, I redirected the stream and the sank into the water. It wasn't as nice as the hot spring below the hills in Aven, but it was still pleasant. It would have been much better with Fionn here, even though it would have been a tight fit.

Actually, the way I was starting to feel, a tight fit was just what I wanted.

I let the hot water soothe my muscles – it would be a while yet before I was back to my old physical condition – and I let the sound of water trickling down the stone wall and across the floor soothe my mind. As much as it could be soothed, anyway.

I pictured that bird wing I'd so carefully drawn as a boy and thought about the other diagrams I had attempted. Daphnis's quiet inquiry, "Will you try to construct functional wings for him?" had hurt even more than the severed connection in my belly. I wanted to do everything for him. For Fionn. And Fionn wanted to fly.

"Fuck," I said to the empty room. Had he really been here the other night, or had I imagined it? Had I been so far gone in sickness and sorrow that I'd grasp anything to believe he still wanted me? And if he hadn't been here, had I really been kissing Daphnis, lying tucked together with him on my bed?

"No," I said, as if saying it aloud would make it more real. "He was here." He *had* to have been here. He had taken the knife from my hand when I'd been lying in this same spot, trying to find the courage to end everything, because I knew I didn't have to courage to go on. And he had told me he loved me and asked me to live. He believed we had a future, and his belief gave me the courage I needed to stay.

He had asked me to steal him away from the Eyrie.

I sat up suddenly, as if to grab my clothes and set out for Aven right away. But that was silly. I had to prepare. I had to get my magic back. And now I had another possible path. I only had to figure out how to request the Vogel include their seer among the party invited for Autumn Balance. Then I could ask Fionn right out, in person, what he wanted me to do.

I lay back in the water, trying to imagine what I would say to him if – when – I saw him. What I would say in public, and how I would get him *out* of public to say the things I really wanted to say.

I pictured him as I'd last seen him, looking ghostly and re-gal here in my bathing room. He'd been naked, slim and sculpted, his hair long down his back and his wings small, their added feathers gone. Was the nudity a side effect of spirit flight or had he been naked in the Eyrie? Had his hair already grown back? His pale skin had glowed in the dim lamplight and even with no moon he had seemed to be outlined in silver. His bluish freckles, sprinkled across his cheeks and nose, his chest and shoulders and belly and the tops of his thighs – even his chin and the tips of his delicately pointed ears – made him look younger. But his silver eyes made him look older. He had smiled that gentle, heart-rending smile at me.

He had looked like someone who should be worshipped.

Later, borrowing Daphnis's body, but looking only like himself, he had kissed me. He had pressed his mouth hard against mine and probed his tongue deep into my mouth as if he couldn't get close enough. He had left me breathless and feeling like I might dissolve into a puddle on the floor. And he had made me want to drag him under the covers with me so I could touch and taste every bit of his skin and feel him do the same to me.

He had pushed me back on the bed, hands stroking my chest, my belly, my ribs, and I knew if he'd been there for real and not using a dryad's shape, he would have leaned over me to kiss me again. He would have wrapped a long, beautiful leg over my thighs and bent to lick my neck, to kiss the hollow of my throat, to nibble first one nipple, then the other.

He'd have moved his hands lower, to push my thighs apart, to reach for my cock and find me already hard, wanting him so desperately I dribbled white fluid onto my own belly. He'd stroke me, wriggle down the bed to press his lips to my thigh and slide his soft wet mouth over my erection and tease me until I tangled my fingers in his hair – grown long enough for me to grip in both fists.

And then he'd lift his mouth away, smile when I begged him to keep touching me, and move one hand under the back of my thigh, to bend my knee and push it up close to my chest. He would fit his slender hips between my legs and press his perfect cock against my asshole.

"I want to be inside you," he would say in his soft, husky voice, blushing even though he hadn't said the same filthy words he liked me to say to him.

"Yes," I would say. "Fuck me, pretty bird. Fuck my ass and make me yours." And he would blush again, but he would also thrust his hips against me, push his hard length into me, and half-close his eyes like he wanted to be lost in pleasure but didn't want to lose sight of me.

He'd fan his wings – his perfect little wings, not the embellished and added-to things he'd been forced to wear in the Eyrie – softly at first. Then he would move them faster, beating at the air to gain leverage. And he'd curl his long fingers around my cock, and stroke me while he fucked me, and make me come hard and long as he pulsed into my ass once, twice, three times. And after the fourth pulse, he'd collapse on top of me, nestle close against my chest, whisper my name and tell me he loved me.

10
Fionn

THERE WERE RAISED eyebrows all around the council room when I walked in. I was impeccably dressed, made-up, and had a feathered serpent decorating each shoulder. The King wasn't there yet, but the rest of the councilors were. Councilor Rocsh met my eyes, smiled, and rose far enough to bow.

<Welcome, my Seer,> he said.

One of the others, a larger man with dark green wings who had been among the first to accept my presence in the council, also half-rose and bowed. <We didn't expect you, so soon after your illness, my Seer,> he said. <But welcome, indeed.>

Another man muttered, <We didn't expect you at all,> and I met his eyes coolly. He flushed and hastily bowed. The rest of them immediately followed suit.

<I am still weary, I admit,> I said. <But my mind is perfectly intact. I'm sure I can function well enough for a council meeting.>

Councilor Rocsh stood then, and beckoned to his attendant, who stepped forward from his place against the wall. <A chair for our Seer, please,> he said. I made note of the "please." Most noble Vogel seemed to treat their attendants and other servants as automatons; that Rocsh didn't told me good things about his character, and I felt more sure that I could trust him if I needed to.

The attendant nodded and hurried from the room. When he returned, I thanked him and Councilor Rocsh both. At previous meetings I had been forced to stand at the King's left hand. Feeling as I was, I hadn't been sure I could manage that today, whether the King preferred it or not.

The chair was smaller and plainer that those the Councilors sat in, and looked almost primitive next to the King's enormous, thronelike seat. It wasn't especially comfortable, either, but at least it was something.

No one spoke much until the King came in, then we all stood and greeted him with a bow and a, <My King.>

<I thought I said you didn't need to attend today, Seer Tokka,> he said, one eyebrow aloft on his forehead.

<You did, my King,> I said mildly. <But I believe it is important, if I am to be an effective Seer, that I attend every meeting I'm able to.>

He nodded and the meeting began. As he had said the night before, it was not an interesting or important discussion, but I was able to make several comments that sounded like I knew what I was talking about, and the Councilors even voted to implement one of my suggestions. So, while it was an insignificant event in the course of life at the Eyrie, I felt it was very successful in my attempts to be a good Seer.

I left exhausted but pleased.

Afterwards, the King took my arm as we walked back into the living area of the palace, up several long staircases to the highest inhabited floor. Our guards and attendants followed behind, just out of hearing range of our conversation.

<Have your noon meal with me, little seer,> the King said.

My stomach clenched, but I replied, <If it pleases you, my King.>

<I was hoping to please *you*, my Seer.> He leaned closer as he said it and his voice dropped.

<Of course you do, my King.>

He gave a terse order, and someone scurried off to make sure enough food for two was delivered to the King's rooms, and none at all to mine.

When we entered his sitting room, he sent our attendants away, as he always did, and gestured for me to sit. <You look tired, Tokka,> he said. <Perhaps you shouldn't have come to the meeting.>

<I'll rest after we eat, my King. I was glad to have been useful.>

He looked at me for a long moment. <You have become quite good at making yourself useful.>

I knew, from the way he said it, that he wasn't entirely pleased, but probably didn't have an articulate reason for why. He wanted me to be decorative, symbolic at best. I smiled, as if I didn't understand the implications of his words or his tone of voice.

<It is my purpose as a Seer to serve my people however I can,> I said.

Then the food arrived, and I didn't have to say anything at all while dishes were laid out and uncovered, and the servants scurried out again.

I made it through the meal, but I must have looked exhausted because the King only kissed me gently. When he took my hand to help me to my feet, I expected him to caress me or to lead me towards his bedroom and I prepared myself mentally for what would inevitably follow. Instead, he led me to the door of the anteroom.

<Get some rest, my Seer,> he said, bending to kiss the top of my head.

<Thank you, my King.> I hoped I didn't sound too relieved when I said it.

Days went by with little for me to do and the King must have been busy, because he didn't call on me either, though he did send me a bottle of apple wine one evening, and a basket of candied fruits and other delicacies another. To keep busy, I began spinning and weaving again, and even set up a space for dyeing – after convincing Neeka to find me a drop spindle and a loom – and rediscovered the simple delight in making something with my own hands. Neeka was unimpressed by the dyepots but agreed that at least I kept them on the balcony and not in my sitting room. Each night before bed, I scoured every book in the library that seemed likely, to find mentions of fever and salt-leaf trees.

Plenty of volumes referred to the great fever that had swept the Vogel Monarchy generations ago, killing royalty and commoners alike, and a few more recent books had a line or two given to the Queen's death. Several mentioned the wholesale cutting of salt-leaf, too, but none said anything about how it was to be used. My only real clue was the rhyme.

<Neeka,> I said, setting aside yet another book that had little to say on the subject, and nothing at all useful.

<My Seer?> She was poking halfheartedly at a piece of embroidery but didn't really seem to be enjoying it.

<Can you get me some salt-leaf bark? And some leaves?>

She set her hoop aside. <It won't be easy,> she said.

<There's so little growing in Aven now, especially near the Eyrie.> She tapped her fingers on the arm of her chair. <I have a cousin… Well, an old family friend, really. He might know where to get some. Do you plan to try the old folk remedies? The Princess hasn't become sicker these last few days, and no one else is ill.>

I stood up and stretched, arching my back, and spreading both wings as wide as I could in the confines of the room. Once, it would have been easy, but with all these extra feathers glued on to make me look presentable, I had to be careful. Finally, I resorted to stretching one at a time.

<I think the feather-worker is gathering new feathers for you,> Neeka said. <I overheard him telling the head cook to save the best feathers from the geese he was preparing.>

<Lovely,> I said. <Goosefeathers.> I flipped my wings into place against my back. I still wasn't used to the weight of them or the way they stirred the air at the slightest movement. <How soon can you go to see your cousin? Even if no one else is sick *now*, it seems like a good idea to find out if it will even help, and maybe we can see to it that the Princess recovers fully. Also, I think it would be good to find somewhere that harvesting some won't threaten the very tree with extinction.>

Neeka stood and stretched, too, and her movements were much less awkward, like she just knew where her wings were at all times and didn't have to watch to make sure she wasn't going to knock over a vase. <I can go now, my Seer, if you don't mind me leaving from the balcony. It'll be a quicker trip to the village if I don't have to go through the palace and back around.>

<You can come and go however you please,> I said, and followed her out the door. She stepped up onto the railing.

<I'll be back before the evening meal, Seer Tokka.>

<Take as much time as you like. Stay overnight, even. Get

a good visit while you can.>

She grinned, then dove from the balcony, opening her wings and soaring away before she hit the water. The sun gleamed on her brown and black wings, turning them almost gold, and as always when I watched one of my people fly, I felt a vicious stab of envy. But at least I had spirit flight.

Bright sad, said Smoke, curling up my leg from where she had slithered out of my room on her belly, all three sets of wings tucked close.

Not fly, said Flame, curling around my other ankle.

Someday fly, said Smoke.

I looked down at them. "Just because I can't fly doesn't mean you two have to crawl," I said. I spoke Islish to them most of the time, though they understood me perfectly well no matter what language I used.

Too heavy, said Smoke.

"Did you eat too much?" I teased. "You know, you needn't eat everything Neeka offers you. She won't be insulted if you refuse."

Too full, said Flame, but her tone sounded sly.

Not food, said Smoke.

"Then what are you full of?"

Eggs. Smoke sounded smug.

"Eggs!" I bent to lift the serpents, one in each hand. They did seem oddly thick. "But you were flying yesterday. You were chasing each other around the bathing room and splashing water everywhere." They wriggled out of my hands to coil up my arms to my shoulders. One nestled under each side of my jaw, tickling my earlobes with their feathers.

"Wherever did you find another serpent?"

Flame began to purr, then Smoke joined in.

"You're not even two years old yet," I said.

Old enough, said Smoke.

Many serpents on beach, said Flame.

We chose, said Smoke.

Mine was fastest, said Flame, sounding pleased with herself.

Mine was smartest, said Smoke, sounding even more pleased.

"Goodness." I looked over the side of my balcony but had no glimpse of the beach. "Don't tree serpents lay their eggs in spring? You can't be fat and lazy all winter."

Lay soon, said Smoke.

First clutch, said Flame, as if that explained everything. I suppose to her, it did.

I went back inside to perch on a stool with my spindle in hand. Spinning always settled my mind and kept my hands occupied so I wouldn't fidget. And the yarn I was spinning was for making a gift for Kiernan, though who could say when I'd be able to give it him. It was the softest wool I could find, from an area in the mountains where they had a rare breed of fine-wooled sheep, and I had dyed it a deep forest green.

Smoke and Flame had both been part of a clutch laid on my tower roof at the Abbey of the Moon, just when the days had been starting to get warm. I had watched their parents incubate the eggs all spring and saw them hatch as the days turned to summer. But perhaps tree serpents could lay eggs twice a year?

Fret fret fret, said Smoke, gliding off my shoulder to my lap, and from there to the basket of wool at my feet.

"You can't sleep there," I said. "Unless you want me to spin you into yarn."

Silly Bright, she said, yawning. She curled up right in the middle of the wool.

I sighed as Flame followed her sister into the basket.

First eggs always autumn, said Flame, looking up at me.

"Is that bad?"

Not bad. Won't hatch.

"Oh. Do they never hatch when they're laid in autumn?"

Too cold, said Smoke.

"What if you made a nest for them by the fire, instead of laying them outside?"

Serpents wild, said Flame.

"I know you're wild, but what if?"

Might hatch. Flame didn't sound interested. They both curled tighter into the wool and ignored me. I wondered if anyone had even written a book about the lives of feathered serpents. I wondered if anyone would read it, if I wrote one.

I set my spindle aside and went to my bedroom to rummage in my desk for the notebook I had been using to write down useful information I came across in my reading. I had to set that aside, too, when a knock came at the door.

<Healer Kah says… Oh!> A distracted-looking Vogel woman in an infirmary smock looked up and had obviously not been expecting me to answer my own door. Her eyes widened. <Oh. My Seer, I didn't think…>

I smiled to reassure her. <What does Healer Kah need?>

<The Princess…> she said, and I felt dread in my belly.

<Is the fever worse?> I said, with a calm that bore no resemblance to what I was actually feeling. I pushed aside the silly notion that Neeka's casual remark about no one being sick had cast an ill luck charm. <Take me there,> I said.

<She doesn't require your presence,> she said. <She only wanted to inform you.>

<Nevertheless, I may be of some use.>

She nodded and looked a little reassured, but bustled away, not even waiting for me to follow.

Halfway across the palace another Vogel approached me, hurrying down the hall and looking relieved to have found me. I recognized him as Councilor Rocsh's attendant, but I didn't know his name.

<My Seer,> he said, bowing slightly.

<I'm on my way to the Princess,> I said. <Please relay your message while we walk.> I was afraid of losing sight of the infirmary attendant and ending up lost.

<My Seer, Councilor Rocsh sent me to beg your help. He has received a… a messenger, I suppose.>

I was distracted enough I didn't think about the odd phrasing until I had already said, <Can it wait?> I hurried to keep up with Healer Kah's associate. The part of the palace where the royal children lived was still confusing to me.

<I… He really could use your help as soon as possible.> The Councilor's attendant twisted his fingers together when I looked at him. He seemed to really care that his master needed my help. <It's a message for the King, we think, but with our King occupied…>

"We think" struck me as curious, but I wasn't sure why. Perhaps Rocsh was as unconcerned as I was with proper hierarchy in the palace.

<All right,> I said. <Come with me while I speak to Healer Kah. I'll be as quick as I can. Then you can take me to the Councilor.> It would also solve the problem of finding my way back to familiar halls.

<Thank you, my Seer.>

I entered the Princess's rooms to find a scene much like I had seen when she first fell ill. I paused in the anteroom to change into a white infirmary smock and mask, then walked cautiously into the room.

The Princess looked tiny on the huge mattress, her face flushed and thin. The King sat on the edge of the bed as he had sat days ago and, as I watched, Healer Kah put a hand on his shoulder and said something to him. The King nodded and stood and when she drew back the sheet, he lifted his daughter into his arms and turned towards the bathing room. He met my eyes briefly and I saw fear and anguish.

Healer Kah turned to see where he was looking. She frowned when she saw me.

<You didn't need to come,> she said. <I don't want a repeat of last time.>

<I won't stay,> I said. <But I need to speak to you.>

<A moment.> She followed the King into the bathing room, where I could hear water running. A short time later, she emerged and crossed the room.

<I...> I hesitated. She had been dismissive of the idea of salt-leaf as a cure, and I didn't want her scorn now. Worse, I didn't want her to forbid me to try.

She raised her eyebrows, waiting.

<I believe I have figured out how salt-leaf can be used to cure the fever,> I said. <Or at least help treat it.>

<This again.> She looked at me impatiently.

<It was used wrong last time there was a major outbreak.> I pressed on, knowing I had to say this now, or give up, and I wouldn't give up. I might not love my King, but I didn't want him to have to watch his child die. <But the rhyme is true.>

She sighed. <Even if you *are* right, we have no salt-leaf on hand. It is very rare, no thanks to that last outbreak you mentioned.>

<I know. But Neeka has gone to see if she can find some. She knows someone. Healer Kah, I must try. If I'm right, it should only require a small amount.>

<So not only do you claim a folk cure is correct, but you also think the tree was needlessly harvested until there was none left?>

<Yes,> I said, with more confidence than I could possibly feel. I lifted my chin and refused to look away from her eyes.

She sighed again and her shoulders sagged. <Well, your

cool bath idea worked. Not enough, but it kept her alive this long.> She waved a hand. <Return when you have a cure to test.>

<Thank you, Healer,> I said, and I wasn't sure she even heard me, because she was already heading back to the Princess's bathing room.

Councilor Rocsh was waiting in the Council Chamber, frowning at a large wooden box in the middle of the table. A rustling noise came from inside the box, and then a sharp tap.

<Councilor?>

<Close the door.> He attendant obeyed, pulling the door to quietly. To my surprise, he didn't take up a place against the wall, but instead stood next to the Councilor.

<Your attendant said you had received a message?> I glanced at the other man, who had deep red-bronze feathers and eyes to match. He wasn't handsome, exactly, but he had a friendly look, and I couldn't help smiling. He smiled in return, then looked away. <I'm sorry,> I said. <I don't know your name.>

<Nikna, my Seer,> he said. His facial feathers told me he was widowed, with no children, and was not seeking a partner.

When I looked back at Councilor Rocsh, he was looking at me with a slightly amused expression.

<It isn't so much a message,> he said, <As a *messenger*.> He gestured at the box. <It flew into the King's rooms. One of his guards caught it and brought it to me. It speaks, I think, and there is a paper tied to its leg, but I haven't the gift to understand it, and it won't let anyone near to read the message.>

<It… What is in the box?>

Let me out, you pea-brained fop, said whatever was in the box.

<Perhaps you could open the box?> I said.

<Are you certain?>

I nodded and Councilor Rocsh gestured to his attendant

who leaned over the table and gingerly removed the lid.

A very annoyed black and white bird with an absurdly long tail hopped onto the edge of the box and looked at me from a shining dark eye.

The Prince of Morven Forest sends his regards, it said.

COUNCILOR ROCSH had to help me to a chair and I realized I had just made myself very, very vulnerable to him.

If he hadn't suspected already, he would now be certain that my feelings for Kiernan hadn't changed. I could only hope he was the ally I suspected he was.

After an elaborate preamble listing the names and titles of what seemed like the entire Sidhe royal family but was actually only the Queen and her three heirs, the magpie allowed me to untie the message from its leg. I handed it to Councilor Rocsh and he unfolded it and handed it back. It was written in Sidhe.

I smiled, trying to hide it, but only half succeeding. Kiernan could not have found a more certain way to make sure I would read the letter than composing it in his own language. I wasn't fluent, by any means, but I had been studying, and I was good with languages. Both the King and the Council had had me translate for them before, though not Sidhe until now. And he had used formulaic phrases such as you might find from one member of royalty to another in any language.

<You are hereby cordially invited to the Sidhe court in Morven Forest to attend Autumn Balance festivities,> I translated. Where I encountered an unfamiliar word, I made my best guess according to what was most likely. The gist was, the Vogel King was invited to send a small delegation to Morven

to enjoy Sidhe hospitality and discuss the possibility of opening trade relations.

When I had finished translating to the best of my ability, the magpie looked at me expectantly. I didn't know if it wanted a reward or a reply.

<I wonder what the Sidhe Queen would do if we sent a reply in Vogelspek,> Councilor Rocsh said, amusement in his voice.

<Please wait here a moment,> I said to the bird, and stepped out of the room. <My Seer,> said Konta, stepping forward from his place guarding the door. He always seemed to know when I needed something as soon as I glanced in his direction.

<Could you find a dish of water and some nuts for our… guest? Some dried fruit, perhaps? I'd send Neeka, but she's away.>

He looked puzzled but nodded and left in the direction of the stairway to the kitchens.

I looked at Rocsh, who had followed me outside. <What do we do?>

He paced down the hall and I hurried after, Trikta and Nikna coming close behind.

<The King will not be interested in this as long as the Princess is still ill,> he said. <Less now that she has relapsed.>

<But how long can we wait to send a reply?>

<It would be rude to wait more than a day or two.>

<Can the Council make such a decision in the King's absence?> As I said it, I realized that Councilor Rocsh had not chosen to send for any of the other Councilors when he needed help; he sent for me. Perhaps it was only because he thought I could speak to birds, but it still felt strange. In a good way. <Trade with Morven and the goodwill of the Sidhe seems too

important to let slip by.>

<I agree.> He paused where a balcony opened in the wall and stepped out into the sun. It had a similar view to my own balcony, only it was much closer to the water. <Whatever the Council's decision, I'm sure the King will accept it.>

<Do you think the other Councilors might vote against sending a delegation?> I leaned on the balcony railing and looked out to sea.

<Some of them believe the King would prefer to keep us isolated. He doesn't even like having to deal with the Alfar.>

<That's because the Alfar are our overlords, and their tithe requirements are excessive.>

He leaned on the rail next to me, all elegance. I realized it was him and not the King that I emulated, whenever I tried to look as properly regal as a Seer should. He looked at me appraisingly. <You've come a long way from the frightened boy who first arrived at the Eyrie in the claws of one of the King's Guard.> He said. His voice was rich and kind.

<I would like to go,> I said. <With the delegation.>

He didn't look surprised. He glanced at his attendant and when I followed his gaze, I saw the other man was hiding a smile behind his hand.

<Not because… because of what you think,> I said, though it was only partly true. <I believe it would show goodwill. And trust. If I went.>

I looked away from his eyes, back out to sea, where a small fishing boat was heading in towards the City Beneath the Cliff. <According to that book,> I said, <The one about seers that I found in the library, our seers were once not only spiritual advisors and healers. They were also negotiators. They spoke to the spirits on behalf of their people, and to their people on behalf of the spirits. And they worked with other seers to make sure all peoples could flourish.>

I dared to look at him again, but he was watching his attendant, something soft on his face. Nikna nodded, almost imperceptibly, and Councilor Rocsh turned back to me.

<I do believe you've done your research,> he said. <And I think your reasoning is sound. I will support you in Council, and argue for you with the King, if it comes to that.>

He looked out over the sea again. <I believe I should go along, as well.> His attendant glanced at him in surprise, and moved to stand beside him, covering one of the Councilor's hands on the rail with his own.

<Thank you,> I said, trying not to stare at Rocsh's elegant hand, fingers twining with the thicker, stronger fingers of Nikna.

He looked at me and smiled. <But I do not believe for a moment that you don't also wish to see your Prince again.>

I almost managed not to blush. <I —>

He held up his free hand. <It's okay, Seer Tokka. I understand what love is. I even know what a heart bond feels like.> He looked at Nikna and then away. <I can't say I entirely approve, but not because he isn't Vogel.>

I bit my lip, wondering if I should try to deny everything. But I realized that, by holding Rocsh's hand, Nikna was telling me something. He was saying the Councilor was not my enemy. <Then why?> I said.

He touched my shoulder lightly, briefly. <Because I would hate to see you hurt, and it is hard enough to witness you struggling to do what our King requires of you.> I knew he didn't mean my duties as Seer. He looked at Nikna again. <At least the man *I* love is not forbidden to me, nor does he live in a far-off realm, even if it is frowned upon for a noble – however minor and thin my blood – to take up with a commoner.>

<You and Nikna?> I said, as if it wasn't obvious.

<For more years than you have been alive, my Seer.>

<Since you were widowed?> I said to Nikna.

He smiled, but there was an undercurrent of deep sadness in the expression. <Since many years before that,> he said. <Our laws don't allow same-sex marriages, even though relations are permitted. And they don't allow… more than two.>

<I – *oh*,> I said, and Councilor Rocsh laughed. His mirth was tempered by sadness, too.

<We would all three of us have married, had it been possible,> he said. <But at least two of us could, and the three of us could be together.>

<But now we are only two, and still can't marry,> said Nikna.

<I'll add that to my list of laws to change,> I said.

<You do that, my Seer,> said Rocsh.

<In the meantime,> I said, an idea suddenly occurring to me and making me flush with excitement, <If you are going with the delegation, why not marry in Morven? The Sidhe don't allow more than two to marry, but as long as both are consenting and have reached their majority, they don't care which two.>

Councilor Rocsh's smile grew. <First we have to get the Council in its chamber and get them to agree to send a delegation at all.>

<And I have a new treatment for fever to test,> I said, suddenly filled with energy. I grinned, completely forgetting I was supposed to be the elegant, serene Seer of the Eyrie in public.

Both the other men looked startled. <Whenever did you find a new treatment?> said Rocsh.

I looked at my feet. The paint was starting to flake off one of my claws. <Actually, it's a very old treatment, but I'm hopeful I can change it from a folk remedy to an effective medicine.> I turned to go back inside.

<I hope you're right,> said the Councilor. <Or our King

might lose his treasured daughter.>

11
Kiernan

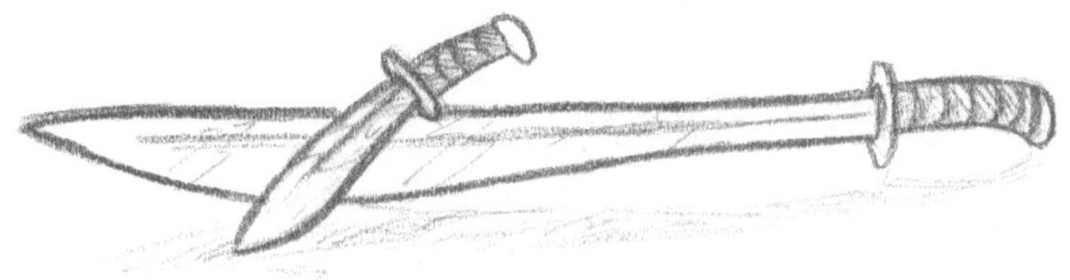

There was more than a moon before Autumn Balance, which should have been plenty of time to prepare for a diplomatic visit. In an emergency, it would have been possible to offer hospitality on no notice at all.

But I wanted this to be perfect. Even if Fionn didn't accompany the delegation, I wanted him to understand, when his people reported back, that I had worked hard to give them a wonderful experience.

My Queen gave me leave to arrange things as I chose, even to the extent of redecorating the guest rooms, if I deemed it necessary. And with me doing everything, she didn't have to be bothered herself, and she didn't have to spare any of her own staff. She only required me to report to her every few days so she could know everything that was and would be happening.

«I had a thought, my son,» she said, after I had given one of my reports. I had decided on a few upgrades to the main guest suite to better accommodate the taller Vogel.

«My Queen?» I replied. She had not invited me to sit, and in the Hall it would have meant dragging over a chair from the edge of the room anyway, so I stood before her throne, hands clasped behind my back. My cousins stood in their usual places behind the Queen's throne, one on each side, but my sisters had left when I arrived, claiming to have better things to do than listen to me.

«Your sisters each have their own personal guards, as do I.»

My stomach fell. I didn't need more staff following me around, trying to help me. But I didn't say anything.

«I believe it is time you assembled a guard of your own,» she said.

«My Queen,» I said, carefully. «I don't require a guard. I'm perfectly capable of defending myself.»

«Of course you are,» she said. «But the purpose of a personal guard is not, as you seem to think, to guard you.» She leaned back on her throne and waved her hand in the general direction of Sean and Padraig. «Do you think I need these two, or any of their comrades, to guard me?»

«No, of course not, my Queen.» My mother had never been interested in weapons, but she was the most powerful magic user in Morven Forest, maybe even on the Isle, and therefore feared nothing and no one.

«Their purpose is symbolic.» She tapped her finger against her lips. «I'll give you one of mine, already trained, and you can build your own company over time.»

I tried not to sigh too loudly. «How many, my Queen?»

«Oh, not too many. Six or eight, perhaps. Enough that they have time to sleep and holiday and not leave you unguarded.»

I licked my lips, thinking carefully about what to say. I knew she wasn't giving me a choice. «Who did you have in mind?» I said. Whoever it was, I would need to be very careful around them; no doubt they would continue to work for her. I wondered if there were six people anywhere in the court I would actually be able to trust with my life.

«Your cousin Padraig,» she said, and he looked startled, but said nothing. «You may select any others you require from the Palace Guard.»

At least it wasn't Sean. I might even be able to trust Padraig, eventually.

Then my Queen smiled, and my stomach plummeted. «I think I shall be generous and give you *two* of mine.» Her lips curled even more, showing the tips of her long canines. «Sean nicFia shall be yours, too.»

Sean opened his mouth to protest, but Padraig jabbed him in the ribs behind the throne before he could get any words out.

«My Queen,» I said, carefully. «I am fairly certain my cousin Sean would still like to see me a corpse on the end of his sword.»

She only smiled. «He would. Which is why he will be very careful to keep you alive.»

«My Queen?»

She didn't look behind her, but I suspected her words were for Sean as much as they were for me. «Everyone knows he wants to kill you, so if you die, he will be blamed, even if he wasn't responsible.» She tapped the arm of the throne. «And you know the penalty for killing a noble fey.»

Not the same as the penalty for killing a werewolf. But I didn't say it. I didn't dare.

«And,» she said, before I could protest further. «Everyone knows you would be pleased to kill *him*. You may be a Prince, but you are not *entirely* above the law.»

I had no idea what the use of, and emphasis on, "entirely" meant, but I noted it for thinking about later.

«When will you transfer them from your employ to mine?» I said.

She waved her hand again. «They'll need new livery. I suppose you've gone with green and grey for your servant?»

The Palace Guard were outfitted in green, grey, and russet brown, and her personal Guard had added embellishments in deep blood red. I nodded.

«A few days, then, to get them outfitted properly.»

A few days of relative freedom. It wasn't enough. I needed to get my magic back and get away from here before her grip choked me to death.

I bowed my head. «Of course, my Queen.» I turned to go.

«And Kiernan?» It was her use of my name more than anything that made me turn around instead of just pausing. I couldn't remember the last time she had used my name.

«My Queen?»

«I'm pleased with your work. Let me know as soon as you have an answer from the Vogel.»

«I will, my Queen.» She nodded and I knew I was dismissed.

Daphnis followed a few steps behind me until we were away from the palace and deep under the trees. I had taken as much time as I could the last while to walk in the forest and try to re-learn it from my new perspective of no magic.

I thought I was doing rather well, at least as far as destinations within a half-day's walk of the palace were concerned.

"I'm sorry, my Prince," Daphnis said, taking advantage of his longer legs to catch up and walk closer behind me. When we reached the meadow, he moved up beside me.

"For what?" I breathed a little easier. We weren't far from the palace, but few noble fey came this way. It was too close to a village full of werewolves, humans, and other "lesser" peoples.

"I know you value your privacy. It will be harder to be alone with two guards following you around."

"Harder than with you following me around?"

He clasped his hands together. "You could return me to your Queen," he said. "Or send me back to the gardens."

"You know I won't do that."

"My Prince, I had a notion."

I headed across the meadow and Daphnis seemed to suddenly realize where we were.

"Why have we come here, my Prince?"

"Dec had tools and wood. I need tools and wood."

"You could not acquire them at court?"

"I don't need the whole court gossiping about their Prince taking up a handcraft."

I walked around the cabin and stood at the bottom of the shallow steps, looking up at the door. Now that I was here, I didn't want to go in. I didn't want to see Dec's absence written in dust and a cold, untended hearth.

"Fuck." I continued around the cabin to the other side. There was a second, smaller door that led directly into the cellar. It was a quicker way to where I wanted to be, anyway, and would have fewer painful reminders, since Dec had seldom allowed me into his workshop.

I just hope Dec's family hadn't come to clear out his things. But of course, they probably would have. Good tools were expensive, and Dec had refused to use anything but the best.

"What was your notion?" I paused at the door to try to reach a pocket on the inside of my jacket. With my sword strapped across my chest, it was hard to get into and I struggled with buttons until Daphnis moved closer and pushed my hands aside. He shifted the straps of my sword rig, unbuttoned the top buttons of my jacket, and reached into my pocket.

It felt intimate, and I longed so badly for intimacy. It would be easy to give in. Easy to do something I would spend the rest of my life regretting. I almost jerked away. I breathed carefully and made myself stand very still until he handed me the two thin, sturdy wires I had been trying to reach.

"Thank you."

He stepped away and I turned to pick the lock on the door. Dec had always joked about how easy he would be to rob, but he'd never bothered to upgrade to a better lock, even when I had offered to have it done for him as a birthday gift.

"What was your notion?" I repeated, once I had the lock open and my lockpicks stored in my pocket again. And this time I managed the buttons on my jacket myself.

"You need magic, my Prince," he said, and I managed not to flinch.

"I need to break my mother's spellwork," I said.

"I know that, but…" He hesitated, then went on, quickly as if to get it all out before he changed his mind. "I may be able to give you my magic."

I had been struggling to pull open the door, which had swollen with the moisture of three years of abandonment, and which was thoroughly stuck. Daphnis laid a hand on the boards and, after a moment, it came easily free.

"Dryads are good with wood," he said when I looked at him.

"I can't borrow your magic, Daph," I said, even though the idea of having magic again – any magic – was thrilling.

"It wouldn't be a loan," he said.

"In that case, I definitely can't take it."

"At least consider the idea," he said. "And in the meantime, perhaps your Seer Siona could draw magic through you, to ease the ache."

"To what?"

"When you were a child, you learned to draw the magic of the Realms into yourself, yes?"

"Yes, of course."

"A skilled magic user can direct that flow of magic first through another, before drawing it into themself. I'm certain Seer Siona could do it."

"Even with the Queen's spellwork cutting me off?"

"I believe so, yes."

I looked into the cellar. It was so dark even I would have trouble seeing, and I had no way to summon light. I should have thought to bring a candle.

"How could you give me some of your magic?"

"Not some, my Prince."

"It would… what would you do without magic?" I took a step into the dark and almost jumped when a wisplight drifted past my shoulder to cast a dim light over the steps. It was greener than the wisplight I conjured. *Had* conjured, once.

I glanced back at Daphnis, and he simply looked back at me expressionlessly.

"I am enslaved, Kiernan," he said, omitting my title for the first time since the Queen had ordered him to serve me. It made me feel naked, vulnerable, as if the word "Prince" had clothed me, hidden me from his regard. I turned back to the steps and moved cautiously down.

"I have no hope of freedom, because my people can never be freed according to Isle law. So I have no use for magic," he said.

"You seem to have had quite a few uses for it," I commented. The steps creaked under my weight but seemed solid.

"Only to serve you."

"What about children?" I said. "Isn't it dryad custom to pass on their magic when you reproduce?"

"The magic we aren't supposed to have?"

I laughed softly. "I've found a few references to dryad culture from before the founding of the Monarchies."

"You assume I wish to reproduce."

"Don't you?" His wisplight illuminated the large open space below Dec's cabin and I took a deep breath, and when I let it out, it was shaky.

His tools were here, oiled and each hung in their proper place, as if he had only just put them away for the day. Except for the dust. There was even wood stored in racks close to the ceiling where heat from the room above would have helped keep it dry.

A wool sweater hung from a peg near the narrow stair that led up to a hatch in the corner of the kitchen. I moved closer, brushed it with my fingers, and bent my head to smell it. I had to grab the stair railing. I couldn't breathe. It still smelled like Dec. This place reminded me of him so much, and it *hurt*.

I made myself take slow, careful breaths, and moved away from the sweater on its peg. Slowly, in and out, I breathed until I felt less lost. Dec was three years dead and I had said my farewell, even though I had never cried for him. It hurt to think of him, but he was my past; Fionn was my present and my future, and Fionn was why I was here.

I ran a hand over the tools. I had no time to get to work now, not with all that still had to be done before Autumn Balance, but everything I needed was here. If I couldn't be near my beloved, at least I could work on a gift for him for that future of ours, until I either found a way to regain my magic or my time ran out and I was required to travel to Dudoon. And then I would run for the Eyrie, to steal him, and live as an outlaw if I had to.

"As I recall," I finally said, choosing a few tools and laying them on the bench to wait for a free day when I could lose myself in experiments and invention. "Dryads pass on their magic when they impregnate a partner. Or so the book said."

"Yes."

"And once their offspring is rooted safely in the soil, they begin to wither until eventually nothing is left, or else they root themselves and become a tree."

"Yes."

"So how did you plan to pass your magic on to me?"

"Our magic, when we reproduce, is concentrated in our pollen."

"And I would, what? Consume your pollen?" I sorted through a rack of wood, standing on the workbench to reach, and pulled out several long thin pieces that would work for what I intended to try.

"That would give you a small amount of magic," he said. "Until your digestive fluids destroyed the pollen." He was waiting for me at the bottom of the stairs, like he didn't want to intrude in this space, or on my work.

I climbed down from the bench to rummage in a drawer, looking for wire.

"It would have to be… implanted," he said.

When I looked up, I thought he might be blushing, but the dark and the uncertain, wavering wisplight made it impossible to tell.

"Implanted how?"

He looked down at his hands. "I thought, perhaps, if your Seer visited in spirit again, and borrowed my body, it could be done then."

Finally, standing there with a spool of brass wire in my hand, I realized what he was telling me. Even then, it took a

long moment to process.

"You'd have to fuck me," I said, and he didn't look up from studying his fingers. "You'd have to concentrate your magic in your pollen, all or nothing, and you'd fuck me, and ejaculate it up my ass." He still didn't look up, even though I was deliberately more vulgar than I needed to be. I wanted him to react. I wanted him to be *angry*, to see the absurdity of what he proposed.

"Yes, my Prince," he said, his voice calm.

"And then you would wither away to nothing? Shrivel and slowly die?"

"If it was allowed, my Prince," he did look up at me then, and his eyes shone in the green wisplight. "I would choose to root in the forest and become a tree."

I stared at him, but I was thinking, absurdly, about the triple-trunked salt-leaf tree hidden behind the Eyrie in Aven, that the Vogel peasants called the Dancing Dryads.

"Daph, how is a Mother Tree created?"

He blinked at me, unprepared for the change in subject. "They say our Mother Trees were once dryads who rooted in the earth with their magic intact, and over many lifetimes became further infused with the magic of our people.

"And the Mother Tree in Aven was a salt-leaf?"

"Yes."

I didn't know what this meant, if any of it meant anything, but it pricked at my thoughts, and I wished I could talk to Fionn about it. He would have ideas, suggestions that would clarify my stray notions.

"Why do you ask, my Prince?"

"I don't know," I said, and pushed away the thought. "And as for implanting your magic, my answer is no. I haven't so many friends that I would sacrifice one to claim magic that isn't even mine."

I put the spool of wire next to the saw and drill and chisel I had laid out on the bench. "And even if I were filthy rich in friends, I would never use them that way."

"Of course, my Prince."

"And," I said, walking closer to look up into his impossibly deep brown eyes, "I made a promise to Fionn. I'm his, and only his, unless he tells me he doesn't want me." And I pushed him firmly aside to climb the steps again.

He followed and closed the door. I heard the click of the lock and turned to watch him withdraw his finger from the keyhole, a thin tendril of green resorbing into its tip.

"You could have done that in the first place," I said.

He almost smiled. "I wasn't sure I wanted you to know all that I can do, Prince Kiernan."

We walked back across the meadow, heading for the palace. Until we heard back from the Vogel, I didn't like to be away too long. I wanted to receive the magpie with its reply personally, because who knew what might happen if it flew back to Padraig with only Sean around. I would not be surprised if Sean tried to sabotage my careful plans in order to make me look bad to my Queen.

"You know your beloved is not capable of keeping that same promise," Daphnis said gently.

I stopped and whirled around to face him. I know he was not intentionally cruel, but he'd managed to wound me anyway. He took a step back when he saw my face.

"Do you think that because he is required to let his King fuck him that I should break *my* promise?" I said, anger infusing every word. I tried to find calm, because I knew Daphnis was trying to be kind, but it was harder and harder to do these days. I had not realized how volatile I would be without my forest to gentle me.

"I only meant…"

"You meant I should feel free to take my pleasure where I find it," I said. "Or did you think that if you convinced me that he's happy servicing the Vogel King that I would turn to you for comfort?"

"My Prince." He took a step back but something on his face changed. He looked… guilty.

"Daphnis?"

"You know I… I care for you, my Prince. I don't like to see you suffer."

"So you would comfort me, and then give me your magic and leave me alone again, with no one but my cousins for company."

His eyes widened. "I –"

"Daphnis, you *are* my friend, but I can't love you the way you want me to. My heart belongs to Fionn. And if you give me your magic and plant yourself in the forest as a tree, I will have no one here I can truly trust.

"You would still have Seer Siona."

"She is like a mother to me," I said. "But she belongs to my Queen, and I cannot ask her for her loyalty without endangering her."

"I think you underestimate her, my Prince."

"Don't bring this up again," I said, turning for the palace.

"No, my Prince."

"I need you, Daph. Maybe not the way you want me to, but I need you."

"Thank you, Prince Kiernan."

He followed me in silence for a while, before venturing, "I think the design with leaves in place of feathers is the soundest, my Prince."

I glanced at him, then noticed Sean and Padraig hurrying out of the palace.

"I was thinking the leather one, like bat wings."

"It would be heavy, but maybe you could find something lighter for the membrane."

"Silk, maybe? We'll try both."

"We, my Prince? Will you let me help you, then?" He dropped back as we headed for my cousins, taking his proper place.

"You said you were good with wood."

"Yes, my Prince."

That was all we had the chance to say, as Padraig caught sight of me and almost ran across the lawn. He held out a rolled message, wax seal still intact. "The magpie returned," he said, eyes bright and cheeks flushed.

Sean scowled, "I still say you should take that to the Queen immediately."

"Don't forget to polish her shoes with your tongue before she dismisses you," I said. I took the paper from Padraig and looked at the elegant script on the outside. "It has my name on it, not hers. I'll read it and not bother her with any but the most relevant information."

I broke the seal and carefully unrolled the paper, trying not to show my excitement. It had a greeting at the top in Vogelspek, of which I could only read the gist, but the rest was in Islish, written in an impossibly neat hand. I imagined Fionn sitting at a fancy writing desk, forming the perfect letters with a quill dipped in vivid shell-purple ink. I forced myself to keep my face bland, to not let through the smile I wanted to give the world.

"They're sending a delegation," I said. "They don't give names, but ask if two representatives of the King, two experienced trade negotiators, two attendants, and four guards would be an acceptable number."

Finally, I allowed myself a grin at Padraig. He grinned back. "Congratulations, cousin," he said, and I'm pretty sure he meant it.

12
Fionn

Neeka returned the next day with a sack of leaves and bark — it was a smaller amount than I had hoped, but if I was right, it should be enough.

<I'm sorry, Seer Tokka,> she said when she handed it over. <But my cousin wouldn't harvest any more. He wouldn't even tell me where he got this; he just disappeared into the wood yesterday and came back after dinner.> When I told her the Princess had relapsed, she replied that even that wouldn't have been enough to convince her cousin to harvest more salt-leaf.

<It's okay, I understand. This will have to be enough.>

I took the sack into my bathing room, where I had a long counter I could work at, dumped the contents out, and sorted it.

There was plenty of outer bark, which the tree naturally shed, peeling off in long orange-red strips all year long, but most intensively in late summer. Unfortunately, it was — if I was correct — the least useful part of the tree for treating fever.

I set it aside for later, when I might have more time to work on trying to induce spirit flight.

The next most plentiful was leaves, which the tree would also shed naturally all year. About half the amount was dried leaves, and half fresh. I separated them into two piles.

And last, there was a regrettably small amount of pale green inner bark.

<Neeka?>

She appeared behind me with a mug of tea in each hand and I smelled my favorite mix of winterleaf and sweet bean pod.

<My Seer?> she said, handing me one of the mugs.

<Good visit?>

She grinned and nodded. <But that's not why you called me.>

I sipped my tea and closed my eyes as the steam soothed my eyelids. I had been too excited by the prospect of traveling to Morven Forest – of seeing Kiernan – to sleep well. I had spent most of the night going over and over the arguments I would have to present to the council, and maybe to my King, trying to think of the best way to convince them.

When I opened my eyes again, she was looking at me closely. <What happened while I was gone? You're nearly shaking, and you look like you haven't slept at all.>

<Could you go to the infirmary and borrow a pot? One of the ones they use for boiling down decoctions? I need to make one and it doesn't seem like a good idea to do it in my tea kettle.>

She frowned at me, pretending to be angry. <Not until you tell me what has you so agitated.>

I sipped my tea again and laughed at the expression she made. <There was a messenger yesterday,> I said.

Her eyes widened and she waited for me to continue.

<From Morven Forest.>

She shrieked and then covered her mouth with one hand. Her eyes were huge, and dancing with glee. <What did the message say?>

I turned back to my counter to contemplate the leaves and bark arranged in neat piles on its surface and pretended to be unconcerned.

She poked my shoulder, and not gently. <Seer Tokka,> she said, in the tone of a nanny scolding a child, or an older sibling chiding a younger. Or how I imagined those characters would sound, at least; I had no experience of either. <Tell me.>

<You know, I don't think it was really that exciting a message after all.>

<Tokka!> she said, exasperated, and I finally relented.

<They've invited the King to send a small delegation to Morven Forest for Autumn Balance, to enjoy their hospitality and to begin to negotiate a trade arrangement.>

<That's… that's amazing, Tokka!> she said, her voice rising again. <But what's Autumn Balance?>

<It's what the Sidhe call the Autumn Equinox. It's the third of their harvest festivals. Apparently, they eat and drink a lot, and have music and dancing.> I looked at the plant materials on my counter again, because I couldn't look at her. <People exchange gifts,> I said. <And often there are weddings after the main festivities.>

She put an arm around my shoulders. <You're thinking of him, aren't you? Of the possibility of seeing him again?>

<He's the one who sent the message. His Queen has appointed him ambassador.>

<Will you go then, with the delegation?>

<The council has yet to decide if there will be a delegation at all.>

<Not the King?>

<He's too preoccupied,> I said, taking another sip of my tea and setting it aside.

<Of course,> she said. <How bad is the young Princess?>

<Still alive, but rapidly getting worse.>

She set her teacup down. <I'll go find you a pot while you get started here. The sooner you have a treatment, the sooner you can convince the King to let you go to Morven.> She turned away.

I was hoping not to have to ask the King at all. <Councilor Rocsh agrees that I should go to Morven,> I said.

She glanced back at me from the doorway. <He does?>

I nodded. <But the King won't like it, if we have to ask him. I need to convince the Council if I'm to have a chance.>

<And that's why you haven't slept.> She shook her head and left.

When she was gone, I turned back to the bark. I rummaged in a drawer to find my favorite blade for chopping herbs. I had gradually begged and borrowed small pieces of equipment from Healer Kah so that I was able to do a little healing work of my own. She told me I was welcome to work in the infirmary, but I always felt more comfortable alone. Except Neeka. She never bothered me, even when she offered to help.

I cut the green strips of bark into thinner pieces, the better to get all their healing properties out. When I was done, and because of the small sample it didn't take long at all, I scooped the result into a bowl and set it to one side.

Half the leaves, starting with the dry half, I dumped into a pestle and began to grind them up. They crumbled easily, but I needed a paste not a powder, so I gradually added small amounts of daggerleaf oil. It was a greasy relative of the winterleaf I used for tea and was mostly inert but had minor cooling properties. It should make a good base to help consolidate the salt-leaf into a poultice. When I was done, I spread a tiny amount on the back of my hand and my skin immediately chilled until I had goosebumps.

I scraped the mess out of the pestle and onto a square of tightly woven linen, wrapped it up, and put it next to the bowl of bark. Then I added the fresh leaves to the pestle and began to pound them with the mortar. This time, the leaves pulped and quickly formed into a paste without the need for added oil. Again, I spread a little on my skin, this time farther up my arm, and as before, I felt the instant cool and goosebumps.

Like the first poultice, I wrapped the herbs in a square of linen and put them aside. The first would be good for cooling, but the second was so strong it would only need be used sparingly. I paused to stretch.

Make a poultice of the leaves
for cooling feverish skin.

That was the easy part, of course. It was the part of the treatment I had no doubts about, now that I had felt the effect of the leaves on my own skin. The rest, I was not so sure of, though I had thought it through carefully, taking into account everything I had read and everything I knew about herbs and medicine. From what I had been able to puzzle out of the scant references, salt-leaf was usually made into a tisane, or tea, and given to a feverish patient to drink. It had effects similar to birch bark; it helped reduce a fever, but not enough to make a difference with this particular fever.

Inner is for outer could mean to use the inner bark for treating what seemed to be a heat on the outer body, as the references indicated had been done. But what if the ancient Vogel, from whom the rhyme had presumably been passed down, understood more about illness than we assumed? What if they knew that fevers came from *within* the body? That would seem to mean that I should use the outer bark to treat it.

Except the one thing we already knew for sure about salt-leaf was that the outer bark caused a person to feel warm *inside*.

Outer is for inner – the outer bark causes heat within.

So, instead, I was going on the assumption that the inner bark would cool the body from the inside out, driving the fever to the surface, so to speak. Where it could then be cooled with the poultice of leaves.

Inner is for outer heat, then, meant that the inner bark moves the heat, the fever, outward.

The actual healing, I was convinced, was simply the body's own defenses being able to function at full capacity once they didn't have to fight the fever. And I wondered if perhaps the Royal Plague wasn't some unique and terrible sickness but was instead something more common. Fevers of various sorts were hardly unknown. So perhaps it was an ordinary illness somehow made worse by specific circumstances. It would explain why it seemed to simply appear when no one else had been ill, and why it might take time to move from one person to another.

If we could keep the body from burning itself out, it could recover from illness just like usual.

That was why the Princess had lived so long, and why she had seemed to recover. Healer Kah had managed to keep her cool enough to do better, only it had not been sufficient for a full recovery.

Of course, if I was wrong, she would die, and the King would blame me for it.

The only part of the rhyme I had been unable to puzzle out was how using the outer bark to induce fever and allow spirit flight connected to the rest. Perhaps I was being too particular, and it was only included in the same rhyme because salt-leaf was involved. But the other two parts were connected, and it niggled at my thoughts.

By the time Neeka returned with a pot, I had cleaned my counter and tools and had even washed the tea things and put them away.

<Healer Kah is doubtful it will work,> she said. <But she's willing to try anything. The cold baths help, but they're not enough.>

<Did she say how the Princess fares?>

<Alive and barely coherent, and very weak. She fears she will soon be unconscious. Like you were, my Seer.>

<Did she say how the King was?>

<He looks terrible. He didn't even seem to notice me.>

<You went to the Princess's room? Not the infirmary?>

<I went to the infirmary, and they sent me to Healer Kah, who was with the Princess. They said I needed her permission to borrow anything.>

I rolled my eyes and Neeka laughed. Then I dumped the chopped bark into the pot and added enough water to just cover it. Back in my sitting room, Neeka helped me build up the fire and nestle the pot in the flames to heat.

<A decoction is different from a tea, isn't it?> she said, sitting back and watching the flames. I sank onto one of the couches and stretched out my legs. My toes ached and I wished I had Kiernan to rub them for me. I would *not* think about him stroking his finger between my toes. Not while Neeka was in the room.

<It's like a tea, only much stronger.> I considered the pot, which was just beginning to steam. <It's kept on the heat to concentrate the properties of the ingredients. In this case, I'm going to boil it down until it's almost a syrup.> And hope that I didn't use too much heat and destroy the healing properties

I was trying to concentrate. <We must be careful it evaporates but doesn't scorch.>

We took turns getting up to stir the pot and in between Neeka flipped through a catalogue of clothing designs from a tailor in the City Beneath that her cousin had given her, while I moved to my tall stool, took up my spindle, and worked on the basket of wool. Once I had moved my two fat, sleepy tree serpents to a cushion on the hearth instead.

Lay soon, said Smoke.

Soon soon, said Flame. *Won't hatch.*

Might hatch, said Smoke, and they both went back to sleep.

Finally, when the decoction was nearly as thick as I wanted it, there was a knock on the door. Neeka stood to answer it, and I kept spinning.

When she came back, she looked serious. <What is it?> I put my spinning aside and stood. <The Princess?>

She shook her head. <You've been called to the Council Chamber.> She broke into a wide smile. <They're going to discuss the message from Morven.>

She hustled me into my bedroom where she had me change from my everyday clothes to something a little more grand. Then she quickly applied makeup to my face – not as much as if I were going to make a public appearance, but enough to make me look put-together. And to hide the lack of sleep.

<I'll look after the decoction,> she said.

I nodded. <When it's thickened, let it cool. Then take it and the poultices to Healer Kah. Tell her…> I paused, hoping I was right. I *had* to be right. <Tell her to give the Princess the syrup. Just a spoonful at first, because she's small.>

<There isn't going to be much more than a spoonful in the pot when it's done.>

<Then it's good that she's small. She'll get very flushed. That's when Healer Kah should apply the poultices to as much

of her skin as it will cover, concentrated on the hot parts —
armpits, groin. She'll know. One of the poultices is stronger, so
she'll have to decide which to use where. It should begin to
cool the Princess immediately. She won't be cured, but it
should give her the strength and the time to get well.>

Neeka nodded and held my hand tightly.

<Good luck with the Council.>

I WAS THE LAST to reach the Council Chamber and when I
walked in every one of the Councilors rose to their feet,
bowed their heads, and murmured a greeting. They waited for
me to sit before seating themselves again.

I was tempted to take the King's chair since it was much
more comfortable than the small one Nikna had brought in for
me, but I knew I mustn't press my luck. It felt validating,
heady, to have gained at least some respect from the Council,
and I didn't want to lose it by doing something stupid.

<Shall we begin?> said one of the Councilors, a man with
such large, flashy feathers in his facial adornments that I
couldn't help wondering if he was compensating for something. According to Neeka, though, he really did have twelve
children.

<A moment,> I said, and carefully uncurled the message
from the Prince of Morven Forest, weighting the edges down
with small leather sandbags I had borrowed from the library.

There was a soft tap at the door, and I called, <Come in.>
It opened, and I saw a brief glimpse of Konta's face before a
black and white bird flew through the gap to land on the table.
Several Councilors got to their feet and their attendants
stepped forward. Councilor Rocsh looked faintly amused.

<May I present the Morven Forest messenger, Councilors?> I said. They looked at me, at the bird, and back at me. One by one they resumed their places. The bird strutted down the table.

<This magpie was sent by the Prince of Morven Forest with a letter for our King,> I said, even though I knew Rocsh would have given them at least the gist of the message's contents. I wanted them to hear it from me, and I wanted to make sure they had the full effect, bird and all.

The magpie carried on down the table, looking curiously at each Councilor in turn. Most of them looked quickly away and I kept my face neutral, not giving in to the smile I wanted to show. It could be disconcerting to be looked at by a bird with such obvious intelligence in its dark beady eyes. The Councilors should be glad Kiernan hadn't sent a raven. *Their* regard could be downright chilling.

<Has the King heard the message?> said one of the Councilors. I had never been properly introduced to any of them, except Rocsh, and still didn't know their names. The King had not thought I needed to know, as I was to be ornamental and not a functional member of the Eyrie's government. I would really have to fix that, and soon.

<He has not,> said Rocsh. <Our King is currently occupied at the bedside of his daughter, who is deathly ill with Royal Plague.> They already knew this, of course, but Rocsh knew it wouldn't hurt to remind them, to keep them from asking unnecessary questions. <In his absence, the bird was delivered to me. I asked Seer Tokka's assistance in communicating with the bird, and again in translating the letter.>

<Translating?> said the same Councilor.

<The letter was written in the Sidhe language,> I said, drawing every eye to me. I would *not* blush.

<That seems a little… rude,> said the Councilor with the

over-large adornments. <Surely, they could have used Islish.>

<It is well known the Sidhe are proud of their culture and language,> I said. <As we are of ours.>

Councilor Rocsh cut in smoothly. <And their Prince knows there would be one here in the Eyrie who could read that language.>

Everyone looked at me again.

<I don't follow,> said the large feather Councilor.

<My thought,> said Rocsh, <Is that he composed the letter in Sidhe because he knew our Seer would be needed to read it.> He tapped his fingers on the table thoughtfully. <He wished to ensure our Seer read it, I believe, because he may not have felt comfortable asking outright for Seer Tokka… Well, perhaps we should hear the contents of the letter first.>

I smoothed the paper in front of me, cleared my throat, and translated as best I could. When I finished, the large, friendly Councilor with green wings said, <Of course we shall send a delegation, but is it wise to include our Seer? It would be a terrible thing to have found a Vogel Seer after so long, only to lose him again.>

<I don't see why we should send a delegation at all,> said another Councilor, one who spoke so seldom I didn't know what his views were on any subject.

I let them argue for a short while, then I stood up. They all turned to stare at me again. My stomach lurched and I wanted to twist my fingers together as I used to do when I was nervous, to make sure my hands didn't shake. But I forced myself calm, let my hands hang at my sides, and faced them all down the long table.

<Here is my opinion,> I said, and I laid out all the arguments for why we needed to send a delegation to Morven Forest, and why we shouldn't bother the king with it, until it was time to leave. For the latter part, it was mostly because he

wouldn't care, with his daughter being ill, and everyone nodded when I said it.

Then I went through every possible objection Councilor Rocsh, Nikna, and I had been able to think of, and refuted them clearly and carefully. Then I stopped.

Councilor Rocsh tapped the table lightly, and everyone turned to him. <Might I suggest we first vote yea or nay to sending a delegation in the first place, before we argue about who?>

<I vote yea,> said the green winged Councilor.

One by one the others voted and I few I thought would vote against begrudgingly voted in favor. In the end, only the quiet Councilor voted nay, but threw his hands up as he said it and said, <Fine, I've been outvoted. Now who do we send?>

<Me, for one,> said Councilor Rocsh.

<Aren't you needed to administrate the Eyrie?> said green wings. <Especially with the King otherwise occupied?>

<My staff are capable of functioning without me for a time,> he said. <*Especially* if the King is otherwise occupied.> More than one of the other Councilors chuckled at that. <But it is *because* I am the Eyrie's administrator that I should go. Unless you think we should send the King himself?> And then he laid his own arguments out as thoroughly as I had given mine, if much more briefly.

<Who else?> said green wings, when no one could come up with any good reasons Rocsh should not go. Many of the other Councilors seemed to defer to the green-winged man, and I was very glad he had taken our side.

<During our late Queen's time,> said Councilor Rocsh, and several around the table murmured a traditional blessing on the dead, <Pairs of trade negotiators were sent to other Monarchies to initiate communications. One such pair visited Morven Forest and though ultimately nothing came of their

visit, their experience was positive. Both have since retired, but both have agreed to accompany the delegation.>

<Excellent,> said big feathers. After first objecting, he now seemed to have warmed up to the whole idea. I couldn't help but wonder how Councilor Rocsh had got in contact with the retired trade negotiators so quickly.

<And I do believe we should send Seer Tokka.> He put up his hand against the inevitable protests. <Please, Councilors, let me explain why.> And he then presented all the arguments I had made to him the day before, only much more eloquently. When he finished, many of the men around the table were nodding, but some stirred uneasily.

<The King won't like it,> said the quiet Councilor. <In fact, he may forbid it.> The look he turned on me was not unkind, exactly, but it was not at all comforting. <I think I we all know how he feels about our Seer.>

Something in the way he said it made me feel soiled, like he knew exactly what the King and I did together in his rooms and did not approve. I didn't suppose it would help if he knew I didn't approve, either, but did what I did because I had no choice.

I leaned on the table and studied my hands. I had hoped no one would bring up the King's… feelings for me, and I knew I couldn't even answer directly, especially since the Councilor hadn't himself spoken directly. I didn't want to answer at all; I wanted to crawl into a hole and disappear.

<The King has his daughter to look after,> I finally said, and made myself look up at the Councilors and not shrink from their eyes. <And to be very blunt, I believe he has been… distracted with me.> I met Councilor Rocsh's eyes and he inclined his head very slightly. <With me away, working for the good of our Monarchy and our people, perhaps our King will be able to focus on governing again.>

The Councilors only stared; none dared say anything to that. I knew I may have gone too close to criticism, but it wasn't anything they didn't already know. I met each of their eyes, one by one around the table. And one by one, they nodded.

<Well then,> said green feathers. I really needed to learn their names if I wasn't going to be a figure only brought out for show at appropriate intervals. I think I had surprised the King – and not in a pleasant way – when I turned out to have a brain.

<Councilor Rocsh, Seer Tokka, and two trade negotiators,> said green feathers.

<Plus our two attendants,> said Rocsh. <And two Seer's Guards.>

<Better add two King's Guards as well,> said big feathers.

<Yes,> said Rocsh. <Thank you for the reminder.>

<That should be suitably grand, without making it look like we're taking advantage of their hospitality,> I said, though "grand" was probably not the right word. Not even close. <Shall I compose a reply?>

<You, my Seer?> said the quiet Councilor. <We can send for a scribe.>

I smiled. <I was raised in an Abbey, Councilor. I believe I am a more than adequate scribe. And as the letter was in the Prince's own hand, I believe the reply would best be written in mine.>

As I said it, I realized I had slipped. Councilor Rocsh gave me a sharp glance. Because how would I know what the Prince of Morven Forest's handwriting looked like? Only a few people knew exactly how I had arrived at the Eyrie, though most knew that Kiernan had somehow been involved in my rescue. No one but the King and Councilor Rocsh, and my own guards and attendant, knew Kier and I had been lovers.

But none of the Councilors seemed to notice. I had to hope none of them would think of it later.

Nikna brought me paper and pen and a bottle of royal purple ink, and I carefully wrote out a reply, following Councilor Rocsh's dictation of the appropriate opening lines in Vogelspek. Then I switched to Islish for the rest, and without too much fuss we had a final draft of which everyone in the room approved.

I rolled up the paper, applied the seal of the Royal Council, and said, <If it please you, magpie, I have your reply.>

About fucking time, it said, and I was glad no one else in the room had the magic to understand bird speech.

I tied the paper to the bird's leg, opened the door, and it launched from the table and was gone.

In a very short time, I would be leaving the Eyrie for Morven Forest.

In a nineday or a little longer, I would see Kiernan again.

II: MORVEN FOREST

13
Fionn

THE DAY WE WERE TO depart began bright and sunny, though the air had turned crisp over the last nineday and the leaves were vivid colors in Aven Forest, deep reds and oranges and golds against the darker backdrop of the conifers that lined the mountain slopes.

I had spent as much time away from the palace as I could; with the King still busy with his daughter, who was improving again but not yet well, I just had to convince Councilor Rocsh to allow me to visit the City Beneath the Cliff. And Councilor Rocsh seemed pleased that I was taking an active interest in the lives of our people and only insisted I take at least two guards with me.

I visited as many different businesses as I could — tea-houses and bakeries, vegetable market stalls and clothiers, butchers and wagonwrights, even an herbalist and a book shop — and spoke to both proprietors and customers. I wanted to know how their businesses were faring and what concerns they might have, and especially what opinions they had on trade with other Monarchies and how it might benefit them. Most of them were hesitant to say much at first, and kept treating me like some untouchable holy figure, but I made sure to purchase something where I could with the small allowance Councilor Rocsh had arranged for me and eventually they seemed to realize my interest was sincere. And then they answered my questions eagerly.

I was also interested, more for future reference than for immediate consideration, in spiritual topics. I asked how they worshipped and what they had done to celebrate without a Seer to guide them. I learned that most Vogel simply carried on with the customs they learned from their elders, speaking the simple dedications to local spirits when leaving food offerings or trinkets. What excited me most was that there were many small practices surrounding textiles, that there were charms to say while spinning and weaving, and that spun and woven articles were often considered the most important offerings. That this focus existed even in the city, where few people even did their own spinning and weaving, seemed remarkable and exciting.

By the time that last day in the Eyrie dawned, I had a lot to think about.

Councilor Rocsh had decided not to inform the King about the delegation until we were ready to leave. It was his opinion that there was no point in bothering our Monarch with something when his input wasn't needed. He would have to *know* of course, but not beforehand.

I think he also knew the King might forbid me from going and he was trying to make it more difficult for him to refuse.

<Are you not worried he'll be angry?> I had said, when I asked him about it.

<He *will* be angry,> was his answer. <But if I wait to tell him, he'll be angry for a shorter time.>

<I never thought to see you choose to do something the King wouldn't like,> I said. Councilor Rocsh was the King's main administrator; usually he and the King were alike in thought, or so it had always seemed before. Now I wondered.

He smiled and turned to the small case he had open on his sitting room table, half-filled with clothing. Nikna brought him something from their bedroom and he added it to the top, carefully tucking in a stray fold of deep green silk.

<I believe I told you once, that while I will not openly defy our King, my main concern is for our people.>

<Not telling him his Seer is joining a diplomatic delegation is 'not defying' him?> I had managed not to think too much about how the King would react by throwing myself into my work with the people of the City.

<If he doesn't know, how can I be defying him?> he said. His voice was, as always, almost without inflection, but I was beginning to learn how to detect emotions and other hints in it that he might not have wanted obvious. Or maybe my abilities as a Seer were developing. At any rate, he sounded amused. <The worst that can happen to me is dismissal,> he said.

<And then I shall have to be the main wage earner,> said Nikna, delivering another item of clothing. He leaned over to kiss the Councilor's cheek. Since they had revealed their relationship to me, he was much more openly affectionate with his beloved, and it warmed my heart to see. It gave me hope that love could flourish even where it wasn't approved of by our rulers.

<Besides,> said Rocsh, <Since you arrived in the Eyrie, *you* are the primary focus of my loyalty, my Seer. Your happiness and wellbeing are far more important to me that any royal's.>

<Though you mustn't say that to the King,> scolded Nikna gently. I wasn't sure if he was warning me or Rocsh.

<But —>

<You are the hope of our people, and our people are my true masters,> Rocsh said.

<But what if I want to help *all* people,> I said, hesitantly. <Not just ours?>

<Will you be the champion of the downtrodden everywhere?> he teased, allowing it to touch his voice.

<Yes,> I said, tilting my chin up to meet his eyes.

He smiled. <Just don't wear yourself out, my Seer. You can't help anyone if you don't first help yourself.> He gazed absently out the window. <And, though it seems contrary to the advice I just gave, be sure you continue to be worthy of their regard.>

<I'll do my best.>

<I know you will.>

Now I stood in front of my balcony door, hands on the glass, looking out over the sea. In a few hours, I would be on a ship sailing north. I was terrified. Neeka had told me stories of storms and shipwrecks and seasickness all last evening, and what if I threw up in front of all those sailors? They could hardly respect a Seer who puked all over their deck.

I was startled when Flame zipped in from the bedroom and landed on my shoulder. Smoke followed close behind. I had thought they were still curled up asleep in my basket of wool, tucked close to the bedroom fire.

Lighter now, said Flame, draping her tail over my shoulder and butting her head against my jaw. I reached up to stroke her tiny head.

We fly again, said Smoke, headbutting the other side of my face until I petted her, too.

"Where did you lay your eggs?" I said, because they had both returned to their previous slender shapes.

Fireplace, said Smoke.

Is warm, said Flame.

I aimed one more glance out at the sea, where a cloud was gathering to the east, but far off. My bags were already on the ship, and all I had to do was get myself and any last minute personal effects there before the tide turned. And my tree serpents, of course.

I went to the bedroom fireplace and knelt down. There, in a spot where one brick was lower than the rest at the edge of the fire, were five eggs. They were deep olive green and speckled with dark spots of bronze. Four of the eggs were tiny, but the fifth was so big I wondered how the serpent had managed to lay it. Though Smoke and Flame were obviously old enough to reproduce, they hadn't reached their full growth yet. I wondered if that was another reason a tree serpent's first clutch didn't hatch, because they were small enough for a half-grown serpent to lay, but not large enough to be fully developed.

No good, said Flame. *Those ones*. She nudged the smaller eggs with her nose, pushing them to one side.

"What do I do with them?"

Eat, said Smoke.

"I can't *eat* your eggs."

We eat, then, said Flame.

One grows, said Smoke, and Flame nudged the large egg. *Not to eat.*

"Who laid that one?" I bent closer to look and touched it gently with one finger. It was warm and gave slightly to the touch.

Smoke or Flame, said Smoke.

Don't know, said Flame.

"How can you not know?"

Laid all together, said Smoke.

Five eggs, said Flame.

Ours, said Smoke.

Ours both, said Flame.

I shook my head. Maybe they didn't know or maybe they just didn't want to tell me, for reasons that would make sense only to a feathered tree serpent.

"We leave today," I said. "What do we do with it?"

We bring, said Smoke.

Only one, said Flame.

Keep warm, said Smoke.

For Dark, said Flame.

"Yes, we'll keep it warm in the dark," I said, trying to think of a way to protect the egg while we traveled. And to keep it warm. Maybe a small, strong basket lined with wool, that I could tuck inside my cloak.

Not in *dark*, said Flame, glancing up at me from the hearth, where she had been rubbing her face against the larger egg.

For Dark, said Smoke. *Is gift*.

"Wait," I said, realizing finally what they were telling me. "You want to give your egg – your offspring – to Kiernan?"

We love, said Smoke.

He needs, said Flame.

Love and love, they said together. *Bright and Dark*.

A LITTLE LATER, as I was altering a small herb basket I had begged from Healer Kah so I could wear it on my belt or put it on a strap over my shoulders, there was a tap at my door.

<Come in,> I called. Neeka was off making sure our things were properly stored on the ship and saying her farewells to her beloved. I didn't expect to see her until I got to the ship.

<Did you intend to sneak away without saying goodbye, little seer?>

My stomach lurched and I slid off my chair to my knees,

bowing my head. <My King,> I said. <I thought you were oc-cupied with the young Princess.>

<Not so occupied I didn't hear whispers of a delegation setting out today. I'm disappointed you didn't tell me.>

Smoke and Flame slipped away from where they were draped along the back of my chair. They didn't like the atten-tion the King paid to me, but they knew they weren't permit-ted to attack him, so they usually went flying when he visited my rooms. I had left one of the balcony doors ajar, now that they weren't too fat to fly, so they could come and go.

<My King, I – > I shut my mouth when the King took my chin in his hand and turned my face to look up at him. He looked exhausted, his face thinner than it had been, and his eyes shadowed.

<I should be very angry with you, little seer,> he said.

<I'm sorry, my King. The Council –>

<Yes, the Council made a decision. I'm not going to fight them over it.> He looked at me until I had to turn my eyes from his. He was in one of his moods when I couldn't read his expression, which meant he was either about to be very angry, or he was going to take me to bed. Or perhaps both.

I wasn't eager for either.

He moved his hand to the back of my head and pressed me close to him. Kneeling the way I was, my cheek was against his lower belly.

<I should be very angry with you,> he repeated. <But Healer Kah tells me it was your hard work and cleverness that saved my daughter's life. So, I suppose I'm to thank you, in-stead.>

<You needn't thank me, my King. It was my duty as Healer and Seer to try to find a cure.>

<Your duty. Of course.> His voice was flat, and I thought I might have phrased that badly. His fingers combed through

my hair and suddenly tightened. The strands had regrown, so it was long enough for him to hold on to. He kept me against him, his sheath pressing next to my face so I could feel him stirring inside it.

<I will let you go, little seer, but there are things you must promise me.>

My stomach clenched and I felt a little sick, but I would do whatever he asked to not have this trip taken away from me.

<Anything you require, my King.> I lifted my hands from my sides to lay them on his hips, hating that I did it, and knowing that I had to.

<Take my belt off,> he said. I fumbled for the clasps and pulled his belt away. He tugged his tunic aside. <Remove my undergarment.> I pulled loose the tie and the fabric slid down his legs.

He cupped his free hand under my chin and tipped my head up again. <You belong to me,> he said.

<Yes, my King.>

<You will behave as a proper Vogel, with decorum and poise, and make our people proud.>

<Yes, my King.>

<You will not be tempted to run to the arms of your former lover,> he said.

<You cleansed me of him, my King. He is nothing to me now.> I hoped he was distracted enough not to look for a lie. <You are my everything.>

<Then show me how much you will miss me.> He slipped his thumb into my mouth to pry it open. I didn't resist. I closed my eyes and used my tongue, my lips, my mouth in all the ways I knew he liked, but the whole time it was Kiernan I imagined I was kneeling in front of, Kiernan who made me hard inside my sheath.

The illusion was broken when the King pulsed and tasted

sickly sweet instead of salty and his fingers gripped my hair so hard it hurt. Another pulse and another, and then he was instructing me to re-dress him in undergarment and belt, to set his tunic to rights.

<Be a good boy, little seer, and I will make sure your life is a long and pleasant one. Defy me and – >

He didn't finish the sentence and for the first time, I wasn't afraid of the things he might threaten. I realized he didn't actually have a way to finish that sentence. He *needed* me. Now that people knew I existed, he needed me. Perhaps I belonged to him, and perhaps I had few choices, things I was required to do and could not refuse, but I also had a certain amount of power. If I could figure out how to use it, I wouldn't need to trick him into letting me be a proper Seer.

<Of course, my King.>

<Good.> And he left, and I didn't care that he hadn't even tried to give me pleasure. I didn't want it from him, and I was suddenly determined to figure out a way that I would never have to provide it for him again either. Even if it really did mean asking Kiernan to steal me away.

B EING ON BOARD a ship was a lot more boring than Neeka had made it out to be, and after the first hour, as I held her shoulders while she vomited over the rail, she confessed she had never actually been on so much as a rowboat before.

When she was done heaving, I gave her some of Healer Kah's tea for seasickness and sent her to bed. When she was settled, I put my hand on her forehead and she muttered, <I guess it's a good thing I haven't wanted to be a sailor since I was a child.>

I was about to send her to sleep with healing magic, but I remembered Kienan teasing me about how often he had woken from an unconscious state I sent him into and asked her first.

<Will it help with the puking?> she asked.

<It should. When you wake, the nausea should be gone, or at least much less than it was.>

I stood out on the deck that whole first day, once Neeka was asleep, watching the scenery pass by, eager to see anything new. The Isle was thickly forested in most places, with little villages here and there, and cleared fields showing where the soil was rich enough for farming. I had never seen it from this perspective before, and I was mesmerized, especially when I noticed that the landscape was slowly changing. From the long sandy beach near the Eyrie, the shore slowly became rockier, and then the trees came right down to the edge of the sea.

The trees, too, began to change, with more oaks and fewer birch, more fir and fewer pine. I stared and stared, enchanted, but also hoping I might spot the reddish bark of salt-leaf.

On the third day, when I was again at my post, watching the Isle slip past, Nikna approached and leaned against the rail next to me. <The Captain tells me we make good time,> he said. <The wind is in our favor, and we should arrive a few days ahead of time.>

<Won't we find the Sidhe unprepared for us?> I said.

<I'm told there is a good harbor to the north where we can anchor and wait on board, if necessary,> he said. <But they'll probably be watching for us.> I must have looked uncertain, because he added, <Sea travel is never precise in timing. Early arrivals and late are both quite expected.>

I nodded, wondering why he had chosen to come talk to me. Perhaps simply because we were companions on a voyage, and we hadn't had the opportunity to speak on a personal level. He felt comfortable, though. Solid.

<I'm afraid,> I said softly, and he looked at me in surprise, like he wasn't expecting me to be so open. *I* hadn't expected to be so open, but I was glad I had when he put his hand over mine, squeezed, then moved it back to the rail.

<You have your guards,> he said. <And I don't believe the Sidhe intend us any ill. You'll be safe.>

I watched as a huge white bird eased closer to watch us, its wings open in effortless flight. Before I left, Councilor Rocsh had arranged to have the feather worker replace the colorful feathers in my wings with all white. I was told some of them had come from swans – not geese as Neeka had teased – and some from sea birds. I wondered if any of my new feathers had come from a bird like the one that now eyed us with suspicion.

The wind caught at my wings, my new white feathers, and tugged. My wings weren't functional, though, and I envied that bird.

<That's not why I'm afraid,> I said.

<I know.>

When I looked back at him, he was gazing down the deck to where Councilor Rocsh was speaking to the Captain. He looked comfortable on the swaying deck and held only lightly to a nearby rope.

<How can he always look so elegant?> I said and Nikna chuckled.

<It's almost infuriating, isn't it?>

I looked back at him, and his face was soft.

<I read somewhere,> he said, <That the Sidhe allow people to choose their sex, that they can change it from what was assumed at their birth, if it doesn't fit. That they can decide to be called 'he' or 'she' or something else entirely. And no one cares what their… what their anatomy looks like.>

<I've heard that,> I said, and wondered why he had brought it up. Kiernan had explained once, and I had thought it must be wonderful, to be able to say for yourself who and what you were, instead of letting others decide for you. Even though I had never felt I was anything other than the man my sex organs indicated I was, if I had been, it would be nice to be able to say so.

<I think Rocsh would have chosen 'they' if he had been given the option.>

<Maybe one day he'll be able to,> I said.

He looked at me and smiled. <You still have hope,> he said. <That's good. Maybe you can make the world better for everyone.>

<I'm only one small person,> I said.

<One person who has gained the respect and friendship of many in only a short time.> He touched my shoulder. <And there are others like you.> He paused to watch Rocsh pick his way across the deck to speak to a group of sailors, and then turned back to me. <I only have a small amount of magic,> he said. <But I do have the rather useless gift of being able to sense heart bonds.>

<That doesn't sound useless.>

<It is, because heart bonds are rare, for one thing. And most people who develop them already know.> He laughed and leaned on his forearms, looking down at the white spray our ship kicked up. <Rocsh and I are heart bonded,> he said, something like wonder in his voice. <And so was our wife. It's supposed to be impossible for more than two to heart bond. And yet...>

<It's supposed to be impossible for Vogel and non-Vogel, too.>

<And yet...>

<Do —> I stopped, not sure if I wanted the answer. If it was "no," it would hurt.

<You needn't be afraid, my Seer. The magic that connects you may be blocked, even severed, but you *are* heart bonded, and it will recover. You will find his love for you as strong as it ever was, and every bit as strong as yours for him.>

14
Kiernan

I WAS STRIPPED to the waist, sweaty, and wrestling with a long piece of wood that kept slipping out of the jig I was trying to force it into when the Queen's messenger found me.

«My Prince?» His voice was hesitant, barely loud enough to reach me in the cellar beneath Dec's cabin. I turned to glance at the stairs up to the door and the wood slipped again and would have cracked me in the side of the head if not for Daphnis's quick reflexes.

"You mustn't force it, my Prince," he said. "Let me try."

I scowled – at the wood, not Daphnis – and went to see what the messenger wanted. He stood, one of the young fauns I had seen in the Queen's sitting room, trembling at the top of the stairs. I wondered what my Queen was thinking, using such a timid little thing to send messages. But then I had never known what my mother was thinking.

I wiped sweat from my face and neck with my shirt and climbed the steps rather than forcing him to come down.

«My Prince,» he said again as I came into the light, and

dipped into a bow so low his knee pressed into the earth and his hair fell forward over his face. He straightened and snuck a look at me. And stopped to stare, his mouth half open as his eyes took in my chest and arms. I was a little more muscular than most fey, but his wide-eyed look was making me feel self-conscious. I pulled my shirt over my head, and he shifted his gaze to my face, his cheeks flushing pink. He looked terrified.

«What's your name?» I said, keeping my voice low, aiming for the kind of gentleness Fionn would have used.

«I'm no one, my Prince,» he said, so quietly even my keen Sidhe ears could barely catch his words. «The Queen sent me.» He stopped again when I put a hand on his shoulder, intending to be reassuring. But he went stiff and still, like he wanted to pull away, but was afraid to, afraid to anger me. Why the fuck was he so afraid of me?

He trembled under my hand and immediately went stiff again. How badly had he been mistreated? Or was he merely extremely shy?

I dropped my hand back to my side, and he relaxed a tiny bit. He still looked like he wanted to flee.

«You must be someone,» I said, still quiet. «Everyone is someone, and I would bet money your mother gave you a name.» I smiled, aiming for gentle again.

He met my eyes and quickly looked away. He opened his mouth, then closed it again.

«He is called Erith,» said Daphnis, coming up the steps behind me. «My Prince.»

«And what message does the Queen send you with, Erith?» I said, tucking my shirt into my pants and snugging up my belt. Daphnis held out my jacket for me and I heaved an exaggerated sigh – getting me a curious look from Erith – and stuck my arms into the sleeves so he could settle it on my shoulders. And then I had to undo my belt because it needed to buckle *over* my coat.

«The… the Vogel have arrived, my Prince,» said Erith. His Sidhe was awkward and formal, and he flinched when I looked sharply up at him.

«Why was I not told sooner?» I said, accidentally letting irritation slip into my voice and regretting it when Erith seemed to fold in on himself. «The lookouts must have seen their ship at least a day ago,» I added, returning my voice to quiet and even.

«I don't know, my Prince,» said Erith. He sounded like he wanted to cry but was trying very hard not to. He suddenly knelt at my feet, making his already small form look tiny.

«Our Prince will not punish you for not knowing an answer you could not possibly know,» Daphnis said. He managed gentle much better than I did, and Erith looked up at him with wide eyes.

I glanced at Daphnis, and he made a minute motion that might have been a shrug, sighed softly, and knelt next to the faun. I wanted to run full tilt for the palace, first to find out if Fionn had come with the delegation, second to apologize to said delegation for not being there to greet them, and third to find out who had decided not to tell me the delegation's ship had been spotted and make them understand how bad an idea that had been.

But my Queen's messenger, kneeling at my feet and trembling, looked like he was waiting for a punishment he didn't deserve, and my desire to get back was overwhelmed by burning anger at how he must have been treated to make him so afraid. Even overlying that, I felt compassion like a soothing hand on my back – like Fionn was standing next to me – and I just wanted to make this poor young man feel better.

«Erith?» I said, putting every ounce of gentleness I could muster into my voice. I knelt in front on him and touched under his chin with one finger so he would look at me. He started, then froze.

«I'm sorry, my Prince.» Moisture was gathering in his eyes, and he blinked quickly to keep it from turning into tears.

«You have nothing to be sorry for.»

«I… I don't know how to answer your question,» he said. «They say you are very good with knives. That… that you use them to punish your servants and that's why you have so few servants.»

«Because I killed them all?»

«Oh, Goddess Below, I shouldn't have said that. I'm sorry, my Prince. I'm sorry.» He burst into tears and tried to bow lower, to press his face into the dirt, only I was kneeling in front of him, and he ended up with his face in my lap.

He went very still, and a tiny, terrified sound leaked out of his throat.

«Erith,» I said. «I'm not going to punish you. I'm not going to hurt you.» I put my hands on his shoulders, lifted him carefully up, and looked into his eyes. They were russet brown with gold flecks, and wide with fear.

«I don't know who told you I punish my servants by cutting them, but it was a lie. I've only ever had one servant, and he's kneeling next to you.» I looked at Daphnis. His face was unreadable, but there was something soft in his eyes. They were directed at me, though, not Erith. I switched to Islish, thinking the faun might be more comfortable speaking the common tongue. "Have I ever cut you, Daphnis?"

"You've never punished me at all, my Prince. Though you've snapped at me once or twice when you were in a foul mood."

"You see," I said. "You're safe with me."

"But it *can't* be a lie," Erith said, looking from me to Daphnis and back. "Sidhe can't lie."

Daphnis touched Erith's arm lightly. "Who told you these things about our Prince?" he said.

Erith looked at his hands, clasped so tight in his lap that his knuckles were white. "They were Queen's Guard. They laughed when I was happy to be chosen to deliver the message. They said I must be eager to get… to get…" He blushed fiercely and bit his lip.

"What words did they use?" I said, squeezing his shoulders with just the lightest pressure.

"'Our Prince is very good with those blades he carries,' one said."

"Not a lie," I said.

"And…" Daphnis prompted.

"And one said, 'Don't you ever wonder why he has so few servants?'" He looked at Daphnis, who nodded encouragingly.

"That's not a statement, so no outright lies," I said. "And it's true I have few servants. I used to have none. I don't like making other people do things I could do myself."

He looked back at his hands clenched in his lap. "I don't… I can't say out loud what they said next." The tips of his little pointed ears were bright pink. I could probably guess what it was they said that he wouldn't repeat.

"Tell me," said Daphnis, and bent his head so the faun could whisper into his ear. When he straightened, he laughed softly.

"Are you going to share the joke?" I said, though I didn't really need him to. I already knew what they said about me, what the rumors were at court. But I wanted him to say it so Erith would know he needn't be afraid to tell me anything.

The faun stiffened under my hands, so I let him go and sat back. He relaxed a little, and then a little more when Daphnis put an arm around his shoulders.

"One of them implied you like to fuck your servants," Daphnis said, and Erith flushed red again. He seemed to be trying not to look at my chest.

I sighed. "I suppose everyone thinks I'm fucking you," I said, though of course I knew they did. Daphnis's expression didn't change, but something flickered in his eyes.

The faun looked up at me again, through reddish lashes spangled with tears. He had soft brown hair combed back from his face, small black horns, and a face that should have held smiles, not terror. Once, I would have invited him to bed – if he were a little older. Now, I had no interest in anyone other than Fionn.

"Then," he said, and Daphnis and I turned our attention to him. He shrank a little but continued. "One said you probably use the servants who refuse you to practice your knifework on. And she… she did this." He drew his hand, held flat, across his throat.

"It's true the Sidhe can't lie," I said, "But you should have learned by now that they will try to make you believe untrue things by stating facts and saying 'I wonder' and 'did you notice' a lot."

"I haven't been at court very long, my Prince," he said.

"The Queen decided she wanted faun servants while you were away, my Prince," Daphnis said. "Around the same time she returned many of her dryads to the palace from the garden."

"How old are you?" I said.

"Nineteen, my Prince," Erith said, blushing again.

"The age of majority for fauns is the same as that for humans, my Prince," said Daphnis. So he was of age, but only just. And fauns were a free people, so I wondered how my Queen had lured hers to court.

"My Queen," I said, and bit off the rest of what I was going to say. It was angry and unwise. And I needed to get back to the palace, not blurt out to a poor servant that his mistress was a dangerous and terrible person. If he hadn't figured that out already, he was in deep trouble at court.

It was still early morning and I had planned for the welcome feast to happen in the evening, when both the day-dwelling Vogel and the nocturnal Sidhe would be comfortable awake. I needed to let the palace staff know to begin preparing for tonight. They wouldn't be happy about having to work through the day, but I had promised them all extra pay and time off once the Vogel delegation had departed.

"Was that the whole message?" I asked. "That the delegation has arrived?"

"Oh! Seer Siona has had them shown to their rooms so they may rest before the feast and has had apologies sent for you not meeting them when they arrived. And informed them that the feast is tonight."

"Did you see them arrive, Erith?" I got to my feet and Daphnis followed, pulling the faun up with him. Erith pressed close to Daphnis' side, and I had to hide a smile.

"No, my Prince," he said, meeting my eyes and looking considerably less terrified. "But the other servants say they are very tall."

I smiled and he *almost* smiled back. "Most of them are tall, yes." I was thinking of the one Vogel who was not tall, though he would still seem so to Erith. He was tall next to me, and I loved the fact that I had to tilt my head back for him to kiss me.

"You may go now, Erith," said Daphnis and I raised an eyebrow at him for the presumption, then smiled. "Remember in future," the dryad said, "You need not fear our Prince. He is surprisingly difficult to anger, and generally hits pillows and other inanimate objects when he does get angry."

"I did set my mother's hair on fire once," I said.

Erith's eyes got very big, and Daphnis's brief smile appeared and was gone.

"I was four, and she wouldn't let me use a real sword in practice."

"You learned swordplay when you were four?"

"I started as soon as I could walk," I said. "I didn't get so good with blades by accident."

"I can throw a knife pretty good," said Erith, then he clamped both hands over his mouth, his eyes wide.

I patted his shoulder, and he only flinched a little. "If you ever want pointers," I said, "Let me know."

He nodded solemnly and turned to go.

Then I said, "Wait," and he froze. "Do you belong to the Queen, or are you a paid servant?"

He looked confused. "I'm a faun, my Prince."

I looked at Daphnis. Obviously, I had been away when the Queen brought fauns to court, so I had no idea what the arrangements were. He said, "Fauns are offered room and board in exchange for indentured service, my Prince, and the possibility of education, if they show aptitude."

"I see. Do you wish to be educated, Erith?"

"Oh, yes, my Prince," he breathed, then looked at the ground like he thought he might have overstepped.

"What would you like to learn?"

He bit his lip and Daphnis touched his shoulder. "Mechanics, my Prince. And… and how things work."

I felt a smile grow on my face. "That seems like a very practical course of study. Shall I put in a good word for you?"

"Oh!" That one small exclamation stabbed my belly like a knife, it was so like Fionn. I thought Fionn and Erith would get along very well.

"Go on now, Erith," said Daphnis. "Let the Queen know the Prince is on his way."

The faun scampered back into the forest, and I closed and locked the door to Dec's cellar.

"You can't save us all, my Prince," Daphnis said.

I sighed, and it felt like it came from the depths of my bones, from beyond where the emptiness of magic lay. "No, but I can try."

He smiled his almost-not-there smile. "One at a time?"

"If I have to."

WHEN I GOT BACK to the palace, I discovered that someone had already informed the kitchen staff that the feast was to be tonight and when I asked the cook who, he shrugged.

«One of the Queen's Guard. No, sorry, they're Prince's Guard now, I suppose, my Prince.»

«Which one?»

He looked embarrassed. «I'm afraid I can't tell the two of them apart, my Prince.» That was fair, I supposed. Sean and Padraig looked very different to me, but I had known them all my life, and for me, telling my cousins apart was vital – I needed to know which one might try to kill me, and which was only aiming to put me in my place as youngest of the royal brats. To others, they looked almost like twins.

I went back to my rooms and washed off the sweat and grime of the night's work, then let Daphnis dress me in what he thought was most appropriate. Before the feast, he would make me change into something even more grand. When I went outside to cut around to the entrance most convenient to the guest suite, I caught sight of a flash of red fur and paused.

Siona's fox Ember trotted out of the underbrush and across the lawn to sit at my feet. She yipped at me, but with no magic, I couldn't understand her. I didn't even know if she could understand me.

Daphnis must have noticed my frustration, because he said, "She says she'll take you to Seer Siona, if you would follow. I am to wait here."

So there was another bit of magic dryads probably weren't supposed to have. And another bit of *my* magic I would have to do without.

I ached and wondered if Siona meant to draw magic through me, to help me make it through the feast. After Daphnis had described how it could be done, she had eagerly tried, even knowing it would likely not please our Queen. And it *had* helped. It wasn't enough, but it helped.

I left Daphnis to his own thoughts and followed the fox into the forest. I was clumsy without my magic, and she had to keep stopping to wait, when once I would have kept up with her easily. But I had been learning how to move better without magic and I was improving. At least I hadn't left any of my hair behind, tangled on branches, when we came out on the hillside near the sacred caves of Morven Forest.

Siona was sitting on a rock, part of a tumble of mossy boulders that hid the cave entrance. It was a place only Seers were permitted to go unless given explicit permission, but Siona had granted me leave to come and go a long time ago. I hadn't taken advantage lately, and perhaps she was reminding me I needed to take care of my spiritual health alongside my physical.

«My Prince,» she said, smiling and rising from her seat to put her hands on my shoulders, and then my face. Even with no magic left in me, she could still sense my presence. Padraig and Daphnis had both said I was a void to them, like I didn't exist at all.

«Seer Siona.» I pulled her into a hug.

«I had a thought,» she said when I let her go.

«The delegation is here,» I said. «I should try to sleep before the feast.»

Her smile grew. «Sleep below,» she said, and gestured at the boulders. «The spirits and our Goddess will ease your mind and your heart. You will rest better there.»

She had an odd look on her face that made her smile look a little sly. But I knew better than to demand answers. She couldn't be broken by begging or even by reason once she had made her mind up about something. Even when I was a child, before blindness afflicted her, my big green eyes had never swayed her.

And I knew I could trust her. If she thought I needed to visit the shrine, she had good reason, and it very likely *would* do me good.

«Very well,» I said. «Oh esteemed Seer of Morven Forest.»

She swatted my shoulder lightly.

«But what if I oversleep?»

«I'll send Ember in plenty of time to wake you to prepare for the feast.» Then she gave me a little push and I climbed the boulders and eased myself into the cleft in the earth that led to the cave shrine, wishing I had left my sword in my rooms.

As I climbed down, I stared at the rocks, looking again for any signs that this was the same sort of shrine as the one Fionn and I had found beneath the hills of Aven, or the one under the Eyrie. I saw nothing but natural stone, and soon the daylight faded. It was long climb, but not a difficult one, which was good, since I hadn't stopped to take my boots off, and once I got past the farthest reach of dim sunlight, I would be blind.

Halfway down, I wished I had a candle. In the darkness beneath the earth, even a Sidhe's eyes can't see, and I had no magic to make wisplights with. But as the daylight dimmed and vanished, I was able to pick out a diffuse glow. Siona had left a lamp burning for me at the bottom.

So when I reached the end of the vertical climb, and turned to face into the cavern, I was expecting to see the first sacred pool and the passage into the next cave.

I was *not* expecting to see someone kneeling beside the pool, their back to me, wisplights drifting lazily over their head.

I must have made some noise because they stood and turned and… I couldn't breathe.

"Oh!" he said, his voice soft and gentle, a little husky.

I opened my mouth and no sound came out.

He took a step towards me. He was dressed in a long tunic of soft white wool over pale blue linen trousers and shirt. There was a darker blue cloak pooled on the floor where he had been kneeling. The garish blue and green feathers they had put on him in the Eyrie were gone, and his wings and tail, his facial adornments, were composed of pure white feathers to closer match his natural silver plumage.

His hair had grown out since I had last seen him and seemed determined to creep between the feathers to tickle his face. His large seer-silver eyes were wide in surprise and his pale pink lips were slightly parted. He was perfect, magnificent. Untouchable and sacred. I wanted to worship at his feet.

"Seer Tokka," I said, mustering enough brain power to stop gawping at him. I think my voice was even normal.

He took another step closer, his white brows pinched together, his hands clasped in front of him, fingers twisting around each other like he did when he was anxious.

"I'm still your Fionn," he said, in a voice that was at least half sorrow.

I felt my knees hit the stone before I realized my legs had given out. "Goddess Below," I said. "Fionn." I stared up at him and resisted the urge to grovel and kiss his feet.

This was not how I had imagined our first meeting would go, when I saw him again. First, we would have met publicly and pretended to hardly know one another, to be proper and formal. Later, I had thought we would meet privately, and I would say, all cocky and certain, "Will you kiss me, pretty bird?" and everything would be as if we had never parted.

He knelt slowly in front of me.

"Fionn," I said again, because apparently that was the only word I could pronounce. But then I managed another. "Beloved."

A smile broke through his anxiety. He put his hands on my face like he was trying to make sure I was real. "Kiernan," he said, and I wanted to melt from the way my name sounded in his mouth. "My Kier. Beloved. I missed you."

I stared into his eyes, utterly lost. "I hoped you would come."

He stared back. "You made sure I would read the letter." His lips curled.

"I was really hoping no one else in the Eyrie could read Sidhe." I finally managed to make my body function and put my hand over his where it cradled my face.

"*I* can barely read Sidhe," he said. "And I've been practicing."

"I tried to find a Vogel grammar, a dictionary, anything, but we have no references to Vogelspek in our library."

"I'll have some sent to you," he said, and I felt a tiny stab of pain at the thought that he would have to leave me again. But then I was kissing him, pressing my mouth on his, and he was responding just as fiercely.

After what felt like a very long time, the urgency eased, and his hand slid from my face to my chest. I kissed him carefully then, brushing my lips over his, tracing them with my tongue, chuckling when he moaned and opened his mouth to me.

His hands had made fists in the front of my coat and several buttons had popped open when I pulled away to breathe, just far enough to rest my forehead against his.

"I missed you," I said. "Fuck, Fionn. I missed you so much."

"I missed you too, Kier." He unclenched his hands and smoothed my jacket over my chest.

When he started to do up the buttons, I said, "I was hoping you'd take this *off* me, not put it back on."

He laughed softly and stopped buttoning.

"Why are you here?" I said. "In the cave shrine?"

"Your Seer brought me here," he said. "She asked your Queen permission to exchange knowledge with me, which I gather is what happens when Seers meet. She said this was the place to begin, that I should come here and rest before the meetings start." He paused, touching one of the moonsilver buttons on my front. "She told me no one visits here after they're introduced to the spirits when their magic first comes. Except Seers, but she's the only Seer currently at court."

"It's true. No one visits here without permission. It's too sacred, too full of magic, and it makes most people uncomfortable."

"But not you." He touched my lips with his fingers, and I darted my tongue out to lick them. He sighed and smiled as I kissed each fingertip.

"Not me." I didn't say anything about currently having no magic to feel uncomfortable *with*, because it was irrelevant. With or without magic, I had always loved coming here.

"There are no fish," he said. "You told me there were cave fish."

I smiled at that memory, of how I had told him the beauty of cave fish had made me weep after he had said he was pale and strange like they were. "Not in this cavern," I said. "The next one." I got to my feet and helped him up after me. "Come on, I'll show you."

I couldn't bear the thought of not touching him – and that was going to make the next ninenight difficult – so I laced my fingers through his and led him through the passage to the next cave. It was a squeeze for his big wings, but he didn't get stuck. His wisplights drifted in front of us.

"You're getting very good at those," I said.

"I had a good teacher."

We crossed the cave, down its gentle slope to where three pools, each nearly round, cascaded one into the next. The last pool was the largest and it vanished back into the depths of the cave, ceiling getting lower and lower until it met the water.

"Float a light over there." I pointed.

His wisplights drifted across the surface of the largest pool and as they moved, they caught silvery reflections. At first there were only a few, and then hundreds.

"Oh!" he said in that soft, wondering way he had, and he moved closer to see better. In the pool, reflecting back the light from their colorless scales, were hundreds of tiny fish, pure white and eyeless, swirling in the water like a storm of snowflakes.

"Oh, Kier," he said, turning to look at me. "They're beautiful. Just like you said they were." His eyes were full of tears and as I watched one spilled over to run down his cheek. I moved closer and brushed it gently away with my thumb. "They're so beautiful," he said.

"Yes," I replied. "And so are you."

15
Fionn

I was expecting Morven Forest to be much the same as Aven Forest, and in many ways I supposed it was. But it felt somehow deeper, darker. More ancient. It felt very much wilder and even without having seen Kiernan here, it felt like him.

I blurted out something to that effect when Seer Siona invited me to walk with her, after we were settled into our guest rooms to rest before the welcome feast. I wanted to find Kiernan, but of course I couldn't do that; I had to be patient and wait for the proper time.

So I took Seer Siona's arm and she directed me under the trees, following the bright red tail of her fox, and I said, "It feels like him here." I didn't even need to tell her who I meant. He must have told her about me, about us, as he had told me he would.

She smiled and patted my arm. "Perhaps it is more that *he* feels like Morven," she said. A few steps later, she added, "He is a true child of Morven." I didn't understand what she meant, but before I could ask, she directed me onto another path that required me to pay attention to where I was going, or risk losing an eye to a sharp branch. And though she kept hold of my arm, Siona really didn't seem to need my help to know where to put her feet.

When we came out on a meadow and headed across, I said, "He told me you're more a mother to him than the Queen." I kept my voice low, in case anyone might be listening. In the Eyrie, it was easy to see when you were alone; here I had no idea if someone might be behind a tree or around a bend in the path.

She smiled again and said, "He is the son of my heart." It echoed something I had once told him when we'd first met, and it made me feel warm inside. "He was three months old when our Queen tired of nursing him and gave him to me to find a wet nurse."

"Oh," I said softly, aching for him. I had never known my mother at all, except in one too-brief vision of her from before I was born, but I thought being rejected by a mother might be even worse than not having one.

"I couldn't find anyone willing," she continued. "No Sidhe women at court had infants, and the local non-fey women were too afraid of the Queen." Her Islish had the same rich accent as Kiernan's and it made me long to hear him speak again.

"What did you do?" I said.

"You know we ride deer in Morven Forest?" she said.

I nodded, then remembered she couldn't see the motion; she was so sure-footed it was hard to remember she was blind. "Yes," I said. "Though Kiernan – Prince Kiernan's stag was gone by the time we got into Aven Forest."

She nodded. "They're not the most intelligent creatures. The stag showed up here some time later and we feared our

Prince had been killed." She squeezed my arm comfortingly. "I think the version of your journey between the Abbey of the Moon and the Eyrie he told me was a little different from the very factual report he gave the Queen." She laughed. "To begin with, I doubt he confessed to her that he had fallen quite in love with the handsome young Seer he rescued."

I blushed hot.

We walked on for a few moments and then she picked up her story. "Luckily, my doe had just given birth a few days before Kiernan was given to me. It was an early birth, so close after Midwinter, though not unheard of, and she'd had twins, but one was sickly and died. The other fawn grew into the stag Kiernan rides. My doe had plenty of milk and didn't mind sharing, and though he was too tiny to nurse directly from her, he was happiest if left to curl up with her fawn after drinking from his bottle."

"He's milk brothers with his own stag?" I said, finding the idea strange and wonderful at the same time, like one of the old tales I had read in a book in the Abbey library.

She laughed. "He is. And not only with his stag. I worried, you see, that deer milk might not be enough for him. He always seemed to be so *hungry*. So, when one of our hunters brought me an injured she-wolf to heal, and she proved to have recently had cubs, I asked her if she would nurse a small Sidhe child, and she agreed, on the condition that I find her cubs and bring them to her while she healed from her injuries."

"Did you find her cubs?"

"I sent the hunter who had brought me the wolf back to where he found her trapped by an illegal snare and told him to scour the nearby forest. At first he refused to believe a wolf would have cubs so long before the spring thaw, but he returned with three strong wolflings; two female and one male."

"So somewhere in the forest, he has wolf siblings, too?"

"And perhaps a wolf mother, although she was not young even then. But our wolves live longer than those elsewhere. They say the werewolves can take the shape of wolves because their ancestors were wolves, that Morven wolves and Morven werewolves know they are close cousins, so they never attack each other."

"Everything here is like a fairytale," I said. "Two animals had their offspring earlier than usual, without which Kiernan might not have lived."

"It doesn't make you think less of him, to know he was raised by animals as much as by people?"

I smiled and shook my head. "It makes me... it fills me with wonder," I said. And it made me miss him more, to learn these details of his childhood.

We stopped at last near a pile of boulders and Siona said, "This is what I brought you here to see."

I looked around, seeing nothing unusual. "I –"

She laughed and I thought it was a sound I could listen to every day and never find it less enchanting. I could see why Kiernan spoke so fondly of his Seer, why he loved her like a mother.

"Climb to the top of the boulders," she said. "And you will find a cleft that leads down, deep into the earth. At the bottom you will find our sacred shrine. This is where we bring our children to meet our Goddess, when they come into their magic. And this is where Seers come, to learn to listen to the spirits. I hope, Seer Tokka, that you and I can speak often while you are here, because I believe there is much we can learn from one another."

I looked away, feeling suddenly shy and inadequate. "I think I have much more to learn from you than you could possibly learn from me," I said. "And... if you could, at least in private, call me Fionn."

"Fionn," she said. "I confess I was worried, when he told me of you, that he would end up getting hurt because you can't be together."

The words made my stomach ache.

"Our Kiernan doesn't love easily." She let go of my arm and stepped back. "He makes friends more easily than he realizes, and he cares so much more about everything than he lets show, but love… I've only known him to fall in love once before, and when Dec was killed, it nearly destroyed him." She sighed. "He's so very strong, our Kiernan, and so very, very fragile."

The name Dec plucked at something in my memory, but I couldn't make it come to the fore. I felt like I should know that name, but I couldn't say why. Had Kiernan mentioned him? I didn't think so, but why else would it seem so familiar?

She had moved away to sit on a rock on the edge of the pile of boulders, her fox friend by her feet, and I made my way over, suddenly feeling weary.

"I don't want to hurt him," I said. She took my hand and gently squeezed.

"Then don't let yourself be taken from him."

"I don't know how," I whispered. "I want…"

"It's okay," she said. "I can read it in your heart." She let go of my hand and rose, touching my shoulder. "Remind me to teach you how to shield yourself from others who can read you. We seers are not the only ones who can, and even though seers are loyal to each other, some of us have other obligations we cannot refuse."

She pointed at the boulders. "Go below. Rest. Meditate. Sleep. There is a bed in the farthest cave for when new seers are trained. I'll send Ember to you when it's time for you to return to the palace and prepare for the feast."

THE CLIMB DOWN the cliff was easier than squeezing through the tighter parts of the Aven caves. I only had to be careful where I put my feet, and keep my wings tucked. Only once, when I thought I was getting close to the bottom and tried to climb faster, I got my left wing wedged between two of the boulders that filled the cleft and couldn't get free.

I clung to the rock and struggled, pulling desperately on my wing until my breath grew short and choppy and tears threatened to spill over. It felt like that moment in the caverns beneath Aven Forest, when I got stuck in a tight passage, and Kiernan had to crawl past my feet to get behind me, and gently pull my wing free of where it was stuck. He had spoken softly to me, telling me how brave I was and how I only needed to hold still, and he would get me out.

I closed my eyes and remembered his voice, so calm and gentle, and his careful hands on my wing, and gradually the panic ebbed away, and I held still. Then I eased myself back up a step on the boulder, then another, then tugged on my wing again, and it pulled free.

I was much more careful of where I was putting all my limbs as I descended the rest of the way and made wisplights when I reached the bottom. I looked around. It was a simple cave, with no carvings like the caves under the Eyrie and fewer flowstone formations than the Aven caves. But a pool of water spilled over the floor on the other side of the cavern, and I went there and knelt next to the edge. I could feel spirits pushing close as I had been able to do since my King had taken me to the death shrine under the Eyrie and I had nearly crossed to the afterlife by accident.

"Hello, spirits," I said, my voice barely a whisper. "And greetings, Goddess Below, if you're here." I felt the slightest brush against my mind of something very large and old and I shivered. The spirits seemed to swirl away from the presence, but returned when it withdrew. "I came to learn more about this forest," I said. "And about the magic of our Isle, and I hope I can be welcome here." They swirled around me again, and it felt like I was being examined, and then they drifted away, leaving behind a feeling of warmth and belonging. "Thank you," I whispered, and gazed into the pool.

I had been hoping this was the place Kiernan had told me about, but I saw no fish in the water. Still, it was calm and beautiful, and I felt completely at peace. I didn't even feel inclined to explore farther, to look for the sleeping chamber Siona had mentioned.

I don't know how long I knelt there, but it was long enough that I felt so serene I didn't even startle when something made a noise behind me, and I realized I was no longer alone in the cave.

I stood, keeping serenity wrapped around me like a cloak, my wisplights gathering to spill light across the stone floor. And I froze, all calm rushing away until I felt it was only willpower holding me still, keeping me from flying apart in fragments. I had to force myself to keep breathing. I must have said something, but there was a rushing in my ears that drowned out my own voice.

He took a step towards me, his deep green eyes examining me from the top of my feathered facial adornment to my travel-dusty feet. He looked tired, shadows under his eyes and cheeks thinner and sharper than they had been. He was dressed in green and grey, wool coat tailored to fit perfectly, so I could see how broad his shoulders and chest were, how trim his waist, and how powerful his thighs.

I couldn't read his face, and I couldn't look away once he met my eyes. I felt flushed all over.

The green around his eyes that looked like makeup but wasn't was faded, browner, like leaves turning in the fall. I wondered if the tattoo on his arm that marked his magic would be the same, or if it would be gone entirely.

He looked beaten down but not broken, weary but still strong. He looked so handsome I felt myself stir in my sheath, so magnificent I wanted to fall into his arms and let him protect me for the rest of my life.

"Seer Tokka," he said, in his rich smoky voice, and I almost cried out. He might as well have slapped me. I was not, should not ever be, Seer Tokka to him. Not in private.

I heard my own voice as if from outside my body, petulant as a spoiled child. "I'm still your Fionn."

He dropped to his knees as if his legs had been cut from under him, but hardly even seemed to notice. "Goddess Below," he whispered. "Fionn." And it was as if saying my name released me from a trance. I crossed the cavern to him and knelt in front of him.

"Fionn," he said again, like he couldn't believe I was there. And then he said the word that made my heart soar. "Beloved."

I must have grinned like an infant given too many sweets. "Kiernan," I said. "My Kier. Beloved." I had to stop to breathe. "I missed you."

K IER SEEMED, THEN, to return to his old self. He got to his feet and took my hand, lacing our fingers together as if to make sure we didn't accidentally get separated. He showed me the way to the next cave, where three pools spilled one into the other and the tiny white fish that filled the third pool made me weep, they were so beautiful.

Then he led me on into the next cave, which was deep but filled with water save for a platform of white stone in the middle. We stepped across and Kiernan said, "This is where we are brought when we come into our magic. First, we spend a night in the first cavern, where the Seer presents us to our Goddess. Then we spend a day in the second cavern, where she reads us, to see what magics we are likely to develop. Then we come here to practice drawing on the Realms."

"How old are you when this happens?"

He turned to face me and took my other hand, and we stood smiling stupidly at each other.

"It can happen at almost any age, though almost always by the time we're twelve or thirteen. The youngest I know of was three, which is too young to really work on developing magic."

I bent my head to rest my brow on his. I wanted to press my whole body to him, but I also wanted to wait, to draw our reunion out until I couldn't stand it anymore. "Three is so young," I said. "I was three when I had my first vision, and I didn't understand what was happening. I remember screaming a lot."

He nuzzled my cheek. "Three is young. I believe Siona presented him to the Goddess and then just tried to teach him control. She left the full initiation until years later."

I studied his face. His mouth kept curling up and he kept smoothing it out. "How old were *you*?" I said.

He broke into a grin. "Three," he said. "I was six before I had any control to speak of, and not much even then, and that was when…" He stopped and licked his lips. "I was a terror and set things on fire that weren't meant to burn."

I laughed softly. "Was Siona proud?"

"I think my *Queen* was proud. At least until I set her hair on fire. Soon after that she took my antlers and sent me to my father." He spoke softly, evenly, but I knew the hurt that was behind his words. The first real betrayal of his belief that she loved him. I wondered if he knew she had given him to Siona to deal with as an infant.

He freed one hand from mine to touch my face and I closed my eyes and pressed my cheek to his palm.

"Will you kiss me, pretty bird?" he said, his voice somehow even lower and smokier. I felt pressure in my sheath and my breath came quicker.

"Always," I whispered, and pressed my lips to his, softly, carefully. I feared I would be nervous, as I had been in the first cavern, as I had been when we first kissed at the Abbey of the Moon. But as soon as I felt his mouth on mine, all uncertainty fled.

He moaned softly and I chuckled, butted my nose against his, and kissed him again. He moved his hand from my face to my hair and pulled me closer, pressing his mouth to mine more firmly, sliding his tongue deeper.

"I've thought about how I'd kiss you again every day since I left the Eyrie," he said, moving his hand to my neck, then reaching to trace my ear with his fingers.

I put my hand flat on his chest, and saw where I had pulled some of the buttons open on his coat when we first kissed in the cavern.

"Please don't button those," he said.

"Can I unbutton them?" I touched his deep green shirt where it showed in the gap his jacket revealed.

"Yes," he breathed. "But first let me show you the last cavern." He stepped away, but kept hold of my hand, and we crossed over the water on the other side of the chamber and slipped into a narrow tunnel that led steeply upwards. I had to squeeze through the last part, but then we emerged into what looked like a simple ordinary bed chamber, except for its odd shape.

"Oh, now I see," I said, teasing. "You just want to get me into bed."

He grinned and hooked a finger into my belt to pull me closer. "I hope, one day, to have a home that's ours, with a very big, soft bed in it that I can get you into."

"Our bed?" I moved his hand to my belt clasp and watched as his clever fingers figured out how it worked, and my belt fell away. He caught it and hung it on the back of a wooden chair against the curved wall.

"Yes. Our house, our bed, our dishes and spoons. Our firewood and our chamberpot."

I started to unbuckle the strap across his chest that held his sword in place, but he took my hands and moved them around behind him. "Bottom first," he said, "Or we'll end up with a naked blade on the floor when the whole thing tips upside down." When I'd done that, he said, "Thighs next," and I trembled as I reached for the first buckle that held his knives strapped on securely.

"Can we have plumbing?" I said. "I'd rather a commode with running water than a chamberpot."

He watched me undo all his buckles. "The chamberpot will be for emergencies," he said.

"I'd like a bathtub." I unbuckled his belt next, and he shrugged out of the whole array of leather straps with a familiar motion. He hung it on the chair with my belt.

"We'd better build our house near a hot spring, then," he said, tugging my tunic over my head. "Because I'm not fond of hauling cauldrons of water."

I worked at his coat buttons while he draped my tunic over the chair. "But you would, though, wouldn't you?" I said, looking at him from under my lashes. "For me?"

He slipped out of his coat and put it with the rest of our things, then he stepped out of his boots and pulled his socks off with his toes. He smiled at my teasing, but when he answered, it was serious. "I would do anything for you, pretty bird." Then he stepped closer, pressed against me, and slid his hands up my back and under my shirt. I felt his fingers in my feathers, stroking softly, slipping through to find my skin.

I must have made a noise, and he tilted his chin to look up at me. "I love the little sounds you make when I touch you," he said.

I tugged on the laces at the neck of his shirt with one hand while I traced the shape of his ear with my tongue. He pulled up the hem of my shirt, then stopped, and frowned.

"How do I get this off you?" he said, and I laughed.

"There are buttons," I said. "Under my wings." I squirmed as he felt for them. "That tickles."

"Does this tickle?" He slid his foot over mine and poked his big toe between my toes and I gasped. Sensation shot up my leg to my crotch and the pressure behind my belly muscles increased.

"I think you're obsessed with my toes," I said, when I could breathe properly again.

"You have pretty toes."

He slid my shirt over my head, and I pulled his off him. We added them to the pile on the chair.

"There are buttons at my ankles, too," I said.

"Mmm." He knelt and undid the buttons, then stroked the top of my foot and slid a finger between my toes. I made a noise and groped for his antlers, grasping them and stroking with both hands.

"Goddess Below," he said, voice rough. "Be careful, pretty bird. They're sharp now."

I touched the moonsilver carefully and felt the tingle of foreign magic. "This is how she did it?" I said, softly, not wanting to hurt him.

But he only replied, mildly, "Yes."

"I'm so sorry."

He stood slowly, eyes taking in every detail of my chest and arms, hands following where his gaze had gone. "My Fionn," he said. He met my eyes. "I love you."

I moved my hands to his face, then his neck, his muscular shoulders. "I love you, Kier."

He traced a finger down from my collarbone, between my pectoral muscles and over my abdomen. He smiled when his fingertip poked into my belly button, and I squirmed. He stopped with his finger hooked into the waist of my trousers.

"Do you want me?" he said. It seemed such a simple question, one lover to another, but it felt like so much more. I thought he might not be asking me if I wanted him right then, but if I wanted him at all, forever. And he might not just be asking if I wanted to share a bed with him, but if I wanted his love, his companionship, a life with him.

But it didn't matter how complicated the question was; the answer was simple.

"Yes." I tugged open the buttons on my trousers and let them slide down my legs, and then I did the same to my undergarment and stepped away from them, just a single step back from him. I wanted him to look at me, but I didn't want to be too far away. "I want you Kiernan. I want you now and always."

He licked his lips and moved his hands to his waist, slipped off his trousers and his undergarment and took a half step back. His bronze skin gleamed in my wisplights and I had to force myself to keep looking at his face, to not glance down to see if he was hard for me.

I bit my lip and saw something soften in his face.

"My beautiful Fionn," he said, more breath than words.

"Do you want me?" I said, trying to make my voice as even as his had been, trying not to sound desperate.

"Yes," he said. "Now and always." Then he grinned and

gestured at his nether region, and I had to look. He was erect and magnificent. "As if that wasn't obvious."

Then he closed the space between us, reached for my face, and pulled me to him to kiss me.

16
Kiernan

GODDESS BELOW, I could have done nothing but hold Fionn's naked body against mine and I'd have been happy.

When I pulled his head down to kiss him, he made one of his pretty love noises as he opened his mouth against mine and combed his fingers through my hair to pull me closer, to kiss me deeper.

I remembered how hesitant, how nervous he had been the first time we kissed, and he'd been the one to make the first move. But now, all the tentativeness was gone, replaced by something more confident. He was still as sweet and gentle as always, and my heart sang to think he wanted *me*.

I let my hands slide down his arms, long and slender, but sculpted with toned muscle, and I took a step back towards the bed. He followed me, his fingers tangling in my hair as he tried to get his tongue farther into my mouth.

When the backs of my legs hit the edge of the bed I pulled slowly out of the kiss, not really wanting to stop, but also very much wanting to put my mouth in other places. I sat on the edge of the bed, rested my cheek on his hip, and ran my hand over his belly, savoring the feel of every muscle under my palm. He trembled when I reached the soft feathers over his groin and his hands moved from my hair to my antlers when I traced a finger over the seam of his sheath, touching him so lightly I barely stirred his feathers.

I turned my head to kiss him and felt his belly muscles tense under my lips. "You smell so good," I said and kissed him again, moving closer to his sheath opening, stirring the feathers with my breath.

I traced his seam again, felt it part slightly under my finger, and he moaned very softly.

"Kier," he said, his voice gone even more husky than usual.

"Mmm?" I answered and ran my tongue over his seam.

He made a strangled noise and tightened his hands on my antlers. I stroked my palm over his hip and thigh, then back up, and ran my tongue over his seam again. I felt his belly muscles tighten with the effort of keeping his sheath closed and I hid a smile in the crease of his hip. He liked me to tease him, to touch and caress until he couldn't keep his cock in any longer. And I fucking loved teasing him.

I slipped a hand between his legs to nudge his thighs apart, then licked him again and he clung to my antlers, arched his back, and cried out, soft and sweet. He was so sexy I could probably get off just listening to his reactions. There was a soft, wet, sliding noise, all moisture and slickness, and his erection emerged from his sheath, glistening with lubricant.

Not for the first time, I marveled at how beautiful his cock was. He was a little longer than me, but slenderer, with a distinct upward curve and an almost pointed tip. His skin there was as pale as the rest of him, but his tip was darker, a silvery blue to match the freckles that scattered his body everywhere the sun would touch him most, if he was in habit of walking around naked. He had a row of large, flexible scales protecting his upper surface, in the same darker silver-blue.

And he self-lubricated, emerged from his sheath slippery and gleaming. I wanted him inside me so badly my ass ached.

I curled my fingers around him and looked up at his face to see his eyes closed, his head tilted back, revealing his long pale throat. His wings were clamped tight to his back and his tail folded into a thin strip of feathers. I stroked him, up and down, then ran my tongue over his underside and he whimpered.

"Kier," he said again.

"Mmm?" I sat up straighter so I could reach him better, and wrapped my lips around his tip, teasing him with my tongue as I slid farther over him, taking him as deep in my mouth as I could.

"Goddess Above," he said. Then, "Wait."

I stopped moving but didn't take my mouth away.

"Not yet," he said. "I haven't even touched you."

I did move my mouth away then, so I could smile. "I like making you feel good, pretty bird."

"I like making you feel good, too," he answered, and pushed me back onto the bed, climbing on after me. For a moment, I had an odd memory of him pushing me onto my back on my own bed. But he had never been in my rooms. It plucked at my memory, but then Fionn was licking my neck and I forgot everything except the feel of his tongue on my skin.

He sat astride me, his cock rubbing against mine, and seemed determined to taste every inch of my neck and shoulders. He sat up to stroke his hands over my chest and to grin wickedly when I gasped as he tweaked both nipples at once.

Then he leaned over and licked one of them, nibbled it, and traced the outline of each of my abdominal muscles with fingers and tongue. He pushed my knees apart with his and I sprawled, helpless, on the bed. He could touch me any way he wanted to, and I would beg him for more.

He ducked his head between my legs, scooped his tongue under my testicles, and sucked one of them into his mouth. I held onto the bedsheets like I might implode if I didn't have something solid to touch. Then his tongue flicked over my asshole and away.

"Oh, fuck. Fionn," I said. And he slid his beautiful mouth over my cock, and I couldn't make any more words come out. I could feel it building, the pleasure, and I knew if I didn't stop him I would come hard and it would be amazing and for a moment, I almost let it happen.

Then I gasped out, "Wait," and he raised his head to meet my eyes. I lay limp, only my cock hard and twitching. "Goddess, Fionn," I said. "I want…" I took a few deep breaths. "Will you fuck me?" I finally said. "Please?"

He leaned forward over me, and his erection bumped against mine. "I'll do anything you want me to," he said, and kissed me, and I could taste salt on his tongue. I could taste *myself*. When he met my eyes again, his silver gaze burned into me, leaving me helpless to do anything but what he wanted.

He touched my face softly with his fingertips, ran them over my cheekbone, my neck, my chest, and my hip. He nudged my legs farther apart and I pulled my knees up, let him pin one between his arm and mine, and wrapped my other leg across his back. My ass cheeks spread open with my legs and I couldn't let go of the sheets beneath me; I thought I might float away or dissolve into a puddle if I let go.

He reached down to stroke my cock, to transfer some of his lubricant onto me before stroking me again. His slippery hand felt divine on my hardness, and I could feel my orgasm building.

"Please, Fionn. I'm so close."

He bit his lip and cocked his head slightly. "Tell me what to do," he said, and I knew he wasn't saying it because he didn't know how to fuck me. He wanted me to say all the words that had been forbidden to him in the Abbey of the Moon, to tell him in the filthiest way possible how I wanted him to take me.

I almost couldn't get words out, I was so far gone, but I took a couple of panting breaths and said, "Put your hand around your own cock, pretty bird." He did so, keeping his eyes on my face. "Press your tip against my asshole." I tore my eyes from his to watch him touching himself, dipping his cock between my legs, and then I had to close my eyes when his tip touched me.

"Oh fuck," I said. "Yes. Rub me with it. Massage my ass, pretty bird. Make me open for you."

"Don't stop," he said.

"Push yourself inside me," I said, and cried out when he did. "Oh, fuck. Just your tip. Just… just there inside my ass." I was panting; we were both panting.

"Don't stop," he said again.

I made a strangled noise. "Fuck. Fuck. Fionn, push your cock inside me. Farther. Farther. Goddess Below." He kept going until he was filling me, until he couldn't get any deeper because he didn't have any length left to push into me.

He twitched suddenly and I felt his first pulse move through him from the base of his cock to his tip, and it was his turn to cry out.

"Fuck me, pretty bird," I said. "Fuck me hard and don't stop until you're done."

He half pulled out of me and pushed in again, and again, faster and harder and I clung to the bedsheets and pushed my ass up to meet him. He pulsed again and moaned into my neck.

Then he pushed his chest away from mine, propping himself up on one arm so he could touch me, could grip my hardness in his fist and slide over my lubricant-slick cock, matching every thrust of his hips.

His wings half opened as his third pulse hit him and I wanted to weep at his beauty, his magnificence. He was fucking perfect, wings stirring the air around us as he thrust against me, desperate now.

It had been like this the first time he had fucked me, except then it had been only his own small wings beating furiously at the air. He had been perfect then and he was perfect now, gasping with each thrust until I couldn't hold back anymore, and I let my pleasure out in a yell and splattered spunk all over myself, from belly to throat. And I watched as his beautiful eyes widened and he said, "Oh Kiernan," and his fourth pulse felt like it was tearing through me, from my asshole deep inside.

And then I had to let go of the sheets to catch him, to lower him gently to the bed beside me.

He made a sleepy, contented noise and looked at me from half-closed eyes and smiled.

"Feel good?" I said, kissing his damp forehead.

"Mmm." He snuggled closer and lay an arm across me, then opened his eyes and said, "You're sticky."

I laughed softly and said, "That's your fault, beloved."

"Is it?" He blinked, then blushed. "Oh!"

"I love you, pretty bird."

"I love you, my Prince."

I WOKE IN DARKNESS so complete it was indescribable. If you've never been at the bottom of a cave, you've probably never experienced the true absence of light, but this was it.

I was nestled close against Fionn's back, my face buried in the feathers between his wings. He felt wonderfully warm and *here*. Goddess Below, Fionn was *here*.

I uncurled carefully from him and stretched, wondering if there was a candle or a lamp. I had been too otherwise occupied when we came in here to notice.

Fionn stirred next to me and asked, "Why is it so dark?"

"We're in a cave, beloved," I said. "Can you call some wisp-lights?"

"I thought I was dreaming," he said, as he rolled onto his back and called up a wisplight into the palm of his hand, set it floating over us, and rolled the rest of the way over to face me. "But it's real. You *are* here. And we…" He flushed pink.

"You were magnificent," I said, and the flush spread from his cheeks to the tips of his ears. I grinned and kissed him.

"How much time do we have?" he said, propping himself up and putting his free hand on my chest. I untangled my arm from the sheets to put my hand over his and he saw my tattoo. It was too late for me to hide it, and anyway I didn't want any secrets from him, even though seeing it would make him worry.

He called another couple of wisplights and sat up in bed, taking my arm in both hands, turning it over to look carefully at the leaves and tendrils curling across my skin like they had grown there.

"I don't know when it started," I said, as he examined how the green leaves were turning brown at the edges, some of them faded so much they were almost invisible. "Probably as soon as she took my magic. But I was feverish and delirious for days, so I don't know. Daphnis might have noticed."

"Daphnis?" He looked up and met my eyes and I felt a surge of guilt in my belly, even though I hadn't given in to temptation. I hadn't even ever really wanted to.

"He's a dryad. My mother gifted him to me after she took my magic and I wasn't in any state to refuse. Now that I am, he's asked me not to return him to her."

"Did you… Do you…?" He looked away, brows pulled together just a little.

"No, pretty bird. I'm not fucking him. We were… we were boys together, and yes, I *have* fucked him, but it was a very long time ago. I've kept my promise to you."

He glanced up again, startled. "Kier, I never expected you to be celibate."

"Maybe not," I said, touching his face. "But I don't want anyone other than you."

"But I can't –" he started to say, and I prepared to explain that him being required to share his King's bed didn't break any promises he'd made to me, because I knew it wasn't his choice, but he suddenly stopped and said, "Oh! The dryad. Daphnis. I remember!"

I frowned at him, puzzled. "You remember what?"

"You were… You wanted to die. Because your Queen took your magic. And I… There's a raven, only it's white not black, and it said you needed me, so I flew and you wanted to die."

I waited until he slowed down and put my fingers against his lips. He scowled at me but stopped talking.

"You're not making any sense."

He took a deep breath and pushed my fingers away. Then he started at the beginning, with meeting a raven on his balcony. And as he talked, I started to remember, too. Thinking I was imagining the sound of wings outside my window, the caw of a raven, Fionn, transparent so I thought he was a ghost, then gone completely, and only Daphnis could see him. He had visited me in his spirit body, but without magic I was unable to see him, so Daphnis had let Fionn borrow his body to talk to me. To kiss me. How could I have forgotten that? But it was a part of the magic to be forgotten until the right time, Fionn said.

"But why now?" He just shook his head. "You should tell Siona about this," I said, when he told me he was trying to find a way to induce spirit flight so he could visit me whenever he wanted. And that was why I must get my magic back, so we wouldn't need to ask Daphnis to borrow his body. So we could touch, because he was sure my magic would make his spirit body solid to me.

Then he told me about salt-leaf and how he thought it held the answer. He was excited about working on the problem, about the prospect of finding a solution, and his eyes shone, and he gestured with his slender hands, and all I could do was listen, smiling stupidly at how happy he was. And grin back when he told me how he had figured out how to treat the fever, even with so little salt-leaf to experiment with.

"And you think spirit flight might also be related to the fever treatment?" I said, when he finally paused. He'd been the one talking, but I felt breathless. I wanted to pull him into my arms and never let go, and I wanted to listen to him talk about something that excited him for the rest of my life, even if I only understood half of it.

He nodded. "I can't explain why, but it feels like it should be connected. And they're in the same rhyme."

"Maybe Siona can help you figure it out. And Fionn?" I smiled and kissed his hand. "If you need salt-leaf, we can get you some. It's common in Morven, especially along the coast. Make it a part of your trade requests."

He smiled so wide I almost laughed. "Oh yes! I will."

He stretched and his back popped and suddenly his face

changed, his eyes going distant.

"Are you okay? That sounded painful."

He blinked. "Oh, no. I'm fine. But Kier?" His voice held excitement again, only it had a different quality.

"Yes, pretty bird?" I kissed his hand again.

He smiled and it lit up his face. I would do anything to make sure he could smile like that, over and over his whole life. "I remembered. Before I went on the spirit flight, I had a vision. Or a bunch of smaller visions."

He lay down next to me and put his head on my shoulder, then pulled the blankets up. I put my arm around him and turned so I could kiss his forehead.

"What was in your visions?"

"In one, we were on the beach below the Eyrie, walking and talking. I can't remember about what." He turned his face to kiss my shoulder, then settled again. "It was a different kind of vision than usual, because it wasn't something that happened or might happen."

"What then?"

"I think it was symbolic. You kissed me and gave me a bouquet, but instead of flowers, it was salt-leaf branches. I think… I think it was meant to tell me I could get salt-leaf from you, from trade with Morven."

"Have you had symbolic visions before?"

"I don't think so."

"Maybe you're developing your Seer abilities, if you're having new types of visions. Getting stronger."

"Maybe. Then I had another vision, a more normal one, of us in a possible future. We were on top of a hill looking down on a… an encampment, I suppose. And you said the people were there for me, and I said they were there for you. And I called you General."

"General?"

"General Druison."

"That's… odd. My father has always been General Druison to me. Was it a distant future?"

"No, it felt very soon. A year. A few years maybe. It's impossible to tell, really, except your antlers were different. Not bigger, just different."

"You're sure it was me?" I teased and he poked my ribs to make me squirm.

"Yes, it was you. You teased that you wanted me to call you General while I…" His cheeks turned pink.

"While you pleasured me?"

"Anyway, there was no moonsilver on your antlers."

"So there is a good possibility I'll escape my Queen's spell-work."

"Yes. And the green around your eyes…" He paused to trace a careful finger under my left eye, barely brushing my skin. "It was bright and healthy again. I didn't see your tattoo, though." He curled his fingers around my forearm, as though he could stop the disintegration of the leaves there.

Then his eyes turned bright again. "And I *did* have a distant future vision, too. My back popping reminded me." He traced my cheekbone and then my lips with his gentle fingers. "We were old men," he said, and he looked like he thought that was the best thing he could imagine. And I would not disagree.

"I'm looking forward to seeing you as an old man, someday far off," I said.

"We were in a house. Our house, I think. And your hair was long, and braided, and some of it was white." Then he reached up to touch one of my antlers, carefully. "And your antlers were much bigger."

He looked so happy; I couldn't help but smile. But then his eyes went sad.

"Did something bad happen? In your vision?" I said.

"No." He shook his head but wouldn't meet my eyes. "But Kier, you were… you were…"

"What is it, pretty bird?"

"You were blind." He looked like he was going to cry, so even though his words hit like a gut punch, I didn't react except to kiss his forehead and stroke his shoulder.

"A very smart Seer once told me that visions of the future are only possibilities, because the future is always changing."

"Yes," he said. "That's true, but…"

I shifted position so I could look into his eyes. "Once I was stuck in an Abbey full of people who see my kind as the enemy," I said. "And I was blind. And a very kind, gentle healer took care of me. And I didn't feel helpless, Fionn. I can't say I'd ever *want* to lose my sight, but if you were with me, I wouldn't be afraid."

He swallowed and tried to smile.

"And you've shown me that we *can* have a future together, and there are a lot of things I'd give to have that happen." I tucked my face against his hair. "Now tell me what we were doing in our old man house in the future."

"You were in a big chair in front of the fire," he said. "And I was sitting in your lap, my stupid long legs hanging over the side."

"Your long legs are not stupid," I said. "Your long legs are very nice. Especially when they're wrapped around my head and I'm –"

He smacked my shoulder and I laughed. "I thought you liked to hear the filthy words," I said. "And I'm pretty sure you like it very much when I put my mouth there."

"Of course I like that," he said.

"What else?"

"I kept sliding off your lap and you kept pulling me back on. And then you said…"

"Will you kiss me, pretty bird?"

"Yes."

"And that's all?"

"Well, presumably more happened after, but that's where the vision ended."

"But did you kiss me?"

He smiled. "I will always kiss you."

"Did you still want me? To make love to me? Even though I was an old man?"

"I will always want you."

I nuzzled his hair.

And almost got cracked in the teeth when his back seized and his head snapped back and he was gone, fallen into a vision, and all I could do was hold his head so he didn't hurt himself.

17
Fionn

WHEN I WOKE IN THE DARK with Kiernan curled up against my back, I could have wept. He was *here*. We were together. I knew it was temporary. In a nineday or so, I would have to return to the Eyrie, and he would have to stay in the forest.

But in the meantime, we were together, even if we had to be careful. I didn't know what would happen if my King learned I had disobeyed him, that I had lied to him, and had gone straight to Kiernan. It was against Vogel law for me to be with Kiernan, and while I might be the only, precious bird folk Seer, I was not above the law.

Nor should I be above the law, because no law was much use if it only applied to less important people. But it was a stupid law, and I didn't care if I broke it; I hoped many people were breaking it.

I tried not to think about how soon I would have to go back to being my King's good little Seer; there was so much I wanted to tell Kiernan, and so little time to do it in. And my body didn't want to talk, it wanted to kiss him, to touch him, to feel him inside me. I wanted us to take as much pleasure in each other as we could.

When I sat up in bed and he lay next to me, smiled as much with his deep green eyes as with his lips, it was all I could do not to lean over and put my mouth on him. But I resisted. If we were truly going to mean anything to each other, we needed talking as much as fucking.

He listened while I told him about the Vogel Princess falling ill with fever, and he took my hand when my voice broke as I told him how she wasted away and nearly died, and there had been nothing I could do. He smiled when I got so excited about the salt-leaf and the treatment that had finally saved her that I started babbling and probably making no sense. And he asked careful questions that helped me explain better, and good questions that made me think. I wished he had been in the Eyrie while I was puzzling out the fever cure, because with him to ask the right questions, I might have found the answers sooner.

I told him about my visions, too, of us in the future, as old men, and his face went soft and dreamy, like he was imagining that far off time. His eyes shone when I told him we had been in our own house, sitting in front of our own fire, and the way he smiled made my heart so full I felt I might burst. I felt like I could surely defeat his Queen's magic with only the strength of my love.

But life is not a fairy tale, no matter how it sometimes felt like one, and I could not kiss him and break the spellwork.

But when I told him he was blind in my future vision, he said, "If you were with me, I wouldn't be afraid," and I felt like maybe I really could be as strong as he needed me to be. If I could cure a deadly fever that had plagued my people for generations, then maybe I could find a way to get Kiernan's magic back.

"Did you still want me as an old man?" he said, teasing. He ran a finger across my collar bones and made me shiver. "Did you still want to make love to me, even though I was old and white-haired and blind?" I lay next to him, and tucked my face close against his shoulder, thinking of how beautiful he had still been in my vision, how strong, and how my body had still burned as brightly for him as it did now.

"I will always want you," I answered, and he turned to kiss me, only there was a tightness in my scalp, behind my eyes, and in my neck, and my back spasmed and seized and then there was darkness.

Then firelight. I was sitting astride his lap, my fingers buried in his long curls. They were like ringlets, except where his hair was braided, down past his shoulders, and I made my hands into fists to pull him closer and angled my head to get my tongue deeper into his mouth.

Goddess Above, how I wanted him. Years, decades, together and I still ached for his touch the way I had the day we met. And deep in my belly I felt the connection to him that the Vogel call "heart bonding" and it told me he craved my caresses as much as I yearned for his.

I shifted the way I was sitting so I could feel his hardness against me. I fanned my wings for balance, and they swept forward, still too small for flying. But I had other ways of flying, now.

"My beautiful Fionn," he said, when I could bear to move my lips away from his.

"How do you know I'm beautiful?" I teased. "You haven't seen me in years. I could be wrinkled and ugly by now."

He laughed and put his hand gently on my face and traced the shape of my cheekbones and chin. "You feel exactly the same," he said. "And I think even with wrinkles you would be beautiful. Even bent and swollen-jointed and cranky, you would still be my beautiful Fionn. And besides –" He shifted his weight, hands steadying my hips, and I found myself sitting on his erection, my sheath seam threatening to part. "You still make those pretty little love noises."

I leaned over and bit his earlobe, but not hard. At least, not *too* hard.

"And I can see the shape of your magic, in here." He tapped the side of his head. That was an ability only seers were supposed to have, but I didn't tell him that. He probably already knew anyway. He had been raised by a Seer, and used magic the way we did, always asking, never commanding.

His hands on my hips lifted me to slide over his hardness. I tried not to cry out, but I couldn't help it. I wanted him fiercely.

"Beloved," he said, and as I felt my erection slide free of my sheath, the darkness came back and he was gone. A blue-black, frothy ocean slipped beneath me. It was night and windy, though not quite storming. My wings were stretched open and I was trying not to fall into the sea, beating against the air. I was terrified, but it was not the cold, unforgiving water below that frightened me.

There was a jerk and a stabbing pain in both shoulders that reminded me of when the King's guards had plucked me off the cliff above Aven Forest, leaving Kiernan dangling on a rope, only this time talons broke my skin and tore into muscle until I couldn't hold back a scream, and Goddess Above please don't make me go back.

Then blinding light in my eyes and the ocean was below me again only it was sunny, near noon, and I stood on a hill overlooking a huge bay dotted with islands. My shoulders ached and my feet hurt and I was scared. Everything felt so huge, but Kiernan was beside me, holding my hand, and I knew I could believe everything would be okay.

I turned to him and he met my eyes and smiled. His hair fell into his face and when I reached up to push it back he flinched, then closed his eyes.

"I'm sorry, pretty bird," he said. "They still hurt. Like I'm missing part of my skull."

His antlers…

The dark returned and swirled me away again and made me so dizzy I had to put my hand out to steady myself on the counter in my bathing room.

<Seer Tokka?> Neeka said. <Are you okay? Maybe you should lie down.>

<There's still one last thing to try,> I said. <I won't let anyone die if I can help it.> I looked at the clutter on my counter. Crushed leaves and bark, bottles of syrup boiled down from salt-leaf bark, and one precious bottle boiled down from sap.

Neeka put her hand on my forehead. <You feel hot, Tokka. If you get the fever, you won't be able to help anyone else.>

<I must try.> I looked at the one part of the salt-leaf tree I still hadn't dared use. The outer bark was, I now knew, used to allow seers to separate their spirit body from their physical body. But I hadn't dared yet to use it for treating the fever. It was the only element left, though, so it had to be the key.

<Would you put the kettle on while I package up the latest poultices and tisanes?> I said.

She nodded, looking at me sidelong, like she suspected I might be up to something.

<If I do fall ill,> I said, and she narrowed her eyes as if expecting her suspicions to be confirmed by whatever I said next. <If I have seizures, like when I'm having a vision, tell Healer Kah not to use her muscle-relaxing tea on me.>

<Are you sure? It stops you from thrashing around.>

<When I wake, it feels exactly the same as when she doesn't use the tea. Like my muscles are still seizing, even if

I'm not moving,> I said. <And I think it interferes with my visions.>

She frowned, but nodded, and while she was in the sitting room hanging the kettle over the fire, I quickly packed up my latest batch of remedies and then put some of the crumbled outer salt-leaf bark into a linen pouch and carried it with me to make tea.

Smoke and Flame watched me from my spinning basket next to the fire, eyes bright.

You go, said Smoke.

We follow, said Flame.

I shook my head, glad that Neeka couldn't understand them. I had tried to teach her to speak to feathered serpents, but it seemed her magic didn't include that gift.

I sat on my favorite couch and pulled a blanket over my lap. It had grown cold over the last few ninedays and soon it would be deep winter. I wondered how Kiernan was and if he was any closer to regaining his magic, and how things were going in Dudoon and Great River City, because he must be there by now.

<I'll take the latest batch of remedies to Healer Kah,> Neeka said, pouring hot water into the teapot. <If you agree to rest for a while.> I could smell my favorite blend of winterleaf and sweetbean pod.

<Thank you,> I said. <Take the rest of the day off. I need you rested, too, if we're to do any good.>

She nodded and put her hand on my forehead again.

<I'm not feverish,> I said. Not yet. <Only tired.>

Finally, she left and I got up to lock the door behind her. It wouldn't keep the King out, but I could hope he was too busy doing his job and helping organize the efforts to keep the fever from spreading.

I dropped the bag of salt-leaf bark into the teapot with the other herbs. I didn't know how strong it would need to be, or if the winterleaf and sweetbean would affect the results, but I could only try. I knew I could just chew it, but I feared that would make it too strong, and perhaps not long enough lasting. A sharp scent, almost like wood smoke, immediately arose from the pot, and the tree serpents stirred in their basket. They crawled out and looked up at me as I poured tea into a cup.

We follow, Smoke said.

We keep safe, said Flame.

"You can't follow me this time, little friends," I said and sat back on my couch to sip my tea. It was too hot, but I drank it as quickly as I could, and as soon as I set the cup on the table, Smoke and Flame went to it and lapped up the last drops. Then they moved into my lap and curled up together.

"I should get in bed," I said, but it was too late. My whole body felt flushed and suddenly I was standing, looking down at myself and the two little balls of feathers and scales curled up on my lap.

My back twitched – not in my spirit body but in my physical body – and then one of my wings. I looked undignified, sprawled and spasming irregularly, and I had to look away. I hoped Kiernan never had to see me like that.

Except he had, hadn't he? He'd held my head and watched over me while I had a vision, and he still loved me. He still wanted me.

Tok. There was the sharp tap of a huge beak on the glass of my balcony window. I went to the door and struggled with it, before remembering I could just walk right through it.

Wait, said Smoke.

We follow, said Flame.

And I turned to watch, hardly believing what I saw, as the two tree serpents left their own physical bodies to flit around me in the air in their spirit shapes.

"I didn't expect that," I said.

You can never tell with tree serpents, said the raven as I closed my eyes and stepped through the glass.

When I opened my eyes, the serpents were gone. My balcony was gone, and the sea, and the Eyrie.

Tok, said the raven. *That wasn't supposed to happen.*

The light was dim; only one wobbly wisplight hovered somewhere behind me to light the space, and I realized I was in a cave.

No, not *a* cave. *The* cave. The cave under Morven Forest where I had begun to have the vision in which I drank salt-leaf tea. Was this a vision within a vision?

You seem to have learned a new way into your spirit body, said the raven. It sounded amused. And proud.

"I had a vision where I left my body," I said. "Is that why?" I couldn't make my brain understand how that could possibly have worked. Unless *this* was just more vision, and I wasn't actually here in my spirit body. "Am I still in that vision?"

You're not in a vision at all, said the raven. *You're in your spirit body, like I said.*

I turned around. "Oh!" I lay on the bed, limbs sprawled, twitching. Kiernan held my head in his lap, stroking my face.

"I'm here, pretty bird," he said. "You're safe. I'm right here."

It seems this time, you need him, said the raven, and it made a sound that might have been laughter.

I was still naked, and so was Kier; our clothes were piled on the chair where we had left them. But he had covered me with blankets and every time I twitched, he pulled them back into place. He didn't try to restrain me, he just made sure my seizures didn't tumble me to the floor or crack my skull against the headboard of the bed. And he kept covering me so I wouldn't get cold.

The wisplight faltered and almost went out and I realized it was *my* light, because Kiernan couldn't summon lights without his magic. How it was still going while I was trapped in a vision, I had no idea.

I stepped over to the bed and touched my own shoulder, expecting to be drawn back into my body. But my hand just passed right through me, and my spirit body stayed separate from my physical form.

"What's happening?" I said.

I turned back around, but the raven was gone. Fear stabbed my belly, and I was almost glad my connection with Kier was broken, because I didn't want him to feel it. I didn't want him to worry.

I looked at him, at us, and studied his face. He knew this was what happened when I had a vision, and he didn't look afraid.

Drool leaked from one corner of my mouth, and I felt a flush of embarrassment. But Kier's lips twitched, and he said, "You're leaking, pretty bird," and wiped the saliva gently away with a corner of the blanket.

He stroked my hair back from my face where it had crept through my feathers, moved his hand away when a back spasm twitched my head violently, then gathered me back into his lap and wiped my mouth again.

"I love you, Fionn," he said quietly. "I know you can't hear me, and I know I've already said it, but I'm going to keep telling you I love you for the rest of our lives."

It had been so hard for him to admit, the first time, but now that he'd managed it, it came easily. And every time I felt full and warm, just like I had the first time.

"I love you so much it hurts," he said. "And I fucking hate that you have to be so far away from me."

My body twitched and he waited for it to stop, then settled

my arms and legs into a more comfortable position. It was mortifying, to have to watch myself this way, but the way he cared for me made me want to wake up so I could kiss him.

"I'm so sorry I left you with your King," he said, leaning away from my flailing wing, then tucking it back under my shoulder. "I'm so fucking sorry he makes you share his bed when you don't want to." He sighed and touched my face again. "If he ever hurts you, I will fucking cut his head from his arrogant fucking shoulders."

My arm twitched and my fist hit his thigh, hard, but he didn't flinch.

"I love you, and if he hurts you even a little, I will kill him."

And then my leg kicked out and hit my spirit body and I felt myself drawn in…. to darkness and cold.

I was shivering, violently, and I didn't recognize where I was.

"Kier?" I said, my voice small and uncertain. My breath came out in plumes of white.

"I'm here, pretty bird. The fire went out and I can't get it started."

"Your magic?"

"I can't stop shaking enough to call up a flame."

I sat up, pulling the thin blanket around me. "Let me help. I can call flame."

He smiled. "I know. I was just hoping my magic was strong enough I could do it myself."

"I'd love that," I said. "But I'd also love if we didn't freeze to death while you try."

My hands were so cold my fingertips had gone numb, but I took his hands in mine and rubbed them to warm us both. Then we called magic together, mine strengthening his so the flame we eventually released onto the tinder came from both of us.

He leaned over and kissed my cheek, his lips cold and my skin colder. But the tinder caught and then the kindling. He called up another tiny flame to dance in his palm. "This is sure a long way from setting the Queen's favorite couch on fire."

I pulled the blanket over both of us, and we huddled together. "We'll be okay," I said.

"Well, if we die, at least we die together."

"Don't, Kier. Don't joke about that. I almost lost you twice. I can't do that again."

He pulled me closer and, despite the cold, his touch brought heat to my skin. "I know, beloved. I'm sorry. I have a terrible sense of humor."

"I think I like your penis jokes better," I said, and he laughed.

When he kissed me again, his lips on mine were no longer cold. They were hot, and I was hot with the fire between us — and not the one that now burned in its ring of stones with a merry yellow flame.

The fire that lived in my heart, in my belly, in my groin, that flared up when he was near, and became an inferno when he touched me, was just beneath the surface.

"I'm yours," he said.

And before I could reply, darkness swirled around me again and carried me away to somewhere just as dark, only it smelled like fir needles and autumn leaves, and the cold was only a sharp chill and not a bone-aching freeze.

I was crouched in a tree, looking down on a well-used path, listening for footsteps. I balanced easily, my toes wrapping around the branch I perched on like a bird's, holding me steady. I heard movement somewhere, but it was too dark for my day-dweller's eyes to make out much beyond the shapes of trees. I hoped I would be able to see well enough to do what I needed to do.

A soft footstep carried to me on the night air. I reached for the knives strapped to my thighs and slid them free, one in each hand. Their hilts were shaped to Kiernan's hands, not mine, but they felt comfortable, oddly familiar, like they recognized me, almost.

Soon.

There. More footsteps. I probably would never have heard them, except the person making them was wearing ridiculous, fancy court shoes with tall heels that made silent walking impossible. Then almost below me, a gleam of dark red hair and I loosened the grip of my toes on the branch and prepared to drop.

A shift again and I was in the cave, kneeling in front of the pool of blind fish, and a tall, shadowy shape rose out of the water. She had long hair like blood and shadows, huge antlers curved and sharp, and eyes that glowed like a fox's in the wisplight.

"Silver bird," she said, and I shivered. "Let me help you save him."

And darkness came again and I was back in my body, headache coming on fast, feeling like my skull would split open and spill my brains out onto the bed. And it would be a relief.

I felt my limbs shiver and my back spasm one last time and it *hurt*. It hurt so much I gasped. But then it was gone and I was limp, curled on my side on a bed that smelled like Kiernan. Like Kiernan and me and sex.

And I knew what I had to do to save him, to return his magic to him, so I was smiling when I opened my eyes and saw a fox the color of a bed of well-tended coals watching me from an amber gaze.

18
Kiernan

Iheld Fionn's head in my lap and stroked his hair and told him all the things I hadn't wanted to say to his face, because I didn't want to upset him.

I told him I hated that he had to be so far away, and hated even more that I had left him with a King who required his Seer to also be his pleasure boy. I told him I would kill his King for him, and I wasn't being hyperbolic. Maybe my Queen had despaired of me ever developing a casual attitude towards killing – I would never have that. But for Fionn, I would kill and feel no regret.

I held him gently, put his arms and legs and wings back into comfortable positions when his back seized or his muscles flailed, and wiped drool from his mouth. He looked adorable with saliva dripping down his chin, but I would never tell him so. And I told him I loved him, that I was there, and that nothing would make me leave while he needed me.

Knowing he couldn't hear me made it all easier to say, even though none of it was secret.

His wisplight hovered over us, uncertain and flickering, but somehow still burning, as if – even lost in visions – he knew I'd be in complete darkness if he didn't keep a light going for me.

And even though I was worried that the vision was going longer than I thought was usual for him, I was happy. He needed me. Watching over him while he was vulnerable was something I could do for him, and I wanted to be the one keeping him safe always. Selfishly, I wanted to be the *only* one he trusted to guard him while he was gone.

"I love you, pretty bird," I said, and dared to brush a kiss on his forehead.

A hint of movement caught my eye and I looked around to see Ember at the cave's entrance. She trotted across the space and looked at me expectantly.

«I can't, Ember,» I said. «I can't leave him.»

She looked at Fionn, moved closer to poke his side with her nose, then leapt back when he twitched and one arm flailed out.

I tucked his arm back under the blanket. «He's having a vision,» I said. «You'll have to go get Siona. I can't leave him.»

She looked from me to Fionn and back. I didn't know how much she really comprehended even when I had my magic. Could she understand me at all without it?

She turned and left the cave, quickly disappearing into the dark.

I wanted to kiss Fionn again, as if maybe he could feel me there even if he couldn't hear me, but his back spasms had grown more frequent, so I didn't dare. I didn't mind if I took a crack to the skull, but I didn't want *him* to be hurt. So I just held him gently, kept him covered so he wouldn't get cold, and rearranged his limbs as they needed it.

I seemed like forever before I heard movement in the cave

again, and I was really beginning to worry about the length of Fionn' vision. Even if the vision itself was safe, his muscles were going to be in agony after.

«What's happened?» Siona said as she stepped quietly into the cave. There was warmth in her voice and in her eyes when she turned her sightless gaze towards me.

«He's having a vision,» I said. «But it seems long. Too long.»

«You told me he had seizures,» she said. «But I didn't realize they were so severe.» She moved closer to lay a cautious hand on his forehead, then shook her head. «If I stop them, it will interfere with the vision, perhaps wake him too soon. And it's never a good idea to wake a Seer in the midst of a vision.»

«What do I do?» I said. «How much time do we have before the feast?»

«You will go to the palace, and bathe, and dress in clothing even your mother would approve of, and you will be a gracious host.»

«I can't leave him.»

«You must. If you're both late to the feast, or don't make it there at all, there will be talk. And worse, you will insult our guests. I will stay and watch over him until he wakes and then I'll take him back to the guest suite. As far as our Queen knows, he was spending the day with me, anyway.»

«Please, Siona. You can't make me leave him. He needs me.»

She sighed and sat on the edge of the bed. Ember jumped up, too, but kept her distance from Fionn and his twitching limbs.

«Son of my heart, what he needs is for you to keep your tryst secret. Not from our people, but from *his*.»

«But —»

«What will happen to him if his King learns he was with

you, after being expressly forbidden from seeing you in any context besides the official delegation? You know your union is forbidden in the Vogel Monarchy, and you have already told me King Sarkot is jealous and possessive.»

I made a frustrated growl and she smiled sadly. «I know, Kiernan. I know it's hard, and I know your heart tells you to stay and protect him. But Ember and I will watch over him. No outside harm can come to him here, and I am better equipped to deal with visions that you are.»

«Fuck,» I said, but I knew she was right. He needed me to play my role as Prince of Morven Forest more right now than he needed me as his beloved and his protector. I tucked a pillow under his head and stood up, reaching for my clothes. I dressed quickly, not sure if my buttons even lined up, and strapped my sword and my knives back into place.

Then I touched his face gently, brushed a stubborn strand of hair from his forehead, and took a step back, still reluctant to leave. Fionn's back twisted and Siona caught him before he rolled off the bed and settled him back into place. She was so delicate looking that I forgot, sometimes, how strong she was.

«Go, Kiernan. I promise you your beloved will be safe.»

«Tell him I love him,» I said. «When he wakes»

She nodded and I made my way back through the caves, moving quickly even without light, as I had done many times as a boy, having dared myself to walk from the entrance to the bed chamber and back without light, and without walking into a wall.

If I knew where I was going, darkness was no hindrance.

WHEN I ARRIVED at the feast, having collected the Vogel delegation on my way, the Queen and her entourage were already seated. My sisters sat to one side of her, and my aunt and uncle – a dour and silent noble Sidhe I rarely spoke to – sat on the other. An empty place waited for Siona.

I made the introductions, running through the appropriate ritual phrases and making sure no one important was left out. When my Queen nodded, a surprisingly pleased look on her face, I showed Councilor Rocsh to his seat near the head of one of the tables that made a U shape with the Queen's table, and let an attendant show the trade negotiators their places with the lesser nobles.

"I've made arrangements for your attendants and guards to eat after the feast, Councilor," I said, low enough my Queen wouldn't hear. "I'm afraid it would offend the sensibilities of our nobles to have them dine with us, though I would prefer they did, myself."

"Would you, indeed?" he said, and inclined his head graciously. As I left him, I noticed he turned to his attendant, presumably to relay the information, and the man looked at me with open curiosity.

My own seat, on the other leg of the U, directly across from the empty place left for Fionn, was to the left of my sisters. They ignored me, as I expected they would.

Sean was seated to my left, leaving us to spend the whole meal bumping elbows, since he was right-handed, and Padraig was on his other side.

"When next we feast, my son," my Queen said, once I was sitting, "Perhaps you will have your cousins standing behind you as your guards, as is your right." I noticed my aunt scowl and let one corner of my mouth twitch up. She looked away.

I could hardly blame her, though. As the Queen's sister was officially a Princess of Morven Forest, her legitimate son

should by rights have been declared a Prince at his birth. I could only assume my mother enjoyed tormenting her sister by withholding the title. Or maybe she thought Sean was as much a waste of respect as I did.

"I'm not sure I want Sean where I can't see him, my Queen," I said.

She smiled, showing teeth, and said, "I know your feelings on the matter, my son. But he and Padraig are your Prince's Guard, and you should start treating them as such."

She turned away from me and waved a hand, and servants began to deliver wine and other beverages as the last arrivals to the feast settled themselves.

"What has happened to your Seer, Councilor?" she said, lifting her cup to her lips as soon as it was filled and ignoring the dryad who had filled it.

"A vision, Queen of Morven," Councilor Rocsh said. "We are hopeful he will join us soon."

"I presume my Seer is with him?"

"That is my understanding," Rocsh replied.

"Is your Seer often indisposed when taken with visions? Mine tends to have them quickly and return to her normal duties immediately after." Her voice was mild, showing only polite curiosity, but I think Rocsh heard the rebuke in it as clearly as I did. I wondered how much his King and my Queen were alike.

He glanced at me, then away, and said, "Our Seer was born… traumatically, Queen of Morven." *His* voice was also mild but held its own soft warning. He seemed a very even-tempered man, but I wouldn't want to get on his bad side. "He is small compared to other Vogel, and frail. His visions are accompanied by seizures."

I would hardly call Fionn *frail*; he was strong, even if he was short next to others of his people, and pale, and small-winged. I took a strawberry from a plate a servant held towards me and stuffed it in my mouth to keep from speaking up in Fionn's defense. The two King's Guards stationed behind Councilor Rocsh watched me with narrowed eyes, as if they suspected me of something nefarious, and were just waiting for me to slip.

The sound of the main palace doors opening and closing had nearly everyone looking that way, me included. I tried not to stare as Fionn and Siona walked between the tables, his guards and attendant following. But he was the only one I saw. He was dressed in pure white – a flowing moth silk tunic over fine linen – and his face was carefully made up to hide the shadows under his eyes and to give his cheeks color. His big silver eyes were outlined in blue like the Seer I had seen pictured on the walls under the Eyrie. He looked like a being from some other world, like a deity come to walk the mortal lands.

He met my eyes and held the look for a heartbeat before looking away. I could tell by the way he moved that he was in pain. His back muscles were probably strained, and he always got a headache after a vision. I wished I could take him away from here, to somewhere private where I could rub soothing salve onto his back and make him a cup of tea.

Despite the aches, he moved like something ethereal, and even my Queen was watching him with something that could have been awe when I shot a glance at her.

When they reached the table, Siona bowed her head and Fionn sank into an elegant curtsey. "I hope I may be forgiven my tardiness, Queen of Morven Forest," he said, and even his voice sounded unreal. It hardly seemed the same voice as the one I had recently heard moaning my name and begging me not to stop touching him.

"Of course, Seer Tokka. I do hope you're feeling better.

Please sit and enjoy the feast my son has arranged for you." He glanced at me again, then moved around the table to his seat when she gestured. Siona touched his shoulder gently as she passed, and he smiled at her. I felt warm inside to see the two people I loved most interacting so.

It was hard not to stare at him, sitting directly across from me, hard not to keep meeting his eyes, and smiling. It was even harder not to completely ignore him, which would have been just as suspicious – more so, since I was known for trying to seduce every pretty visitor to my Queen's court.

Only once, just before dessert, did I slip, and then it was only a secret smile across the open space. But Padraig noticed and leaned across Sean to say, "I hear you talked *that* pretty morsel into letting you fuck him while you were in Aven. I'm sincerely impressed, cousin."

Under the table, I reached across Sean's lap and pricked the inside of Padraig's thigh with a knife. I said, smiling pleasantly and keeping my voice light, "Speak of him like that again, and I'll remove your tackle for you, and your father will have to will his estates to your closest cousin, if he wants to keep his line intact."

Sean took my wrist and moved my hand away. «You're both disgusting,» he said. «And I'm pretty sure *I'm* his closest cousin.»

"Or *I* am," I said, sheathing my knife and picking up my cup of wine. "And speak Islish; it's rude to use a language our guests can't understand."

"I think your sisters are," said Padraig, entirely unbothered by having just had my knife in his crotch. He hadn't learned, yet, to tell when I was joking and when I wasn't. He ought to pay a little more attention to Sean, who had learned that lesson a long time ago.

As the feast went on, Fionn looked like he was having

more and more trouble focusing on the conversation around him, and I wished there was some way I could make this easier for him. I raised my voice to carry across to the opposite table and said, "Councilor Rocsh?"

"Yes, Prince Kiernan?" the Councilor said, turning away from the noble Sidhe next to him who had been saying something tedious about the products produced by his estates.

"Would you and your people join me for the morning meal? I've scheduled a meeting for our trade negotiators to begin talks, but I was hoping we could start our own discussions more informally."

"I would enjoy that, Prince of Morven," he said, inclining his head. "May I inquire which of us I should bring with me?"

"You and your Seer," I said. "Your attendants. Your guards if you like." I glanced pointedly at the King's Guards and then away. The corner of his mouth twitched.

"Speaking of guards," said the Queen, and everyone at the head table went quiet. "Perhaps our guests would like to see a demonstration of Sidhe sword skills."

"Now?" I said. "I had thought leading up to Autumn Balance we would have a show of skills."

She smiled. "Why not now? There's plenty of room between the tables." She gestured to the space in the middle of the U shape, which I thought hardly qualified as "plenty."

"I would enjoy a demonstration," said Councilor Rocsh, perhaps sensing the tension between us. If she was going to have me arrange this thing, she should just let me do it. But she was Queen and anything she wished to happen would.

"Which guards did you have in mind, my Queen?" I said and felt my stomach sink as her smile grew.

"Our two best swordsmen, of course," she said. "We don't want to offend our guests with a show of inferior skills." Her smile was so wide she was showing her sharp canines.

Fuck.

"Tell me, sister," she turned to my aunt, who looked sharply up from her plate, startled to be singled out. "Who are our two best with the sword?"

My aunt spoke quietly, barely audible to anyone not at our table. "My son," she said. "And yours."

"I think you mean *my* son first, and yours second," the Queen said, and once I would have felt proud that she thought me a better swordsman than Sean. Now, I didn't care *what* she thought. I had been able to beat Sean regularly since I returned from my father's stronghold when I was sixteen.

"Come now!" The Queen clapped and servants hurried to clear dishes and bring more wine.

I glanced across at Fionn, who looked like he was barely holding himself upright. But he was watching everything with bright, intelligent eyes.

I looked at Sean, who bared his teeth at me in something resembling a smile. Or maybe it was a grimace.

"I'll fucking kill you," he said.

"Not unless you want to answer to our Queen," I said. "And not unless I suddenly get struck down by a falling tree branch and lose the use of all my limbs." I stood and lifted my sword from where it hung on the back of my chair. "I'll hand you your fucking ass, cousin. Again."

And I hopped directly over the table and into the clear spot between, drew my sword, laid the sheath on the table, and waited.

"Really, my son," said the Queen, after a long moment of silence. I prepared for her to chastise me for jumping over the table. "Have some respect for your tailor."

I glanced at her in surprise and cursed myself for reacting at all. "My Queen?"

"Your vest. It's lovely work. It would be a shame to damage it."

"You assume I'm going to let Sean get that close." But I unbuttoned my elaborately embroidered vest one-handed and slipped out of it. It was covered in a pattern of oak leaves, deep green at the bottom and gradually becoming more yellow, then orange, and finally red at the shoulders. I had chosen it because I thought Fionn might like the thread work – he was a spinner and weaver, not an embroiderer, but I knew he appreciated textile work of all kinds. I handed the vest to Daphnis, who was standing behind my chair.

While I waited for Sean to finish unbuttoning the seemingly endless row of tiny silver circles on his jacket, I swung my sword a few times to warm up and assess the space. It was tight, and we would be fighting close enough for our swords to touch at almost all times.

"Our Prince Kiernan is the finest sword-wielder in Morven," my Queen said. I wasn't certain that was true, since I suspected the Captain of her guard – who had trained both Sean and me since we could stand upright – could still take me down if he really wanted to. But if she could say it, she obviously believed it herself. It felt strange, to think she was proud of something I had accomplished.

"He's not *that* good," said Sean, showing that he, at least, still believed he was better than I was. He walked around the table slowly as if to point out how uncouth I had been for jumping over it.

The Queen ignored him. "He was trained here in Morven Forest, as well as by the human court in Great River City and the fortress of Dudoon."

"He's also pretty good with a knife," muttered Padraig, rubbing his thigh under the table, and I almost smiled at him. Instead, I raised an eyebrow, and *he* smiled.

Sean stood next to me, and we faced the Queen and

bowed, then turned to the Vogel delegation and bowed again. Everything in this court was a ritual, a show. Once, I had enjoyed playing my role; now I just wanted something real.

The Queen stood, and when most of the room would have stood also, she held out her hand. "Oh, relax," she said. "My guests." She raised her voice. "Members of the Vogel delegation, members of my court and my council, and all the rest of you, I present my two best sword fighters."

She gestured to me and then Sean. "Prince Kiernan Druison nicFia nor Dudoon nor Morven." I bowed and flashed a cocky grin, as the audience expected me to. I could only assume she was including my father's surname and origin because she was planning to send me to Great River City soon and wanted to remind her court why I was chosen as ambassador. "And Sean nicCraig nicFia nor Morven." He scowled. It had to sting that she hadn't granted him the title Prince yet, even though he qualified for it.

She looked around the room, and all eyes were on her. I looked away, met Fionn's eyes instead, and let a smile curve up the corners of my lips. He looked exhausted, and his hands were tight around the stem of his glass, like it was all that kept him upright, but there was heat in the look he gave me, and I felt my skin warm, like it had spread from him to me.

I made myself look away before I did something stupid like mouth, "I love you." I almost winked – I was known as a flirt, so it wouldn't have roused suspicion, but I resisted anyway. It would be too easy to cross the space between tables and drag his mouth over to mine.

"The rules are simple," said the Queen. "The first one disarmed loses. Anyone who draws blood loses." She smiled coldly. "Bruises and broken bones are acceptable."

I took a deep breath, glad I had been working on my disarming techniques since I got back from the Eyrie. Once I regained enough strength to swing a sword. I was an efficient killer, but less good at non-lethal combat.

The Queen sat back down. "Prepare," she said, and Sean and I faced each other and took one long step back. It was all there was room for. "Begin."

I held my sword ready, balanced in fighting stance, but didn't move. Neither did Sean. We stared at each other across the small space that separated us. Or, at least, we *seemed* to stare at each other. I was actually watching the triangle made by his head and shoulders – any hint of movement would show there first – and I knew he was doing the same to me.

"Oh, come *on*," said Padraig, and he flung a candied blackberry at my head. I sidestepped easily, caught the morsel, and popped it into my mouth. And then Sean was moving, striking quickly and smoothly.

I head Fionn's sharp intake of breath behind me, and then I was moving too.

Sean was good with a sword, I had to admit, but he had been fighting the same way since childhood, and I knew his every tell, his favorite strikes and counters, the way he kept his balance.

Of course, he knew mine, too, and he knew I knew his. He tried to move differently than I would be expecting, to lead with his left foot instead of his right, but it made him just the slightest bit awkward. I was one of the only people he couldn't easily defeat with his usual attacks, so he rarely practiced anything else, but I had to respect him for trying.

As for me, once I started moving, I didn't stop. I knew that was *my* weakness – I never let myself rest – but it was also my strength. I kept moving and I never stopped changing the *way* I moved. And today, I chose to fight him right-handed, when he would have been expecting me to use my left.

We had trained with the same swordmaster in my mother's

court, but I had also trained with my father. I had brawled with werewolves, learning how to be quick enough that my smaller size wasn't a disadvantage, and I had thrown knives with fauns and learned how to hit a target when I didn't have time to think about where that target even was.

I learned everything I could about edged weapons from anyone who would teach me, until my knives and my sword were like extensions of my own body. And I had then trained my body mercilessly.

I broke Sean's nose before his blade got anywhere close by stepping inside his guard instead of away. He still expected opponents to try to flee from his sword, even now, when there was no room. A quick punch with my right hand, wrapped around the hilt of my sword, and I heard bone crunch. I didn't care that I'd lose if his nose started to bleed; I just wanted to humiliate him.

He stepped back, out of my reach, and though his nose was crooked, it didn't bleed. And, to his credit, be didn't let the blow slow him down.

"You really need to learn some new tricks, cousin," I said, and let his next strike come close enough to give him some confidence. I hated him, and I didn't intend to let him win easily, but if he was going to be guarding me, I wanted him as good a fighter as he could be.

He lunged and I slipped away, noting that he wasn't aiming to disarm me at all; he was aiming to kill.

19
Fionn

I COULDN'T HELP BUT WORRY when the Queen of Morven Forest announced a swordfighting demonstration, with Kiernan as one of the combatants. I knew he could look after himself, and that he was very good with a sword, but naked blades in the cramped space between tables seemed like a very bad idea, even if the Queen decreed that no blood would be shed.

I had tried not to watch Kier too closely during the meal, but my eyes were drawn to him, over and over, and I probably drank too much wine trying to hide the fact that I was staring at him.

I was exhausted and finding it hard to concentrate on the conversations around me, but when he jumped over the table and drew his sword, all eyes turned to Kier and I didn't have to hide my glances anymore. If I looked away, I would be the only one *not* looking at him.

And he was beautiful. I had never seen him do much more than practice swings; this was something else entirely. He moved like quicksilver, slipping past his cousin again and again, making the other man look slow and clumsy, even though I could see he was also skilled.

"Well, I'm bored," said his other cousin – Padraig, I think I remember the Queen calling him. "Kiernan's just playing with him." I didn't think that was *quite* true; though it didn't look like Kier was in any danger of losing, to my untrained eye, his opponent seemed to be holding his own.

"Would you like to give your cousin some help?" said the Queen. Her voice was amused.

"Which cousin?" Padraig stood and removed his coat. Kiernan tilted his head slightly, like he heard and noted the movement, but he otherwise didn't react.

"Which one do you think needs help?" said the Queen.

"I don't need help," snarled Sean, executing a very neat strike at Kiernan's head. Kier slipped aside, but it looked like Sean had come closer to hitting him than I felt comfortable with. Sean looked like he was trying to injure Kier, not disarm him.

Padraig rounded the table and Kiernan slipped away from Sean again, so he didn't end up caught between them.

"No bloodshed," said the Queen, as Sean lunged again, sword aimed at Kier's gut, while Padraig slashed at his blade, hitting it hard.

I held my breath to keep from making some sound that would reveal my worry for Kier. A sound that might distract him.

So fast I almost couldn't follow, Kier moved around Sean's blade, grabbed his wrist with his free hand, and pulled his cousin past while he batted Padraig's sword aside. He put his back to the table, so close to me I could see the damp skin on the back of his neck, and switched his sword to his left hand, drawing one of his knives with his right. One of the knives I had been holding in my vision.

I was starting to wish I hadn't eaten so much. I was definitely wishing I hadn't had so much wine. I clutched the stem of my glass to anchor myself and tried to keep my breathing even. I wanted to scream at his cousins to leave him alone, and I wanted to jump over the table and kiss him.

"He's stopped dancing around," said Padraig. "He must be getting tired."

"I'm just trying to keep both of you in sight," Kiernan said.

This time, it was Padraig who lunged while Sean engaged Kier's sword, and though he twisted away, Padraig caught the fabric of Kier's shirt with the tip of his blade.

"Nice one," Kier said, sheathing his knife, ducking under Sean's wild swing, and slipping right out of his shirt, leaving it flapping on the end of Padraig's sword.

My chest felt suddenly tight, like I couldn't get enough air. I knew I was staring but I couldn't help it. Kiernan's chest and arms gleamed with a thin sheen of sweat, and muscles bunched and flowed under his skin with every movement. I felt myself getting hard inside my sheath and clenched my belly muscles desperately.

I had seen him shirtless before, of course. I had seen him completely naked and panting with desire. But this… this was different. He was deadly, and I was reminded of the dangerous killer he could be, that I had only seen once before, and then it had been in the dark of night, and I had hardly been able to see him or the knife he killed the Alfar scout with.

Now, the light was clear on his bronze skin, picking out each muscle and vein, turning the movements of his sword to a dazzling trail of silver in the air, and I felt a prickle of fear. *This* was who he really was. This calm, skilled, deadly warrior. My erection very nearly pushed its way out of my sheath, and I had to clench my teeth not to whimper.

He drew his knife again and waited, balancing his weight

between both feet, to see what they would try next. I let my gaze slip from his chest to his eyes and had to swallow, hard, and look quickly away. He had met my gaze and, though he didn't react outwardly, I had seen in his eyes the same look he had right before leaning over to kiss me. Or to put his mouth somewhere else on my naked skin.

Both his cousins lunged at him at once and he looked away from me just in time to see them begin to move. He met Padraig's blade with his sword and Sean's with his knife, and then he had his back to my table again, and Padraig was rubbing his wrist with his free hand.

"Ow," he said. "You hit hard, cousin."

"I didn't realize I'd have to go easy on you," Kiernan said, his smoky voice sending a zap of desire right to my crotch. I needed to find some calm, and quickly, or I was going to embarrass myself.

Padraig laughed and adjusted his stance and Kier moved, spinning towards his cousin, and sheathing his knife again so he could take the sword right out of Padraig's hand.

"Fuck," the other man said, staring at his empty palm. Kier shoved him out of the space between tables with his shoulder and turned to face Sean again.

For a moment, Kiernan held both swords in his hands, as if testing their balance together, but then he tossed his cousin's blade behind him, as if trusting the other to catch it.

"Your turn," he said, and Sean lunged. Kiernan stepped aside and tripped Sean on his way by, then chopped his forearm onto his cousin's wrist. Sean cursed as his sword dropped from his hand.

When Kiernan put his sword on the table and bowed to his Queen, I felt like I could breathe properly again. I carefully unclenched my hands from my wine glass and made myself look at the color of the beverage instead of staring at Kier's muscular shoulders.

He turned, then, to our delegation and bowed again, and I saw the little quirk at the corner of his mouth that meant he was trying not to smile when he looked at me.

As he straightened up, I caught movement behind him and stared too long, wondering if I was really seeing a knife plunging past Kier's shoulder. I started to push myself up from my chair. "Kier —"

He turned his head in time to see Sean's dagger descending. From the angle I was at, I could tell Sean wasn't aiming for Kiernan, though from nearly anywhere else in the room it would look like he was. His blade was headed towards where I had just been leaning on the table.

Desperately, I reached for Kier, but he was already moving, spinning around as Sean's knife grazed his shoulder. His cousin froze with Kier's fingers around his neck.

"That's hardly sporting, cousin," Kiernan said, and twisted further to grab Sean's knife hand and dig his fingers in. Sean dropped the knife onto the table. There was blood on it, and I hoped it was only from a superficial wound. I was afraid to look, to make sure Kiernan was okay.

Sean pulled abruptly away, and Kiernan straightened and faced the Queen again, and I sagged back into my chair.

"Our winner," the Queen said, clapping her hands. "Prince Kiernan nicFia!"

As the crowd clapped, I dared to turn and meet Kiernan's eyes. The look there told me he had noticed Sean was aiming for me, too, even if the Queen had chosen not to see it. Even if the Queen had chosen not to reprimand Sean for attacking after he had lost the fight.

I tore my eyes away from Kier as he turned to bow to the crowd and pretend everything was fine.

Back in our guest rooms, I made myself a strong pain relief tea – the kind with a sedative in it – knowing I would sleep badly without it. I let Neeka undress me, and run a bath for me, and help me into bed.

<You must be exhausted, Seer Tokka,> she said. <You're not even *trying* to do everything yourself.>

I'm not even sure I answered her, I fell so quickly into sleep. I didn't wake all night, but I had nightmares about Kier's cousin Sean attacking me with a knife, over and over. In some of them, his blade sank deep into my flesh while Kiernan watched helpless, unable to reach me in time. In others, Kiernan *did* reach me, and Sean's knife struck his heart, and he died in my arms as I screamed for help.

Finally, the nightmares faded, and I slipped into a strange sequence of what seemed like memories of flying, and of meeting Kiernan before I ever possibly could have.

I woke feeling as if I had not slept at all, but I refused Neeka's offer of concealing makeup. I wanted to look like myself when we had the morning meal with Kiernan, not like Seer Tokka.

He welcomed us to his rooms with a handclasp for each of us, including our attendants and guards – only my own guards came with us, fortunately. I was certain his hand lingered on mine, and his fingers brushed my palm as he let go.

"It must be quite an adjustment," Councilor Rocsh said, his Islish smooth and cultured. "Having to play host to day-dwellers such as we are."

Kiernan shrugged and poured tea, handing us cups with his own hands. His attendant dryad was nowhere to be seen. "Most think of the Sidhe as night-dwellers, but we love the twilight hours the best."

"Which is why you scheduled our meetings in the early mornings and evenings, when we're all comfortable."

Kier smiled and sat next to me on a couch, keeping a respectable distance. "Exactly. I'm afraid the Autumn Balance celebrations are a night-time event, however. I've left the day before clear, so you'll be able to rest."

The rest of the talk as we ate was similarly inconsequential and didn't require much thought. I found myself relaxing and simply enjoying the company, and the way that Kiernan treated our attendants and guards exactly the same as he treated Councilor Rocsh and me soon had them relaxing, too.

Even Konta took off his bird mask and sat on a chair with a plate balanced on his knee. He eyed the array of dishes on the table with suspicion.

"You don't have anything here for cleaning your fingers, do you?"

Kiernan's eyebrows drew together slightly and I thought he looked confused. "There are napkins." He pointed at a pile of neatly folded linen squares.

"I don't think even Konta would eat *those* by accident," said Trikta, earning an elbow in the ribs from the older Seer's Guard.

Kiernan's frown deepened. "I think I missed something," he said.

Neeka looked at Konta and then at Kiernan, a cheeky grin on her lips. "After the welcome feast," she said, ignoring Konta's poisonous look, "When we were eating with the rest of the attendants and guards, Konta ate the fruit slice out of one of those bowls they put by each plate." Her grin grew and she chuckled. "Then he drank the liquid and said it was delicious." She put her hand over her mouth but couldn't hold in her laughter. "He asked for more, in a bigger bowl." She leaned on my shoulder and turned her face to muffle her mirth in the sleeve of my shirt.

Konta's tanned cheeks flushed red, and he stared down at

his plate. "Why would anyone put fruit in water meant for washing in?" he said gruffly. "The whole rest of the evening the palace staff asked me if I'd like to eat various inedible things." He scratched the back of his neck and a hint of a smile tugged at his mouth. "'Here, Seer's Guard,' they'd say. 'Try this shoe. The leather is fresh and delicious.'" He snorted.

"I could see how the staff would find that amusing," said Kiernan carefully. I could tell he was trying not to smile.

"By the end of the night," said Neeka, "They were all saying, 'Do Vogel eat this?' or, 'Do bird folk eat that.' Finally, Konta just stood up and said, 'Didn't you know Vogel will eat anything?' and stomped off back to our rooms. For the rest of the meal, I kept hearing people say, 'Didn't you know Vogel will eat anything?' like it was the funniest thing they had ever heard."

"I suppose it *was* pretty funny," said Konta.

Kier looked at me and I met his eyes. "I'm sure they didn't mean anything by it," he said. "But it does seem unkind."

"It's not entirely untrue, though," I said. "Vogel digestion is very strong. It's helpful, when the peasants are starving, that we can eat rancid meat and moldy fruit and not get sick."

Kiernan cocked his head, his brows gathered in a frown again. "I'm sorry that ever has to happen." He took my hand and squeezed my fingers before letting go.

"Well, it makes for a good story to tell the other guards back home," said Konta, finally reaching to pile food on his plate.

After we had all eaten well and talk began to lag, Councilor Rocsh stood, and everyone else stood, too. "Thank you for a very pleasant morning," he said, and Kiernan nodded.

"I was happy to speak with all of you away from the formalities of court."

"I'll check in with our negotiators, and see you at the next joint meeting?"

Kier nodded. "I've good hope we can wrap up whatever needs negotiating in the next couple of days so you can spend the rest of your visit enjoying our hospitality."

Rocsh clasped Kier's hand and then turned to me. "Seer Tokka." I thought I saw the slightest smile touch his lips. "In the interest of, as Prince Kiernan says, wrapping things up, I thought you might outline your trade requirements as healer this afternoon." He looked back at Kiernan. "And perhaps Prince Kiernan can suggest the best approach for our meeting with the negotiators."

Kiernan blinked in surprise but didn't otherwise react. "Of course. I'll help in any way I can."

Rocsh nodded and gestured for Neeka and my guards to precede him out into the hall. "If I may borrow your guards?" he said.

"Oh! Of course."

Trikta and Konta looked like they might protest, but Neeka said, "I'm sure Prince Kiernan and his exceptional sword skills can keep our Seer safe."

"Thank you," said Kiernan softly as everyone filed out and the Councilor paused, Nikna hovering next to him, one hand touching the small of Rocsh's back.

"I do understand," Rocsh said, and looked at Nikna, who smiled and dropped his eyes.

"At the Eyrie," Kier said, his hand on the outer door. "You said you didn't approve."

"I said it was forbidden," Rocsh said. "And I hoped he would recover once you were gone. But one doesn't get over a heart bond." Then he turned and left Kiernan and me alone in his sitting room.

I stood in the middle of the room as Kier closed and locked the outer door, and then the one to the anteroom. I suddenly didn't know what to do with my hands. Or my face.

He stood for a moment with his back to me, as if he was as unsure as I was. As if we hadn't been intimate so short a time ago.

"How's your shoulder?" I finally said, just to break the silence.

He turned. "One of our healers treated it. It'll be healed by tomorrow."

"I… He was aiming for me," I said.

He took a step towards me, then another, and put his hands on my shoulders. I had to work not to collapse into his arms.

"I saw," he said, and I breathed easier. It was hardly comforting, of course, that one of Kier's own guards wanted to hurt me, but it was nice to know I hadn't imagined it.

"He also looked like he was trying to hurt *you*," I said. "Not disarm you."

"I noticed that, too." He pulled me close and wrapped his arms around me, careful of my wings. He laid his head on my chest, and I rested my cheek against his hair. He was so strong that I forgot sometimes that I was taller.

"Keep away from him if you can," he said. "I'll make sure Sean is watched."

"But why? Why hurt me? Why hurt you?"

"I don't know. He hates me. He hates non-fey. Maybe that's enough."

I realized I had my hands clenched in the fabric of his shirt, and I made them relax and smoothed the material over his back. "Are we really going to talk about trade?"

He laughed into my tunic. "We can if you want to." He let go of me and stepped back. "How are your feet?"

I looked down at my toes, as if I'd forgotten they were attached. "They're –" I stopped myself from giving an automatic, and not really true, answer. "They're a bit sore. It was a long walk from the ship."

"Sit." He pointed to a couch and went to the sideboard where he had poured us tea and rummaged in the cupboard. "Do you want more tea?"

"No," I said. "I think you've already fed me a whole pot. I might start sloshing if I have more." I sat on the couch.

He turned around, smiling. "Where are your serpents?" He sat on the table in front of me and opened the jar he'd taken from the cupboard. I smelled swordleaf.

"I left them on the ship." I leaned back on the couch and let myself relax as he lifted one of my feet onto his lap and began to rub salve on the sole.

I squeaked when he dug his thumbs into the muscle, and he chuckled but rubbed more gently. I laid my head on the back of the couch.

"And they agreed to stay there?"

"No. I mean they did, but I don't expect them to be patient. They'll appear any moment and scold me for leaving them behind."

He smiled, but kept his attention on my foot, rubbing until my whole body felt limp. Then he put that foot on the floor and picked up the other one.

"They have a gift for you," I said, letting my eyes droop closed.

"For me? What is it?"

"I promised not to tell. I'm to give it you at Autumn Balance, assuming they don't appear to gift it themselves."

"I won't be able to understand them," he said, softly.

"I know." I opened my eyes again. "I had a vision of us as old men again. And another where I was back in the Eyrie, and the fever had broken out." I didn't tell him about *seeing* myself in a tree with his knives in hand, waiting to kill someone for him.

His hands stayed gentle on my foot. "We'll make sure you have as much salt-leaf as you need," he said. "And I'll see if Siona has any ideas for making it more effective."

"I think I was trying to figure out how spirit travel could possibly be part of the cure."

He looked up but kept rubbing the sole of my foot.

"In my vision," I said. "I made a tea that allowed me to leave my body, to move in my spirit body instead, but before I could figure out how to use the ability to help cure the fever, I… I traveled away. To here."

He slipped a finger between my toes, and I couldn't hold in a gasp. Why did him touching me there feel so erotic?

He smiled and moved his fingers away. "Did you save me again?"

I shook my head. "I only *saw* myself in the cave. But… last night I dreamed… I've started to remember, Kier." I sat up and put my foot on the floor. "I had terrible dreams, but then… I started to remember all the times I've spirit traveled before. I thought it was only once or twice, but it was more."

"You came here when my Queen took my magic," he said, thoughtfully. "And you borrowed Daphnis's body."

"Yes. I thought that was the first time, but it wasn't. I've done it before. And I only had to borrow his body that time because without your magic, you couldn't see me. Or touch me."

I leaned forward and put my face in my hands. There was so much to tell him, and so little time. He touched my hair, then moved his hands to my shoulders.

"Take off your shirt and lie on the couch, pretty bird," he said. "Let me rub your back. You must be sore after your vision yesterday."

"I'm *remembering*," I said.

"Tell me whatever you need to," he said. "Talk about it as much as you can and maybe the memories will come clear. And while you do, let me ease your pain."

My back *did* ache. I pulled off my tunic and shirt and lay on my belly on the couch. My legs hung off the end, and I didn't know what to do with my wings.

Kiernan rose and crouched over me, a knee on each side of my hips. He stroked both hands down my back, then began to rub the swordleaf salve into my shoulders, working the muscles with his thumbs. For a long moment I just lay there, feeling his touch and trying not to become aroused.

Then I said, "The first time I had a vision of you, I was three, and it terrified me."

"You told me," he said. "You *saw* my mother take my antlers."

"Yes. It was the sort of vision when I *see* things as they're happening."

"Mmm." He pushed his hands down the muscles along my spine and I felt like I might melt into the couch. "Does this hurt?"

"A little, but it feels good, too."

His fingers splayed out to rub the muscles between my ribs, moving carefully over and around my feathers. Then he lifted one of my wings in one hand, and gently rubbed with the other, careful to only move with the direction my feathers lay.

"Oh!" I said. "That feels lovely."

He switched to my other wing.

"That was the first time the raven came and took me out of my body. Later, all I remembered was the vision, and being afraid."

"Where did the raven take you?" He moved his hands back to my shoulders, then down to the small of my back, slipping between my feathers and making my skin feel hot.

"Dudoon," I said.

His hands stopped. "When I was six, my mother took my antlers and put me on a horse and sent me to my father, in Dudoon. The day I arrived, I learned I had an older half-brother. I was so excited to meet him." He paused and resumed rubbing my back again, working more salve into my lower back, careful not to let it clump my feathers together.

"Half a day later, I learned my brother hated me before we even met, because our father divorced his mother to marry mine."

"He beat you," I whispered.

He kept stroking my muscles, so gently it almost tickled. "That first night, I lay awake in my bed. I wasn't used to sleeping at night, and I was alone in a fortress of human soldiers, disappointed that my father was distant and my brother, who I had wanted so much like me, didn't want anything to do with me. I wanted so badly to go home. I was afraid, and unwanted."

"You cried."

"Yes." He shifted his weight to my thighs and began to rub the muscles in my hips. "I lay in my bed, curled up as small as I could make myself – and since I was still a child, and Sidhe, that was pretty small." He laughed, but it sounded sad. "And I stared into the dark, trying to find the courage to run away. And… a little boy came into my room, so pale I thought he was a ghost at first. But then I saw that he had wings, and I thought he was a spirit of air."

His hands paused on my hips, then began to rub again.

"He wasn't a ghost or a spirit," I said.

"I remember he looked as lost and afraid as I felt, and I wanted to comfort him. So I uncurled myself, and lifted the edge of my blanket, thinking he might be cold."

"I got into bed with you," I said. "And you put your arms

over me and said you would keep me safe."

He laughed again, softly. "I was bigger than you were, then." He slid his hands all the way up my back to my shoulders, then bent to lie against me, his lips brushing my neck. "In the morning, you were gone, and I thought you were a dream. By the next night, I had forgotten you came at all. But I gathered my courage and asked my father to teach me swordfighting, so I could protect people who needed protecting."

He kissed my neck and I shivered. "He laughed at me. I was so tiny, my request must have seemed ridiculous. So, I took a sword from one of his guards and told him I'd started to learn bladework as soon as I could walk, in my mother's court, and I challenged him to fight me. I had no hope against him, of course, but he could see that I at least already knew how to *hold* a sword, even if the one I'd taken was much too big for me. So he taught me, and that gave me the strength to stay, to learn what I could from him. For a few years, anyway."

I wriggled under him until he sat up to let me roll over. I couldn't meet his eyes for a moment, but I made myself get out the words that flooded my mouth. "I think I've loved you ever since you put your arms around me and told me you'd keep me safe."

"You were my first friend," he said. "The first person who saw *me* and not a Prince."

"You were mine, too."

He smiled, his beautiful full lips curving into my favorite shape. "I suppose, if your Councilor is right and we're heartbonded, it didn't happen nearly as quickly as we thought it did." He touched my cheek. "I only wish we could have met in person sooner."

"At least we remember now."

He leaned over and kissed me, softly, wonderingly, and I buried my hands in his hair and pulled his mouth harder against mine.

20
Kiernan

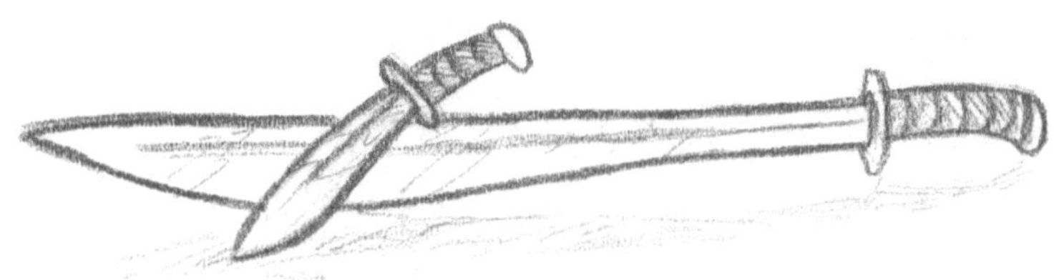

As I rubbed Fionn's back and felt his muscles relax under my hands, I thought about what it would be like to have a life where I could do this for him every time he had a vision. Or even if he'd just had a long day.

That was all I really wanted: a quiet life where Fionn and I could look after each other. And as I massaged each muscle and listened to his soft sighs, I realized it was a life I would fight for – both for myself and for others – if I could figure out who or what I needed to fight in order to get it.

When he rolled over under me and looked up at me with his beautiful silver eyes that could probably see into the core of my being, I wanted to tell him I would take him away from the Eyrie if he'd let me.

Except I knew he cared about his people. I knew he was worried about his vision of fever spreading. And I couldn't do much of anything until I got my magic back. So I leaned down and kissed him softly, tasted his lips, amazed that I was privileged to even touch him at all.

His dug his hands into my hair and pulled me closer, and I was lost. I would always be lost, every time I kissed him. Every time he smiled at me, or held my hand, or said my name.

"You have too many clothes on," he said, so I tugged my shirt over my head and kissed him again, pressing my skin against his.

"Can I touch you, pretty bird?" I said, when I lifted my mouth from his to look into his eyes again.

"You don't have to ask," he said.

"I want to hear you say it." I kissed his neck, and he tilted his head back so I could reach more of his skin with my tongue.

"Touch me, Kier," he said.

I sat up and stroked both hands over his chest, marveling at the softness of his skin over the firmness of his muscles. He made a noise in his throat and arched his back under my touch.

"Can I taste you?" I shifted backwards on the couch and tugged open the buttons at his waist.

"Taste me," he breathed.

I lifted his hips to slide his trousers down, did the same to his undergarment, and he kicked them free of his legs.

"Take yours off, too," he said, so I stood and undid the tie of my trousers, letting them slide off. "All of it," he said, so I smiled and did the same with my undergarment, then stood still a moment while he looked at me. He held out a hand, and I stepped closer. He stroked his palm over my cock and his lips curved into a smile. "You're so hard for me," he said, then scowled when I stepped away again, to kneel beside the couch and run my hands over his skin.

I leaned over and kissed his abdomen, poked my tongue into his bellybutton to make him squirm, then moved the end of the couch, glad this one didn't have arms so I could get between his legs.

He lay back, watching me as I kissed the inside of one knee, then the other, and worked my way up his thigh with my tongue.

"Tease me," he whispered when I licked the crease where his thigh met his pelvis. "I want you to tease me."

"Beloved," I said into his hip, and touched the tip of my tongue to the very top of his seam and felt his muscles tense.

"I like that," he said softly as I traced his seam with my tongue, then my finger, then my tongue again. I licked him a little harder and felt his sheath start to open for me, tasted the sweetness of his lubricant. I slipped my tongue inside his sheath, and his seam opened, and I stroked along the length of his cock as it emerged.

He arched again and groped for my hair, wrapped his hands around my antlers, and fuck that felt good. He pulsed as soon as I slipped my lips over his cock and sweet spunk flooded my mouth.

"Tease me," he said again, so I moved my mouth away and traced his length with one finger, then my tongue, feeling the shape of him, the near point of his silken tip, the smoothness of the flexible scales that covered his upper surface. I felt him tense and slid my mouth over him as he pulsed again, filling my mouth with his honey sweetness.

I shifted so I could touch him with my fingers, too, could slip them into his sheath to coat them in his lubricant, then traced backwards, between his cheeks to his perfect, deep pink asshole.

He gasped and arched against me. "Kier," he said.

I lifted my head to study his face. His eyes were closed, his head tipped back, his lips parted. "Tell me what you want, pretty bird."

"Taste me," he said. "Don't stop."

I flicked my tongue over his tip and rubbed my fingers around his asshole. He whimpered.

"Yes," he said, when I pushed my fingers against him. "Oh, yes."

When I slipped two fingers inside him, he cried out softly and thrust against me, burying his cock in my mouth and pulsing again, shooting his spunk down my throat.

I rubbed him, massaged him from the inside and knew the moment I found that spot that feels so good because he moaned and thrust helplessly against my mouth.

My own cock was painfully hard, but I ignored it, wanting only to bring him pleasure. I could wait.

But he opened his eyes and said, "Please, Kier. I want to feel you inside me. I need to know… I need to remember that you fucking me isn't the same as –" He stopped himself from finishing the sentence, but I already knew the end.

He needed to know I wouldn't fuck him the way his King fucked him.

I pulled my fingers slowly out of him and crawled up the couch. He wrapped one of his long legs around my back and bent the other to press his foot into my shoulder. I turned my head to kiss his ankle.

"Hurry, please," he said. "I need to… I need to finish."

"Guide me in," I said, nibbling on his perfect ear. "Cover me in your slick and put me where you want me."

When he had me coated in lubricant and my tip pressed to his asshole, I gently pushed forward inside him, then shifted my weight so I could wrap my fingers around his cock at the same time.

"Please, Kier," he whispered. "Please."

"Faster?" I said.

"Yes."

"Harder?"

"Yes. Please. Make me… make me pulse again. One more time."

I matched the thrust of my hips to the strokes of my hand, feeling my own pleasure build as I watched him lose himself in my touch.

"Goddess Below, you feel so good," I said, and then I couldn't say anything else because he was pulsing in my hand and I was falling over the edge of my own orgasm, throbbing and spurting into him.

I braced myself, bowed over him, panting, my forehead against his chest, and listened to his breathing, quick and gasping.

"How do you always make me feel so good?" he said, and I lifted my head to meet his eyes.

"I love you," I said, and his beautiful smile spread over his face. I would never tire of seeing him smile like that, and I would never stop trying to find ways to make it happen.

I CARRIED FIONN INTO my bedroom after and tucked him into bed, then got him a cup of water, which he insisted on sharing with me. Then I climbed in with him and held him against my chest, his wings snug between us.

I thought he had fallen asleep, but he stirred and rolled over to face me. He put one arm under the pillow and put his other hand on my chest. His palm was warm.

"When I was six," he said. "The raven came for me again, and took me to Dudoon, to that same cold stone room."

I put my hand over his and he turned his over to lace our fingers together.

"I was nine," I said. "After three years of my father training me, I was better with a sword, and better at hiding, but my brother still hit me more days than he didn't."

He wriggled closer, moving our joined hands to rest on his thigh so he could press his chest to mine and put his face against my hair. He hooked one leg over mine.

"You were angry," he said. "Pacing back and forth across your room, kicking the furniture. I thought… I didn't remember you at first, didn't remember I had visited you before, and I was afraid."

"I wasn't really angry," I said, nuzzling my face into his neck and breathing in the musky sweet scent of his skin. "I was scared. I had decided to run away for real that time, and I was terrified my brother would stop me. That my father would be disappointed. That my mother would send me back as soon as I got home."

"You stopped pacing when you saw me. You just stared at me, and I wanted to cry. But crying meant punishment at the Abbey, so I held in my tears and said, 'Why are you angry?' and you crossed the room and put your arms around me and said you were sorry for frightening me."

"Fionn?"

"Mmm?"

"Why are we remembering this now?" I shifted back so I could look at him. He bit his lip and his pale eyebrows drew together, making a little crease between them. I wanted to touch it, to smooth it away, but one hand was pinned under my head and the other was still holding his.

"When I visited you after you lost your magic, I asked the raven why I didn't remember ever visiting you before." He let go of my hand to rest his palm against my hip, and I reached up to touch my fingertip to the thinking wrinkle between his eyebrows, then cupped his cheek.

"Did it tell you?"

"It only said I would remember when it was time. It didn't say time for what."

"Do you think –" I shook my head.

"Do I think what?" His hand slid over my hip and up to my ribs.

"It seems an awful lot of visions and traveling and magic just to help two boys become friends."

"It does. It's almost like… like we were meant to fall in love."

"But you don't believe in destiny." I didn't either. I hated the idea that my choices might mean nothing.

He frowned again and shook his head. "I don't. If we all have a destiny to fulfill, then what's the point in doing anything? What's the point in choosing?"

I watched his face, loving how every shift in thought and every passionate word showed in his eyes, in the way his mouth moved.

"I'm a seer. I *know* the future changes. The things I *see* in the future are only possibilities, not fixed. We can choose to work towards those possibilities, or we can refuse them."

"But what if… what if something bigger than we are is… I don't know."

"Trying to make things happen?"

I nodded. I didn't like the idea of being a pawn of Gods or spirits. I especially didn't like the idea that I loved Fionn because I was *supposed* to love him.

"I don't know. Why us?"

I smiled then. I couldn't help it. "Well, you're the first Vogel Seer in generations, so it's obvious why you're special."

He echoed my smile. "If I'm so special, why aren't I normal?"

"That doesn't make any sense, pretty bird. And anyway, how is any seer normal?"

He bit my earlobe, probably because his free hand was busy stroking my back so he couldn't poke me.

"I mean my wings. My height. I have seizures when I have visions. None of that is normal."

"Who cares about normal? We're all weird in our own way. And I've decided I don't care if we're being manipulated by Gods or spirits or anything. I care that I love you, and that you love me, and if you don't stop touching me, I'm going to have to pleasure you again."

"I do love you." He didn't stop touching me. In fact, he pulled his arm out from under the pillow to stroke my skin with both hands.

"When I was six and you were nine, I spirit traveled to Dudoon and we stole a horse together and ran away across the river to Morven Forest," he said, picking up the story again.

"And you vanished from the horse halfway back to the Heart of Morven."

"When I was ten, the raven took me to Morven Forest to hold you when you passed out from the pain of —" He stopped and met my eyes, his hands going still.

I knew my breathing had gone ragged and not because he was touching me. I forced it slow and even. "I wedged my antlers into a tree and tore them off myself," I said, my insides churning but my voice calm. "I thought my father would be more likely to accept me without antlers, since that's how my mother had sent me, before."

His eyes shone with tears. "After that, I don't remember visiting you. Not for years, except in visions."

"You might have," I said. "There might be more to remember." Then I said, "I missed you," and wiped away a trail of moisture from his cheek. He blinked quickly to keep more tears from falling. "I can't help thinking there's something we're supposed to learn from remembering now."

"Midwinter," he said softly. "Three years ago."

I felt tears gathering behind *my* eyes now. "My cousin murdered Dec," I said.

"You loved him."

I didn't want to answer that, even though it wasn't phrased as a question. Absurdly, I wanted him to believe *he* was the only one I had ever loved. But I couldn't lie to him. I wouldn't. I also couldn't make words come out, so I nodded.

"I wanted so badly to make everything better for you. To help you stop hurting."

"You did, pretty bird. You spoke to his ghost, let him borrow your spirit body. You let me say goodbye."

He swallowed. "The raven brought me because you needed me. That's what it told me."

"You gave me the courage to keep living, Fionn."

Suddenly he wrapped his arms around me and pulled me close, clinging tight. I hugged him back just as hard.

"I didn't just help you, Kier. *You* helped *me*. You gave me the courage to continue on, alone and different in that fucking Abbey."

"If I could spend my life giving you courage, pretty bird, I would."

"Will you?" he said, pulling back to stare into my eyes. "Will you spend your life with me?"

"I will."

Then he looked away, staring over my shoulder at nothing. "If a person makes a spell, does that spell continue after they're dead?"

I felt dizzy from the sudden change in subject, but I knew he wouldn't ask just on a whim. "It depends on the spell. Some can be attached to an object and continue after death, but that takes a lot of magic and leaves the spellworker drained for a long time after." I touched his face gently and he tucked his head into my shoulder. "Most spells end when the spellworker dies. I think. I don't know much about spellwork. My Queen chose to pass that knowledge to my sisters, not to me."

Then I realized what he was really asking, and I took his face in both hands so he'd look at me again.

"Fionn. Beloved. You mustn't think that. She's out of my reach, even if killing her could give me my magic back."

"Would it? Give you your magic back?" He tilted his chin up in defiance and I remembered what Seer Moira had told me about treating him like a child. He wasn't one, and he was smart. Smarter that I would ever be. I just had to make sure he knew how dangerous this path of thought was.

"I don't know for sure. Probably. But she did enspell the moonsilver on my antlers, so maybe not. But… promise me you won't pursue this."

"Would you kill her, if you could?"

That gave me pause. The Queen was my mother, and I had loved her and hated her, sometimes – often – both at once.

"I don't know," I finally said. "But please, pretty bird, put that thought out of your head. I'll find a way to get my magic back. I promise. And I'll go to the Eyrie and steal you away, and together we'll find a way to make a better life."

He nodded.

"We'll become those two old men fucking in a chair in front of their fireplace."

His face took on a wicked look, and his hands moved over my skin again. "I thought we agreed my visions of the future are only possibilities?"

"That's one possibility I'll be working towards with every-thing I have." I reached for his ass and pulled him closer, but he resisted, keeping space between us so he could trace the outlines of my stomach muscles. By the time he reached my cock I was so hard for him I could hardly think.

"How about we practice being two young men fucking in a bed while everyone thinks they're discussing trade in medicinal herbs?" he said.

I explored the roundness of his perfect ass, and he twined his leg over mine. "Yes, please," I said.

21
Fionn

THE NEXT SEVERAL DAYS were full of meetings. We talked about trade, of course, but I also spent a lot of time with Seer Siona. We were supposed to be exchanging ideas and techniques, but mostly she was teaching me about seer magic, since I had no one to guide me as I grew up and had only recently met Seer Moira in the werewolf village. My King had promised a human seer tutor I could meet in the City Beneath the Cliff, but so far that hadn't happened.

On the subject of medicinal herbs, though, I felt a little closer to her equal, because I had spent my childhood studying in the Abbey library, and growing whatever I could in the Abbey garden. Siona had more practical knowledge, of course, and many more years of experience, but at least I felt I had information to add to our discussions. We met, those times, with other healers, and I left the meetings feeling as if I had contributed nearly as much as I had learned. My notebook was soon crammed with ideas and methods of preparation, and my pack was filling with carefully labeled samples.

Siona had even demonstrated a method of making a thick syrup from tree sap that could concentrate its medicinal properties. At my request, we tried the method with salt-leaf sap, and created what I hoped would be a more potent treatment for fever.

I only saw Kiernan in passing, and never privately, so we were forced to be courteous but distant. I wanted to tell him about all the things I was learning but could only do so in the form of idle small talk the few times our delegation shared a meal with him.

I was getting fidgety, to have him so close but so untouchable, and even Neeka's teasing didn't make me laugh as it usually did.

<It will be Autumn Balance tomorrow,> she said one day. <I'm told it's normal for couples to sneak away during the festivities. Perhaps you'll have a chance to meet with your Prince then.> She was attempting to keep my hair from creeping through my feathers to fall into my eyes. It had been so much easier to tame when it was long, even if it did have the tendency to get snagged on things.

<I hate this,> I said, and winced as the pin she was trying to wedge into my hair poked my scalp. <We're nearly halfway through our visit, and I've only really seen him once.>

<Twice, I think, my Seer,> she said. <But maybe the winter storms will come early, and we'll be trapped here until spring.> She smiled and tried to get me to smile back.

<Don't you miss your sweetheart?> I said. <Aren't you eager to get back?>

Her eyes slid away from mine in the mirror.

<Neeka?>

She blushed. <There's a very pretty guard,> she said.

<A Sidhe guard? Is she a Queen's Guard?>

<One of the Palace Guard.> She added another pin to my

hair, and I thought I might end up with more metal than hair on my head. I raised my eyebrows and she laughed. <You don't get to tell me how liaisons between Vogel and non-Vogel are forbidden,> she said, tugging one of my feathers back into place and pinning another section of hair.

<Just be careful,> I said. <And what about…?>

<Sifka. We… weren't getting along and we agreed my coming with you would be a good time for us to consider our future.>

<Oh. I'm sorry to hear that.>

<She believes my loyalty should be for our King above all else.>

<It probably should.>

She pinned one more strand of hair into place and stepped back. <I agree with Councilor Rocsh. Our true masters should be our people. Or maybe *all* people. The ones without the power to speak for themselves. And you represent our people, so I believe my loyalty should be to you first.>

<You're an idealist,> I said, finally smiling at her passionate words where I hadn't been able to smile at her teasing.

<So are you.> She poked my shoulder gently.

I turned around and looked and her and we both laughed.

<What if your pretty Palace Guard is fiercely loyal to the Sidhe Queen?>

She cocked her head. <I've been talking to a lot of the staff, while you and Councilor Rocsh have been in meetings.> To Neeka's disgust, many of the meetings we had attended were for our negotiators and representatives only, and attendants were expected to keep occupied with other tasks. Only royalty, it seemed, had attendants with them at all times in Morven Forest – though I had noticed Kiernan seldom brought his dryad along.

<What have you learned?> I said. I heard all the Eyrie's

news and gossip from Neeka, so I had no doubt she could gather all sorts of information here in Morven, too. She was friendly and easy to talk to, and I had already noticed her frequently waving or saying hello to all sorts of people as we made our way through the halls each day.

<Most of the Guards are loyal, of course,> she said. <They swear oaths and all that. But...> She paused and sat on the edge of the bed. <I think... They seem to be very fond of Prince Kiernan, and more afraid of the Queen and her daughters than anything.>

I must have blinked in surprise or made some face, because she laughed. Seer Siona *had* told me that Kier made friends more easily than he realized, and I wondered if this was what she meant.

<They like him very much, my Seer,> Neeka said, getting up to pour tea. <Many of them hope to catch his eye.>

I looked down at my hands.

<But there has been considerable consternation that he hasn't been as free with himself as he was before he left for Aven.>

I met her eyes again and hers crinkled at the corners.

<Some think he's bedding his dryad servant, but most of them speculate that something happened while he was away.>

<What do they think happened?> I took the cup of winterleaf tea she handed me and sipped. Sweet bean was hard to come by in Morven, but their winterleaf was sweeter and very nice all on its own. I made a metal note to mention tea to our negotiators as another possible trade item.

<Opinion is divided,> she said, sipping her tea and trying to hide a cheeky grin. <Most of the staff think he fell in love and had his heart broken.>

I almost choked on my tea.

<The guards have a different idea. They mostly think that,

among the other injuries he sustained at the hands of our Vogel King's men, Prince Kiernan was gelded.>

This time I did choke, inhaling half a mouthful of hot liquid and coughing so hard my head hurt. Neeka rubbed between my shoulders until I could breathe again. <What do people think of the Queen's punishment?> I said, setting my cup aside.

She moved to the window to look out. <Some are afraid that if their Queen would do something so terrible to her own son, for something that most of them think was not even a crime, that it could happen to them, too.> She glanced back at me. <They're worried, and many are angry. I think it has made your Prince more allies, in the end. I think many who usually prefer to stay out of the squabbles of royalty decided their Prince is more worth their loyalty than their Queen, even if she terrifies them.>

THE AUTUMN BALANCE celebration began with a solemn ritual in the Queen's Hall, high in the branches of the Heart of Morven. Siona led a small group of Seers who had gathered at the palace especially for the event, in a blessing of the royal family and of the whole of Morven Forest and its people.

It ended with a procession of the entire court, followed by everyone else who had come to attend, following the Seers two-by-two to lay offerings around a sacred stone on a nearby hilltop. Siona and the Seers led the way, their arms full of produce and other gifts. After them came the Queen, flanked by her guards, then the two Princesses and their guards.

To my surprise, I found myself paired with Kiernan. He held out his arm for me to take and we fell into step with his guards and mine close behind. He was dressed in a perfectly tailored coat of grey wool, with trousers and accents of deep green. He looked so handsome I had to stare at my feet instead of meeting his eyes. I was sure I was blushing, and even felt heat in the tips of my ears.

"Once the offerings are laid," he said, "there will be bonfires lit on the palace lawn, and food and drink free for anyone who has come to celebrate." His smile was formal and polite, but I thought I could see something more personal in his eyes when I could finally bring myself to meet his gaze. "I hope, Seer Tokka, that you won't be put off by the wildness that follows."

"Wildness, Prince Kiernan?" I shifted my hand on his arm and let my thumb brush the inside of his elbow before settling my grip more firmly in place.

"It's an excuse for everyone to let off some energy," he said. "Just like every festival and celebration. People will eat too much and drink too much. They'll dance until they fall over. Drinking, dancing, and debauchery is normal at Sidhe celebrations, once the sacred part is over."

He wasn't looking at me when he said it, but I snuck a look at his face and the corner of his mouth was quirked up.

"I see."

"There could be duels, though not on palace grounds. Fist fights, perhaps. But mostly a lot of eating and drinking and fucking."

I stared ahead at the backs of the Princesses' guards and ignored the snort from one of Kiernan's cousins, walking behind him as his guards. "Our Prince does like the fucking," said one of them.

"Mind your mouth in front of our guest," Kiernan said without looking around.

"And *is* that your favorite part, Prince of Morven?" I said, making my voice light, as if I didn't actually care.

"It used to be," he said, but didn't elaborate. "Sometime between the offerings and the… wildness, it's traditional to exchange gifts with friends."

"As they do at many celebrations," I replied. I kept my voice free of the excitement I felt at the thought of giving my gift to Kiernan. Would he like it? Or would he only say he did because I had made it for him?

Smoke and Flame had their gift for him, too, and I wouldn't be surprised if they chose this evening to finally decide they were tired of waiting at the ship and come to find me. I was a little surprised they had waited this long. Perhaps they had believed me when I told them the Queen of Morven Forest liked to make accessories out of serpent skin.

When we reached the hill, Kiernan showed me where to stand and then left me to wait for the rest of the delegation while he turned to join his Queen. As he let go of my arm, he said, "Perhaps I'll see you at the bonfires, Seer Tokka?" He smiled. "It's not a formal affair, just tables of food and drink anyone can help themselves to."

"Perhaps," I said, not daring to meet his eyes, because I felt like I might do something stupid if I did.

The laying of offerings was a brief ceremony, and I only understood a little of the ritual language, because it was all in Sidhe, where the earlier blessing had been repeated in Islish. But I felt the presence of spirits swirling around and through the crowd and lingering near the stones as if to examine what had been left for them. They felt ancient, unknowable, but not hostile. I wondered if, were I alone here, I could speak to them as they say seers once did.

After, Seer Siona approached our delegation where we waited for the celebrants to head back to the palace.

"I hope that wasn't too dull for you," she said, clasping

Councilor Rocsh's hands, and then mine, and leading us away from the hill. "It's not our most exciting ritual."

"Not at all," said Rocsh. "It was lovely, even if I didn't understand the words. We have very few large celebrations at the Eyrie these days, though I understand our people once celebrated many festivals."

"Do you suppose," I said, feeling suddenly shy, but wanting to ask, "That our people once had similar ceremonies? Our climate is not so different from yours; perhaps once when we had seers. More of them, I mean."

"I was given to understand the Vogel only ever had one seer at a time," said Siona. "But there is a copy of the founding laws of the Nine Monarchies in our library that contains a list of the obligations a Seer has to their Monarch. And there is a short history of seers that might answer your question."

I gripped her hands tighter in my excitement. "Might I be permitted to read them while we're here?"

She smiled and squeezed my hands back. "I'm surprised you haven't consulted your own copy of the laws – every Monarchy should have one. But I'll request permission for you to use our library. Prince Kiernan goes there often; I'm sure he'd be happy to show you where to find everything."

She smiled at the eagerness that must have showed on my face. "The history is a hand-written manuscript, and not very rich in detail, but it does offer an intriguing outline of the role of seers among the different peoples of the Isle. Perhaps I can get the Queen's permission to have it copied for you."

"I would like that very much."

When we reached the palace, Siona said, "If the celebrations become too rowdy for you, feel free to return to your rooms. No one will be insulted if you don't wish to eat and drink obscene amounts or dance until you fall over. In fact, most of the court will retire to their private quarters early on and leave the revels to the common folk."

"Thank you," said Councilor Rocsh.

"On the other hand," said Siona as she turned to leave, "If you *do* want to join in, you and your attendants and guards are all most welcome. The Queen ensures there are wards in place on the palace grounds to prevent violence, so you will be safe, even if things do become rowdy."

"Prince Kiernan said sometimes there are duels and fights," I said.

"Away from the palace, yes. But stay close to the food and the bonfires and you'll be fine."

I nodded and glanced at Councilor Rocsh. <Shall we eat, Councilor, or would you prefer to return to our rooms?>

He looked around at the tables laden with food and drink that had materialized while we were observing the offering, and the people milling about with plates and napkins and cups.

<It seems even the staff are given leave to celebrate,> he said, and I looked more closely at the people around us. Servants and guards still in livery, craftspeople with their aprons and smocks over their best finery, as if this event required them to be recognized for what they were, but also encouraged dressing up, moved around the tables and helped get several small bonfires going.

Most of the nobles seemed to have withdrawn to an area near the roots of the Heart of Morven where chairs had been set out for them. They watched their lessers with looks of scorn or amusement.

<Except dryads,> I said. The tree-folk seemed to be the only ones still filling their roles of servitude and I didn't see a single one take so much as a bite of food or a sip of drink. Instead, they took away empty plates and delivered full ones, picked up refuse, and made sure the jugs of wine and cider

were kept topped up.

Councilor Rocsh sighed. <It doesn't seem right, does it?>

<No,> I said. <It doesn't.>

We moved carefully between groups of celebrants to the food table, and I chose a goblet of apple cider and a crispy slice of bread with soft cheese and fish paste spread on it.

<I think I'll take a plate back to our rooms,> said Councilor Rocsh.

I nodded. <I'd like to stay a while, if that's okay. I want to see the dancing.>

<I'll stay with you,> said Neeka, but I could see her gaze drifting away, probably looking for her pretty palace guard.

<We'll stay, too,> said Konta.

I shook my head. <Look around. All the guards are joining the feasting and celebration, not guarding their masters. There's no danger.>

He frowned.

<Either go back to our rooms and rest or join in and have some fun.> I pointed to where a group of musicians had begun to set up near one of the fires, and people were gathering to dance. <Why not join in?>

<You go with the Councilor, Konta,> said Trikta. <I'll stay with our Seer.>

I let them discuss it, and wandered away to the fire, listening as the musicians tuned their instruments. One of them, who played an unfamiliar stringed instrument, smiled at me.

"Seer Tokka, right?" she said.

"Yes." I finished my piece of bread and sipped my cider.

"Do you like to dance?" She played a jaunty tune, but quietly, and some of the others joined in, just as soft, as if waiting to hear what I would say.

"I've never danced before," I said, feeling heat creep up my neck.

"Now *that* is a tragedy," said a smoky voice that made my breath catch. I only just managed to keep my reaction off my face.

I turned to face him. "Prince Kiernan."

The music increased gradually in volume, making me have to step closer to hear him.

"Dance with me, pretty bird?" he said, and held out his hand.

"I don't know how." I fiddled with my goblet. He smiled, took it from my hand and drained it, then handed it to one of the musicians, who saluted him with it and used it to tap the skin of his hand-drum.

"It's easy. I'll show you."

I bit my lip and took his outstretched hand.

"Tonight," he said, "No one cares who dances with whom or who gets drunk and falls asleep in the hedge. We can eat together, and dance, and find a quiet place to talk, and it will only be two young men having a good time at harvest."

He pulled me closer, showed me where to put my hands, and walked me through the steps slowly. And then the music reached full volume and everyone around us was suddenly moving, swirling and twirling, and we were moving along with them. I was awkward, and he was patient. I stepped on his feet, and he only laughed and swung me around. The very music seemed to seep into my being until it became a part of me, and it was so very different from the solemn tunes my King preferred to have played at the Eyrie.

This music made me want to leap and twirl, made me laugh out loud when Kiernan spun me around, made me lean into his arms. I was ridiculous, but I didn't care. Kiernan's hands were on mine, his breath on my neck, and the rest of the world slipped away as we twirled around the fire.

When we stopped, I was breathless and dizzy. I felt drunk

and I hadn't had more than a few sips of cider.

"See," he said, grinning at me. "You did fine."

"I made a fool of myself," I said, but I smiled back.

"You're a lovely fool. Let's get something to drink."

We moved away from the fire to find a table with beverages and then found a bench away from the crowd where we could sit and rest and watch the people.

"Oh!" I said. "I didn't see where Neeka went."

"I think I saw her flirting with one of the Palace Guards," Kiernan said. "I hope she knows not to get caught. My people won't care, but I worry about those King's Guards of yours."

"They've gone with Councilor Rocsh, Nikna, and Konta, back to our rooms."

"So only Trikta's got his sharp eye on you."

"What?" I looked around.

"Over by the fellow in the very large hat, trying to disappear behind that unfortunate topiary." He nodded in the direction of a short man in a tall conical hat and a bush clipped to look like… well, I wasn't sure what it was supposed to look like.

"Oh dear." Trikta was holding a drink and looking like he was trying to blend into the scenery. "I told him to have some fun."

"He cares about you," Kier said.

"Perhaps too much," I replied, sipping my cider. It was cool and tart and perfect.

"You know he loves you, then?"

I met his eyes. "I know." I waited a heartbeat and then said, "You know Daphnis loves you?"

He sighed and took a long drink from his cup before answering. "I know," he said, softly.

I touched his knee, briefly. "And you know I love you," I said, my voice just above a whisper.

He leaned sideways so his shoulder pressed against mine, then straightened. "You know I love you," he said, just as quietly.

"I have a gift for you," I said. He turned to look at me. "I hope it's not inappropriate. I wasn't sure if gifts at Autumn Balance were… Well, I didn't know who gave gifts and to whom." I stumbled to a stop. "And it will be your birthday soon."

"Autumn Balance is about prosperity and abundance," he said. "Wishes for a good winter, free of hunger or strife. Parents give gifts to children, of course, and friends to friends, lovers to lovers." He looked at me, then away, and he was smiling. "I have a gift for you, too, but I left it in my rooms."

"Are you trying to get me into your bedroom again?" I said and he snorted.

"I will never stop trying to get you into my bedroom."

"Can we… Is it safe to go there?"

"Can you find your way? We should go separately, so no one can carry tales to your King's Guards." He turned his cider cup in his hands and lifted it to tip the contents into his mouth.

"I know where it is," I said. "Shall I climb in the window?"

He laughed. "I think it should be safe to go through the door." He set his cup on the end of the bench and leaned back on his hands to look up at the sky. "I –" But whatever he was going to say was left unfinished as he sat up straight, his face going from soft to surprised to delighted.

I looked where he was looking and suddenly the air seemed to be full of serpents, swooping and diving and chittering, even though there were only two.

Dark and Bright together, said Smoke.

Love and love, said Flame.

22
Kiernan

OING SOMETHING AS simple as dancing a peasant dance with
Fionn had me so giddy I felt drunk.

The way he laughed every time I spun him away from me,
hands clasped over his head, made me want the evening to go
on forever. Every time I pulled him back and his hand found
my shoulder and mine nestled against his hip, every time he
stepped wrong and landed on my foot, every time he threw his
head back as we turned, I wanted to fix in my memory and
treasure.

When we stopped and moved to the edge of the crowd, he
paused bent over, hands on his knees, to catch his breath.

"So how do you like dancing?" I said, and he turned his
beautiful smile on me.

"I made a fool of myself," he said. "But I liked it very
much."

"You make a lovely fool."

When he agreed to meet me at my rooms, I wanted to rush
away immediately, but I also didn't want to attract attention by

leaving too early. I was the Prince who liked to drink and dance and carouse with the common folk; sneaking away before the carousing had properly gotten underway might make people talk, and talk could get back to the Vogel King's Guards. I wanted Fionn all to myself, but I wouldn't endanger him to do so.

No matter how much I wanted him to stay, I knew he would have to leave, and back in the Eyrie, he was at his King's mercy. I would not give his King reason to be angry with him. So when he and his guard Trikta left to take plates of food back to their rooms and join the rest of their delegation, I stayed where I was, seated on the bench we had shared, watching the crowd.

I thought about getting up to get another drink, or maybe to dance with a few pretty men and women, but I spotted Padraig heading my way, a drink in each hand and a determined look on his face.

"Can I join you?" His jacket was unbuttoned, and his shoulder-length hair mussed and creeping out of the clip that held it back, but his sword was in its place on his back and his step was steady.

I shrugged and took the drink he offered me, staring into it thoughtfully.

"Poison isn't my style," he said. "And besides, I think I might actually like you, even if you did threaten my tackle with a very sharp blade a mere handful of days ago."

"If you expect an apology, you'll be waiting a very long time."

"No." He sat down and rested his forearms on his thighs, considering his own drink. "I probably deserved it."

I sipped the beverage cautiously and thought that there was one more useful thing I could have done with magic once; I'd have been able to tell if the drink had been tainted by magic or poison. It tasted fine though, cool and tart. I took a longer sip.

"You still care for him, don't you?" Padraig said.

I contemplated all the possible ways I could answer. It would be easy to lie, to tell him he was an idiot. I could probably be very convincing. But I hated lies. I was so *tired* of lying. I decided to just not answer at all.

"Half the palace thinks you got your heart broken in Aven, and the other half thinks you got gelded when the Vogel guards beat you." He turned to look at me, and I found myself wishing he didn't look quite so much like Sean. It would have been easier to like to him, to consider him a friend, even. He snorted and turned back to his drink.

"I think you fell in love and stayed that way," he said. "But don't worry. It's not obvious. I just have a knack for seeing that sort of thing. Feelings."

"I thought you couldn't see me at all with your magic," I said.

"I can't. But I can see him."

I sipped my cider again, relishing the way it cooled my throat and made my muscles relax. "That doesn't seem like a particularly useful talent, reading emotions."

"You might be surprised. Being able to tell if your father is angry or merely annoyed can be extremely useful."

I couldn't dispute that. There were times I'd have found it helpful to know what my Queen was feeling. A lot of times. "I don't care what people think happened to me," I said. "I don't care what people think of me."

"I think you do care," he replied. "And don't give me any manure about not being able to lie. It may not be common knowledge, but *I* know your human half lets you speak untruths."

I opened my mouth to tell him I really *didn't* care, but he held up a hand, so I finished my drink instead.

"More importantly," he went on. "You care what people think of *him*, and that alone tells me you love him."

"What do you want?" I said, setting my cup next to the one I'd emptied with Fionn.

He fiddled with his, sloshing the last of the liquid around in the bottom and finally tipping it to his mouth to empty it.

"Padraig?" He wouldn't meet my eyes. "Maybe you came over here just to be friendly, but I can tell you want to ask me something, and it has nothing to do with who I may or may not care for."

"It does, a little," he said.

I growled under my breath, and he laughed.

"They say you had a wolf for a wet nurse," he said.

I snorted. "Will you just come out with it?"

"I need a favor," he said, looking at his empty cup.

"What have you done?" I said, and he looked at me sharply.

"Why do you assume I've done something?"

I raised my eyebrows and waited.

"I have… a friend in service to the Queen. He's sweet and well-intentioned, but shy. Clumsy when he's nervous and our Queen makes him very nervous. I'm afraid he'll be dismissed with his indenture still owing. Or worse."

I watched his face and said nothing. I was fairly sure I knew exactly who he was referring to, but I wanted him to say it. He looked away.

"Why can't he ask for reassignment?"

"He can barely form words when she looks at him, he's so afraid of her. I… I think she may have done something to him." He set his cider cup aside and sat up straighter. "He's a faun. They need permission to shit once their contract is signed, and… Have you ever read a contract of indenture?

They're the worst kind of exploitative. He didn't know what he was getting into when he applied to work at the palace, he just saw that he might qualify to be educated and signed his fucking life away. He wants to learn, Kiernan. So badly he'd work himself to death for it."

"How do you come to know a faun so well?" I kept my voice even. I didn't want him to think I was judging him, but I also wasn't ready to admit how much I empathized.

"He's from a village near my family estates. I think… I think he came here to be… to be closer to me." He jerked his chin up to meet my gaze, his nostrils flaring. "And you haven't got a fucking exclusive right to non-fey friends."

"Friends?" I said, letting a little skepticism creep into my voice.

His nostrils flared wider, and he didn't look away.

I let the corner of my mouth curl up. "His name is Erith," I said. "And he's terrified of me. Or he was the one time we met."

"He's more terrified of the Queen." He didn't look surprised that I knew his faun's name.

"So, *you* help him. You're just as noble as I am, descended from the same great grandfather. *You* petition the Queen to sign his contract over to you."

"First of all, my Prince, you should be the first to know that letting our Queen know you want something is the best way to ensure you never get it."

I had to concede that point.

"And second, I can't hold a servant's contract while I'm in service myself. Which I am, until my term as Prince's Guard ends, which isn't for at least three years. I looked it up."

"You think the Queen is going to sign his contract over to me just because I ask? I refer you to your own point number one."

He leaned back on his hands. "So, make her think she's inflicting him on you against your wishes. Didn't she say you need more servants?"

"As befits someone of my station? She may have said something to that effect."

"Well, find a way. They say you're a clever shit. So be clever."

"Why not ask Sean? He has the Queen's favor already. I'm just her unwanted son."

"I'm not even going to answer that. Sean can fuck himself."

"As far as I can tell, he *is* the only one he thinks is good enough to fuck him."

He barked out a laugh. "I think he's angling for one of your sisters."

"I hope to all three of the Goddesses he isn't *that* much in our Queen's favor." I sighed and looked up at the sky. Even with the bonfires so close and dozens of wisplights drifting about, the stars were still brilliant. "Erith is a nice kid," I said. "He –"

"He's not a kid." Padraig's voice was heated, and I looked at him, letting him see my smile. He scowled when he realized I'd set him up, that I had already figured out why he was really asking me to help.

"Okay, he's not a kid, but he *is* a bit young, don't you think?"

His eyes widened and he stared at me. "Fuck," he said. "How?"

"Don't worry, I'd never have guessed until a few sentences ago." I straightened to stretch my back. "I've already been thinking about how to get Erith out of our Queen's clutches. Daphnis tells me I can't save everyone, but no one should have to be that terrified every day. Or ever. I'll try, but I can't guarantee I'll succeed."

Talking to Padraig left me both hopeful and irritated. Hopeful that maybe I'd finally found someone at court I could trust, could count as a friend. And irritated that he might very well just be one more person being nice because they thought they could get something out of me.

And depressed because there were too many like Erith at court, and in the estates of every noble in Morven Forest. Too many like Daphnis. People trapped in a life that wasn't anything like what they would have chosen, simply because of the circumstances of their birth.

I couldn't save them all, but if I could try to find a way for me and Fionn to have a better life, then I could find a way for other people to have better lives, too.

But to do either, I needed magic, and so far, the only two possibilities I'd found were to wait for my Queen to decide I'd suffered long enough, or to let Daphnis sacrifice his own magic – and his life – to give it to me. Which would also mean letting him fuck me.

I was getting up to get another drink, to maybe let myself get a little drunk and forget before I met Fionn in my rooms, when I spotted a familiar figure near one of the bonfires. Tall, burly, but a little bent and grey with age. He wouldn't want to see me, but I found myself unable to look away, unable to resist walking over to him.

Another werewolf in the group he was with nudged him and he turned around. I tried not to flinch away from his startling sky-blue eyes, so like his son's.

"Papa Winterborn," I said, then faltered, because I couldn't think of anything I could possibly say to him that he would want to hear.

"My Prince," he said, and started to sink to one knee.

I caught his elbow and pulled him upright. "Please, Papa, don't."

He stood straight, staring at me, and I was the first to look away. I could stare down anyone in this court but the Queen, but I couldn't face the eyes of my dead lover's father.

"Can I do something for you, my Prince?" he finally said, when I didn't speak. And what the fuck had I thought I could say to him? I may not have wielded the sword, but it was my fault his son was dead.

"I – How are you? Is there anything you need? How's Mama?"

He frowned, but softly, like he felt he should be angry, but couldn't quite make himself feel it. "I don't think you ought to call us Mama and Papa anymore, my Prince." His eyes were empty, his face still with no trace of the smile I had been so used to seeing there.

"I miss him," I said. "I can't imagine how you –"

He grabbed my arm, hard, and I snapped my mouth shut. "Don't lad. This is a celebration of abundance. Now isn't the time to mourn."

He met my eyes again and his face softened. His grip on my arm eased until it was more a comforting squeeze. "I don't blame you, lad. Some of the others do, but I never did. I saw how you loved him. But don't you see that folk like me even talking to you puts us in danger?"

"It shouldn't be that way."

His face softened even more. "You ever want to leave this court for good, you come talk to me," he said, his voice gentle. "Until then, it's best you stay away."

I nodded, even though it hurt. For one wonderful year, the Winterborn family home in the village had been a place of refuge for me, as much as Dec's cabin had been. And one moment three years ago had stolen all of it. But now, the more my Queen found me useful, the more a danger I was to my non-court friends.

"Do you mean that, Papa?" I said.

He scowled at me, but it slipped into a grin, and then vanished. "I mean it."

I nodded again, then turned away to wander between fires, greeting people I knew, flirting a little, and even dancing with a few of the younger court fey. But the delight I had felt dancing with Fionn was gone, slipped away against a tide of unhappy thoughts.

And I suddenly found myself face-to-face with Padraig again. He was drunk this time, and grinning.

"Dance with me, cousin!" he said, and grabbed my hands before I could say anything, leading me in a very wobbly round that had both of us laughing by the end. Then he dragged me away to one side, into the shadow of a tree.

"You've had a few more ciders," I said. "Be careful not to have too many."

He laughed. "You haven't had nearly enough." He put a hand on the side of my neck, playing with the ends of my hair with his fingertips. "But I'm afraid I'm going to have to kiss you now."

"Please don't," I said, laughing too.

"But you see," he said, leaning close to speak quietly into my ear. "I'm not actually drunk." He leaned back and grinned. "Or at least not very."

"Really?" I raised an eyebrow.

"And –" He leaned close again. "It occurred to me that if you and I are both… are both in love with people not befitting our station…" He leaned on my shoulder and laughed into my shirt. "Fuck, cousin, you do have *such* a substantial chest."

"And you are not at all easily distracted."

He snorted. "I was getting to the point." He took a deep breath. "We are both… desiring people not deemed suitable for those of our elevated rank, so obviously we should let everyone think we're fucking each other." He looked at me expectantly, like he had just proposed something brilliant. Despite his assurance, he was definitely drunk.

I shook my head. "If you want people to think we're fucking, why are we hiding under a tree? I'm fairly certain that everyone in this court would agree we're perfectly suitable liaisons for each other, anyway."

"But we have to *pretend* to be secret, without actually being secret, so people will notice, and remember, and then *not* notice when we actually *are* being secret."

Maybe I'd had one too many cups of cider, after all, because he was starting to make an odd sort of sense.

He stepped closer, put his hand back on my neck, and pulled me towards him. I thought about resisting; even when he wasn't drunk, I was stronger than he was. But it might not be a bad idea to let people spread the rumor that we were fucking, as a cover for both of us sneaking away.

"Please Kiernan, my Prince," he whispered. "It'll help protect those we love."

"Who said anything about love?" But I let him press his mouth against mine and tasted cider on his lips. And then I took over, because if I was going to kiss Padraig, I might as well make it worth the effort. I slid both hands into his hair, now completely loose of the clip he'd had it held back with. The strands were silky soft, though not as soft as Fionn's. He moaned quietly and parted his lips, letting me slide my tongue into his mouth, and grabbed my jacket with both hands to pull me closer.

He was lean and strong, not unlike Fionn in build, but

shorter. I lifted my mouth from his when I felt his cock start to wake up against my leg. I definitely didn't need to take this ruse *that* far.

He stared at me for a long moment, studying my eyes. Then he said, "Fuck, Kiernan. If you kiss him like that it's no wonder he let you take him to bed."

I let my mouth twitch into a grin. "That's only the barest hint of how I kiss him," I said, touching his sharp cheekbone and then stepping away.

"Fuck," he said again.

I snorted. "See you tomorrow evening," I said. "And don't get caught smuggling Erith into your room."

I RETURNED TO MY ROOMS to find Daphnis depositing an array of food and drink onto the low table in my sitting room.

"I thought you were attending your dryad rites," I said.

"Not until the feasting ends and the palace lawn has been cleaned up. Until then, the palace dryads are required to work."

"You should go root in the garden while you have a chance," I said.

"You wish to get rid of me, my Prince?"

I sighed. "I wish to have privacy, Daphnis."

"You're nervous," he said looking at me strangely. "Has something happened?"

"Nothing has happened," I said. "Except every time I have a chance to see Fionn alone, I know it might be the last." I sat down and picked up a slice of bread. I had hardly eaten at the feast, and all the cider I'd drunk made my head spin.

"And… you mean to meet him tonight?"

"I'm not used to having servants, Daph." I looked at the bread in my hand and tried to convince myself to finish it. "I'm not used to someone being *here* all the time. I only want…" I almost put the bread down but made myself take a bite instead.

"You wish to meet him here, so you need me to leave," he said.

"Daph…"

"I probably could use to root for a while." His voice was brisk. Perhaps I had only imagined the hurt. "When shall I return?"

"Our next meeting is early evening tomorrow."

"I'll be back before that to help you dress."

"Enjoy your rites, Daphnis."

He inclined his head but didn't say any more.

When he had gone, I tried again to eat, but just ended up tearing the slice of bread to pieces and scattering crumbs on the floor. I was just about to draw my sword to work out some of my nervous energy in practice when I heard a noise from my bedroom.

I went through, closing the door behind me, and found two tree serpents flitting about, investigating everything from my bathing pool to my wardrobe. They headed directly at me as soon as they saw me, and twined themselves around my neck, chittering loudly.

"I wish I could still understand you, little friends," I said, scratching both their chins until they purred. "Is he coming in my window?"

I leaned on the sill and looked out.

"Oh!" he said, looking up at me and smiling sheepishly. "I don't remember it being quite so high."

"Didn't you get your spirit body stuck last time?" I leaned farther out and held out my hands. "I thought you were going to use the door."

Fionn let me pull him up and through the open casement. When he was standing safely inside the room he said, "I was going to, only the King's Guards were stationed outside our rooms, so I climbed out my window. And then it just seemed to make sense to take the shorter route to your window."

I touched his face and he smiled hesitantly. "I'm glad you came," I said. I took his cloak off to find him dressed only in night clothes. His sleeping tunic was sleeveless and only reached to mid-thigh, giving me a nice view of his long slender arms and legs.

"Stop staring," he said. Pink spread from his cheeks down his neck.

"I like looking at you," I said. "Are you hungry? Daphnis brought an entire feast to my sitting room."

He shook his head. "Is he here?"

"No, he's gone to the garden."

He stepped closer, making me tilt my head to look up at him. A piece of silver hair escaped to fall over his forehead and I reached up to tuck it back behind his feathers.

He closed his eyes and rested his forehead on mine. "I don't want to go," he said. "This past nineday has felt so..." He shook his head. "Even with having to meet secretly, it's the closest we've been to having a life together and I don't want it to end."

"I know, pretty bird," I said, slipping my hands around his waist and pulling him snug against me. "I don't want you to go. Or maybe I want to go with you." I sighed. "I saw Dec's father tonight. At the feast. I thought he would hate me."

"Declan's death wasn't your fault."

"I think he offered me an escape." I laughed softly. "If I wasn't trapped with no magic, I'd be tempted to take it."

He shifted against me, tugging on the laces at the neck of

my shirt to loosen them.

"Neeka says the staff here, and even the guards, are, well, not happy, I suppose. She says they feel your Queen's punishment was excessive, and that… that they're more loyal to you than to her."

I pressed my fingers to his lips. "Don't repeat that, beloved. My Queen won't like to hear anything that sounds of treason."

"I know." He touched his tongue to the tip of my finger, then slid his lips over the whole digit, sucking gently before sliding away again. I made a noise in my throat and pulled him closer.

I tried to keep my breathing even as he pulled my shirt over my head. "I want to put my tongue somewhere I've never put it before," he whispered, and I shivered. I grasped his hips and pulled him tighter against me, then slipped his tunic over his head.

"*Is* there somewhere you haven't put your tongue?" I said, helping him pull my trousers down, then my undergarment. Then his undergarment.

"Turn around," he said, his husky voice dipping lower.

I turned and he pressed himself against my back, sliding his palms over my chest, teasing my nipples until I arched under his touch and leaned my head back against his shoulder.

I let him push me slowly towards the bed.

"Tell me what you want me to do to you," I said, and he laughed quietly in my ear.

"I want you to do what I say," he said, and I remembered the first time he'd fucked me, when he'd asked hesitantly if he could be in charge. There was that same slight hesitation this time when he said, "Get on the bed and lie on your stomach."

I crawled onto the mattress and looked over my shoulder at him. My cock was already hard and would probably start leaking onto the blankets any moment now, with the way he was looking at me, like he wanted to devour me whole and make me enjoy every bit of it.

I lay on my belly and watched as he climbed onto the bed after me, kneeling between my legs, nudging my thighs apart, and stroking one hand down his own belly to the soft feathers that covered his sheath.

"Goddess, Fionn," I breathed as he met my eyes and then looked down at himself. I followed his gaze and watched as he parted his feathers with his slender fingers. I groaned when he stroked his seam again and it opened and his beautiful cock slid out, glistening with lubricant.

"Is my ass *that* spectacular?" I said, and he just smiled, bent close, and spread my ass cheeks open with both hands. And then he bent down even more to put his tongue where he definitely hadn't put it before.

III: HOMEWARD

23
Kiernan

I WOKE WHEN FIONN stirred next to me and sat up, but I didn't want him to feel like he was disturbing me, so I kept my eyes closed and lay still, curled warm and comfortable in the blankets.

When he got out of bed and started to dress, I thought at first that he must be cold, and I almost got up to stir up the fire, but something kept me still. I listened to him pick up my belt and buckle it around his waist, fumbling to get the straps snug on his thighs.

By the time he was climbing out the window, I was concerned, worried, but I didn't have anything solid to attach my worries to. He was being quiet, sure, but that might only be because he didn't want to disturb me and not because he was sneaking around. And besides, Fionn didn't have any deceptive tendencies that I had ever noticed; he had only ever been truthful, even when it pained him to be.

I had to just trust he was okay, that he had a perfectly normal reason to be borrowing my knives and climbing out my window. I had to trust he hadn't decided that the theft of my magic had freed him by breaking our connection, leaving him able to sneak out and meet someone else.

But no, I wouldn't follow *that* thought. I would not hurt him with my doubts. And anyway, even if he did want someone else, that didn't change how I felt about him. There was no one else for me.

After he had gone, I sat up and climbed out of bed, going over to the window to lean on the sill and gaze out into the darkness of the forest. The serpents stirred on the pillow and chittered softly at me.

"I wish I could still understand you, little friends," I said. They made sleepy sounds and curled more tightly together, apparently unconcerned that Fionn had left them with me.

I could still hear the echoes of revelry, of drunken singing and music. It would likely continue until dawn as it did nearly every feast day. Once, I'd have been out there still, drinking and dancing and fucking anyone who asked. Now, I found myself craving quiet, simplicity. Exactly the things I could never have as Prince of Morven Forest.

I wondered what my Queen would do if I told her I had changed my mind, that I didn't want legitimacy or a title after all. I wondered if I would survive telling her such a thing.

I braced my elbow on the windowsill and put my chin in my hand. I hadn't bothered to dress, relishing the cold air even as it raised goosebumps on my skin and made me shiver.

And then, after staring out into the night for what felt like a long time, I spotted a shadow, darker than the rest, and moving. Then I saw the flash of a pale ankle, revealed and then hidden again, and a glint of silver-white hair as his hood shifted. I felt my lips curve into a smile as I watched Fionn slip along the palace wall toward my window. Once, he'd have had no idea how to remain hidden. Now, he would have escaped the notice of most of those who lived in the palace.

I was proud of him, and my belly felt warm, and I didn't care anymore that he had snuck away, thinking I was asleep. I had begun to teach him how to move in the woods, how to be quiet, when we escaped the Abbey of the Moon, and he had proved to be a quick study.

But I didn't know if that was something I should tell him. He had been treated like a child most of his life – his King *still* treated him like a child – and I didn't want him to think I was praising him just to make him feel better. He was smarter than I'd even be, and capable of making his own decisions. And now he was getting good at sneaking in the dark. I would keep my pride to myself and enjoy it secretly.

When he looked up and met my eyes, I knew I couldn't keep all my worry off my face – the palace was safe tonight, but if someone saw him, they might assume the worst.

"I thought you'd gone back to your rooms," I said. "Though I couldn't figure out why you'd take my trousers and my knives." I smiled to let him know I wasn't angry.

"You were awake," he said, just the smallest note of accusation in his voice, and I wondered if I should have let him know when I woke up, after all.

"I couldn't imagine where you'd be sneaking off to," I replied, careful to sound teasing, and not like I was accusing him of something. "I almost said something, but I didn't want you to think I was trying to tell you what to do."

"I wasn't sneaking," he said. "I forgot your gifts in my rooms and went to fetch them." He took my hands when I leaned out the window to help him back in.

"Was it so important you couldn't wait for morning?"

I wanted to undress him as soon as he was safely back inside, to kiss him and take him to bed and show him with my mouth how glad I was to have him back with me. But I made myself be patient.

"Don't you worry about strangers climbing in your window?" he said.

"The palace is warded." I pushed his hood back and cupped his face in my hands. "And before I lost my magic, I warded my own windows and doors on top of the general wards."

"But I could get in," he said, undoing the clasp at his throat and slipping his cloak off. He had a basket slung over his shoulders that he set aside, along with a paper-wrapped package.

"My windows are specifically not warded against *you*." I kissed his chin and said, "Why are you wearing my pants?"

"I didn't think you'd mind. I wasn't really dressed for the weather."

"I like when you get into my pants," I said, and went through to my sitting room to make a pot of his favorite tea and fetch the gift I had for him. I heard him settling himself in bed with Smoke and Flame and when I returned with the tea, he pushed the blankets aside for me to join him.

I put the cups on the table and handed him my gift. I watched as he examined the cloth I had wrapped it in, waiting for him to realize what it was.

"Don't you recognize it?" I said, sipping my tea. He looked more closely at the fabric, deep green and clean, but stained with rusty red-brown patches. He frowned, and then I saw his eyes light when he figured out it was cloth cut from the shirt I'd been wearing when we traveled from the Abbey to the Eyrie.

"Oh," he said. "Your shirt." I flushed with heat at his voice.

"I love watching how your face changes when you figure something out."

His lips curled and he touched the gray ribbon that held

the package closed. I could hardly breathe waiting for him to open it.

"You have two gifts to open," he said. "So you have to go first." He handed me the paper package he had brought from his room.

"I used to always cut strings and ribbons," I said as I worked at the knot. "Until I met Dec."

"What changed?"

"I learned that people who aren't given everything they desire value even the simplest things more. Dec would save any piece of string long enough to use again and he would use it until it fell apart. And then he'd use the fiber for tinder."

I pulled the string away and coiled it around one hand and put it on the table next to my cup. Fionn sipped his tea and watched me.

"He re-used everything, so he didn't need to buy much. Every bit of money he had went to buying tools. He was a hunter, grew up in a family of hunters, but he wanted to be a craftsman, so he saved and bought good tools and whenever he had time, he made things."

I looked up from the package and met Fionn's eyes. "When he was murdered, he was just beginning to be known for the quality of his woodwork." I swallowed. "And I've never forgotten what he taught me about the value of something well made by a craftsperson who cares about their craft."

"I'm so sorry," he said, voice gentle.

I smiled. "You're the only one I've really talked to about Dec. I... I know you probably don't want to hear about my previous lovers, but..."

He shook his head. "Most of them, no I don't. But you loved Declan. And I... I liked him, too."

I blinked in surprise. "I keep forgetting you spirit traveled there, that you talked to his ghost and helped me say goodbye." I sighed. "It was years ago, and yes, I loved him, but it was nothing like what I feel for you."

"It doesn't matter," he said.

"It does, Fionn. I didn't know it was possible to love someone the way I love you."

"Daphnis said…" he stopped, and I wondered when he had spoken to the dryad.

I looked up from studying the folds of paper in my lap. "Daphnis said what?"

"I… ran into him on my way to my rooms and he said…" He sighed and let his shoulders slump. "He said he saw you kissing your cousin Padraig. That it… that it looked passionate."

I laughed and he looked up at me. "Yes, I kissed Pad. He was drunk and had the mad notion that if people thought we were fucking they'd never suspect I was really sneaking away to see you and he was sneaking away to see *his* inappropriate lover."

I folded back one side of the paper.

"You don't… want him?"

"Goddess, no. For one, he may be a distant cousin, but he's still too closely related for my taste. And for two, he's not you."

I folded back another corner of paper, then looked at him again. "Were you jealous?" I teased.

"Maybe for a moment," he said, pretending to be unconcerned. "But I trust you, Kier."

"There is no one for me but you." I folded back the rest of the paper to reveal deep blue-green woven fabric inside. I slipped the fingerless gloves over my hands and reveled in the warmth and softness of the wool. He had spun and dyed and woven me a hood, cleverly shaped to fit around my antlers, and the gloves, and a pair of ankle-warmers – things to keep me warm over the coming winter – and if there wasn't magic in them, there was caring and love.

"Open yours." I said, after staring speechless at the things he had made me for far too long.

He tugged open the bow on the ribbon and folded back the cloth. It was books. One was bound in pale blue leather and silver-grey silk with an image of a drop spindle blind embossed on the cover, and the other was old brown leather and maroon cloth with a worn gilt title that said *Folklore of the Textile Arts of Aven, Morven, and Tronven*. He stared at both for a long time before looking at me.

I touched the folklore book with one finger. "I found a copy in the palace library and sent messengers to three different cities looking for a one I could buy."

"This is… this is perfect," he said.

"This one," and I touched the blue and silver book, "I asked our Archivist to make for you. I meant it for you to take notes in, but I kept finding things in the palace library I thought you would find interesting." He traced his fingers over the embossed design and then lifted the cover. I had half-filled the book with my own handwritten notes and sketches.

"Beloved?" he said, something hesitant in his voice. "Will you… will you keep this with you? And keep adding notes to it? And give it to me again when it's full?" He looked away from the book and met my eyes.

I touched his hand where it rested on the cover. "Of course. Do you want to keep it for now? Read what's in it so far, then leave it with me when you…?" I suddenly couldn't get any more words out. I didn't want to finish that sentence.

"Yes," he said, turning his hand over to squeeze my fingers.

Then he handed me a little basket on a strap, stuffed with soft grey wool, and I held it in my cupped hands. It was warm, as if it had been hanging near a fire, or cradled close to Fionn's body. I liked the thought that he had maybe carried it from the ship slung over his shoulders, tucked under his cloak, maybe even next to his skin.

Smoke and Flame uncurled themselves from their spots on the pillow and watched me carefully pull away the wool to see what was inside. I saw olive green, speckled with bronze, not shiny but with a soft matte finish that barely reflected the wisplights that Fionn had floated over our heads.

I carefully upended the basket to roll the egg into my palm, where it nestled against the wool of the fingerless gloves I was still wearing.

"This is a feathered tree serpent egg," I said, not sure I was even audible. "One of theirs? I… they want me to raise their child?" I blinked and felt moisture trickle down my face. Fionn leaned over to kiss my cheek, to lick away the tear.

"They won't tell me which of them laid it, but they agree that you needed to have it."

"Thank you," I said, to the serpents or Fionn I wasn't sure.

When I nestled the egg back in its basket and hung it near the fire – checking with Smoke and Flame that it was an appropriate distance from the heat – I looked up to Fionn staring at me, one hand over his mouth. He was trying not to laugh.

"What?" I said, looking down at myself to see if I had something stuck to me.

"You're naked," he said, laughter in his voice.

"I like being naked," I said, standing up straighter. "I thought *you* liked me naked." I pretended to pout.

"I do," he said. "Very much. Only, you still have gloves on."

I looked at my hands, clad in the softest wool I'd ever touched, in a color that reminded me of the deep forest at night.

"I don't think I'll ever take them off," I said.

"Oh, but you must." He put his books on the table next to

the bed and put the other gifts on top of them.

"Why must I?" I watched as the serpents dragged a cushion across the floor to the hearth, where they curled up to guard their egg, and then looked back at Fionn. He had a wicked gleam in his eyes.

"Because I want you to put your hands on my skin, and I don't want anything in the way."

"Oh," I said. "I suppose in that case I could make an exception." I pulled the gloves off slowly as I approached the bed and put them on the table.

He lifted the blankets and I said, "You'll have to take that tunic off if you want my hands on your skin."

He dropped the blanket and stripped off his sleeping garment, flinging it at me with a cheeky grin.

I climbed into bed, grabbed him, and found the ticklish spot on his ribs, and he shrieked and squirmed but went still when my lips found his.

He slipped his tongue into my mouth and for a long moment we did nothing but kiss, tongues tangling and teeth bumping. Then I pulled away and settled him against me. He wrapped one leg over mine and I felt the feathers that covered his sheath brush against my cock.

"Will you put your tongue somewhere you've never put it before?" he said, looking at me from under his long silver lashes.

"Do you want me to tongue-fuck you, pretty bird?" My words made his cheeks flush pink and his breathing speed up.

"Yes," he whispered.

"Will you say it?" I knew he liked to hear me pronounce words he thought were filthy, things he'd have been beaten for saying at the Abbey, but I wasn't sure if *he* wanted to say them, too.

He bit his lip, and I smiled. "You don't have to," I said. "If you want my tongue in your ass, I'll do it, whatever words you use."

"Please," he said, and I kissed him again, then rolled him onto his belly and burrowed under the blankets. I stroked a hand over his tail, gathered the feathers together, and gently pushed it aside. He held it up, making a tent of the bedcovers so I didn't have to fight blankets to reach him.

"Kier," he said, as I crept between his legs and kissed the back of his left thigh.

"Mmm?" I nibbled my way over his ass and as far under his tail as I could get, until my tongue was tracing his crack.

"That's nice," he said, shifting his legs farther apart.

I poked my tongue in deeper, licking him from between his thighs as far up as I could go without making his tail flex uncomfortably. I felt the blankets shift as he made fists in them and stroked my hands over the soft skin of his behind, pulling his cheeks apart. I kissed him, just a light touch of my lips to his asshole, and then a deeper, harder kiss, ending with my tongue slipping inside him and pushing in as far as I could reach.

He cried out and arched his back, and I heard the soft wet sound of his cock slipping out of his sheath and felt the throb as he pulsed.

"Pretty bird," I said against his ass, then speared my tongue into him again, and again, and again.

He moaned into the pillows and pulsed again, and I nudged him up onto his knees.

"Do you want me to keep fucking you with my tongue?" I said. "Or do you want my cock inside you?" I slid my hand between his legs to stroke his hard length and flicked my tongue over his asshole again.

"I want you…" He hesitated, as if he wasn't sure what words he wanted to use. "I want you to orgasm, too."

"Don't worry about me, beloved," I said. "Tell me what *you* want."

He started to twist away, annoyed, then moaned and moved back to where he had been, ass spread, so I could put my tongue on him again. "I want you to orgasm, too," he said again, more firmly. "Please. I like it when you… when you come."

I smiled and traced my tongue over him again, then sat up and moved my hand, slick with his lubricant, to my own cock and rubbed myself until I was slippery.

"Please, Kier," he said, panting. "Don't stop before I'm done. Please."

"I'm not stopping," I said. I reached around him to stroke him again and he cried out and pulsed, hot and throbbing in my hand.

"Please," he whispered.

I pushed myself against him, rubbed his asshole with the tip of my cock and then pushed him open, spread him wide to thrust inside.

"Oh, Goddess, yes," he said. "Kier, don't stop."

I'm not sure I could have stopped if I'd wanted to. The blankets had been shoved away and he knelt before me, wings half open and tail cocked to one side, ass cheeks spread, and I disappeared into him, slid out, plunged in again.

"Fuck," I said. "Fionn, you're… Oh, fuck." I buried my face between his shoulder blades as I stroked and thrust and he pushed back against me, tilted his pelvis against my fist, and then I was coming, thrusting helplessly against him, stroking him, and he pulsed in my hand and for a moment we were both lost in pleasure.

When I could catch my breath, I helped him lie down, away from the wet spot he'd made, and tugged a corner of the sheet up to cover the damp so I could lie next to him.

We lay quietly for a while, curled together, hands absently stroking skin, just for comfort. Then he stirred and said, "If you regained your magic tomorrow, what would you do?"

I thought for a moment and then replied. "I would tell my Queen I wanted to give my place as her heir to Padraig and be released from my duties to her."

"Would she accept that?"

"No, I very much doubt it. But at least she would know why I left."

"You would leave?"

I traced the feathers around his face and wondered what other Vogel could read in them. "I really think I would."

"I would kill her for you, if I got the chance," he said, and for a moment I wasn't sure I'd heard him correctly.

"No, pretty bird, you mustn't do that." I cupped his face in both hands and kissed his forehead. "Seers mustn't take life, and even if they could, I would never wish that stain on your spirit."

He took a ragged breath but didn't try to argue with me. Instead, he said, "Would you take me with you? If you left?" He wasn't looking at my face; instead, he watched his own hands where they rested on my chest.

"Would you like me to?" I said. "It would make us outlaws."

"Could we still help people?" he said. "Could I do… could I do good for people who need it, if I was an outlaw?"

"You could do whatever you wanted to, pretty bird."

"I wonder if I could accomplish more away from the Eyrie than locked inside it," he said thoughtfully, and then he did meet my eyes. "I wonder if I could unite people to help each other."

I smiled and touched the tip of his nose with one finger. "I think you could," I said. "Maybe that's what your visions have been telling you. Maybe we run away together and travel the Isle helping people."

He laughed softly. "It's a nice dream." Then his face went serious. "But if we did that… What if we started a rebellion by accident? People would be hurt. People could die."

"If it gets to the point where people are willing to rebel, then I think they usually believe there's something worth dying *for*."

"*Is* it worth dying for?" he said. "Freedom? The ability to choose who to love, who to marry, what to call yourself?"

"The freedom to choose the path of your own life? Ask Daphnis," I said. "Ask any dryad. Ask the werewolves, who don't have any say in how they're governed. Or the fauns, whose only hope of a better life is to sign a contract of indenture. I think many of them would say it *is* worth dying for."

"What about you?" he whispered, touching my face, his fingers tracing my cheek and jaw. "Do you think freedom is worth dying for?"

I smiled and kissed his fingertips. "Beloved," I said. "I think freedom is worth *living* for. It's worth suffering for."

"Oh," he said. "Sometimes living is harder than dying, isn't it?"

I rested my forehead against his. "Living is always harder than dying."

"Will you live?"

"I promised you I would." I pulled him closer against me, checking to see that his wings were tucked comfortably. "If I die, it won't be because I chose it. Not anymore."

He made a sound almost like a sob. "I choose to live, too," he said. "For love, and freedom, and the possibility of a better world."

"For love," I said, and closed my eyes to listen to him breathe.

24
Fionn

WHEN I CLIMBED out Kiernan's window to go back to my room as dawn was breaking, I was filled with equal measures of hope and anxiety. I was tired enough, though, that I fell asleep as soon as I got into bed after making sure Neeka had made it back from the revels safely.

I slept late – our next meeting wasn't until evening – and woke when Neeka brought me tea and toasted bread with blackberry preserves. She looked as groggy as I felt, but she was grinning.

<Did you meet with your pretty guard?> I asked, as she set out my clothes for the day and fussed with the makeup on my dressing table.

<Maybe,> she said. <Did you want to bathe before you dress? I believe Councilor Rocsh and Nikna are finished in the bathing room.>

<I suppose I'd better bathe,> I said, unable to hold in a grin over *why* I need to bathe. Though I'd washed before I left Kier's rooms, I was sure I must still smell of him, of *us*. <I'll tell

you what gifts Kier gave me if you tell me about your evening.>

She blushed and held out a robe for me to put on over my sleeping tunic. I dutifully put my arms in the sleeves and let her tie the belt.

<I'm *not* giving you details,> she said. <But we danced. And we talked. And we kissed. And she promised to write to me, after we go.>

<So you didn't break any Vogel laws?> I teased, following her into the bathing room, where she ran me a bath and insisted on handing me soap and washcloths and towels.

<Not yet,> she said. <But we have a few more days.>

<Just be careful,> I said, happy for her, of course, but worried about those King's Guards we had with us, that were, I was sure, observing everything to report back to our King as soon as we arrived in the Eyrie.

<You, too.>

We looked at each other seriously for a moment and then both grinned. <It's worth it, though,> I said.

<Yes,> she agreed.

Once I was dressed, we emerged into the sitting room of our delegation's suite to find Councilor Rocsh waiting for us.

<I've been invited to visit the nearby village,> he said. <It seems the people there are mostly day-dwellers, unlike our hosts, and they have local craftwork they would like to share.> He tilted his head to one side to look at me, as if he could see my late night under the makeup Neeka had carefully applied, but he didn't comment, only let a brief smile touch his lips.

<You're welcome to come along,> he continued. <But you've had a message from Prince Kiernan asking if you would like to see the palace library. It seems he doesn't mind waking during the day for your convenience.> Again, he let a little smile slip onto his lips, only this time it grew, as if he al-

ready knew which option I would choose.

<I *would* like to see the local textiles production,> I said. <But Seer Siona mentioned some books in the library I would very much like to consult before we leave.> I bit my lip, then made my mouth relax. I thought I saw amusement in the Councilor's eyes.

<I'm happy to make note of any spinning or weaving, my Seer,> he said. <And there may be time yet for you to visit.> He paused. <If you mean to consult a copy of the Founding Laws, I believe that should take precedence.> He frowned. <I can't imagine where the Eyrie's copy has gone. It isn't supposed to leave the library, and I consulted it only just after you arrived when I needed to look up a detail on tithes owing to the Alfar.>

The King's Guards accompanied Councilor Rocsh and Nikna, leaving me with my own guards and Neeka to follow me to the library.

We found Kiernan waiting just inside the door, talking to a small, bent old Sidhe who looked at him with fondness. Kiernan looked exhausted, but I couldn't tell if it was from our long night together, or from the strain of living without his magic.

"Seer Tokka," he said. "This is our Archivist."

"Hello," I said, shaking the frail-looking hand the Archivist held out to me. Their grip was firm and much stronger than I had expected. "What do I call you?"

"Archivist is fine," they said and laughed. "I think I might fall down from shock if anyone called me by my given name after all these decades."

"They've never told me what their name is," Kiernan said to me, smiling.

"No, I haven't, young Prince. Because I'm not very fond of it." Their lips curved in a smile. "Now, what can I find for you, Seer Tokka?"

I looked at my hands, then met the Archivist's kind hazel eyes. "You could call me Fionn," I said, shyly.

They smiled. "And what can I find for you, Seer Fionn?" they said.

"Seer Siona said there is a book about the history of seers. And I'd like to consult your copy of the Founding Laws. Our copy at the Eyrie seems to have gone missing, and I haven't had a chance to look at the section that outlines a Seer's duties to their Monarch."

They nodded and looked thoughtful. "Seer Siona has asked me to have a copy made of the history. It's in manuscript, and as far as I am aware has never been available in a printed edition. I'm afraid it will have to be sent to you at a later date, but you're welcome to look at the original now."

"Oh!" I said. "If I'm to have a copy, I can wait."

"Then, if our good Prince will lend me his strong arms, I'll fetch the Laws. There are tables that way where you may sit." They pointed to an area that was more brightly lit than the rest of the dim, comfortable room.

Trikta and Konta arranged themselves near the door, while Neeka and I found a table and sat down.

"You don't have to stay," I said. "I know how much you love historical research."

She laughed. "I'd rather do embroidery," she said.

"I *like* embroidery," I retorted. "Though I'm not very good at it yet."

"Yes, but you have patience," she said. "I'd rather learn how to use a spear or a sword. As if I'd ever be allowed."

I poked her arm. "Maybe your Sidhe guard will teach you."

She stuck her tongue out at me.

"Go talk to the palace staff," I said. "Or watch the guards train, if any of them are awake at this hour."

She hesitated until she saw the huge old tome Kiernan brought to the table, and then she stood up quickly.

"Take Konta with you," I said, and she nodded and left.

Kiernan set the book on the table, careful with it despite its large size. It looked like it may have been rebound since its original creation, but it had been well cared for and when I opened the heavy cover, the pages were still soft and supple, and the ink bright.

Kiernan stood next to me, leaning over the book to peer at the writing. "There's no index," he said. "But the Archivist tells me the section on Seers starts about halfway through."

"Is this in Islish?" I leaned closer to study the text.

Kiernan leaned closer, too, and I felt a lock of his hair tickle my cheek. "I find it very difficult to read this old hand, but it doesn't look like Sidhe."

I turned pages and stopped at a heading that looked like the word "Seers." "I'm familiar with a lot of hands," I said. "From studying at the Abbey."

He turned so his forehead just brushed mine. "I'd wager you can write them as well as read them," he said, making the words sound like a declaration of love instead of an ordinary comment.

"I can." I lifted my chin so my lips brushed his earlobe as I spoke and he drew in a sharp breath.

I turned back to the book. "It's Old Islish," I said. "I can read it well enough, though some words have changed spelling, and some have changed meaning."

"And some just don't exist anymore." Kiernan pointed to a line.

"So," I said, standing so I could better see the huge page. The book took up the full width of the table and nearly half its length. "This says…" I paused to scan the lines, translating them into a more modern wording in my head. "Oof. There is a lot of very formal language that really doesn't mean much."

"So, not a lot has changed, then." Kiernan glanced at me and smiled, then looked back to the book. "I can almost read this," he said, frowning.

We worked through the text quietly for a while, slowly turning the big pages, both of us running a finger under each line to help keep our place. After the third page, I started to get a sick feeling in my belly.

"What's wrong?" Kiernan said quietly, studying my face, and I realized he'd just asked me about a word he couldn't make out and I hadn't answered.

I traced my finger back over a line of text near the bottom of the page and he looked at it more closely.

"This says a Seer belongs to their Monarch," I said.

"We knew that," he replied, looking back at my face.

"It uses a word for possession to mean that a Seer has duties to their Monarch that are absolute, not in the sense of ownership, like a slave is owned."

His dark eyebrows crept closer together as he looked from me to the page and back.

I ran my finger under another line. "A Monarch may dictate which Seers among their people will work directly for the Monarchy, and which will be assigned to other nobles or villages or cities, and they may change those assignments at any time."

"Yes," Kier said softly.

"A Monarch must ensure all Seers among their people are provided with food, clothing, and shelter." I paused. "And that every Seer is given a wage according to their abilities. If the Seer's magic increases over time, the amount they are paid should also increase."

He touched my hand when I stopped to swallow the lump in my throat. I turned the page and sat staring at it, not seeing the words. "I should be getting *paid*, Kier. Not just a few coins here and there to buy trinkets at the market, but a proper wage."

I looked up at him finally, and his eyebrows were crowded as close together as I'd ever seen them, but he wasn't looking at me, he was running a finger under a sentence in the book. His nostrils flared. "I'm not sure I'm reading this right," he said, and his voice was tight and clipped. Whatever he had read had made him angry.

I looked at the sentence, read it, and clamped a hand over my mouth.

"Keep reading, pretty bird," he said, so softly I almost couldn't hear him over the roaring in my ears. I read the next sentence, then the next.

"I need to throw up," I whispered. He put his arm around me.

"Do you want to go and find a bathing room?"

I shook my head and swallowed hard. "No," I said. "No, I'm all right." I took a deep breath and turned back to the text. "A Monarch can only give a Seer orders that aid in the running of the Monarchy and the physical or spiritual wellbeing of its people," I said, and then I had to sit down.

Kiernan put a hand on my shoulder and squeezed.

"A Monarch may forbid a Seer to marry or have children, as those things can interfere with their duties," I said, much more calmly than I felt. "But they may *not* forbid a Seer from forming friendships or even intimate relationships so long as the wellbeing of the Monarchy takes precedence."

"Beloved," Kiernan said, his voice just audible. His hand tightened on my shoulder again and he bent and kissed the top of my head. I looked up at him when he straightened and felt tears gathering in the corners of my eyes.

I swallowed again. "A Monarch may not dictate with

whom a Seer shares their bed," I said, not sure sound was coming out of my mouth anymore. "And it is inappropriate for a Monarch to take any of their own Seers as lovers, as it could create a conflict of interest." The tears spilled over, and the words blurred on the page. I leaned away from the table to avoid wetting the ancient text.

I tried to blink away the tears. Trikta shifted his position across the room, but Kiernan was between us, and I was glad my loyal guard couldn't see me.

"All this time, *he* was breaking the law," I whispered.

"You never have to share his bed again, beloved," Kiernan said, brushing tears from my face with gentle fingers. "You don't have to be afraid to go back."

I looked at the huge old book, then back at Kiernan. There was a hardness to his face. He was angry. Furious. But not at me. He was angry *for* me. I stared at him, realizing I had never seen him truly angry before.

"I –" I looked at the open pages on the table. "Councilor Rocsh said he consulted the Eyrie's copy of the Founding Laws in the library not long after I first arrived, but I know I've never seen it there."

"Do you think –" Kiernan hesitated.

"*He* must have taken it," I said. "The King. Only a few people have a key to the library."

"He didn't want you to know," Kier said softly.

"No, he didn't want me to know." My belly felt cold inside, but I didn't feel like throwing up anymore. I was too angry. "My King likes young boys," I said. Something flickered in Kiernan's eyes, but his face didn't change.

"You're not a boy, young or otherwise," he said, tracing my cheekbone and wiping away the last of my tears. "You're very much a grown man, beloved."

"But I'm small for a Vogel. Stunted, some have said. I'm

the *size* of a boy, compared to my people."

He shook his head but didn't interrupt.

"I'm small and my eyes are too big and I was afraid when I first arrived at the Eyrie." I slide my gaze away from his. "And inexperienced." I bit my lip. "He could pretend I was a child."

He sighed. "But you've reached your majority, so fucking you wouldn't break any Isle laws. You must have seemed like a gift from the spirits."

"Except for the ancient law no one seems to remember, that Monarchs may not have relations with their own Seers."

"And if the only book stating that law couldn't be found, then no one could be reminded."

We stared at each other.

"He must have the book somewhere. Even he wouldn't dare destroy it." I put my hand on the page in front of me. "I need to find it, to show the council, or it will only be my word opposing his, and as King his word is truth."

"Show this to your Councilor," Kier said. "Both your King and your Council trust him, or he wouldn't be here negotiating an important trade deal."

I nodded. "Yes, I'll do that." I looked up at him.

"Are you okay, pretty bird?"

I couldn't nod or even shake my head, so I just stared at him. "I'm angry," I finally said. "I thought… once I thought I might have loved him, or at least desired him, if I wasn't to be allowed to have you. When I thought you were lost to me."

He smiled a little and stroked my cheekbone with his thumb. "And I thought that if you accepted his advances that he would protect you. Treasure you. Make you happy if I couldn't."

"When I found out *why* he wanted me –" I felt tears threatening again and had to stop or else have my words turn into a sob.

He moved his other hand to cup my face.

"And when I learned he wanted to plunder our past and not learn from it –" I went on.

His kissed my forehead.

"I knew I could never feel for him. Not even as a friend. Even if I hadn't had to watch you sail away from me, taking my heart with you."

"If he touches you against your will again, pretty bird, I *will* kill him."

That evening, I managed to appear serene and collected, as if I was above everyone around me, untouched, even though inside I was screaming.

I think Neeka could tell I was unsettled, because she kept frowning and studying my face, but she must have sensed my mood, because she didn't ask.

When I requested that Councilor Rocsh read the section of the Laws pertaining to Seers, he agreed and didn't ask why. I think he could also tell I didn't want to talk.

The meeting that evening was to present an outline of the trade possibilities we had discussed to the Queen, so there was very little for me to do except be there, for which I was grateful. I only had to observe and listen as our negotiators described our requests and the Sidhe negotiators described theirs. The Queen nodded graciously at each point, asking for clarification from time to time, but everything went smoothly.

Kiernan's job was to introduce each speaker and sum up the whole of the negotiations. As he was finishing up his comments, the Queen held out her cup for more wine, and a nervous-looking faun scrambled forward with a pitcher, tripped, and spilled dark liquid over the table.

Everything in the room seemed to stop for a moment, until the Queen stood and backhanded the servant, sending him sprawling to the floor.

I glanced at Kiernan and there was a darkness, a hardness in his eyes as absolute as he had expressed when we discovered my King's transgressions. I had only seen something close when he had talked about his cousin Sean murdering Declan Winterborn. For just an instant, I saw pure hate there, and it terrified me.

But then it was gone, and he was gathering up the stained tablecloth like what had just happened was inconsequential.

"I think you need new servants, my Queen," he said, stepping around the faun cowering on the floor to wipe up a little more wine.

"So it seems," the Queen said lightly, as if she hadn't just viciously struck another person. "But what am I to do with this one?"

Kiernan shrugged. "I don't want servants, yet you insist I must have some. Give him to me, and I'll add him to the dryad I didn't want that you gave me when I was too ill to protest."

"My son has a weakness for the less fortunate," the Queen said, turning to our delegation. None of my people had moved, too shocked to react. Councilor Rocsh recovered first and nodded politely.

"Scribe!" the Queen said, and a Sidhe with a portable desk strapped around his shoulders stepped forward, pen poised. "Fetch this creature's contract from the Archivist and sign him over to your Prince." The scribe bowed and hurried from the room.

The Queen looked at Kiernan and smiled, an expression with too many teeth to be comforting. "It's your problem, now, my son. Perhaps you have the patience to housebreak it."

Then she rose and said a polite farewell, and the meeting was over. One by one the other Sidhe left the room after their Queen, and then our delegation, until only Councilor Rocsh and I were left with Kiernan. And the faun, sobbing on the floor and trying to muffle his cries against the woodwork.

Kiernan tossed the bundled-up tablecloth in a heap on a chair and knelt next to the faun, who flinched away. I put my hand over my mouth to keep from making an unfortunate noise.

"Erith," Kiernan said gently, putting his hand on the faun's shoulder. "It's okay, she's gone."

"I'm sorry," the faun whispered. "I'm so clumsy. So stupid. Oh Goddess, I'm sorry." He pressed his face harder into the floor.

"Hush now, Erith, you're okay." Kier gathered the young man into his arms, and at first the faun went stiff with fear. I caught a glimpse of his eyes and the terror in them. But then he seemed to realize he wasn't about to be hurt again and he relaxed and turned to bury his face in Kiernan's chest. His thin shoulders shook with sobs, but he made no sound.

"It's okay, Erith. You're safe."

"I can't –" the faun whispered. "She'll dismiss me, and I'll never pay off my indenture. She'll... she'll beat me. I can't go back."

"Hush, little one," Kier said, stroking the faun's hair. I felt tears gather in my own eyes, at the faun's misery and Kier's gentleness, and I felt like an intruder. I turned to go, but Kier looked up and caught my eye and I stopped. His lips curved into a smile, there and gone.

"You don't work for the Queen anymore, Erith," he said.

"I – I don't?" The young man finally raised his head and I realized he was older than I had thought at first. I wondered if that was how people saw me.

"You work for me now," Kier said, keeping his voice low and calm.

"Oh. I – Oh, that's better." Erith scrubbed his face with both hands. "But… what if I spill wine on you? I'm so clumsy." He started to cry again, but gently.

Kiernan shifted to pull a handkerchief from his pocket and wiped the young man's face. "I promise I will never hit you for spilling wine."

Erith bit his lip and seemed to suddenly realize there were people in the room besides him and his Prince. He looked down at his hands and flushed deep pink.

"I'm a terrible servant," he whispered.

"It's hard to be good at anything when you're terrified all the time," Kier said. "But you needn't be afraid anymore."

Erith looked at him again, eyes wide.

"You told me you want to learn," Kiernan said.

"Oh, yes!" Hope warred with the fear and misery on the faun's face.

"Then you shall learn." Kiernan smiled at him and Erith's face lit up so he looked like the happy young man he probably was before he arrived to work for the Sidhe Queen.

"And Padraig is one of my Guards, so you'll see him every day."

The faun's smile grew wider, and he blushed even more, and I saw something on his face I'd seen on my own face in the mirror: love. Deep, unconditional love. Some of it for Kiernan, perhaps, but mostly for Padraig. I hoped Kier's cousin was worth the devotion on Erith's features.

"Thank you, my Prince," he said. "I owe you my life."

Kiernan smiled and stood up, helping Erith up with him. "You do not, Erith. You only owe it to yourself to live the best life you can."

Then he looked at me and he might as well have been speaking the words to me alone.

I nodded. "Yes," I said, softly. "Oh, yes."

25
Kiernan

Between the two of us, Daphnis and I had finished a proto-type of artificial wings in Dec's cellar. They looked better than I could have imagined but were monstrously heavy.

I wanted to show them to Fionn anyway, so once I had found a new room for Erith, closer to my own rooms, and filled Padraig in on the good news, I sent a message to the Vogel delegation inviting interested parties to come view my invention the next afternoon. I knew most of their party would be getting ready to leave, to head north to where their ship waited to take them back to the Eyrie. And I knew Fionn would know the invitation was mostly for him.

Then I spent the rest of the night trying to read – the Archivist had suggested a volume of fairy tales as a way to take my mind off my lack of magic – but I ended up just staring at the book and not seeing the words. I was too distracted by imagining what Fionn's face would look like when he saw what I had made for him.

Daphnis brought me food and nagged me until I ate, and

when dawn came, he nagged me until I drank a sleeping tea and went to bed.

I woke feeling only marginally less tired than when I'd first climbed under the blankets. I needed to make time to see Siona, and soon, to have her draw the Realms through me to ease the ache of my stolen magic. Being near Fionn helped but it wasn't enough. The hollow feeling left me exhausted and it was beginning to affect my ability to function.

Daphnis's offer of magic was looking more and more appealing, and I hated that I was even considering it.

I dressed slowly. This would be one of the last times I would see Fionn. Later that night would be the farewell ceremony, and the next morning the Vogel delegation would leave. I might convince my Queen to allow me to escort the delegation to their ship, but that would only buy me a day and there would be no opportunity for a private farewell.

So I chose my clothes with care, ignoring Daphnis's suggestions and choosing garments for their fabrics and colors — things I knew Fionn would appreciate — rather than for how fashionable they were. And even though it wasn't truly cold yet, I put on the hood and gloves and ankle warmers Fionn had made for me. Even if I hadn't wanted him to see me in them at least once before we left, their softness and the care with which they had been made gave me more comfort than an inanimate group of objects ought to.

I looked at myself in the mirror and saw, beneath the exhaustion, not a Prince but a warrior, and I had a stabbing moment of doubt. Was it a good thing that one of Fionn's last views of me would be that? Would he prefer to see me as I was most comfortable, as just Kiernan Druison, good with a sword? Or would he rather have the stylish and dashing Prince of Morven Forest?

I sighed. I knew the answer, of course, because it was the

same answer I would give about him. He would see *me*, and it didn't really matter what I wore.

"You look handsome, my Prince," Daphnis said.

"I suppose I'll do." I turned to go but paused by the fireplace to check on the serpent egg. It was warm to the touch, but not over-warm. A couple of times a day Smoke and Flame had appeared at my window to make sure I was taking care of it properly. I had hoped it would hatch before Fionn left, but so far it showed no signs of doing so.

"It is an honor, my Prince, for feathered tree serpents to bestow one of their eggs upon you."

"It is," I said, stroking the smooth shell one more time. "It's an honor for them to show me friendship at all."

"Tree serpents are intelligent. They know a good man when they meet him."

I snorted.

"You *are* a good man, my Prince. I believe Erith would agree with me, and so would your Seer."

I made a noncommittal noise and we left the palace for the forest. Erith had been instructed to bring any of the Vogel delegation who decided they wanted to see my project. My guards, like most Sidhe, were asleep in their beds and would stay there until twilight. I had yet to choose more guards, to provide myself with a full-time entourage, but I knew I would soon have to, or my Queen would choose them for me.

At Dec's cabin, we opened the cellar door wide to let in the sun and lit lamps to drive away the shadows. I had originally thought to move the wings out into the meadow, but they proved too heavy and awkward.

I had another moment of doubt that almost bent me double with anxiety. Perhaps I should have waited until I had something that actually worked, something that Fionn could use, and not just something that looked pretty. It passed, slowly, and I left the cellar, rounding the corner of the cabin to the front steps.

For a long time I just stood, my hand on the solid planks of the front door, remembering the last time I had been inside. It had been Midwinter night, close to four years ago now, mere hours after Dec had been murdered. I had been called before my Queen before I could even mourn, and declared her legitimate son and third heir, given the title Prince of Morven Forest, and I would have refused despite wanting those very things my whole life if I could have had Dec alive again.

I had come back, seeking darkness and solitude, and found his body cold on the floor. I had covered him with a blanket and crawled onto his bed where the bedding still smelled like him – like us – and I had waited to cry.

I had not cried. Not then, and not since.

I rested my forehead against the door. While I had lain there, miserable and heartbroken, unable to weep for the man I had loved, a tall, pale Vogel with perfect silver-white wings had come through the door and told me he saw Dec's ghost. He had let me say goodbye, had even allowed his spirit body to be possessed by Declan so we could touch again, one last time.

And when Dec was truly gone, his spirit absorbed back into the Realms, I still had not cried. I couldn't understand why. When Fionn had been taken from me by the Vogel King's Guards – and he had been alive and safe – I had bawled like a child. Had I changed so much, or did I love Fionn differently than I had loved Dec?

Maybe it didn't even matter. I straightened up, squared my shoulders, and turned to pick the lock on the door. It was cold and dusty inside, untouched except that Dec's body was gone. There was still wood on the hearth, and everything was put away in its proper place. Dec was like Fionn that way – everything had a spot it belonged and must be put away when not in use.

I found a water bucket, long dry but still sound, and picked it up. When I turned around, Daphnis was in the doorway.

"Do you need water, my Prince?"

"I thought I would make tea for our guests."

He held out his hand. "Allow me." He looked at me, expressionless, until I passed him the bucket. "I think you could use a moment."

I nodded and he left me alone. I took Dec's teapot and an assortment of cups from the cupboard and wiped them clean with a dish cloth from one of the drawers. Everything was so familiar, and felt as hollow as I did, empty of that which had once given it life.

I found a packet of tea – probably stale, but if would have to suffice – and then I realized I was just putting off what I had come inside to do. I couldn't have said why, but I didn't want to let Fionn leave until I had made my peace with the terrible things that had happened in this cabin. Perhaps, if I laid Dec's memory to rest along with his ghost and his body, I could be whole again, could be someone worthy of Fionn's regard.

So I crossed to the bedroom door, and looked through. There was Dec's big bed, just as it had been, only the sheets were rumpled and dusty. The bloodstains on the blanket were obscured because it had been pushed aside.

The bloodstain on the floor was a dark and stark reminder of what had happened.

I made myself look at it, at all of it, and let it sink in again.

A soft noise behind me made me turn. I expected Daphnis with the water, but it was Fionn, hesitating in the open door.

"This is Declan's house," he said softly. "I remember."

I held out my hand and he crossed the floor to take it in his.

"You're sad," he said and laid his palm against my cheek.

I turned my face to kiss his hand. "I'm okay," I said. "It was a long time ago."

"Not *that* long." His thumb stroked over my cheek and my eyes were suddenly blurry. I felt, for a moment, like I had been punched in the gut, and then his arms were around me and my tears were soaking into his tunic front.

"Oh Goddess," I said, my voice ragged. "I thought I was done grieving."

"You loved him," Fionn said, softly. "And three years — even nearly four years — is not a long time."

"I'm sorry." I wrapped my arms around his waist and buried my face in his chest and he stroked my hair, kissed the top of my head, and didn't try to stop me from crying.

"You needn't be sorry, beloved."

I laughed, a sharp, bitten-off sound. "I'm weeping for another man. That seems like something I should be sorry for."

He laughed, too, but it was a gentler sound than mine. "I'm not so fragile that I'm threatened by the memory of your previous love."

"You're too good for me," I said, nestling close. My tears had stopped, and I felt lighter. I still missed Dec, but it wasn't so painful, now.

He snorted. "Do you realize," he said, "That I experienced sex for the first time in this house?"

"What?" I pulled back to look at him and he laughed again.

"I let Declan borrow my spirit body and he used it to make love to you. I gave him my permission, of course. But I was… there. An observer, I suppose."

I felt myself flush and was glad my skin didn't show blushes easily. I stepped back and turned away from the bedroom. "Do you want to see what I asked you here for?"

"An invention, you said?" He followed me to the door.

"Erith brought me, but no one else came along. I think even Trikta realized I wanted to come alone."

"I can send Daphnis and Erith back the palace to wait for us."

He twined his fingers in mine as I led him around the side of the cabin to the cellar door. He was right behind me as I ducked inside and climbed down the steep steps. Then I turned to watch him as he noticed the wings on the worktable. He froze and stared, eyes wide, for several heartbeats.

"What is this?" he said and moved closer, touching the polished wood with hesitant fingers. He looked at me. "Kier, what?"

I smiled. "They're not actually functional. Not until I find a way to make them lighter. But I dropped a smaller version from the canopy of the Heart tree, and they worked. They'll carry weight."

He looked back at the wings, moving slowly around the table to study them from all angles.

I turned one of them over, grunting with the effort.

"Oh, they are heavy," he said.

"I need to find better materials."

He touched the underside, running his fingers over the straps. "Why is it built like this?"

I bit my lip and hesitated, uncertain again, then made myself continue. "Your wings fit there," I said. "I had to guess at the measurements, but…" I looked up and he was staring at me, astonishment on his face. "You… well, you manipulate them with your own wings, so your arms are free. The tail piece is the same."

"So… they're like extensions for my wings and tail, only functional instead of decorative?" He half-opened one of his own wings as if to contrast its unusable extra feathers with the contraption in front of him.

"Something like that."

He frowned and looked back at the unwieldy things on the table. They looked bulky and inelegant next to his perfect white feathers, and I began to wonder if I should have showed him after all, if I should even have tried to build them.

He ran a hand over the leather membrane. "Silk would be better, I think," he said. "It's very strong, but light."

"Cloud silk?" I teased, but his face was serious when he turned his gaze back to me.

"Cloud silk would be perfect. It's lighter and stronger than moth silk, or even spider silk. And it's water resistant."

"And extremely expensive."

He flashed me a grin. "Not if I grow it myself." He tugged a lock of the hair that had escaped and crept through his feathers to fall onto his forehead.

"You would withhold your tithe from the Alfar Monarchy?"

He shrugged. "I believe we're planning to escape and be outlaws." His grin grew. "And as it turns out, when Councilor Rocsh consulted the Founding Laws – before the Eyrie's copy went missing – he learned we aren't actually required to send the silk from every Vogel citizen as we have been. Instead, there is a specified weight. We've been overpaying for decades."

"Another lie perpetrated by a greedy King?" I asked.

"They seem prone to it," he replied, his face serious. Then he looked back at the wings on the table and smiled. "And apparently, Rocsh never did send my hair to the Alfar. It's still at the Eyrie, mine to spin and weave as the ancient Seers once did, to make offerings to the spirits."

I laughed. "I like your Councilor Rocsh more every day."

"As for the frame," he said. "There is a reed that grows in Tronven. They say it gets as large as trees in some places. They use it to make furniture and tent frames." He met my eyes again and his were full of light. "It's very light and strong."

He moved the rest of the way around the table and stood facing me.

"Cloud silk and Tronven reeds," I said. "Next time maybe I can give you flight, and not just an inoperable model."

He moved closer. "Will you send Daphnis and Erith back to the palace?" His voice was soft and husky, and I felt it shiver through me to the tips of my toes.

I tilted my face up to his. "I can. Why?"

"You made me wings, beloved. And maybe I can't use them yet, but…" He drew in a breath. "You gave me a dream." He bent and brushed his lips over mine. "Beloved, you're trying to give me the sky." He kissed me again, harder. "Let me give you something in return."

"Your smile is enough." I caught his lower lip between my teeth and pulled it gently away from his gums, then let go. "And you've already given me something so much more precious, beloved. You've given me yourself."

"Then let me give you myself again. Now. Unless… you don't want to use Dec's house that way."

I put my hand on his chest to feel his heartbeat on my palm. "I don't think he would mind."

I stepped slowly away from him and led the way out of the cellar. In Dec's kitchen, we found Erith and Daphnis making tea. The fire was built up in the hearth and the kettle was steaming.

Erith jumped to his feet and bowed when we walked in. "My Prince," he said. "Seer Tokka."

"You needn't be formal when we're alone, Erith," I said.

"But we're not alone." He looked pointedly at Fionn, who smiled.

"Fionn – I mean Seer Tokka – is a friend. You needn't be

formal with him, either."

"Yes, my Prince."

I looked from Erith to Daphnis and before I could say any more, Daphnis took Erith by the shoulder and steered him towards the door.

"Come, Erith. We have things to attend to at the palace," he said.

"Oh, but —" Erith looked at me.

"Go on," I said. "I don't need you here."

"But —"

I looked at Fionn, then back to Erith, considering what I should say. "Seer Tokka and I are... like you and Padraig," I finally said.

Erith's eyes got very wide. "Oh!" he said. "*Oh*. Of course. Daphnis and I have things to do at the palace." Then he grinned. "I am happy for you, my Prince."

Once we were alone, I was suddenly overcome by nerves. I lifted the kettle and poured hot water into the teapot and stared into it as the leaves swirled.

"I don't really want tea, beloved," Fionn said. "We can go somewhere else if it hurts you to be here." His voice was soft, so gentle I could have wept.

"No," I said. "This is... I think I want to drive away the bad memories with new ones. Good ones." I turned toward him and hooked a finger in his belt to pull him closer. "This used to be a sanctuary for me, a place to escape to away from the court, where I was safe and loved. I want it to be that again."

"You *are* loved," he said, pretending to resist my pull until the clasp of his belt popped open and it fell to the floor.

"So are you," I said, tugging on his tunic until he shrugged it off over his shoulders.

"You're wearing my gifts," he said, pulling the hood over

my head and tugging off the gloves.

"Not anymore," I answered, laughing. Then I grabbed him, lifted him in my arms – he was taller than me, but light as a bird – and carried him into the bedroom.

He wriggled out of my arms, leaving his shirt behind, and tugged at my belt until I undid all the buckles holding my sword and knives in place and hung the whole rig from the bedpost.

Then I grabbed him again, pulled him close, and kissed him thoroughly.

When I leaned away, he yanked my shirt over my head and wrapped his arms around me to press our chests together and we stood that way for a moment, just feeling the warmth of skin on skin.

He sighed and traced my ear with his tongue, lingering on the spot where the edge was deeply nicked and tugging one of the rings with his teeth. "I don't want to go tomorrow," he said.

"I don't want you to go." I slipped my fingers into the feathers on his back, relishing the softness and the warmth of the skin beneath. "But I promise I'll come for you as soon as I have magic again."

"That's the only reason I can make myself leave." He found my mouth with his again and slid his tongue deep inside, until I groaned and reached for the buttons on his trousers. He reached for the tie on mine, and we fell together onto the bed, naked and tangled, barely noticing the cloud of dust we stirred up.

I couldn't help but compare him to Dec, just a little. He was as tall, but slenderer, softer, gentler and more giving. But he had his own kind of strength that Dec could never have matched. And where Dec had always wanted to be the one doing the fucking, Fionn liked fucking and being fucked equally.

Dec was a good lover and would have been a fine husband,

but Fionn was… Fionn was my perfect match in every way.

He twined his legs around me and suddenly grinned and twisted, and I found myself flat on my back looking up into his silver eyes, his smile turning his face from handsome to beautiful.

And as he leaned down to kiss me, I caught movement beyond the edge of his wing, heard the creak of a floorboard, and I must have made some noise because he said, "What is it, beloved?"

This time, *this time*, I moved without thinking, tucked him close against me, rolled him under me, and pushed myself up to my knees. I reached for my belt and had just wrapped my fingers around my knife hilt when I felt the sting of a moonsilver blade.

Fionn clamped his hands over his mouth, but only muffled his scream. And for a long moment time seemed to stop, and I could follow his horrified gaze to the length of metal protruding from my belly, stained red.

Time started again and I heard a shout. Padraig. "Sean, what the fuck?"

"You weren't supposed to get in the way, you stupid mongrel filth." That was Sean. Was I the mongrel? What wasn't I supposed to get in the way of?

I met Fionn's eyes. Right. Fionn. He was trying to kill Fionn. Then I remembered the blade in my hand and thanks to Sean's big mouth, I didn't need to see him to know where to strike. I might not have magic, but I did have functional ears and exceptional hearing.

I clenched my teeth, because I knew it would hurt to move, and I struck.

I felt my blade sink into Sean's neck to the crosspiece and when I ripped it free again, he fell, taking his sword with him.

Darkness crept closer.

"Beloved," I whispered.
"No," he said.
"I'm sorry."
"No."
And I sank into the comforting shadows.

26
Fionn

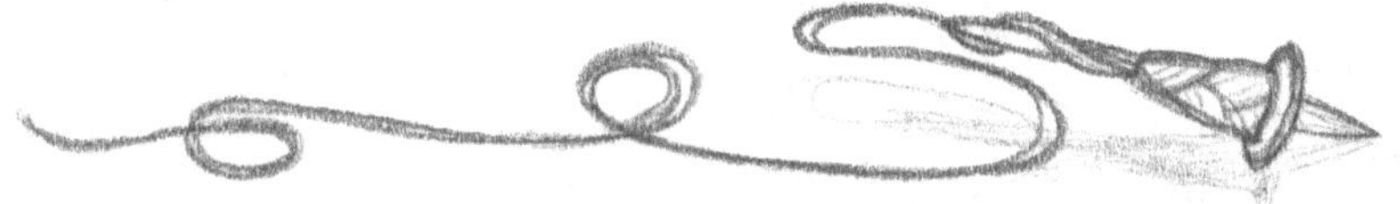

AT FIRST, MY MIND refused to comprehend what I was seeing. That couldn't be right. That couldn't be Kiernan's cousin Sean behind him. That couldn't be a sword.

But then my brain caught up and only by clamping both hands over my mouth was I able to muffle even a bit of the scream that tore out of my throat.

And then I couldn't move. I just lay on the bed, watching as Kiernan drew a knife from somewhere behind him and, without even looking, twisted and stabbed it into Sean's neck. And ripped it free, severing something vital in his cousin's throat. A gout of blood followed the blade and then Sean was falling, pulling his sword with him, cutting Kiernan open as he went.

And then calm seemed to settle over me and I wriggled out from under Kier's legs to kneel in front of him. He didn't seem to be able to focus on me. "Beloved," he said, so quiet I didn't think even Padraig heard, and he was crossing the room to catch Kiernan under his arms, to hold him up.

"No," I said firmly, and reached for Land, Sea, and Sky. Healing magic flooded into me.

"I'm sorry," he said.

"No," I said again, and pushed magic into him. The blood oozing from his belly and back slowed and I reached further, seeking to read his magic, to see his injuries as Healer Kah had taught me, and I saw… nothing.

Without his magic, Kiernan was a blank. I could stop his bleeding, heal the outer edges of the wound, but with no magic to read in him, I couldn't *see* the injuries on the inside. Was this how all hollow people would appear to me, or was it because his magic was stolen and blocked by spellwork?

I couldn't heal him.

He slumped and Padraig struggled to keep him upright.

"We have to get him back to the palace," I said, meeting his eyes. "I can't heal him properly."

Padraig nodded. "I'm sorry," he said. "I didn't know what Sean was going to do."

"He was not trying to kill your Prince."

"No, he wasn't."

"He was trying to kill me." I wiped blood from my hands onto the sheets and dressed quickly, fumbling with my belt until I could have screamed in frustration.

"I know. What I don't know is why."

I tried one more time to sense Kier's wounds, then shook my head. "I can't heal him."

"You stopped the bleeding," he said, lowering Kiernan carefully to the bed.

"But I can't *heal* him." I pushed back the panic that was making me clumsy, making me bite my words off shorter than usual. I reached for calm and found it, somehow. "We have to dress him."

"What?"

I met Padraig's eyes again. "How do you propose we explain it if we show up with him, bloody and naked? Bad enough we must tell your Queen her son is injured, and her nephew is dead."

"Right," he said, and then Daphnis was there suddenly, appearing as if out of nowhere, handing us Kiernan's discarded garments in the order that we'd need to put them on him. When he was clothed again, I pried his knife from his hand and used it to cut holes in his shirt, exactly where they would be if he had been impaled through it. I wiped it clean, slid it back into its sheath, and looked up to find Padraig watching me, curiosity on his face. But he said nothing.

The gloves and hood and anklets I had made I folded up and handed to Erith, who had been hovering in the background, like he wanted to help but also wanted to stay out of the way.

"You're quick, aren't you?" I said as he took the items and held them against his chest.

"I can run fast, yes, Seer Tokka."

"Will you run ahead to Seer Siona and tell her your Prince is injured and needs healers? Have her take them to his room."

"Yes, Seer Tokka."

"And hurry."

He nodded and practically leapt down the stairs and was gone into the woods.

"Daphnis?"

"I'll carry him, my Seer. I'm the strongest."

I nodded. "Go. Hurry. I'll be right behind you."

He scooped Kiernan up carefully and strode away, his long legs carrying him across the meadow and into the forest.

"And what shall I do, oh Seer?" said Padraig. Despite his mildly mocking tone, he did seem to be waiting for me to give him instructions, as if, with Kiernan unable to command him,

I was next in authority.

I looked at Sean, lying in a pool of blood on the floor. He looked younger, dead, and almost heartbreakingly handsome. I could see the family resemblance to Kiernan better now that there was no hate or scorn on his face.

"Can you carry him?" I said.

"He's not light, but I can manage."

He pulled a sheet off the bed to roll his cousin in.

"Will you take him to your Queen?" I picked up Sean's sword gingerly by its crossguard and slid it into the scabbard at his waist without bothering to clean it, and Padraig hoisted him up and slung his cousin over his shoulders with a grunt. We left the cabin together.

"Go on ahead, Seer Tokka," he said. "You're a healer, too. Kiernan needs you. I'll deal with Sean and the Queen."

I hesitated, then nodded, turned for the path, and ran.

Vogel aren't built for running, but I caught up with Daphnis just as he was leaving the forest for the palace lawn, and Siona was already waiting.

"Goddess Below," she said softly. "Get him inside."

What happened after was mostly a blur. Healers crowded Kier's sitting room where he lay on a couch – his wards prevented most of them from entering his bedroom – and magic seemed to fill the whole space.

And no one else could *see* his wounds any better than I had. The spellwork that had stolen his magic and prevented it from returning also blocked the healers' ability to do anything more than pour magic into him and hope it would do something useful.

"Your Queen's spellwork is blocking our healing," I said to Siona, finally, when it became apparent the many healers couldn't do any more than I had done alone.

"We must ask her to remove it," Siona said. "I don't believe she will let her son die." She stood from where she had been sitting next to Kiernan, perched on the edge of the couch he lay on.

"I will do no such thing."

Everyone in the room stopped what they were doing. A few turned to watch as the Queen entered, but most kept their eyes turned away and sank into a bow or knelt in place. Seer Siona and I bowed our heads in respect.

"My Queen," said Siona, "We cannot heal him properly with your spellwork in place."

"Then he must heal himself." The Queen looked down at Kiernan, who kept his eyes firmly closed, though I was certain he was conscious and aware of her. "If he comes near to death, perhaps I will reconsider."

Siona stepped away as the Queen went to her son's side and sat on the edge of the couch. I stayed where I was, near his head, and tried not to stare as she put her hand on his face and he opened his eyes slowly, blinking at her as if he had just woken.

"Mother," he said, something vulnerable showing in his eyes. Then his face went hard. "My Queen. Forgive me for not kneeling."

"Nonsense, my son. Even I am not so cruel." She sat looking at him, her hand still on his cheek, and he looked back at her, face blank. Then he looked away.

"Would you let me die, my Queen? Rather than return my magic?" There was no emotion at all in his voice; it was as if he asked her a simple question, the answer to which had no meaning for him one way or the other.

"I cannot end your punishment early, Kiernan." I thought he might have flinched a little at the use of his name. "But I have no doubt you will find a way to stay alive." She looked around the room. "All of you, out. I would speak with my son alone."

Everyone rose and quickly left the room, almost silent, as if they knew it was folly to make too much noise and disturb the Queen.

"Siona, you stay." She glanced up and caught my eye and I looked quickly away. "And you, Vogel Seer. I'm told you saved my son's life. For the second time, it seems."

I nodded and resumed my place, too afraid to say anything to her. She was so much stronger than me, than any of us, in magic, it was ridiculous.

"I don't intend to die, my Queen," said Kiernan, but it was my eyes he sought.

"Good. Now tell me what happened that I find you in such a state again."

"Sean happened, my Queen."

"He was forbidden from harming you," she said, matter-of-factly. "He would not have broken my command."

"He wasn't trying to harm me," Kiernan said. "He was trying to kill the Vogel Seer."

She frowned, seemingly caught off guard. "To what purpose?"

"The same purpose that had him attack the Seer at the welcome feast under the guise of fighting me, I assume."

"And that is?"

Kier shook his head. "I don't know, but I would be curious about what his father has to say on the matter."

The Queen stood. "My sister is inconsolable, and I have lost a nephew and the man I would have married my daughters to."

Kiernan looked at her sharply. "Then we should be glad," he said, his voice hard. "Sean would have been a terrible King."

"You doubt my judgement?" Her voice was so cold I had

to suppress a shiver. "He would not have been King; he would have been a consort only. But it hardly matters now. He's dead, and I can't even blame you for killing him. Your cousin Padraig confirms your story, and I assume the Vogel Seer does as well?" She turned her terrifying green gaze on me, so like Kiernan's and so completely different, and I pulled all the calm I could into myself and faced her serenely.

"Yes, Queen of Morven Forest. Sean nicFia attacked me for reasons I'm not privy to, and Prince Kiernan stepped between us, taking the blow that was meant for me."

She nodded and turned to Siona. "Heal him as best you can, and let his body do the rest. If he truly comes so near to death he can't escape, then I will remove the spellwork." And she swept from the room.

Siona put a hand on my face and said gently, "I will tell your delegation what has happened. Perhaps they will delay your departure."

"Perhaps," I said, but I doubted it. Everyone but me – and perhaps Neeka – was eager to head home.

Then Siona left, too, and Daphnis returned from where he had been waiting outside the door to carry Kiernan into his bedroom and settle him in bed. As he left again, he spoke softly in my ear. "It must be tonight."

I curled up next to Kier, holding the blankets close around us.

"I'm sorry beloved," he said. He sounded weary and in pain, but at least he was aware now.

"For saving my life?" I said, forcing a teasing note I didn't feel into my voice.

"For not doing a better job of staying alive." He smiled and tucked a stray piece of hair behind my feathers.

"You're not dead yet," I said. "And I intend to make sure you heal."

He closed his eyes. "I love you, pretty bird. Whatever happens, remember that."

I kissed his forehead. "And whatever happens, remember that I love *you*. Now sleep." I touched his forehead lightly with two fingers and used the one bit of healer's magic I knew would still work on him: healing sleep.

And then I strapped his knives to my thighs, wrapped myself in my cloak, and climbed out his window into the darkness, to do what I could to get his magic back.

THIS TIME WHEN I SNUCK out of the palace into the dark night, there was no magical spell to keep violence away, and this time, I knew there were people who wanted me dead, because I could not believe that Sean nicFia could be the only one. From what Kiernan had told me, his cousin lacked the imagination to incite strife between Monarchies, so there had to be someone else. Maybe many someones.

So this time, there was the real possibility of danger, but I would not shrink away from what I needed to do.

Seers mustn't take life echoed in my head, but I pushed the thought away. Kiernan had nearly died for me – he might still die – so I would not shy away from killing for him if I had to, and I could see no other way.

I slipped along the palace walls to the rose garden and through it to where it bordered the forest – farther than I had gone before. A path wandered between trees in a long loop designed to bring peace to a forest creature's heart. It was, Daphnis assured me, the Queen's habit to walk here every night.

I climbed a tree and perched in the branches, letting my long toes and talons hold me steady on the branch, my wings and tail spread slightly to help me balance but not so much that they showed outside the concealment of my dark blue cloak.

And I waited.

Far off, an owl hooted, and I realized I could understand that it – he – was telling his mate where he was. I smelled leaves slowly returning to earth on the forest floor, tasted them with every breath. And I felt spirits around me, some welcoming, some indifferent, and some that seemed to warn me away.

And then, finally, quiet footsteps that would have been inaudible, except the wearer had on shoes of a fashionable design that made it impossible to walk quietly, even on the soft surface of the forest path.

She came into view between the branches, her dried-blood hair catching the reflections of the wisplights that floated around her. She was smiling, just the barest curve of her lips, and the sight made me angry. Her son was injured, maybe dying, and she looked so self-satisfied I could scream.

How could she smile when Kiernan might not live because *she* refused to end his unreasonable, unjust, unearned punishment?

I slipped Kiernan's knives from their sheaths, and they felt familiar in my hands though their hilts were shaped and worn to his wider grip. They were named blades, he had told me, made with magic that adapted them to their owner.

But they seemed to accept me even though they weren't mine and I didn't even know their names. Perhaps they understood, if an object can understand anything, that I loved Kiernan and that I needed them to help him.

When the Queen was directly below my branch, I loosened the grip of my toes and dropped from the tree, striking out with both blades.

I was hit by a wave of magic of such strength I could

barely comprehend it. The closest I had ever encountered was when Kiernan was fighting the magical fire in Aven Forest. I stumbled back and was hit from one side, knocked into the undergrowth by a shape that whispered, "Hide," in my ear. I sprawled under the brush, curled myself behind a screen of ferns, not understanding anything that had happened, unable to parse the sounds I heard. A shout, commands, running. Nothing coming towards me even though I was sure I had been seen.

Then quiet. I lay still for a long time before I pushed myself to my feet and made my slow, cautious way out of the forest, out of the garden, and back to Kiernan's room.

Only as I was climbing back in his window did I realize I no longer had his knives.

I stopped halfway in and almost went back to look for them, but then I glanced over at the bed, where Kiernan lay pale and vulnerable, and I climbed the rest of the way in, shut the window, took off my cloak, and hung the empty knife sheaths and belt where I had found them.

Then I crept into bed next to Kier, burrowed my face into his chest, and let my despair out in a sob.

His arms came around me and he said, "Hey, pretty bird, I'm not dead yet."

"Oh, beloved," I said. "I've made a terrible mistake and I think I may have ruined any hope you had of getting your magic back."

He stroked my back, my wings, my hair, and said, "Why do you have dried leaves stuck to you?"

And it all came out in a rush. How I had a vision that I thought was telling me I needed to kill the Queen to save him. How I had told Daphnis my vision and the dryad had offered to help, to find the perfect place for an ambush. How I had failed.

He held me close while I babbled out my confession and said nothing until I stopped. Then he tilted my face up to his with a finger under my chin and kissed my cheeks – first one, then the other.

"Oh, pretty bird," he said, and I waited for him to scold me like the child I must seem to be. I deserved it, I was sure. But he didn't. He just looked at me for a long moment and when he spoke, he said, "You are so much more than I deserve."

"You're not angry?"

He smiled. "How can I be angry when you were trying to free me, to save my life?" He traced one of my eyebrows and looked at me like he had found a precious gemstone under his pillow. "Did she see you?"

"I – I thought she looked right at my face. But… someone shoved me into the underbrush and told me to hide and… and the guards chased them instead."

"Someone?"

"I thought it was Daphnis, but… he's here, isn't he?"

He slipped out of bed, ignoring my protest that he needed to be still and rest if he had any hope of healing. He opened the door to his sitting room and looked out.

"He's not here," he said. Then, "Come sit out here with me. We'll have tea. If they come for you, let them find us visiting as friends."

I opened my mouth to protest but he smiled and said, "I'll bundle myself up on a couch, and you can make the tea."

"If she did see me," I said, helping him to sit, "What will she do?"

He let me wrap him in blankets and pile cushions around him. "You'll be arrested," he said. "There will be a trial. But if she *did* see you, pretty bird…"

"I'll be executed." It came out as a whisper.

"She might demand your King execute you instead."

"Goddess Above, what have I done?"

"What you thought you needed to, beloved." He took the cup of tea I offered him and squeezed my fingers. "I won't let them hurt you, Fionn," he said. "I meant to steal you from your own King." He laughed softly. "But if I have to steal you from my Queen instead, I'll do it."

"You need your magic first, Kier." I perched uneasily on a couch across from his.

"If I get my magic back, can you heal me?"

"Yes," I said. "I believe I can."

"*Without* burning yourself hollow?"

"You once said you'd burn yourself hollow to save me, "I said. "I would do the same for you."

"I know you would, pretty bird. But can you heal me *without* doing it?"

"Yes," I said. I *wasn't* sure, but I would not doubt myself.

"Then trust that I won't let them hurt you, and we'll find a way through this."

I only had time to nod before there was banging at Kiernan's door, and the Queen's Guard called out that they'd come to arrest me for attempted regicide.

27
Kiernan

WE BOTH STOOD TOGETHER, and I took Fionn's arm to remind him that I would keep him safe. "You're innocent, pretty bird," I said, low and urgent.

"No, Kier, I –" I put my fingers on his lips. I knew he hated it when I stopped him from talking, and I resolved never to do it again. But now, I needed him to listen, to understand.

"I know," I said. "But you must pretend you know nothing. Maybe the Queen saw you, maybe they have proof. But whatever they say, just act as if you did *not* do this."

He nodded and looked at the door when a loud knock boomed out again.

"I'm coming!" I called. "I was almost dead not long ago. Give me a moment!"

Fionn bit his lip, then his chin went up in that stubborn way I loved. "Here, Prince Kiernan, let *me* get it," he said, loudly. He didn't move. "Kier," he said, so quietly I stepped closer to catch every word. "In the cave, when I was having visions… I *saw* myself waiting to kill her. And it wasn't the first time I had that vision. Only – I spirit traveled, and I met your Lady of the Forest. She said I must save you." He looked away from the door to meet my eyes. "She said she would help me. I thought she meant… what I just tried to do."

I touched his cheek to wipe away the tear that slid down it. "No tears, pretty bird. You mustn't let them think you're afraid."

He nodded.

I sat back down on my couch with a sigh and pulled the blanket around me while Fionn went to the door. I saw him pause to breathe, to straighten his spine, and when he pulled open the door, he might almost have been another person: cool, regal, serene.

A Queen's Guard pushed the door open as soon as it was unlatched, forcing Fionn to take a step back.

I stood and let the blanket fall, not caring that I was dressed half in sleeping clothes and half in comfortable travel clothes. I didn't need to look like a Prince for these guards to know exactly who I was.

"What's happened?" I said.

The Queen's Captain stepped around his subordinate. "I'm sorry, lad," he said. "We've come to arrest the Vogel Seer."

"What?" said Fionn, with just the right amount of shock and disdain.

"On what charge?" I demanded.

"Attempting to murder our Queen."

"And when is this supposed to have happened?" I dropped the blanket I was still holding onto the couch and stepped closer to the Captain, reminding him that I was not only his Prince, but also taller and heavier than he was.

"Earlier tonight, my Prince," he said, remembering my title now that I was looking down at him. I *liked* the Captain; he had trained me and had been almost a father figure to me, so I hated to remind him I was higher ranking than he could ever be. But I needed him to understand where I stood.

"Seer Tokka was with me all night," I said. "He spent most of it trying to keep the spirits of death from dragging me away to Tir Na n'Og."

The Captain had the grace to look embarrassed. "I'm sorry, my Prince. The Queen says she saw his face when he attacked her."

"She must be mistaken. He's a *seer*. Seers can't take life."

The Captain sighed. "Seers *mustn't* take life, my Prince. We both know, from personal experience, that they *can*."

I had forgotten that he knew, that he had been the one who found us – me, just a small child, and Siona holding me, bloody knife in her hand, and the fey lord who had tried to kill me and lost his own life instead. Siona had given her eyesight to save me. That had been the price she paid as a Seer, for killing the man who would have ended my childhood.

"It hardly matters," I said. "He was here with me."

"Did you not sleep at all?" the Captain said. "My Prince, these are arguments to present to the Queen. I have no choice but to arrest the Vogel Seer."

I stared at him until he looked away.

"Please lad, don't make this any harder," he said.

"Promise me, Connor nicStane," I said, and he met my eyes again. "He will not be harmed, and I hold you entirely responsible if he is."

He nodded, and I thought I saw the barest hint of a smile on his severe face. "You have my word, Prince Kiernan. Seer Tokka will come to no harm. I'll see to it he isn't even frightened."

I snorted.

He hesitated, then said, "We're to take him to the Queen directly. She wants this resolved now, so as not to delay the departure of the Vogel delegation."

"Does she think the Vogel would still trade with us if she imprisons their Seer?"

"I don't presume to know what the Queen thinks, my Prince."

"Fine," I said. "I'll inform the other Vogel."

"I'll… deliver the prisoner slowly, my Prince," said the Captain and this time I was certain I saw a brief smile.

"Where is Daphnis?" I said, and looked around, though of course he wasn't in the room. He had left shortly after the healers, to give me and Fionn time alone.

"There's only a very nervous-looking faun outside your door, my Prince," said the Guard.

"Erith?" I called and he poked his head around the door, then scurried out of the way as the Captain and the Guard flanked Fionn, escorting him out of the room. Fionn walked with his head up and his nostrils slightly flared, the very picture of serenity slightly disturbed by a wrongful charge.

Erith watched them go with huge eyes. "My Prince?" he said, creeping closer until he was pressed to my side. "Why are they taking Seer Fionn?"

"He's been accused of trying to murder our Queen."

"But that's absurd!"

"Yes, it is," I said, hating the lie. Erith deserved better, but the fewer people who knew the truth, the safer for all of us. I squeezed his shoulder. "I need you to go to the guest suite and tell Councilor Rocsh what has happened. Have him come to the Queen's Hall. And find Padraig."

"Shall I help you dress first?" he asked.

I looked at my mis-matched outfit and laughed, though I felt no humor. "My Queen has seen me look worse than this in her court."

He nodded and hurried from the room. When the door

was shut behind him, I allowed myself to reach for the back of the nearest couch, to brace myself on it. I pressed my other hand to my belly. All the magic the healers had poured into me had closed the wound, back and front, without even a scar. But inside, I wasn't sure they had been able to do anything at all.

They had given me enough to be able to stand, to walk, to pretend to be okay, but I was not. Death still followed me closely, and it was only a matter of time before the spirits took me.

But I didn't have time now to be weak. I pushed away from the couch and went to my bedroom where I stripped off my sleeping tunic and replaced it with a shirt, still loose and comfortable, because I couldn't bear anything too tight. I covered it with a coat and shoved my feet into boots. It took me far too long to pull them on because bending was agony.

Then I reached for my belt and saw the empty knife sheaths. Fionn hadn't mentioned borrowing my knives, but he had done it before.

"Oh, fuck," I said softly. He hadn't just been going to fetch gifts on Autumn Balance night. He had meant to try to kill her then, too, only it wouldn't have worked because the whole palace grounds had been spelled against violence.

"Fuck, fuck, fuck." I didn't know if my knives being missing was good or bad. I strapped on my belt, and had to leave it much looser than usual, buckled the empty knife sheaths to my thighs, and slung my sword over my back.

I reached the Queen's Hall after Councilor Rocsh, who had brought both of Fionn's Guards and his attendant Neeka. My vision was greying around the edges when I walked in the door, and I almost passed out when I paused to kneel.

A strong hand gripped my elbow and helped me stand again when the Queen said my name. I blinked hard, trying to clear my vision, to see who was helping me. I hated the lack of awareness that not having magic brought, made so much worse by my injuries. For a long, awful moment, my dull brain thought it was Sean. But no, it was Padraig.

Sean's body was laid out at the far end of the room, draped with a cloth embroidered with the nicFia stag. His sword – the sword he would have killed Fionn with, that he had nearly killed *me* with – lay atop the cloth.

"My Queen," I said, approaching. "I must protest."

She held up her hand. Fionn was kneeling on the floor in front of her, a Queen's Guard to each side of him, and the Queen was studying him as one might study an interesting insect.

She looked up at me finally. "Do you doubt my eyesight, my son?"

"Of course not, my Queen."

She stood. Servants and attendants knelt, guards dropped to one knee, and Councilor Rocsh inclined his head. I didn't move.

"A cloaked figure dropped out of a tree in front of me, raised knives to stab me, and I saw his face. Pale, white hair, feathers."

"Did you see the weapons, my Queen?" I said, and she snapped her gaze to mine.

"Your knives, my son," she said. "Which I see you do not carry."

"They are missing, my Queen," I said, reluctantly.

"You say he was with you all night?"

"Helping to heal me, yes."

"But he could have left while you slept, taken your knives and crept away to attack me?"

"Perhaps, my Queen," I said, and felt a faint hope flicker in my heart. "But my knives are named blades."

That sharp glance again, that had always made me flinch as a child. Now, I met her eyes calmly.

"So they are," she said, and turned to Fionn. "Hold out your hands, Vogel Seer."

He looked at her, chin high, and held out both hands, palm up. His skin was soft, smooth, calloused on the fingers of one hand, where he held his fiber for spinning.

"Bring my nephew's sword," the Queen barked, and a guard scrambled to lift the sword from Sean's body, handling it by the scabbard.

She took it and looked at it thoughtfully, then held it out hilt-first to the guard. He paled.

"Put your hand on the hilt."

He did, hesitantly, and immediately snatched it away. She grabbed his wrist and examined his palm. It was blistered and red. Then she turned to Fionn and held out the sword again.

"If you would, Seer Tokka," she said.

"My Queen —" I stepped forward and had to stop when pain stabbed through my belly.

"If you believe his innocence, you will not protest," she said.

Fionn turned to look at me. "I appreciate your concern, Prince Kiernan," he said. "But I don't mind a little bit of pain to prove myself." Then he wrapped his beautiful long fingers around the sword hilt. He gasped, a swift but soft inhale, but didn't otherwise react. When he took his hand away and turned it palm up, it was as red and blistered as the Guard's, and I had to force myself not to rush to his side.

"So, Seers aren't immune to the damage a named blade can do to someone not its master."

"So it seems," I said, forcing my voice even.

"So he could not have wielded your knives against me. And yet I saw his face, my son. How do you explain that?"

"I can't, my Queen. But you also saw your attacker holding my knives, which Seer Tokka could not have done." I was glad, then, that my knives were missing and couldn't have been used to test Fionn. Because, as impossible as it should have been, he *could* wield them.

The Queen scowled and handed the sword to me, and I took hold of its scabbard. She sat back on her throne and looked at Fionn, who looked back at her, calm and serene, his burned hand palm up in his lap.

There was a sudden commotion by the door and two Palace Guards, flanked by the Vogel King's Guards, dragged a tall figure between them and flung it to the floor.

"What is this?" said the Queen, sounding almost bored. Her green eyes were sharp, though, and if they had been turned on me, I would have been hard-pressed not to flinch away.

"The Vogel Guards found this dryad in their anteroom, my Queen," said one of the Palace Guards.

I looked more closely at the person they had brought in and almost didn't recognize him. It was Daphnis, but he looked… different.

"We found them trying to hide these in a potted plant just inside the door," said one of the Vogel King's Guards. He held out a cloth, which dropped open to reveal my knives.

"They are yours, my son?" said the Queen.

"Yes," I said. I took them from the guard, one and a time, and sheathed them.

"Daphnis," I said, and he looked up and for a moment I couldn't speak. His face was different, too, his cheekbones softer and his eyes larger. His skin and hair were pale, and in uncertain light, moving, even *I* might have mistaken him for Fionn. Only for an instant, but it might be enough.

"You know this creature?" my Queen said. I turned to face

her again.

"He is also mine," I said.

"This is the dryad I gave you?" She didn't seem to notice he looked different, but then she probably hadn't noticed what he had looked like in the first place.

"He is."

She looked at him for a long time, and he looked at the floor.

"Why did you have your Prince's knives, dryad?" she finally said.

"I stole them, Queen of Morven," Daphnis said, his voice just above a whisper.

"Hold out your hands," she snapped, and he did. His palms were red and blistered.

"Why, Daphnis?" I said.

"You are my master," he replied, and I forced myself not to react. "Our Queen was hurting you, my Prince," he said. "You are wasting away without your magic, and you can't heal properly."

"You are forbidden from harming anyone," I said. "Magically prevented from doing so. Why even try?"

"Because…" He looked up at me and I almost stepped forward to stop him from saying what I knew he would say next. "I love you, my Prince."

The Queen laughed, and everyone observing turned to look at her. "Oh, my son!" she said, covering her mouth with one hand, amusement dancing in her eyes. "If only you could inspire such devotion in your own people as you do in the vermin we share this land with, what a King you would make!"

"Since I shall never be King, my Queen," I said, an unaccustomed bitterness creeping into my voice, "That hardly matters."

"Bring it closer," she said, and the palace guards dragged

Daphnis, still on his knees, to the front of her throne. Fionn moved aside to make room. She leaned forward and put her hand under the dryad's chin to force his face up.

He had made himself look more like Fionn, changing the way his hair lay across his head, making it paler, and growing leaves around his face to resemble Fionn's feathers. Even the structure of his face was different – not enough to make him unrecognizable to me, but enough to make him look more like the man I loved.

But why? Had he hoped that by looking more like Fionn, he could make me love him instead? Or was he simply trying to save Fionn's life by becoming a believable stand-in?

"Perhaps I was mistaken," the Queen said, and more than one of her guards looked at her in surprise, then quickly looked away. From her voice, I guessed someone would pay for her annoyance at being wrong, and that someone would probably be Daphnis.

"Lock this one up," she said. Then she turned to Councilor Rocsh. "I hope you can forgive me for this terrible mistake."

The Councilor bowed his head slightly. "I'm not certain I wouldn't have made the same mistake, Queen of Morven. We take no offense."

Fionn rose to his feet in a smooth, elegant motion. "What I would like to know," he said, and his voice was cool and regal. "Is *why* the dryad chose to impersonate me when he attacked your Queen. And why he was seeking to hide Prince Kiernan's knives in our suite."

The Queen looked at him as if she had forgotten he existed. He looked back at her, acting exactly as if he were her equal in rank and not the least intimidated by her. I was so impressed I wanted to kiss him.

Then she looked at me. "The dryad is yours, my son. See if you can answer the Seer's questions."

I nodded. "What do you want me to do with this?" I held out Sean's sword, expecting her to instruct me to lay it back on his body.

She smiled her toothy smile. "You seem to like using two blades at once. Keep it."

"Its name, my Queen?"

"Foeslayer," she said, the curl of her upper lip showing what she thought of the name. It was marginally better than Heartbreaker, which is what my cousin had named the sword I now wore on my back, before I won it from him. "I trust you'll come up with a better name."

"Brightheart," I said, trying not to look at Fionn.

She waited until Daphnis had been taken away by the Palace Guards and said, "Shall we delay the farewell ceremony until tomorrow night, or are you in a rush to leave?"

Councilor Rocsh answered, "I believe one more day will not affect our schedule too greatly," and the Queen nodded and left the room, followed by her guards. Rocsh took Fionn by the elbow gently, and they left, too, after a quick farewell.

I stood looking at Sean's body until the room was nearly empty, feeling something like regret. Then I shook my head. No. I had tried, and he had refused my every attempt at friendship. and then he had attempted – twice – to hurt the man I loved more than my own life. He deserved what he got. I had only protected Fionn, and finally avenged Dec.

"My Prince?" said Padraig. I hadn't realized he was still there, that's how terrible I felt.

"Why didn't your sword burn my hand?" I said. "When I took it from you at the stupid display we put on at the welcome feast. Is it not a named blade?"

"It's a lesser weapon than yours," he said. "But it is named. But you're my Prince. Perhaps it recognized you as my sovereign the same way it would have recognized *her*."

"She's our Queen. All named Sidhe blades are hers," I said. "And enspelled so as not to harm her."

He shrugged.

None of that explained why Fionn would be burned by Sean's sword, but not by my knives.

28
Fionn

BACK IN OUR SUITE, everyone except the two King's Guards clustered around me while Neeka bandaged my hand, expressing outrage at my being accused of attempted regicide, until I wanted to scream, "I'm guilty!"

Finally, I convinced them all I needed to rest, and only Neeka followed me into my room, where she started to brush my hair. When I was at last able to strip off my clothes, I realized I was still wearing the tunic stained with Kiernan's blood.

Looking at it in my hands, I started to shake. Neeka put an arm around my shoulders and guided me to a chair where I sat and bunched the fabric in my clenched hands.

<He almost died,> I said.

<But he didn't, my Seer. He's alive because you healed him enough to get him back to the palace.>

I looked up at her and whatever she saw in my face made her pull me against her, strong arms holding me while I trembled.

<That blow was meant for *me*,> I said.

She stroked my hair. <He saved your life, my Seer, and I love him for that.>

I leaned away to look up at her again. <You're a good friend, Neeka.>

She grinned. <If you two ever decide to run away together, you better take me with you.>

I blinked at her and she laughed at the surprise I must have shown.

<*Are* you planning to run away?> she teased. <Then you make sure to tell our Prince to hire Màiri nicStane as one of his guards.>

<Is that her name? Màiri?>

Neeka blushed. <I should have been there with you today, my Seer,> she said. <Instead of stealing kisses from someone I'd be arrested for being with at the Eyrie.>

<You couldn't have done anything,> I said, folding the tunic I still clutched in my hands and putting in on the desk next to me. <He might have tried to kill you, too. And likely would have succeeded.>

<Why did this cousin of our Prince want to kill you, Tokka?>

<*Our* Prince?> I said.

She smiled, a little shyly this time, and I had rarely known Neeka to be shy. <He's your Prince, you're my Seer, so he's my Prince, too.>

<Don't let our King hear you say that.>

<Of course not. I may be occasionally reckless, my Seer, but I'm not stupid.>

<No, you're definitely not that. And I don't know why Sean nicFia would want to kill me, only that it's the second time he's tried.>

<The second? When was the first?>

<At the welcome feast. When he attacked Kiernan at the

end of the sword fighting demonstration. He aimed his blow at me, only Kier got in the way then, too.>

<Do you think he meant to stir up discord between Sidhe and Vogel?>

<Perhaps, but why? What would that achieve?>

<I don't know.>

<Me, neither.>

When she had gone, I contemplated climbing out my window and going looking for Kier, but the palace was still busy, and I was dressed in sleeping clothes. So I settled down with the books he had given me, and Smoke and Flame curled on the pillow next to me.

I woke when one of the books hit the floor with a thump. The serpents launched from the pillow and fluttered through the air, circling my head as I sat up and stretched.

We go, said Smoke.

Check egg, said Flame.

I yawned and stretched again. Outside my window, it was full daylight. Tonight, we would have our delayed farewell ceremony and tomorrow we would depart for the Eyrie.

"I'll come with you," I said. I dressed quickly and peered out into the sitting room. No one was there; I supposed they must all have found something to do on our last day, even though our hosts would mostly be asleep. Only Trikta stood guard outside our door.

<Where is everybody?> I said.

<The King's Guards are sleeping,> he replied. <Everyone else went to wander the gardens one last time. Even this time of year they are quite beautiful.> He sounded a little wistful. <I think Councilor Rocsh also intended to look for dryads, to find out how we can help those the Sidhe Queen gifted to our King. They don't flourish in his garden, the Councilor says.>

I thought of the one time I had ventured to the lower garden below the Eyrie, and how without hope those dryads had been. They hadn't enough of their own birth soil to keep them alive for more than a couple of years, though at least they didn't have to worry about being used as pleasure slaves on top of everything else.

<He said you specifically mentioned earth for them to root in as part of our potential trade agreements, but you hadn't had the chance to inquire what else they might need.> His voice was soft and did nothing to ease the flush of guilt I felt.

I had spent a lot of time sneaking away to see Kiernan instead of doing the things I had intended to do. I was ashamed, but also grateful, that Councilor Rocsh had remembered.

I hesitated in the door for longer than I meant, and Trikta said, <Were you going out, my Seer?> He met my eyes with his soft, moss green gaze. <To see your Prince?>

There was no accusation in his tone, but I felt it anyway. Trikta was loyal and kind and, if not for Kiernan, there would likely have been a strong attraction between us.

<Smoke and Flame wish to check on their egg. I thought I would go along and see how Prince Kiernan is healing.>

<Of course, my Seer,> he said, and when I stepped into the hall, serpents draped over both shoulders, he followed. <Will he not be sleeping?>

<I don't think he sleeps very much,> I said. <Being without his magic is… uncomfortable.> I thought about what he had told me the other night, when I had woken in his arms to find him already awake. The lack of magic ached, he had said. He had felt himself drifting apart. And then he had distracted me by kissing me, and slowly, urgently, making love to me, exactly as he had in a vision I'd had before I left the Eyrie.

<My Seer?> Trikta said hesitantly as we approached Kiernan's rooms. He sounded so uncertain I stopped and turned to face him.

<What is it?>

He looked up and down the hall, but most of the palace was asleep and no one was in sight. <My Seer. Tokka> He looked down at his feet, silver bird mask completely hiding his features from that angle. <You know I... I care for you.> He stopped, as if waiting for me to make some response.

<I know,> I said gently. <But – >

<It's okay,> he said. <I understand now, that you and your Prince are heart-bonded. It's only... If you need me, for any-thing, I'm yours to command. Even if... even if it means acting against our own King.> His voice had dropped to the barest whisper as he said the last part.

<Trikta...> I wanted to tell him not to be silly, not to risk his position, his livelihood, with treasonous thoughts. But he was no more a child than I was, for all he seemed years younger than me sometimes. And to be truthful, it felt good to have not one, but *two* friends among my own people who would choose me even over their own Monarch.

So I just put a hand on his shoulder, said, <Thank you,> and carried on towards Kiernan's rooms.

He answered the door fully dressed, as if he had intended to go somewhere, and smiled when he saw me.

Smoke and Flame leapt from my shoulders to his, nuzzled his cheeks, and then disappeared deeper into his rooms to check on their egg.

"Seer Tokka," he said. "I thought you might be resting."

"I was. Now I'm awake. I thought *you* might be resting, but I have questions and not much time left to ask them."

"Come in," he said, opening the door wider. "Trikta, will you have tea? Or cider?"

"No thank you, Prince Kiernan. I'll wait outside the door, as a guard should." Kier smiled at the slight reproach in Trikta's voice that showed what my guard thought of Kier's lax attitude towards this staff and attendants. It was all the more amusing because Trikta had been happy to accept Kier's hospitality only a few days ago.

"Tea?" he said, when I was inside, and the door was closed.

"No," I said. "Kier, why did Daphnis look like me? What was he doing?" I had intended to ask why Sean would want to kill me, but my mouth had other ideas, it seemed.

"I've been puzzling over that myself since the guards dragged him into the Queen's Hall."

"He… he offered to help me, when I… when I did what I did."

He cocked his head at me. "I wonder why?"

"I don't know. I suppose I thought he wanted revenge for his people. Or maybe… to save you."

"He said seers are sacred to his people. Maybe that was enough for him to take your place as the Queen's attacker."

I bit my lip, then quickly stopped, knowing it made me look young and uncertain. I wanted to be strong in front of Kiernan. "He wanted me to convince you that absorbing his magic was the only way to save you. Maybe…" I stopped and shook my head. It seemed too preposterous.

He had been standing a few paces away from me, toying with the hilt of a sword propped up on the couch cushions. Sean's sword, I realized.

"Did you name it for…" Again, the idea seemed too silly to pronounce out loud.

"For you?" He smiled. "Yes. Brightheart is… Yes, I named it for you. And whatever your notion of why Daphnis decided to change his features to look like you, I'd like to hear it."

"He knew it would be a death sentence to admit guilt," I said. "If he could convince the Queen it was he she had seen, and not me."

"And?" It was not a challenge, the way he said it, but an

encouragement to continue.

"And if he was going to die anyway, you couldn't refuse his magic on the grounds that it would kill him."

He smiled, but it was bleak. "My beautiful, intelligent beloved," he said. "That makes perfect sense." He adjusted the sword across his back, leaving the other on the couch to cross the room to me. I thought I saw him wince as his belt pulled across his belly, but it was so slight I couldn't be sure. "Why don't we go ask him?"

HIDDEN BENEATH the Morven Forest palace was a dungeon that reminded me of one I had read about in a book of fairy tales in the library at the Abbey of the Moon. It was dim – the only lights were the wisplights I conjured and the portable oil lamp Kiernan carried. It smelled so strongly of earth I could taste it in the back of my throat.

Two Palace Guards stood outside a large wooden door, looking bored, their own wisplights flickering above their heads. They snapped to attention as soon as they saw Kiernan.

"My Prince," they said in unison.

"My dryad is here?" he said, no warmth in his voice so that he almost sounded like a different person.

"Our Queen felt it best it be kept close until you… until it's punished, my Prince. Else it'd have been locked up in the village where it belongs."

I was watching Kier's face closely, or I might not have seen the barest flicker of anger that touched his eyes when the guard referred to Daphnis as "it."

When Kiernan made to pass by the guards, they stood aside, but one of them said "My Prince?" and he paused. "The dryad is in the iron cell."

A muscle tightened in Kiernan's jaw, then relaxed, and his face might have been stone for all the expression it showed. "Thank you," he said. "Trikta, wait here."

My guard started to protest, but then he looked at Kiernan's face and merely nodded, taking up a place across the hall from the Palace Guards.

"What does that mean?" I said quietly, once the door had closed us into the dungeon. "The iron cell?"

Kiernan stood looking down the hall for a moment, then seemed to recover himself, and we began to walk past a row of barred doors.

"Sidhe and dryads both draw magic from the forest. From the Realms, too, of course." He reached for my hand, and his trembled slightly. "The iron cell is lined with metal plates to prevent that connection. Anyone locked in there is cut off from all magic. It feels like being hollow."

"Goddess Above, that's cruel."

"Yes, it is."

Every cell we passed in the long hall was empty.

"Are there no other prisoners?" I finally asked.

"Since my Queen took the throne, I'm told, there have been very few. At first, her prisoners didn't live long. Eventually, people were too afraid of her to commit crimes."

"Oh," I said.

We turned a corner and followed another long hall, so dark it could have been endless, and I wouldn't have been able to tell.

"How could Daphnis make himself look like me? Or enough like me to convince your Queen he was the one who attacked her? And whyever didn't she notice he didn't look the same?"

His steps had grown slower with what I thought was reluctance until his hand tightened on mine, so hard it hurt. "Kier?"

"I'll be all right," he said, stopping to lean against the wall. "I'm not healed yet, is all."

"You should be resting."

"There's no time for rest, pretty bird." He pulled me closer with the hand that held mine and I leaned against him, letting him feel my warmth. "To answer your second question, most Sidhe – most fey – don't see dryads as people, or even as individuals. I don't think my Queen could tell one dryad from the next, because she can't be bothered to actually *look* at any of them. When she examined Daphnis in her Hall was probably the only time she ever paid attention to a dryad's features beyond what livery they were wearing."

He leaned his forehead against the stone wall, but when I pressed closer to him, he shifted and leaned on my shoulder instead.

"As for your other question… Dryads… most of their magic is suppressed by the spells that keep them enslaved, but they were allowed to keep those magics that make them better servants. And those that make them… more appealing as pleasure slaves."

"Magics like what?" I whispered, not sure I wanted to know the answer.

"They can grow appendages, for one, and customize their tackle to the preference of a lover. And they can change their appearance to some degree, to match the tastes of whomever chooses to…"

"To use them."

He nodded. "Yes."

"The longer I spend outside the Abbey, the more terrible I find the world," I said.

He lifted his head to meet my eyes. This was a conversation we had had before. "It's not all terrible."

"No, I suppose not. It has love, after all."

"And kissing." He kissed the end of my nose, and I couldn't help but smile.

"And dancing."

"Ah, so you *did* like dancing."

"I was terrible at it, but yes. I liked dancing very much." I looked away, down the hall. "Will you take his magic now, as he wants you to?"

"My Queen will expect me to execute him. Probably publicly." He pushed away from the wall, and we continued down the hall.

"Will you do it?"

"I don't know. If I do, Daph won't be able to root in the forest with his ancestors."

"What does that mean?"

"When a dryad passes on their magic – usually to their offspring – they go to the grove of their ancestors and root there and, well, they become a tree."

"That sounds lovely," I said.

"It is lovely. And sad."

"So even if you accept his magic, if you execute him as your Queen expects, he dies and can't root as a tree."

He nodded and squeezed my hand. And then stopped, because we had reached the end of the hall and a small metal door. He put his hand on the bolt but didn't draw it back.

"Should I do it?" he said.

"Execute him?"

"Take his magic."

"What happens to his magic if he dies?"

"It dies with him."

"Will it free you from the Queen's spellwork?"

"Probably not, but it should give me enough magic that I

can be healed properly, at least. And it will make her punishment bearable."

"I thought – the healers seemed sure your body would heal itself, that they put enough healing magic through you to enable that."

"Beloved, the healers can't see what's damaged inside me at all. They gave me enough magic and strength to walk around upright for a few days. That's all."

"Would she let you die?"

He let go of my hand and turned to face me. "Last night, when I went back to my rooms…" He paused, like he didn't want to say what was next. "I shat blood, Fionn. A lot of blood. And this morning I pissed red. I may look healed on the outside, but I'm fairly sure I'm still cut up on the inside."

A deep cold spread through my belly at his words and I wanted to wrap my arms around him, to try to heal him again. "No," I said.

He put both hands on my shoulders. "If you could *see* my injuries," he said, looking into my eyes. "Could you heal me?"

"Me alone?" I was unpracticed in healing magic, but Healer Kah said I had a knack for it. And Seer Siona said my healing magic was very strong. "Yes," I said. I refused to doubt.

He nodded. "Will you –"

"What is it, beloved?"

"Fionn, you know how dryad magic is passed on."

I put my hand on his face and brushed my thumb over his lips. "My Prince," I said, and almost laughed when he scowled. "I do know. And I would rather have to watch a dryad fuck you and have you alive than keep you to myself and lose you."

"I love you so much, Fionn," he said. "Will you… Will you stay with me, when he does it? Kiss me? Tell me you love me?"

"Yes."

"Will you…" A tear slid from the corner of his eye, and I wiped it away.

"I'll hold you, Kier. I'll pleasure you, if you want me to, if it will make it easier. And as soon as you have enough magic for it to be visible to my seer sight, I will heal you."

He turned his face to kiss my palm. "I don't want anyone but you."

"I know."

His eyes met mine, then he looked at the metal door. "We can't do it here. No magic will reach through the iron plates."

"Will they let you take him?"

"They won't dare stop me. I'm their Prince."

"Your Queen will be angry."

"Maybe, but I refuse to die just to keep her happy. Not anymore." Then he let go of my shoulders, reached for the bolt, and drew it back.

29

Kiernan

I HAD BEEN INSIDE the cell once as a boy, when Sean had dared me to go in and then closed the door on me and locked it.

I had been found hours later, throat raw from screaming, huddled in a miserable ball on the floor. I'd had nightmares about losing my magic for moons after.

Now, stepping inside the metal-lined room, I hardly noticed the change. I was already cut off from magic and being cut off *more* made no difference.

But Daphnis looked wilted. He crouched in the middle of the cell, arms wrapped over his head, his hair limp around his shoulders. He didn't look alive; he looked like a wooden carving of a person.

Fionn drew in a sharp breath and stepped back out of the cell. "Kier —"

"You don't need to come in here, pretty bird," I said.

Daphnis raised his head slowly to look at me. His brown eyes were all pupil, the whites bloodshot green with the peculiar tint of dryad blood.

"My Prince," he said, his voice hoarse. I wondered if he had screamed as much as I had. "Is this what it's like for you to have no magic?"

"Come with me, Daphnis."

He rose and I could hear the wooden creaking of his joints. "It aches, my Prince. The absence of magic *aches*."

"Yes, it does."

"Have you come to execute me?"

I looked at him for a long time, my mind crowded with questions, none of which would form into words in my mouth.

Finally, Fionn spoke from outside the door. "We've come to take you up on your offer."

Daphnis turned to look at Fionn, every slightest motion stiff and awkward. I wondered if that was what *I* looked like, trying to get through each day hollow. It *was* what I felt like.

"You convinced him?" Daphnis said, his usually emotionless voice tinged with something like hope.

Fionn shook his head. "You did." When Daphnis only stared, he added, "It's the only way your magic will continue to exist in the world, Daphnis."

"I don't like that you have to die for something someone else did," I said. I looked at Fionn.

"I could confess to your Queen," he said. "I don't like someone else dying for me, either."

"No," I said. "I will sacrifice everything else before I will sacrifice you." Then I turned back to Daphnis. "I don't like it. I don't like sacrificing anyone, especially someone I counted as a friend. But understand me. I *will* do whatever it takes to save Fionn."

Fionn reached for my hand, and I moved closer to the door so he could twine our fingers together. "And I will do whatever it takes to save Kiernan," he said, squeezing my fingers. "And without your magic, he will die."

Daphnis nodded. "You must take me away from here, to somewhere I can feel the forest, and my magic is yours, my Prince. My *life* is yours, as it always has been."

I had meant what I said, about doing whatever it took to save Fionn, even if it meant letting my Queen believe a lie and letting someone else take the blame for trying to kill her. But I still felt guilty for it. I had not become so cold I didn't desperately wish there was another way.

I drew my sword and gestured for Daphnis to precede us down the hall, around the corner, and out the dungeon door.

"My Prince," said one of the guards when we emerged. "The Queen has ordered him held here for punishment."

I looked down my nose at him, glad for once that I was taller than most of my people. "I am taking him to carry out his punishment."

He looked confused and glanced at his companion, who shrugged.

"Will you stop me from putting my own dryad to the sword, after he has committed treason?"

"No, my Prince," he said hastily, and both guards moved aside.

We were leaving the palace when the Captain of the Guards stepped out of the shadow of one of the Queen's hideous topiaries and said, "I can't let you take him, lad."

I narrowed my eyes at him. "And why is that, Captain?"

"I know you and Daphnis are friends. I know you were boys together."

I managed to keep the surprise from showing on my face, I think. Surprise that he knew Daphnis's name and that he called himself "he" and not "they," and that he'd known we were friends, all those years ago.

"He tried to kill my Queen," I said. "My mother." I hated the feel of that word in my mouth. "Our laws dictate that is punishable by death. He belongs to me, so it is my duty to carry out that sentence."

The Captain studied my face. "The young man I knew would have fought to save his friend." That hurt, but I couldn't show how badly he had wounded me.

"The young man you knew has been kicked in the tackle too many times to fight anymore."

He shook his head but decided on a different approach. "It isn't safe to take him anywhere. Carry out your sentence here on palace grounds."

"He can't harm me, Captain."

"He shouldn't have been able to harm the Queen either, and yet he tried."

"And how he did that is one of the questions I intend to have him answer before I execute him, which is why I can't do it on palace grounds." I put my hand on the hilt of one of my knives and knew he hadn't missed the gesture when his eyes flicked that way, then back to my face. I had always hated the rumors that were spread about me, but they had their uses.

That he was willing to believe them stung.

"And you'd carry out your… questioning in front of a Seer, my Prince? That hardly seems fitting."

Before I could answer, Fionn lifted his chin and met the Captain's gaze. With his taller height, he was even more effective at looking down his nose than I was.

"I intend to find out why this… creature… decided to impersonate *me* while committing his crime."

Daphnis flinched at Fionn's choice of words, an almost invisible gesture I would have missed if I wasn't looking at him. I knew it had hurt Fionn to say it, too, but his voice had been as haughty and emotionless as the most self-important noble. It was chilling, even knowing he didn't mean any of it.

The Captain still hesitated, hand on his sword. "Where are

you taking him?"

"He must die for his crimes," I said, "But as you pointed out, he was my friend once. I'll carry out his sentence in the Dryad Grove."

Daphnis flinched again. Taking him to where his forbears had rooted as trees would seem like an undeserved kindness to a fey, as he would die in the presence of the spirits of his people. But it was no kindness at all to him, to kill him in the place where he would have – but now could not – join them.

I raised my sword and pointed it at the Captain's face. "Will you stop me?"

Before he could answer, Trikta stepped forward. "Good Captain," he said, his Islish full of the clipped sounds of his Vogel accent. "I would offer myself as hostage."

The Captain looked at him in confusion.

"If my Seer and his friend, your Prince, fail to carry out the punishment this dryad deserves, I will stand in his stead." He looked at Fionn and smiled. "I know my Seer will not let me suffer for another's crimes."

Fionn managed not to react, but I could see the way he wanted to recoil in his eyes. Trikta might as well have accused him of doing exactly that. I wondered what Trikta would do if he knew the truth.

"I don't like it," said the Captain. "And I don't like who you've become. But I won't stop you." It hurt all over again that he believed my lies, that he believed I was as cold and unfeeling as my mother would have wished me to be, even if I *needed* him to believe it.

He stepped aside and gestured for Trikta to join him, and Fionn and I entered the woods, Daphnis walking between us. Under the trees, I let the dryad take the lead. He was getting what he wanted, so he wouldn't try to flee.

Away from the iron cell, he regained some of his vigor and

all of his calm. He strode quickly along the forest paths and then off them, following a creek that twisted into the dense forest.

I was the one slowing us down now, though I tried to hide it, to conceal how every step sent pain stabbing into my belly, how weak I was. But before long, I felt Fionn's hand on my back and then his arm around my waist, holding me up, keeping me going when I just wanted to lie down.

I knew every part of Morven Forest as well as I knew my own body, but I had seldom been to the grove of the dryads. It was a sacred place for them, and I had not wanted to intrude.

Finally, we left the stream and climbed a hill, with me leaning on Fionn until he was almost carrying me the last few paces. The top of the hill was open and rank upon rank of trees ringed it.

"Are all these trees dryads?" Fionn asked softly.

"Now, they are only trees," Daphnis said. "But once they were dryads."

"There's a tree in Aven," I said, leaning against Fionn, glad we had stopped walking. "Near the Eyrie. The Vogel peasants call it the Dancing Dryads. It's a salt-leaf with three trunks and they leave offerings to the spirits there."

Daphnis turned his deep brown gaze to me. I thought I saw hope in his eyes.

"I think it might be a new Mother Tree growing, slowly drawing magic to itself."

"Thank you, my Prince," said Daphnis.

Fionn shifted his arm around me. "We haven't time to waste," he said. "Let us do this, and quickly."

Daphnis nodded and pulled a handful of something out of a pocket and handed it to Fionn.

Fionn looked at it, puzzled. "Salt-leaf bark?"

"You know what it's for?" said Daphnis.

"Steeped as a strong tisane, it can help induce spirit travel."

"Seer Tokka, you are a strong healer, but even you aren't strong enough to heal our Prince as you are now."

As if to underline Daphnis's words, I swayed and nearly fell. Only Fionn's arm around my waist kept me upright and I was grateful for his strength.

"What has salt-leaf to do with that?"

"In your spirit body, your healing magic will be stronger."

Fionn stared at the bark again and frowned. "That's it!" he said. "That's why the outer bark is included in the rhyme about healing the Royal Plague." He looked at me with excitement in his eyes. "Healing magic can't touch it under normal conditions, but I would wager that healing magic boosted by spirit travel could."

I tried to smile, but I thought I only managed a grimace. "I'm glad, pretty bird. You'll be able to heal your people now, should the fever return."

I swayed again and this time, despite Fionn's support, I slid to the ground.

"Lie down, my Prince," said Daphnis. "We'll help you undress." He looked at Fionn. "You lie down as well, my Seer. Chew the salt-leaf bark and leave your physical body. Be ready to heal him once my magic has been implanted."

Fionn sat beside me. "I promised I wouldn't leave him, Daphnis. If I spirit travel, he won't be able to see me, not until his magic returns."

I stopped my feeble efforts to pull my belt off and took Fionn's hand. "I'll know you're here," I said, even though the thought of enduring this without being able to see him, to hear him, to feel his touch, terrified me.

"Can I borrow your body, as I did before?" he said, looking at Daphnis.

"I need to be in control of my body, at least in part, to concentrate my magic in my pollen and implant it."

"But I could join you in your body, could I not?" Fionn sounded fierce and I wanted to smile but wasn't sure I could make my face work.

"Yes, I suppose we could do that," Daphnis said. "I will mostly need to control the inner workings of my body, and you will wish to borrow my limbs and my voice. Help me with his clothes, then ready yourself."

Daphnis lifted my upper body into his lap, unbuckled my weapons, and drew my shirt over my head. I shivered at the cool autumn air on my skin.

Fionn leaned over me and put a hand on my face. "Beloved," he said. "I'll be here with you. It's okay. Just remember I'm the one touching you."

I tried to smile again and almost succeeded. "I love you, pretty bird."

He smiled back, his face soft. "I love you, too." He leaned forward and kissed me, reaching for the tie of my trousers and lifting my hips to pull them off. He kissed me again, slowly and thoroughly, sliding his tongue alongside mine and leaving me gasping. Then he lay next to me on the mossy ground and put some of the bark into his mouth.

"My Seer," said Daphnis. "I don't think you should be so close. If you have seizures…"

Fionn looked at me, and I said, "Please stay close."

"I'll stay," he said, and Daphnis sighed, but didn't argue further. Then Fionn's eyes closed and his arm twitched, and I took his hand and held it tightly.

Daphnis pulled me higher into his lap and I realized he had undressed while Fionn kissed me. He lifted me against his naked skin until my back was against his chest and I was straddling his lap. If I had been stronger, I might have pulled away.

I held Fionn's hand tighter, not wanting to lose contact with him. I needed to know he was here with me, because I felt more apprehensive than I had ever felt in any sexual situation before. I *liked* sex. I had enjoyed fucking and being fucked, coupling with whomever wanted me, and I had never been the least bit nervous.

But now, I felt anxiety clutch at my belly, adding a new pain to the ache and the tearing already there. I didn't want this, didn't want Daphnis. But if I wanted to live, if I wanted to be able to make Fionn happy, I had no choice.

"Can you see him?" I said.

"He's here, my Prince," Daphnis answered. "He'll join me in my body soon." His arms were snug across my chest, and I felt him stirring against my lower back. I wanted to pull away, but I made myself be still.

"But first, my Prince," Daphnis said. "I need you to know."

I felt ice in my guts. I knew he was going to tell me something I didn't want to hear.

"I love you," he said.

"Please, Daph, don't."

"I have always loved you, Kiernan, since the first day you wandered into the palace garden and caught me conjuring wisplights. I thought you would run to tell the Queen or a guard, to tell them I could do magic forbidden to dryads."

"Daph."

"But instead, you befriended me, and eventually, you wanted me."

"Please don't."

"That summer we spent making love was the best few months of my life, my Prince. You let me see how the world should be."

His hands stroked over my chest, and I had to force myself

to be still, to remind myself why I was here, why I was allowing this to happen.

"My Prince, every day I was in the pleasure garden, fucking fey nobles for whom I was only a living sex toy, I was planning how I could help you make that world a reality – not just for us, but for all dryads. All peoples."

I bit the inside of my cheek, hard, when his hands brushed over my nipples. I wanted to cry out for Fionn, but I kept silent.

"If you find a way to free the dryads, my Prince, my heart, they will follow you. I've made sure of it. They know you will fight for them if you are able. That's why I had to make sure you would live, that you'd have magic and be free of your Queen. Because I love my people."

I didn't even know how to begin to answer that. "Daphnis –"

"It's okay. Your Seer is joining me now. I'll be gathering my magic while he prepares you to receive it."

"Prepares me how?"

"It will implant better if you feel pleasure, my Prince. Your beloved will borrow my body to make love to you, to pleasure you, and when my magic is concentrated, I will… penetrate you and implant it."

"Fionn."

"I'm here, beloved." And I was sure I felt Daphnis retreat, letting Fionn take over his body. It was Fionn's voice, Fionn's sweet breath on my temple. I opened my eyes and looked at my chest, and it was Fionn's hands that touched me.

"Did you hear him?" I said. I knew, of course, that it was Daphnis's body, and that Daphnis was still aware of all that was happening, but it didn't matter anymore. Fionn was with me, was holding me, was kissing my neck.

I craned my neck to see Fionn's pale hair, his facial feathers, and poking above his shoulders, his wings. It was him, and not Daphnis's clever imitation.

"It *is* you." I glanced down again and saw Fionn's physical body close by, his hand still clutched in mine. His back spasmed and I wanted to reach out and arrange his limbs more comfortably and make sure his wings didn't get twisted.

"I'll be fine, beloved," he said. "My body will be perfectly fine while we get you some magic and heal you."

He stroked a hand down my belly, soft over the place I had been impaled. His other hand found a nipple and teased. "Relax, beloved. Let me touch you. Let me make this easier for you."

"I couldn't do this if you weren't here," I said.

"I know." His lips found my neck again and his hand found my cock and squeezed, tugging until I got hard, until I tried to push against his grip, but my belly hurt too much.

"Your wounds pain you," he said.

"Yes. But your hand feels good." I watched him touch me, his long fingers moving quickly in just the way he knew I liked.

"I love you," he said. "So very much."

"I love you, Fionn."

"Daphnis is ready now," he whispered against my neck. "Are you okay?"

I nodded. "Do it." I closed my eyes, felt Daphnis's small dryad cock press against my asshole, felt him grow tendrils around it to make it bigger. And I felt his tendrils open me up so he could thrust inside me.

"Fionn?"

"I'm still here, beloved," he said, his voice doing as much to keep me hard and wanting as his hands.

"Goddess Below," I said, and my back arched involuntarily. Daphnis was filling me, stretching me wide, pushing inside until I wouldn't have been surprised to sprout tendrils from the end of my cock or my belly button.

It felt wrong even as it felt so fucking good. "Oh fuck," I said. "Fionn."

"I'm here," he said. "Beloved I'm here. We're almost done."

I arched again and something tore inside me, and I thought I screamed. A deep heat was building inside my ass, and I screamed again and came violently, spurting all over my legs.

"Beloved, I'm here and I've got you." It was not Fionn's voice, but Daphnis's that purred in my ear. "I love you so much." I opened my eyes, and it was not Fionn's hands on my skin, on my cock, and I tore away from him, scrambling off his lap and not caring about the tendrils that ripped out of my ass or the magic that suddenly overwhelmed me until I couldn't hold on to consciousness as green light and grey shadows filled my vision.

30
Fionn

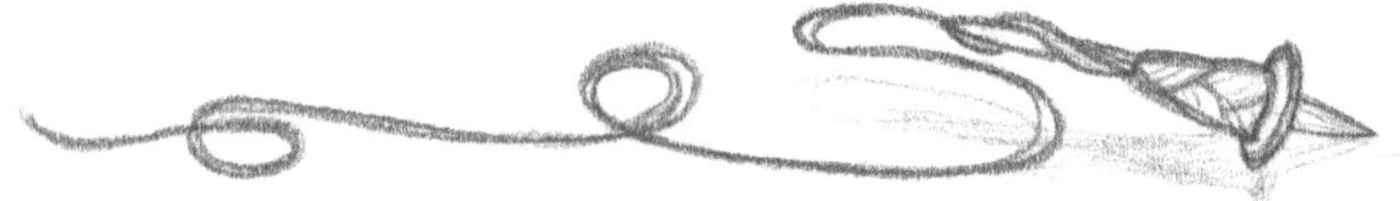

I GATHERED HEALING MAGIC to me, opening myself to the Three Realms, ready to heal Kiernan as soon as Daphnis implanted his pollen.

I refused to think about what that implanting meant for Daphnis, even though sharing his body as I was, I could feel his pleasure building, could feel his orgasm creeping closer.

Instead, I concentrated on Kiernan, talking to him so he would know I was there, that it was me touching him, stroking him, bringing him closer to climax. When Kiernan screamed in pain as his ecstasy worsened his injuries, I wanted to scream with him, but instead I just told him I loved him, that we were almost finished and soon I could heal him.

I felt it when Daphnis had gathered all his magic and infused it into his pollen, strong and green and steady, but when I reached for it, ready to use it to study the shape of Kiernan's injuries I was suddenly hit with an intense disorientation that made me so dizzy I felt about to vomit. I clenched my hands and instead of feeling the skin of Kiernan's chest against them, or the velvet of his hardness, I felt his hand in mine.

I was no longer in Daphnis's body; I was back in my own. I heard Daphnis telling Kiernan he loved him, and I heard Kiernan's half-scream of despair, wordless and feral. He tugged at my hand, and I opened my eyes to see him crawling away from Daphnis, green tendrils pulling out of him, and blood.

Goddess, no. There was too much blood.

I almost sat up, but I forced myself to close my eyes instead, forced calm over my panic, and chewed harder on the salt-leaf bark still in my mouth. And I wrenched myself free of my body again.

My physical body spasmed, hard enough to draw Kiernan's desperate attention away from escape to look at me. At my body. And then he saw my spirit self, crouching over my physical body, reaching for him. He reached back.

I pulled him into my arms, ignoring the peculiar feeling of not-quite-solidity and I looked at him with my Seer's vision, felt for him with my healing magic.

His skin was perfect and unblemished, but his insides had been deeply cut by Sean's sword. The healers' magic had helped, but it had also made things worse. Some parts of the wound had been healed, and some parts hand been healed *wrong*. And, oh Goddess, he was a mess.

I didn't know if I could do this, if I could heal him by myself, but I had to try. Maybe I could at least do enough to keep him alive until we could get help.

I held him tight and pulled healing magic through him, asking the spirits to help, the Goddesses Above, Below, and Around, and even the forest itself. And they answered, pouring healing into me and through me and helping me weave Kiernan back together, to pick apart the things that had been healed wrong and re-heal them correctly.

"Don't use too much magic," he said, his voice small and hoarse. "Please, beloved, don't burn yourself hollow for me." He clung to me, arms tight around my waist, face tucked against my neck.

"You know I would," I said. "I need you to live."

"Please, Fionn."

"I'm okay. I can do this." I eased myself away from the magic, tried to slow its flow, to use it carefully instead of just blasting his wounds with it, and I think if I had been in my physical body, I would have failed. I would have been over-whelmed by it and let it strip me of all my own magic in the process of healing Kiernan.

But in my spirit body I could stand aside and pluck the fibers of magic like I was drafting wool for spinning, and I could weave it as I wanted it, to stitch Kiernan back together.

I could feel him shuddering against my chest, flinching every time I plucked another thread of magic and pieced another mis-healed section of him into place. And then, finally, he relaxed against me and sighed, and I thanked the spirits, the Goddesses, the forest, and tried to separate myself from them.

But in my concentration on healing Kiernan, I hadn't noticed I had also woven myself tight into their fabric.

"Kier?" I said, suddenly afraid.

"What's wrong, pretty bird?" he said, stirring in my arms. He looked into my eyes, and then down at my physical body. I was twitching on the ground, my back seizing, wings snapping open and closed. "Fionn?" he said, and I heard my own fear echoed in his voice.

"I can't pull free," I said.

He took my hand and pulled my spirit body with him as he crawled to my physical body, where he let go to embrace my flailing self. My body fought him – or fought itself – thrashed against him, and he held tighter.

"Kier, I don't think restraining me is a good idea."

"I need you, Fionn," he said. "I need you back in your body." He tucked one wing against my back and pinned it there with his other arm, grabbed my other flailing wing and folded it, his hands strong but gentle. And he held me on his lap, rocked me, and all I could do was watch.

"I need you," he said again. "Spirits, please let him go. Let him the fuck go."

The magic, the spirits, were trying to absorb my spirit body, to make me a part of itself, and keep me from re-entering my body. And I knew I could let go and be absorbed into the forest's magic and become a spirit myself. I could become something ageless and powerful, a being with its own existence but also part of something much greater.

It tugged at me. It would be so easy to let go, to become that bigger thing.

"You will be more than any of your people has ever been before, Seer Tokka," said Daphnis, low and serious.

He still knelt where he had been, his tendrils and sex organs resorbed or hidden wherever they went when he wasn't using them. "I would give almost anything to have that chance."

"Fionn," Kiernan said, his voice breaking. He was hurting, only now it wasn't physical pain. I looked away from Daphnis to watch Kiernan holding my body and I realized that, although he held me still, he wasn't really restraining me. He was just gently tucking my limbs back into comfortable positions every time my flailing muscles jerked them away.

He rocked me in his lap, tucked my face against his chest, and whispered into my ear.

"How can you want me when I look like that?" I said, suddenly disgusted with my physical form, tempted more than ever to let myself be pulled away.

"Let go," whispered Daphnis.

Kiernan looked up from my body, met my eyes in my spirit shape, and smiled. "Pretty bird," he said. "Look at yourself."

"I *am* looking. I'm drooling." I stepped closer, resisting the pull of the forest for a moment longer. "I have swan feathers glued to my wings so I won't look like a stunted freak, but I still can't fly." I met his eyes again and saw tears making the deep green glisten. "I have seizures, Kiernan. Seers are supposed to have visions gracefully, but I black out and flail around like a turtle on its back. I'm too pale and too small and repulsive. And my King likes to fuck me because he can pretend I'm a child and how could *anyone* want me after that and –"

"Stop." His voice wasn't loud or hard or angry, but something in it made me bite off the rest of my words. "Is that really how you see yourself?" he said, and the tears spilled over though he didn't seem to notice.

"I –" Did I really disgust myself so much? I wouldn't have thought so, if I'd been asked sooner. But now… I blinked and looked again at how he was holding me, at the love in every gesture, the gentleness in the way he touched me, at the tenderness in how he was looking at me, watching me puzzle through my own feelings.

"Is it me, beloved?" he said. "Do I make you feel that way? Or was it…" He trailed off.

"My King," I finished for him. I moved closer, knelt next to him, and looked at my body. I wasn't spasming so much now, and Kiernan carefully tucked my wings against my back again. He wiped drool from my cheek with gentle fingers.

"When I look at you like this," he said. "I see the strongest man I know allowing himself to be vulnerable. Allowing me to see him at less than full strength. And I feel so privileged that you let me take care of you."

He met my eyes again and I couldn't resist reaching for him, to wipe tears from his cheeks with not-quite-solid fingers.

"Don't leave me," he said, but he wasn't pleading, he was asking, simply and softly. "You are my heart," he said. "You make me want to be better, to be a good man, a man you could be proud to stand next to."

I moved closer, pressing against his side and bumping my physical leg with my spirit knee. The magic around me eddied and swirled, no longer tugging quite so hard.

"I love you, Fionn," Kiernan said, cradling my physical body and leaning against my spirit body. "It took me too long to be able to say it, and now I want to tell you with every breath." He leaned his head on my shoulder. "I love you."

And the spirits, the magic, the forest, let me go and I sank into myself, stirred in his arms, and said, "I love you, too."

W HAT DO WE DO ABOUT Daphnis?" I said, as Kiernan helped me sit up. Every muscle in my body screamed in agony and my back was twice as bad as the rest.

"I *should* take him back to the palace and execute him as my Queen expects."

He looked down at himself and grimaced, then pulled up a clump of moss and scrubbed at the dried semen on his thighs.

I looked over at Daphnis to find him gone, but he hadn't gone far; he was walking slowly among the trees that ringed the hilltop, moving like he had no energy left. And I suppose he didn't. His magic was gone, and he would soon fade to nothing, to a husk, and then stop altogether.

"I *want* to let him join his ancestors, to root here in the grove."

I looked back at him. "Do you feel the magic now?"

"It feels foreign, but the ache is gone." He smiled. "And I can feel you again." He put his hand on his belly, and I realized I could feel it, too, a faint warmth deep inside that told me he was alive, and well, and mine. It wasn't as strong as our connection should be, but it was much better than nothing. "It will be enough to carry me through until I can regain my own magic. But…" He frowned.

"What is it?"

"My antlers feel strange. Like they're vibrating."

"Is it the spellwork?"

"Maybe."

I looked at my hands instead of watching him get dressed, but I couldn't keep the smile off my face. He was healed, and we were together, even if it was only for a little while longer. But the worries wouldn't be kept at bay.

"Kier… Right at the end, Daphnis banished me from his body. I had to force myself out of my physical self to be able to heal you."

He glanced up from buckling his sword on, looked at Daphnis, and then at me. "He told me he loved me and I… I pulled away from him. I think he wanted you out so he could…"

"He could have you for his own."

"I don't know what to do, Fionn. He was my friend, once, but that –"

"He violated you," I said softly.

He bit his lip and shook his head, but he said, "Yes. And I don't think I can forgive that."

"I know I can't."

He put both hands on my face and looked deep into my eyes. "Could you forgive *me* if I killed him?"

I licked my lips and leaned my forehead against his. "He

knew you wanted me there while he…"

"Yes."

"And he pushed me out, so he could have your pleasure for himself."

"Yes."

"If you didn't keep telling me Seers mustn't kill, I might be tempted to execute him myself." I felt cold, saying those words, terrified of what they meant, that I was capable of violence, of killing, and terrified that Kiernan would see me differently, that he wouldn't recognize the gentle version of me that he loved. But the words were true. Daphnis had done an awful thing under the guise of saving Kiernan's life, and I believed I *could* kill him without remorse, as I had believed I could kill his Queen.

The reproach I was afraid of seeing in Kiernan's look after I said that did not materialize. Instead, there was something fierce in his eyes, and pride, and love, and I felt warm.

"We'll take him back to the palace, then," he said.

We turned and I felt for Kiernan's hand. I should feel compassion for Daphnis – whatever else he had done, he had given his life for us – but I didn't, and it frightened me.

Daphnis stood near the top of the hill, one hand on the trunk of a small tree, but he was looking at the sky. I followed his gaze and saw wings, green and blue feathers bright in the sun, silver bird mask reflecting the light in bursts.

"Konta or Trikta?" Kiernan said.

"Konta. He has more blue in his wings." I shaded my eyes with one hand and watched my Guard approach, circling the hilltop to land on the clear grassy space in the middle. Two thin shapes arrowed towards me, chittering excitedly.

He hatches, said Smoke.

Is now, said Flame.

"Your egg? We have to hurry then," said Kiernan and he

grinned at me, Daphnis forgotten, maybe, or at least no longer the most important thing.

No hurry, said Smoke.

Is here, said Flame, landing on Kier's shoulder and poking his jaw with her nose, He reached up to scratch her chin.

"I'm so glad I can understand you again," he said.

Is good, said Flame.

Konta glanced curiously at Daphnis but hurried down the hill towards us.

Guard has, said Smoke, draping herself around my neck and sounding very pleased with herself.

<I think your serpents wanted me to bring you this,> Konta said, holding out the basket with the egg. <I found them trying to carry it themselves.>

Kiernan took the basket and held it in his cupped hands.

"Islish please, Konta. Kiernan doesn't speak Vogel."

"Sorry, Prince of Morven. I meant no disrespect."

Kiernan smiled. "I do hope to learn someday," he said. "More than the five or six words I know now, anyway."

Konta nodded and glanced at Daphnis again. The dryad was standing next to the same tree, both hands and his forehead pressed to the bark. He looked half tree himself, already.

Kiernan followed his gaze. "We'll return him to the palace after." He nodded at the basket in his hands.

"I should get back, if you don't need me, my Seer."

"Go ahead," I said. "We'll return soon."

Kiernan knelt in the moss, and I sank down beside him and watched as he tipped the egg out into his hands and looked at it closely.

The serpents slid from our shoulders and onto Kiernan's lap, peering at the egg cradled in his strong hands. The olive-green shell rocked and a crack opened, then another, and a tiny snout poked out.

"You got here just in time," I said.

We knew, said Flame.

I leaned my head on Kiernan's shoulder, and he tipped his to rest on top of mine. The egg rocked and another piece of shell detached and fell onto his hand. The snout poked out farther.

"Tree serpents have egg teeth," Kiernan said, his voice soft with awe, and I saw what he had noticed: an outsized fang on the end of the little snout that would fall off later. I had seen Smoke and Flame hatch, but not up close, so it was new information to me, too.

"Is he really that dark colored, or is he wet?" Kier asked. What little we could see of the infant serpent so far was dark grey scales, glistening in the sun.

"He'll be damp, I think," I said. "But he does look very dark."

The egg rocked again and this time it split wide open and a tiny feathered tree serpent tumbled out into Kiernan's hands. I snuck a look at his face, and he was smiling so hard it almost looked painful.

Nyah, said the baby serpent.

"I hope that's tree serpent baby talk," said Kiernan. "Or else I've lost the magic to understand them again."

Is baby, said Flame, nuzzling the little serpent and beginning to groom him, cleaning away the remnants of fluid from the egg.

Will talk, said Smoke, also grooming the tiny creature.

I reached for the basket and pulled off a tuft of wool. "Here," I said, holding it out to Kiernan. "You should help."

He shifted the serpent to one hand and took the wool with the other, and carefully wiped the creature's downy wings. Smoke and Flame backed away to let him take over and the tiny serpent began to purr.

He loves, said Smoke.

Love and love, said Flame.

"He's beautiful," whispered Kiernan. His eyes gleamed, but no tears fell.

Nyah, said the serpent again.

His name? said Flame.

"I can name him?" asked Kier.

You name, said Smoke.

Kiernan gently stroked the tiny wings with the piece of wool, then the little dragon-like head. The baby serpent was, indeed, dark grey with gleams of blue and green, darker than most tree serpents. His wings wouldn't fledge for a while yet, but it looked like they might have some red feathers among the darker colors.

"Coal," said Kiernan. "Is Coal a good name?"

Is good, said Smoke.

Smoke and Flame and Coal, said Flame.

31
Kiernan

ILOOKED AT THE TINY serpent in my hands and he looked back up at me, his eyes red-gold and shining, like a dragon's, if dragons were small enough to carry in one hand.

Nyah, he said, then curled up in the palm of my hand and went to sleep. I transferred him into his basket and held it by the strap, careful not to let it swing too much. I didn't know if tree serpents could get motion sick, and I didn't want to find out. Fionn put his arms around me, and I leaned into him.

"Can we leave Daphnis alone for a little while?" he said. "Can we find somewhere private?"

We watch, said Smoke.

We guard, said Flame.

I looked over at where Daphnis was still standing, forehead pressed to one of the trees in the grove. "I'm more worried that he'll go ahead and root than that he'll run away." I hooked the strap of the basket over a branch and Smoke and Flame curled around the same tree to keep watch.

I took Fionn's outstretched hand, and we walked downhill

to where the trees were thicker and a stream meandered between trunks. For a while, we just walked, and then Fionn said, "How will you get the rest of your magic back?"

I didn't answer right away, but waited until we'd crossed the stream by way of a fallen tree and came out in a little meadow where the ground was too wet for the dry-hill oaks that surrounded us. "I've been doing a lot of reading about spellwork," I said. I didn't want to say that I still had no idea, that I hoped an opportunity would present itself, hopefully before I had to leave for Dudoon.

We crossed the soggy meadow and climbed a rise surrounded by small pines and carpeted in moss. Fionn tugged me to a stop and when I turned to face him, he kissed me.

I smiled against his lips, and he kissed me harder, pressing his mouth on mine until I opened to his tongue, drew it in and sucked on it. He laughed and pulled away.

"We're leaving tomorrow," he said, his smile vanishing.

"I know." I freed my hand from his so I could put both hands on his hips and pull him closer.

"I wanted to spend tonight with you," he said softly, and I met his eyes. His were sad. "But I suspect that won't happen now."

"Because of Daphnis."

"You'll have to take him to your Queen, and…"

"And execute him."

"You Sidhe seem to like to do things very quickly, but also very slowly, with a lot of formal ritual."

I laughed. "And you think it will take all night to deal with one prisoner."

He bit his lip, and I was reminded of the uncertain young man I had first met at the Abbey of the Moon. "You'll have to explain why you suddenly have magic."

I had to admit, that hadn't occurred to me yet, though it

seemed obvious once he said it. "My Queen is bound to notice."

He touched the laces at the neck of my shirt almost shyly. "Let me make you feel good," he said. "Let me remind you of how we can be together."

I smiled and pushed up onto my toes to reach his mouth, kissed him slowly and carefully, then pulled back. "I will never forget how we can be together." I traced the feathers beside his face with the very tips of my fingers. "Beloved, I could spend hours just talking to you, just sitting next to you, and be a happy man," I said, but my lips curved into a wicked grin.

"Are you saying you don't want me?" he said, pretending to be hurt. But then he suddenly went serious. "Is it too soon, after what Daphnis did?"

I slid my hands around his waist and down to his ass to pull him even more firmly against me. "I want you to help me forget what Daphnis did, pretty bird."

He stared into my eyes, searching, maybe to see if I really meant it. "I shouldn't have let him push me out, before you –."

I kissed him again and he growled in annoyance. I had told myself I was going to leave off stopping him from speaking, because I knew he hated it, but I didn't want to hear those words, to be reminded that Daphnis had forced Fionn out so he could be the one to give me pleasure, so he could claim that small victory.

"I'm sorry," I said. "I just don't want…"

"It's okay," he said. "This time. I shouldn't have reminded you."

"Just kiss me, pretty bird."

He did, gently brushing his lips over mine then angling his head to get his tongue farther into my mouth until I was panting when he pulled away.

When we had first met, I had kissed who knew how many

others, but I was his first. And now he could kiss me so perfectly I had trouble catching my breath. I knew no one would ever kiss me that well again, except him.

"Kiss me again," I said, and he smiled and tugged at the buckles on my belt until the whole rig dropped to the moss, sword and knives and all. Then he slipped his hands under my shirt to touch my skin, pulled my shirt over my head, and kissed me, tangled his tongue with mine, none of the shy young man he had been left.

"Do you want me to put my tongue other places?" he said, voice husky and low in my ear. My cock twitched and swelled, and I pressed against him so he could feel it.

"There is no place on my body I *don't* want your tongue, pretty bird," I said, and he laughed deep in his throat. "Though there are some parts of me I maybe ought to wash first."

He laughed again and helped me pull off his tunic and shirt, then reached for my trouser tie. "There's a lovely soft bed of moss here and I think you ought to lie down on it."

I tugged his trouser buttons open and slipped the garment over his hips followed by his underthings. Then I dropped to my knees and pushed my face into his soft groin feathers. "There's something I want to do first," I said, and I ran my tongue along his seam, smiling when he gasped and reached for my antlers.

Maybe it said something about his state of mind, the urgency we both felt that our time was running out, but instead of trying to hold his erection in until he simply couldn't any longer, Fionn let his cock slide out of his sheath as soon as he was hard and urged me to put my mouth on him, clinging to my antlers and panting my name.

I ran my tongue along his underside and slid my lips over him, sucking and sliding until he was gasping his pretty love noises with every breath. When I paused, he looked down at me and said, "Lie down on the moss, beloved. I want to put my tongue on you."

I smiled and wriggled out of the rest of my clothes then lay back on the moss, looking up at him. He towered over me, pale and lovely, so beautiful my heart might break looking at him.

"You're so beautiful," he said, and I laughed.

"I was just thinking that exact thing about you."

He knelt between my knees. "Tell me —" He hesitated.

"I love you, Fionn," I said. "I want you. I need you so fucking badly." I reached down to touch myself, to stroke my palm over my cock, and he made a noise in his throat, bent down, and took me in his mouth. For a moment I just lay still, watching his bobbing head, his perfect pink lips sliding over me. Then he looked up, met my eyes, and lifted his head.

"Roll over," he said, his voice raspy.

I smiled and did as he asked, pushing up onto my knees to give him a good view of my ass.

"Goddess, Kier," he said. "You really *are* perfect."

Then he stroked both hands over my ass and spread my cheeks open as wide as he could, bent over me, and ran his tongue along the space between, from the skin of my testicles, over my asshole, and right up to the divot at the top of my buttocks, almost to where the nicFia stag marked my back.

"Fuck, Fionn," I said, low and breathy. "You should let me wash first. Daphnis —"

"Shut up," he said, "I don't care. Didn't you know that Vogel will eat anything?"

He put his hand between my shoulder blades to keep my upper body pressed to the moss.

"Mmm," I said, the sounding rumbling in my chest. "I like this bossy version of you." Then I twisted to look over my shoulder at him. "Did you just make a sex joke?"

His lips twitched. "I might have."

He pushed his hand between my shoulder blades again and I buried my face against the moss when he bent over me and spread me open again.

For a moment he did nothing, and I could almost feel him looking at me. Then he bent down again and kissed me, his lips wet against my asshole, and I clenched in surprise.

He circled me with his tongue, around and around, and each time, when he pressed a little harder, I moaned, muffled against the moss.

He stopped with just the very tip of his tongue touching me, right in the center of my asshole, and I lifted my head to try to see him over my shoulder, but my own butt was blocking my view.

"Fuck, Fionn. Please," I said.

He removed his tongue. "Please what?"

"Please don't stop."

He dug his claws into my ass muscles, and I grunted. It sent a shiver thought me, though it wasn't even hard enough to hurt. He touched his tongue to me again, pressing harder.

"Oh fuck," I said, as I relaxed enough for his tongue to probe inside me. He pushed his tongue into me until I felt his teeth meet my flesh and he couldn't get in any farther.

I cried out as he swirled his tongue inside me, stretching in, then suddenly sliding out.

"Don't stop," I gasped, and he speared his tongue into me again and again until my ass crack was soaked with his saliva and I was panting with every thrust.

"Fuck me with your tongue, pretty bird," I said, and it was his turn to groan. Just thinking about what he was doing to me made me ache. My testicles felt tight and hot and I wanted him deep inside me.

"Fuck, Fionn," I said. "I want you. Please."

He lifted his head and I moaned softly.

"Tell me what you want," he whispered, and wiped his mouth with the back of his hand.

"Fuck me, pretty bird. Fuck me so hard I forget my own name."

He sat up, knelt closer, and pressed himself against me, using his tip to massage my asshole until I cried out.

"Please fuck me," I begged, not caring how desperate I sounded. "Please."

He pushed me open, thrust into me and opened me wide to plunge into me as far as he could go, until his hips bumped my ass and I moaned again.

"Harder," I said. My hands tightened into fists on the moss, stretched over my head to brace myself against his thrusts.

He pulled out and slammed into me, and I grinned at his sudden intensity, at how happy he seemed to oblige me and fuck me as hard as he could. He pulsed and I groaned.

"I felt you," I said. "Goddess Below, I love feeling you pulse inside my ass."

He grabbed my hips and thrust again and again, crying out when his second pulse hit, and the third came quickly after, and then he slowed, less urgent, but didn't stop. Not yet. He wasn't done, and neither was I.

He wrapped an arm around my chest, and the other around my waist, and slowly pulled me up and held me against him so I was sitting astride his lap, as Daphnis had held me when implanting his pollen. For the barest instant I wanted to pull away, but then I looked down and saw his hands – *his* hands, not Daphnis's – caressing my skin.

"Don't stop," I said, leaning my head back against his shoulder.

He slid his hand down my belly to my cock, curled his fingers around me and stroked, teasing me. And he pushed inside me, thrusting slowly, letting his fourth pulse build.

"Kier," he said.

"Mmm?" I was relaxed against him, only pushing against his hand with my hips, lost in the feeling of his fingers squeezing and sliding over my cock.

"Are you close?"

"I'm close," I said. "So close. You feel so good. So fucking good."

"I love you," he said. "Oh, Goddess." He thrust harder.

"Fionn, I'm so close." I pushed my shoulders back against him to curve my spine. "Beloved –" Whatever I had meant to say next dissolved into a yell of pleasure and I throbbed in his hand, shooting a long string of glistening white onto the moss, from our knees right up to the trunk of the nearest tree.

Then I felt him pulse from deep inside, filling me so full I was sure I would leak.

He collapsed against my back, and I lowered us both to the soft, cool moss, where we curled up together, relaxing into each other, breathing onto each other.

WE LAY CURLED TOGETHER on the moss for as long as we dared. When we had both caught our breath again, we stood up and helped each other dress, taking comfort in holding sleeves out and doing up buttons, smoothing down each other's clothing and picking off stray bits of foliage.

It was astonishing, the amount of joy there was to be found in something as simple as buckling your lover's belt or tucking his hair back into place. And while it wasn't erotic, it was just as much a display of love as fucking wildly on the forest floor had been, and every bit as satisfying.

When we were both dressed, we stood looking at one another for a long time, not speaking, not even moving – just gazing into each other's eyes and grinning stupidly.

Finally, Fionn touched my cheek with his fingertips and said, "Please get your magic back as soon as you can. I don't want to wait moons or even years to hear you say my name that way again."

My heart thumped at the way he spoke those words, and the idea that my voice moaning his name in pleasure turned him on almost made me hard again.

"I don't intend to dawdle," I said. "Because the way you make those pretty little noises when I touch you is one of my favorite things in the world."

"Only *one* of your favorite things?" he teased, lacing his fingers with mine and letting me lead him out of the pines and back across the soggy meadow.

"Well," I said, swinging our joined hands. "I also like the way you tilt your head back and open your mouth when I put my tongue on a certain spot somewhere below your belly button."

He blushed.

"And I like how you clench around me when you pulse while I'm inside you."

He tugged me closer so he could whisper in my ear. "I like how you clench when I pulse inside *you*."

I turned and captured his lips with mine. "Yes, I like that, too."

We climbed back up the hill of the dryad grove.

"Do you know what my most favorite thing is?" I asked.

He shook his head. "When you touch between my toes?"

"I *do* like that, but no."

"When I put my fingers inside you while I'm pleasuring

you?"

I shivered pleasantly. "Goddess Below, that *is* nice. But still no." I stopped next to the tree where I'd left Coal in his basket and turned Fionn to face me. I put both hands on his cheeks and studied his silver eyes, then dropped my hands to his shoulders. "My very favorite thing, beloved, is the way you smile when I do something that makes you happy."

I was rewarded with exactly that smile, the one that made his eyes glow, that made his pretty, handsome face turn beautiful, that told me I had done something right. The smile I would gladly spend my life pursuing.

"You're teasing," he said, his cheeks going a little pink.

"I'm not, pretty bird. Your smile is my favorite thing in the whole world."

He licked his lips and looked away, then met my eyes again. "Mine is when you call me pretty bird."

I almost laughed, because at first he had hated the nickname, but I managed to smile instead. "Is it?"

"It is, because the way you say it is… It's like you're telling me you love me and you want me and you like spending time with me, all at once."

I kissed his nose. "That's exactly what I'm saying when I call you pretty bird."

And I got that beautiful smile again. But then it faded because we both heard the sound: wings.

"Maybe it's just Konta coming back to say we're going to be late for the noon meal," he said.

"I'm pretty sure we've missed the noon meal." The anxiety in my gut, which might have been all mine or might have been his, too, told me it was unlikely to be something so simple.

It *was* Konta returning, only he had Trikta with him. They landed in the clear place at the top of the hill, glanced at Daphnis, still standing where we had left him, and headed towards us.

Instead of a leisurely stroll downwards, Fionn's Guards hurried, their long legs bringing them to us quickly.

"My Seer," said Konta, remembering this time to speak Islish. "There's been a messenger."

"From the Eyrie," said Trikta. He looked at Konta, who nodded. "Seer Tokka, the Royal Plague has hit the Eyrie again."

Fionn shifted beside me, his grip on my hand tightening. "No," he said softly.

"We need to leave immediately," said Konta, and I knew we were out of time.

32

Fionn

I HAD THOUGHT IT WOULD be hard to leave Kiernan behind, but with the urgency of the message from the Eyrie, there was no time to think, no time to despair. And no time to say good-bye.

Konta lifted me into the air with his strong talons around my arms, and we were winging our way over the forest, leaving much more quickly than we had arrived.

When we got to the ship, Councilor Rocsh, our attendants, and the King's Guard were already on board, and sailors scurried about on deck, readying the ship to sail. I knew I should go below, to speak to the Councilor and get out of the way, but I couldn't bear it. I knew I wouldn't see Kiernan as we sailed away, but still I couldn't walk away from my last view of the forest that was so much a part of him.

So I found a spot at the stern, up against the rail, where I didn't seem to be in the way, and I sat down on some sort of large metal fitting that I couldn't imagine the function of. I stared towards the shore, heart aching.

Neeka brought me a cup of anti-nausea tea, which I didn't really need, but I gulped it down anyway and continued to stare at the passing shore.

She leaned against the rail and put a hand on my shoulder. <You'll see him again soon, Tokka.>

<Maybe,> I said. <But it still feels like I'm leaving part of myself behind.>

<That's because you are,> she said. <At least, that's what they say about the heart-bonded.>

I was about to reply when a sudden burning pain flooded my head and I gasped and dropped the teacup I had been clutching. It rolled across the deck and Neeka laughed and ran after it.

"Kiernan," I said, grabbing my head. It was *his* pain I was feeling, and it was so much like what I had felt when his magic had first been taken that I cried out, not loud enough to bother the sailors, but enough for Neeka to quickly make her way back to me. She crouched in front of me and gripped my shoulders.

<My Seer?>

I held my head, trying to separate myself from what Kiernan was feeling enough that I could answer her. <He's in pain,> I said. <It feels like… like his magic is… I don't know.>

<Is his Queen punishing him again?>

I realized that Neeka didn't know that Daphnis had given Kiernan his magic; there hadn't been time yet to tell her.

I shook my head. <I don't know.>

<Will a pain relief tea help?> She dug her fingers into my shoulders, massaging my muscles, trying to help me relax.

<It's not *my* pain,> I said. <It's his.> The burning spread, deeper into my skull, behind my eyes, and my connection to Kiernan seemed almost to vibrate deep in my belly.

And then, from burning to stabbing, worse than anything

I'd felt before, that seemed to rip my skull to fragments and turned my vision red. I think I screamed.

When I became aware of myself again, Neeka was holding me tight to her chest, cradling my head against her collarbone, and a circle of sailors eyed us warily.

<I'm okay,> I said. <I'm okay.> The sailors drifted back to their duties, and I disengaged myself slowly from Neeka's arms. She let go of me reluctantly.

My head throbbed and two points on my forehead burned and ached, but it was manageable. I sat up slowly, then doubled over again when a wave of heat hit my belly.

"Kiernan," I said again, and I felt his anger, his sorrow, his regret. I wished I could see what was happening to him, what made him feel those things. It faded, slowly, to a soft desperation, and I realized our connection was strong again – not the odd, not-quite-right feel it had with Daphnis's magic, but the gentle, warm knowledge that he was alive and safe and mine.

I looked at Neeka and she brushed tears from my cheeks.

<My Seer?> she said, worry in her voice.

I shook my head. <I don't know what happened,> I said. <Something that caused him pain. Something… his antlers, he said they felt strange.> I shook my head again. <But our connection feels normal again, whatever happened.> I tried a smile and she smiled back.

<Maybe he got his magic back,> she said. <And he'll come for you now, to steal you away from our King.>

He *had* promised, but would he really come? He was finally doing work for his Queen that he could be proud of – acting as her ambassador and fostering peace and trade instead of sneaking around as her spy and assassin. And I, too, would be able to do the kind of work as Seer that I should have been able to do all along.

And I no longer needed to worry about my King taking me

to bed. Councilor Rocsh had seen the Founding Laws book, and he knew the Eyrie's copy was missing. He would quietly warn the King that his interest in me was wrong, and if the King wouldn't listen, we would present the issue – and the laws – to the Council.

I looked at my hands. <He might not want to leave his forest, if he does have his magic back.> I gazed over the rail at the scenery slipping by, watched Smoke and Flame play in the ship's wake, and forced myself not to cry. <And I have people to heal at the Eyrie.>

<And yet you both long for each other,> Neeka said. <I can see it on your face. You're heart-bonded, which means that longing will never fade. He *will* come for you, and you'd better take me with you when you go.>

I laughed. Somehow, no matter how I sunk myself in melancholy, Neeka could always find a way to make me feel a little better.

<I think,> I said, <That I'd like to be alone for a little while.>

<Of course,> she said. <I'll let you know when the evening meal is ready.>

I didn't get much time to myself before Councilor Rocsh leaned on the rail and said, <My Seer?> I pulled my gaze away from shore to look at him. <I'm sending the King's Guards ahead to the Eyrie. Can you help me choose which medicines to send with them? And include any instructions for Healer Kah?>

I forced my thoughts away from their desperate spiral. <Of course.> I got up and followed him to his cabin, where the few items our delegation had been able to carry in flight had been stowed.

Seeing my look at the small number of bundles, the Councilor said, <Your Prince's cousin assured me that he and Prince

Kiernan will have the rest of our things sent to us soon, and that they will make our farewells and apologies to the Queen.>

<Of course,> I said again, and shook my head to try to make my thoughts engage properly. I had work to do, and pining for Kier wouldn't help accomplish it any faster.

I opened bundles and sorted packages of herbs and bottles of syrup until I had assembled two piles small enough for the King's Guards to carry without adding a lot of weight. They would need to fly quickly if they were going to do any good. While Councilor Rocsh packed my piles into carry bags, I wrote hasty instructions to Healer Kah. Fortunately, she already knew much of what needed to be done from the work we had accomplished before I left.

I went back up on deck to watch the Guards leave, unable to suppress the stab of envy I still felt every time I saw one of my people fly. Would Kiernan finish the wings he had been making for me? And would they even enable me to fly?

I sat for a long time, watching the sailors work, watching the scenery slip past, but not really seeing any of it. I was almost unaware of slipping into a vision, I was so sunk in my thoughts, and the vision was so like my current reality.

I sat on a metal fitting on the deck of the ship as mist gathered around us and sound faded away. A figure began to coalesce out of the mist and sea spray, hovering over the surface of the sea.

"I told you I would aid you," the figure said, the voice soft but resonant. The shape solidified enough that I could make out a woman, long-haired, with a magnificent set of antlers. She looked like the Sidhe Queen, only somehow *more*, greater than any earthly being.

"Lady of the Forest," I said, unable to bring my voice above a whisper. It seemed impertinent even to speak to one such as she, but I needed to. "I thought you meant for me to…

to…" In the end, I didn't manage to get the words out.

"To kill she who rules my forest in order to save him we both love? No, little silver bird, that was not my intention."

I stared at her, then mustered enough thoughts to say, "You helped me heal him."

"Three times I will help you to help him, silver one. That was the first. Three times my sister of the air will help him help you. And three times… well, that is for another day." And the voice faded on her last words, the shape faded and drifted away into mist and sea spray again, and I was left with a headache behind my eyes and sore muscles in my back, and the distinct impression that I was already forgetting something I really needed to remember.

As the evening drew close and my belly began to complain that I hadn't fed it recently enough, I looked up to see Councilor Rocsh approaching again.

<May I join you, my Seer?>

I nodded and started to get up so he could sit on the metal fixture, but before I could finish the motion, he sank elegantly to the deck to sit with his back against the rail.

He was holding a box in his hands, gleaming wood carved with twisting vines arranged into a knotwork pattern, with a leaping stag on the top. He smiled slightly, then passed me the box.

<Seer Siona asked me to give this to you,> he said.

<What is it?> The box filled both my hands, long and narrow, and it had a clasp of moonsilver on the front that seemed to be locked, but I could see no keyhole.

<She didn't say.> Rocsh leaned his head back to look up at

the pale blue sails billowing above us. <She only said that you will know what to do with it when the time comes.>

I turned the box over in my hands and heard a muffled knock as whatever was inside shifted. I touched the catch curiously with one finger and it sprang open.

<A magic lock, then?> the Councilor said, watching.

I set the box on my knees and carefully lifted the lid. Inside was a wrapping of deep blue-green moth silk – the kind that was nubbly and soft rather than the smooth, slippery kind. I resisted the urge to examine the weave and folded back the edges. Nestled within were two matched sets of antlers.

<I don't understand,> I said softly. I lifted an antler out – it was a little spike, barely the length of my smallest finger. Unthinking, I brought it to my nose and almost cried out. I must have gasped, at least, because the Councilor turned away from the passing shore to look at me closely.

<They're his,> I said, putting the spike back in the box and lifting out one of the larger pair. <They're Kiernan's.> This antler wasn't large, either, but it was forked, and even though it wasn't attached to him anymore, the feel of it in my hand was familiar.

For a moment I remembered the last time I had touched his antlers, when I had clung desperately to them as he pleasured me with his mouth. I bit the inside of my cheek and ignored the heat that flooded my body. I laid the antler back in the box and folded the cloth back over it. There was a folded slip of paper tucked into the front that I hadn't noticed before.

<I didn't think Sidhe shed their antlers as deer do,> Councilor Rocsh said.

<They don't.> I lifted the paper out. <But they can be removed by force.> I looked up at him. <It happened to him twice that I know of.> I closed my eyes. <It must have been excruciating.>

<He must have been very young,> Rocsh said gently. <Those antlers aren't nearly the size he has now.>

<He was six years old the first time,> I said and almost startled when Rocsh put his hand on my knee and squeezed comfortingly. <He was to be sent to his father, who is human, and I suppose his Queen felt it would make him look less… foreign.>

But another thought occurred to me. <Or… Removing a Sidhe's antlers damages their connection to the Three Realms. It doesn't destroy it, but it means they can feel magic but not use it.> I stroked the lid of the box. <He was strong in magic very young, but he couldn't control it. Perhaps it was for the safety of the humans he would be living amongst.>

I unfolded the paper, finally, and began to read.

Dearest Seer Tokka – Fionn – I am sorry we are unable to have a proper farewell. I have had a vision, and though much of it has already faded into forgetfulness, I was left with the knowledge that you would soon need what I send to you in this box.

They were Kiernan's, as I'm sure you've realized. I wish I could tell you for what purpose you will need them, but I trust you will know when the time comes.

He loves you, the son of my heart, and I know you love him. I hope I will one day soon see the two of you together – not for a brief visit, but for the rest of your lives. You and he will change the world, I am sure of it.

My blessings and well-wishes go with you,
Seer Siona of Morven Forest.

I lifted the cloth to touch one of the antlers again, and shivered, suddenly struck by the strangeness of all of it, the sheer impossibility of the things I wanted to accomplish.

And then it was time to eat the evening meal and I had to pretend as if everything was normal when it felt like everything was different, and strange.

LATER, AFTER WE HAD eaten and night was beginning to descend, I was on deck again to watch the sun go down, unable to keep from thinking of Kier, unable to keep the ache of his absence at bay. The ship's Captain approached me tentatively across the deck.

<My Seer,> he said.

<Captain.>

He was short for a Vogel, and muscular, with eyes that squinted even when it wasn't bright. <My people say it is a blessing to have you on board, and I've never had a sailing as smooth as this.>

<I think that has more to do with the weather and the skill of your sailors,> I said.

He laughed. <Maybe, maybe not, but the *Sea Spray*> – he gestured at the deck beneath our feet – <has a Seer for a figurehead, and seers in general are good luck to sailors.>

<I quite like your figurehead,> I said, and felt myself blush. I had only had a few quick looks at the carving on the front of the ship when I'd boarded and disembarked and boarded again, but I had noticed that while many of the other Vogel ships had mermaids, and fish, and busty human women for figureheads, ours had a silver-white bird folk Seer. It was carved with wings outspread behind, cradling the sides of the ship, and the wooden strands of long hair had been made to look as if they were twisting and floating in the wind.

<Can I show you something?>

I followed him forward. He, like all his sailors, had wings and tail trimmed shorter, natural feathers cut neatly so their tips barely reached his knees, and his tail just brushed his ankles. Councilor Rocsh had said they were still able to fly, though not as far or as long as Vogel with untrimmed wings, but they were less like to trip onboard a ship or get tangled in the ropes.

At the bow of the ship, just above the beautiful silver figurehead, a long spar of wood jutted out at an angle, like a finger pointing straight ahead. The bowsprit, I think it was called.

<I've seen you watching the birds, my Seer,> he said. <And you seem sad. If you climb out there and lie along the bowsprit, you can open your wings and it feels as if there's nothing around you but air. It's as near to flying as you can get, save getting in the air with your wings.>

<I can't fly,> I said, my words sharp.

<I know, lad.> He said it more kindly than I might have deserved. <But watch.> He hopped over the rail and onto the bowsprit and I grabbed for a rope as if me holding on would keep him from falling. Then he lay against the slope of wood, wrapped his arms around it, gripped with his toes, and opened his wings. I could see how the wind caught him and pulled at him, and he had to hold on hard. Then he folded his wings and climbed back onto the deck.

<Now you try, my Seer.>

<I don't know.> I looked at the thin bit of wood. It seemed solid enough, and really wasn't any thinner than some of the other parts of the ship.

<Go on.> He touched my back, just a gentle palm between my wings, and then he stepped back. <Just remember to hold on very tight.> He smiled one more time, then left me alone.

I swallowed and put my hand on a rope. I climbed slowly up onto the rail, gripping with my toes and clinging to ropes with both hands. I put one foot gingerly onto the bowsprit and curled my toes around the rope that wrapped around it. I shifted the position of my hands, then put my other foot down.

I could already feel the wind pulling at me, so I clamped my wings and tail tight to my back as I knelt and then stretched out against the wood. For a long moment I just clung there, terrified, but then I set my teeth and eased forward and upward until I was peering over the tip of the bowsprit at the water beneath. Salty spray hit my face as we dipped into a trough and tilted up the other side. Every motion of the little ship seemed exaggerated from here.

I tightened my arms around the bowsprit, and tightened my feet on the rope, held my breath, and opened my wings.

The wind caught me and pulled and if I hadn't been holding so tight, I thought I might have been ripped away and flung into the sky. I shrieked, I couldn't help it, but it wasn't fear, but the fiercest joy I had ever experienced. I opened my eyes wide to better take in the sea and the sky and the white foam. A big white bird soared closer, to fly wingtip to wingtip with me and only banking away when I yelled because I couldn't be quiet.

The ship's bow tipped up and plunged down again as we crested a wave and I realized I was grinning so hard my cheeks ached, and tears streamed down my face only to be snatched away by the wind.

It was as much like flying as spirit flight had been, only I was in my physical body.

Just ahead I could see where – I knew from studying the Captain's maps – the Great River emptied into the sea, turning the water temporarily opaque. Beyond that was Aven, then the Eyrie.

"I'm flying, beloved," I yelled into the wind, not caring who might hear me. And I tilted my head back and laughed. And cried, because even if I had been flying, it was in the wrong direction, away from Kiernan and back into captivity.

33
Kiernan

For the barest instant, Fionn just stared at his guard, then he stepped forward and gripped Konta's shoulder.

"What did the message say, exactly?"

"I don't know. Councilor Rocsh only told me to tell you the fever has hit the Eyrie again.

"Do you know when the message was sent?"

Trikta said, "A messenger arrived but would only speak with you or the Councilor.

I reached for Coal's basket and strapped it across my chest, then touched Fionn's arm. "If you need to go, Seer Tokka, go. I'll deal with the dryad."

Fionn turned away from his guards, and from the edge of my vision I saw them retreat back towards the hilltop and turn away to give us what little privacy they could.

"I'm not ready to leave," he said. "I'm going to miss your birthday."

I took his hand, raised it to my lips, and kissed the backs of his fingers. "I'm not ready for you to go. But your people need you, and you have salt-leaf to take with you." I smiled and held his hand to my cheek. "And you figured out the last part of the riddle; you know how spirit-travel can help cure the fever."

"Kiernan."

"You were going to miss my birthday, anyway. And I'll come for you as soon as I can, beloved. My pretty bird. As soon as I get my magic back, I'll come for you."

"If you don't, I'll just have to escape on my own and find you."

I laughed softly and pulled him into my arms. "We'll have our better future, Fionn. One day we'll be those two old men, still madly in love."

He clung tightly. "I wanted to get you naked one more time."

I laughed again because we had only just been naked. "Me too. But now that you know how to spirit travel, maybe you can visit me. I'll be in Dudoon before the ninenight is over, I expect."

He made a sad noise in his throat and pressed his lips to mine, then pulled reluctantly away. Smoke and Flame curled around him in the air, then circled me.

Feed bugs, said Smoke.

Fat crickets, said Flame.

Nyah, said Coal, poking his head out of the basket.

We walked up the hill, hand-in-hand, and when we reached Fionn's guards, I reluctantly let go. I reached out a hand and Trikta took it. "Thank you," I said.

"For what?"

"For being his friend."

"You don't need to thank me for that."

I shrugged. "Thank you anyway. And you." I let go of Trikta's hand to clasp Konta's. He nodded.

"We're to take Seer Tokka directly to the ship. The others will meet us there with the medicines and our essentials."

I nodded. "I'll make sure anything you can't take now is sent on to you."

Then the guards leapt into the air, beat their wings, and circled the hilltop. Konta swooped low to grasp Fionn's outstretched arms in his talons and then they were gone, winging away over the treetops towards the coast.

I watched them go, heart aching, hand pressed to my belly where Daphnis's magic let me just feel Fionn's anxiety, his worry, and also his excitement at being able to do his job, to be Seer and Healer both, and drive sickness away from the Eyrie.

"It will always be this way," Daphnis said.

I turned to look at him, sorrow warring with anger. He had sacrificed himself for Fionn, for me, but he had also taken something I didn't want to give him, forced me to feel pleasure at his hands, when it should have been Fionn.

"You'll always be watching him leave you, or he'll be watching you leave him," he said. "He's the Seer of one Monarchy and can't be away for more than a few ninenights at a time. And you're the Prince of another Monarchy and have your own duties here."

I continued to look at him, wondering how long he had been plotting to get me to himself, and why he even wanted me so badly.

"I suppose you would be a better match for me?" I said, letting all the cold in my belly frost my voice. He flinched.

"Of course, I cannot be your spouse," he said. "Or even your consort. But I *am* yours — your servant, your slave, yours to command. Unless you dismiss me, I'm yours forever, and you *can* love me and no one else need know."

My jaws clenched and my teeth ground together so hard it hurt. I had to force myself to relax to get words out. "I *don't* love you, Daphnis. I love Fionn, and even if I could change that, I wouldn't." I took a step closer, feeling violence building, making me curl my hands into tight fists. I carefully kept them away from my knives. "And even if I did love you, it doesn't matter now, because you gave me your magic, and without it you must root as a tree, or waste away to nothing."

"There is a way," he said.

"Of course there is." Suddenly the anger was gone, and I only felt tired.

Nyah, said Coal, poking my ribs with his tiny head, distracting me from the tragedy my life had become. I stared at him, and he looked back at me with brilliant red-gold eyes.

"You're hungry, aren't you?" I said.

Nyah.

I looked at Daphnis, who was watching me without expression, then shook my head and turned away. There was grass on the top of the hill, and where there was grass, there were bound to be crickets.

For a few moments I let my other worries vanish as I hunted insects, nabbing a fat brown cricket and holding it up between thumb and forefinger.

"Sorry, little man," I said, and held it out to Coal, who snatched it from my fingers. His egg tooth had already dropped off, and he crunched the cricket between his jaws. I tried to remember if feathered tree serpents had teeth and couldn't. I supposed I would find out soon enough.

"I can return your magic to you," Daphnis said, and I turned from trying to catch another cricket to look at him.

"What?"

"I can return your magic, and then you can return mine, and I shall be your faithful servant."

"My Queen wants you executed, magic or no magic." I refused to acknowledge the excitement that sparked in my gut when he said he could return my magic. It was impossible; it had to be, or he'd have done it already.

Wouldn't he?

"Your Queen can't tell one dryad from another," he said. "You could deliver her any dryad's head and she would accept it."

"Her Captain knows you."

"Her Captain loves you like a son. He won't give us away."

"Daphnis." I met his eyes, searching for the person I had befriended as a boy, wondering if he had always felt this way about me, and I hadn't realized. I had believed we were two lonely boys enjoying each other's company and experimenting with sex. I *had* loved him, but as a dear friend, not as a beloved. "There is no us."

"There has always been an us," he said. "From the day you promised to free me, I knew I meant more to you than you could say. I spent my years in the pleasure garden planning how we could be together."

He moved close and touched my cheek. I pulled away, stepped back out of his reach. Coal poked his head out of the basket and hissed, and I covered him with my hand protectively.

Nyah, he complained and butted his head against my fingers.

"My love, listen to me," Daphnis said, and I shook my head, backing away some more. "I can return your magic. Can't you feel *my* magic working against your mother's spellwork?"

I shook my head again, but I *could* feel something. The tingling in my antlers that I had mentioned to Fionn had been growing, so slowly I didn't notice until Daphnis mentioned it, becoming almost a burning.

I shook my head a third time, not in denial, but to try to

shake off the feeling. "I can't do this again, Daph. Her spell-work almost killed me the first time."

He moved closer, and closer still. "I burns, doesn't it, my love?"

"Daph, stop."

Coal hissed again and tried to squeeze between my fingers. He wanted to protect me, I think, and it made me feel stronger to know that this tiny creature I had only just met liked me enough to want to put himself between me and danger.

Then, a sudden stab of heat in my head dropped me to my knees.

"I can take it away," Daphnis said. "And when your magic is your own again, you can return mine the way I gave it to you. We were meant to be together, Kiernan. You will be King of Morven Forest, and I will be your dryad lover, and together we'll change the world and free all oppressed people."

What he said sounded so close to what Fionn and I planned in some ways that it made me feel sick.

"I will never be King," I said. "And I have no desire for it, anyway."

Daphnis laughed. "If only I could tell you what every dryad knows. If only the Founding Magic didn't prevent me. Oh, my love, my King, my lover."

The Queen's spellwork burned through my antlers as it had done when she first activated it. I had not bargained on it stripping away any new magic I might acquire, but I should have. I knew very well how devious she could be.

And it sounded like Daphnis had known, too.

I looked up at him, my eyes blurring from the pain. I clenched my teeth to keep from throwing up. "Give me may magic, if you really can," I gritted out.

He smiled and it turned his sharp face softer, so handsome it was hard to look at him because I remembered that smile from when we were boys. It was the same smile he had showed me when he confessed he wanted to touch me and I had told him I felt the same. The memory was an ache in my chest I had to shove aside, along with all the others.

Coal hissed and I saw that he had escaped his basket and had crawled along the ground until he was at Daphnis's feet. He reared up as far as his tiny body would allow and opened his fuzzy little wings – all three pairs – to make himself look bigger. I'd have laughed in delight if I could have felt anything *like* delight. Instead, I scooped him up in one hand.

Daphnis moved closer again and touched one of my antlers. It was as if he had pressed a fire poker left too long among the coals to my forehead and I fought back a scream.

"Let me take the pain away," he said.

And finally, *finally,* my brain caught up and I realized how I could escape. How I could remove my Queen's spellwork and regain my magic – connection damaged, but it would heal.

I pushed myself up on my knees and tucked Coal back into his basket.

"Take my antlers," I said.

Daphnis looked startled. "No, my love, we must *defeat* her magic. I can draw on the magic of the dryad grove and use it to free you."

I looked around, the trees that had once been dryads smearing in my blurry vision. "You would kill them," I said.

"They are already dead."

"But they're not. They're trees, alive and growing and full of the forest's magic."

He shrugged. "I would do it for you."

A groan escaped my throat as a wave of heat stabbed down my antlers. "First you would have me kill another dryad to pretend I executed you, and now you would drain your entire grove of ancestors of its life force. Daphnis, what happened to you?"

"Did you know that if I were not a slave, I would be a King?"

"What?"

"Long ago, before we were enslaved, dryads had kings, and I am their descendant."

"So that means every dryad is yours to use? To sacrifice for your own comfort?"

"Of course. That is the way of kings."

"Then you're no better than my mother," I said, spitting out the words. "In fact, you're worse, because she, at least, will spare her own people by sacrificing others. You would sacrifice your own."

He looked startled.

"Take my fucking antlers, Daphnis. I'm not strong enough to do it myself. If you love me as you say you do, tear my antlers off and free me."

"It would be agony, my Prince. I would not cause you such pain."

"*This* is agony, Daphnis."

I forced myself to crawl closer, to kneel directly at his feet, and I took his free hand and put it on my other antler. "If you want to make up for giving me pleasure when I didn't ask for it, then give me pain when I do."

"You wanted pleasure."

"I wanted it from Fionn."

He looked at me, looked at his hands on my antlers, and I tried to keep him in focus, to keep from screaming at the burning that flooded me in waves.

"If you won't do this for me because I ask as your friend," I said. "Do it because I command you as your Prince and your master." I hated the words even as I said them, but I needed him to act now.

"Will you tell me that you love me?" he said.

I spent several heartbeats just trying to breathe and then said, "I will tell you that I love you."

"Will you mean it?"

"I'll mean it," I said, grateful for once that I could lie.

He smiled that precious smile again, and I felt briefly guilty. But if Fionn could say he would kill Daphnis himself if it would help me, and mean it, I could find the strength to say something untrue to an old friend.

Then, quickly, almost easily, showing the incredible strength dryads had that few people ever saw, he wrenched and twisted and there was a crack like lightning that might have come from inside my skull, and I must have screamed. And my old shadow friends crept in and took me away.

I COULDN'T HAVE BEEN out long, because Daphnis still stood above me, holding my antlers aloft, looking at them in what appeared to be disbelief.

But I had toppled onto my side and Coal had escaped his basket again and was pressed to my forehead, his long little body draped above my eyebrows, just below the raw wounds where my antlers had been. He was vibrating, and it crept into my skull and drove some of the pain away, and I remembered being in the Eyrie, searching for Fionn, in pain and almost out of hope, and Flame had vibrated like that and took away enough of my pain that I could keep going. And I had found Fionn and told him that I loved him.

"I'm okay, little friend," I whispered. Coal slid down my face to burrow under the neck of my shirt.

Nyah, he said, softly.

"Thank you."

He purred and I sat up slowly and looked at Daphnis.

"I can't let go of them, my Prince," he said, confusion in his voice and on his usually blank face. He met my eyes and I saw fear in his. "Your Queen's spellwork holds me trapped."

"My Queen always did think of every eventuality." I forced myself to stand even though I wanted to curl into a ball on the moss and sleep for a ninenight, at least.

"What does it mean?"

"It means she thought I might try to have my antlers removed. But I don't think she expected me to ask a dryad to do it, or she'd have had the punishment begin sooner."

He blinked at me.

"Anyone else would still be struggling to pull them off when whatever she spelled into the silver took effect. You were able to do it so quickly her spell didn't have time."

"But I can't let go."

"To be certain you won't escape her punishment."

He looked from hand to hand, each one clutching an antler, and then he looked at me. "What will the punishment be?"

"I don't know. I know my Queen well, but I don't know her every thought."

He shook his head. "You promised you would admit that you love me if I did this for you. And you promised to return my magic."

"I never promised to return your magic, Daphnis. I never promised to fuck you."

"My Prince…"

I smiled gently. "But I keep the promises I do make. I love you, Daphnis."

He smiled and closed his eyes. "I always knew you did."

"I love you as the friend you were to me as a boy. I love you for teaching me to enjoy my body. I love you for saving Fionn."

He opened his eyes again and I saw fear. "Your antlers," he said. "They burn my hands."

"I'm sorry, Daphnis." I lifted Coal from the neck of my shirt and put him back in his basket. "I love you, but not as much as I loved Dec, and nowhere near as much as I love Fionn."

And I stepped back. I don't think he heard the last part over his own scream, as his hands, clenched around my antlers, burst into flame.

"I'm so sorry, Daphnis. I'm sorry things happened this way. Dryads should be free. All peoples should be free."

He screamed again as the flames spread up his arms.

"But I am grateful."

And as he screamed one more long, agonizing sound that tore from his throat, I drew my sword in a smooth, practiced motion and removed his head from his body.

His screaming stopped, but the flames didn't and as I watched, my Queen's magical fire consumed his body, leaving only his head sideways on the moss, looking at me with an un-readable expression in his dark eyes.

And then I made sure Coal was safe in his basket, cleaned my sword on the moss and sheathed it, and ran for the coast, letting out a shrill whistle as I went. My stag was around somewhere, and he would carry me more quickly than my own legs.

About the Author

NICO SILVER LIVES like a hermit on the edge of the woods, but haunts used bookstores like a wraith. They fully expected to be found someday as a mummified old corpse crushed under a toppled to-be-read pile, but the rise of e-books has made that somewhat less likely, though the books will always outnumber even the dustbunnies. Nico will read just about anything, including the instructions on the back of medicine bottles, but has a particular fondness for good stories with a hint of magic. They write dark, sexy urban and romantic fantasy, and sometimes dream in black and white.